SACRIFICE

SACRIFICE

Shane Wesley Shelton

Believing Magic Books

This is a work of fiction. Names, characters, places, and incidents are either products of the author's imagination or, if real, are used fictitiously.

First U.S. edition 2014

ISBN 978-1-941570-17-3

Printed by Amazon CreateSpace

Artwork for all covers in the Believing Magic series purchased on Shutterstock.com

Grammatical and line editing for all books in the Believing Magic Series by:
Karen Robinson – Freelance copy editor and proofreader
Bachelors, English & Masters, English | Texas A&M University, Doctorate, English | Perdue University, Faculty Fellow | Ivy Tech Community College teaching English and Composition

Second Editing and Final Read Through Proofing for all books in the BM series:
Sherri McDougald – English major at University of North Florida
Artist: acrylics, ink, pencil/charcoal, and glass etching
Contact for any work requests at: sherrir30@yahoo.com

Interior book design and ebook conversion by:
Jimmy Sevilleno professional interior book designer and ebook conversion specialist

Cover artwork tweaked and adjusted and prepped for print by:
Jeesun Hwang – Graphic artist and designer

Believing Magic Books
13 Kingfish Avenue
Ponte Vedra Beach, Florida 32082
visit us at **www.believingmagic.com**

Also by the Author

Believing Magic Series:

Believing Magic
Kingdom Come
Sacrifice
Garden of Wrath
All Around the Throne
Devil's Tithe

∞

The Gift
Milina May
Midori
Cinderella, Cinderella
Frank Dobbs and the OtherLands
A Girl Called Grace

Contents

Gannon the Grey

Lightning in a Jar

MIKE AND GANNON were best friends. Four years ago their parents had bought identical two-acre tracts of land set up with identical trailers by some hayseed, backwater, wanna-be developer. "Federation Way" was the grandly overstated name of the rutted up, dirt road these two new families built their simple dreams upon. The closest island of civilization was Valdosta, Georgia, forty minutes away.

Mike and Gannon were the same age. They liked the same music, and thanks to Mike's older sister Mina, who worked at a salon, they both had blue hair *and* blue eyebrows. They both hated school and didn't give a rip if they passed or failed. They both had parents that didn't care what they did or who they did it with, as long as they didn't go to jail, get someone pregnant or eat all the food out of the refrigerator.

And both boys loved the outdoors and 'getting away'. Camping out in the woods was great, but what they enjoyed most was going to festivals or larger gatherings when they could find them. If there was a multi-day outdoor concert, a festival, a rally, or anything that drew a large crowd, Gannon and Mike would be there to hang out, meet people, and mellow with the masses. It didn't take a lot of money the way they did it. They had the process down to an exact science, honed and perfected for just the two of them, but this time they'd stopped at an afternoon pool party before rolling out, and the next thing Gannon knew Mike had a blonde chick attached to his side begging to "*go with*."

"Man, go find someone," Mike encouraged, then went back to sucking face with the girl on the couch beside him.

Gannon lingered beside the couch looking disgusted.

Mike surfaced. "I'm takin' her!" he growled like a swimmer gulping at air before going under again. He resurfaced again a moment later. "Start at the hot chicks and work your way down." His girl reattached.

"Don't just stand there, Gan!" Mike said when he resurfaced. "Go get your own and stop eyeballing mine *cuz I'm not gonna share*." Mike gave his girl a wicked grin and gave Gannon a shove, propelling him off into the party.

Resigned to this change in plans, Gannon moved through the crowded house intending to do exactly as Mike suggested. Why the hell not? It was sound advice. Solid strategy. Start at the top with the hottest chicks. Chicks that were so flaming hot and stuck up they wouldn't even tell their jock boyfriends to piss on you if you were on fire. Start at the impossible, charge through the improbable, plow through the possible, and work down to the frighteningly plump chicks that had too much facial hair.

Gannon let the music carry him deeper into the house, moving with the beat, dancing his way through the crowd. It was a nice party and a nice house, three stories tall backed up to the water. There must have been nearly eighty teens in the house and out around the pool, and there were even adults standing around in key spots to make sure nothing got stolen or broken or pregnant.

Gannon sized up the girls as he eased from room to room. He saw a few sevens, a couple of nines, but no tens so far. He slipped outside onto the pool deck and there they were, all gathered together like a nest of hotties, but one of them stood out like a comet shooting through the sky. Her short hair was dyed an eye popping flare red and pink, the shading making her head look like a struck match. She was pale and super thin with a freckles around her eyes and across the bridge of her nose and on her shoulders and arms. She was dancing with some tall kid wearing gray khakis and a polo shirt. Rich kid.

Gannon didn't think, he just acted. He danced his way out there and began to circle around the couple like a blue-headed satellite as he moved with the music.

"Hey, can I ask you a question?" Gannon asked when he was sure he'd caught her eye. He ignored the boyfriend standing right beside her, glaring furiously as he listened in.

She shrugged. "Sure."

Gannon stopped dancing and so did she and he just asked her. Straight up. No smile, just talk. "My best friend and I were about to head down to Amen Hale, you know, where everyone's camped out and trying to get in to see the witches if they can. It was just going to be him and me, but he found a girl here at the party that he wants to take so now I need to find one too. You're the first girl I asked because you're the hottest girl here and my choices only go down if you turn me down—so what do you say? You wanna come or should I go ask the second hottest girl here? My name's Gannon."

She smiled.

He smiled back.

"What the hell are you smiling about, jackass!?" The country club jock spoke up right on cue. He gave Gannon the standard issue poke in the chest.

"Hey!" The girl frowned. "Cut it out, Kyle! You don't own me." She glared at him. "All we were doing was talking."

"I don't think so!" Kyle said, puffing up. "This guy looks like a punk. Who invited him anyway?"

Gannon gave the girl a friendly but sympathetic smile. "And you'd pass up a weekend with me to be with him?"

"I haven't passed up anything yet," she said.

"Get lost!" The jock shoved in between him and the girl. She glared at his back which he didn't notice. Gannon's grin widened. "And why are you so happy?"

"Because I just stole your girl, you *dick*." He didn't dodge the punch, he even helped it along, falling over into the pool with maximum possible splash.

It was a thing of beauty, watching her stomp her foot and yell at the guy and call him an ass as he paddled his way to the side of the pool. By the time he was out, she was waiting for him and the "adults" were hauling Kyle back into the house.

"You're still smiling," Gannon said.

"My name's Kim," she said as she brushed at the welt he had on the side of his head.

She was still smiling and talking as all four of them got into Mike's car and went to the store for some additional supplies since there would be four people instead of just two. Despite their colorful, cat-dragged-in appearance, both of the girls were impressed at how organized the boys were. They could tell they were in well planned out and competent hands. Whatever else happened, they knew they wouldn't starve, go thirsty, or lack for shelter when they got there.

About ten miles out from Amen Hale the traffic became a nightmare. There were soldiers directing traffic at every intersection and stopped at places along the side of the road. They spent two miserable hours, from three until five, crawling along at a snail's pace as soldiers directed the traffic where to go and eventually where to park. They ended up parked in a huge field miles from where then needed to be.

Envious eyes of other campers scoped out the big wheeled, custom hand carts Mike and Gannon used to haul their huge pile of supplies. They trudged down the dusty trail for almost two miles, past soldiers and tanks and more soldiers until finally, they waded into what used to be a normal street with high end homes on one side that backed up to the St. Johns River facing a giant, open field on the other side of the road.

The houses were set back from the street and soldiers had fenced off the front yards of about eighty homes to create a long greenway just off the pavement where people could set up tents. The large, open field was being used as a fairground where vendors and shows were setting up shop, but campers were squatting on every inch of dirt a tent could fit on and not be chased off by the soldiers policing the area. The boys estimated the crowd to be well over ten thousand people, all spread out across the front yards, fields, and fairgrounds and living in the RV city they passed a mile or so back the way they'd come.

Of course, they people watched as they went. It was easy to pick out the various groups based on their manner of dress. The church people, women in long dresses and men in hot, uncomfortable slacks and white shirts, sweating away as they handed out tracts. Also, the crazier version of the same, wild eyed and untucked, though still wearing a suit.

One of them was standing on an overturned bucket beside the flow of human traffic shouting out over the crowd, red faced and furious. "Repent ye sinful generation! The end is near!"

The steadily moving current of humanity ignored him as they would a street performer in a big city or a bum holding a sign on a freeway off-ramp. His pleading voice blended into the background noises welcomingly, like it belonged there. Background music at Disneyland. There were groups of leather wearing biker types and others that wore robes like priests or witches mixed in with the regular looking everyday folks.

The media was a group all by itself, moving in groups with their cameras and crews. Soldiers were set up at stop points every fifty yards or so, like lifeguard stations at a busy beach, keeping an eye on everyone and everything. Signs had been posted everywhere stating that the area was under military control and that everyone's presence was tolerated but not welcome.

When their group had to clear the road for a convoy of military trucks to pass by, Whip (Mike's girl) asked, "Should we even be here?" but they all kept going. The bedraggled group pressed on and on and on until they came to the gate itself that the military used to get in and out of Amen Hale and turned to the yard closest to the gate just as someone there was pulling up tent pegs.

The girls watched the gear while Gannon and Mike jumped in and helped the biker couple break camp.

"The damn soldiers won't let anyone get through and no one from Amen Hale has come out to get more people since last night. We didn't even get a chance. We ain't seen shit," griped a heavily tattooed man as he tried to arrange tent poles into a pack that looked already full.

"Are you kids trying to get in?" asked the lady who was with him as she eyed them up and down, especially the girls who leaned by the stuff.

Mike answered as he worked. "No way, we're not trying to get into the witches' little city; we're just here for the party."

The woman breathed a stream of smoke through her nostrils like a pissed off dragon then flicked her cigarette into the dirt. "Then you'll probably have a good time if this," she waved her arms all around, "is what you came for." She looked back in the direction of Amen Hale. "Damn witches don't even care enough to come out here and talk to us. They can shove it. Stupid bitches!"

It was almost seven by the time Gannon and Mike had their own tent set up to their liking, and five more minutes before Mike and Whip threw Gannon and Kim out so they could start screwing.

"So what do we do now?" Kim asked a bit nervously.

Gannon held her hand as they walked down the road toward the field where the big tents and vendors were set up like a festival.

"We talk to people. If we see someone we want to talk to, we stop and talk to them. If they're cool, we chat for a while and if not we move on. It's nice to talk to people when they're at a place like this because they're not working or trying to go somewhere or do something or at home behind their locked doors and their guard gates and all that crap. Out here they're just sitting around, chillin' out. Even people who would normally be total dicks and not give a guy like me a second look will talk at a place like this. And not talk down to you either," Gannon said with feeling. "They'll talk to you like you're a regular person. Even if you're young. I've met teachers, doctors, a scientist from some fancy medical company who was so stupid rich he didn't even know how rich he was, and regular people, mechanics, truckers, even homeless drifters."

"It sounds nice." Kim was smiling. "You make it sound so wonderful, just walking around and talking to people." She was looking at him with surprise fixed on her face, but then she looked down as if embarrassed when she noticed him noticing her.

"What?" Gannon asked, worried that he may have weirded her out with all his campfire cult ramblings.

"I just didn't think you were," she shrugged, "you know, a thinker. Deep." She was still holding his hand but not looking up at him as she walked beside him.

"What did you think I was, Kim?" Gannon asked, sure he already knew the answer, and he was right.

"An adventure. Fun. Simple. Nice but average." She said it without making it sound mean or ugly.

"And what do you think now, other than my being 'a thinker' and 'deep'?" Gannon asked, not even meaning to; his mouth said the words.

"WAIT!" Gannon caught her before she answered. "Just hold that thought, and tell me what I am tonight, when we get back to the tent. I want more time to add to my credentials."

She looked up at him, surprised again but smiling. "Credentials?"

He gave her a lopsided smile. "Just because I don't go to school doesn't mean I'm stupid. I want to add to my list before we get back to the tent tonight and you tell me what I am. So far I'm 'a thinker' and 'deep,' right?" He gave her a look.

"Yeah," she laughed out her answer. "And some other stuff."

It didn't sound like that *other stuff* was bad stuff to be, but Gannon nodded.

"I intend to add to the list," he said confidently.

"What are you gonna add?" she asked.

"For starters, 'Expert Tour Guide.'" He pulled her into the stream of human traffic and headed off toward the fair ground and the big tents and vendors. "Before we get wrapped up in the campfires let's go see the fields and the people being stupid and the concerts."

"There's concerts here?"

Gannon laughed. "In a sea of people this huge, there's always concerts, music and dancing!" Gannon knew he wasn't GQ gorgeous or rich or even that good in a fight, but he could definitely dance. And someplace out there, before the night was through, he fully intended to add 'one hell of a dancer' to Kim's list.

He held her hand tight as they moved with the current further into the fairgrounds. The first thing Gannon noticed was how organized everything was, arranged with military precision, rows and alleys and tents all aligned and set up like a big flea market and not scattered about randomly like most unplanned gatherings. All the big vendors were on the same two long rows. The soldiers had allowed them to park their trucks or RVs or catering vehicles along either side of the dirt path and set up shop in front of their vehicles. There were booths selling everything you could imagine: crystals, candles, charms, books, scrolls, bones, jewelry, daggers and knives, capes and hats, beer, chicken on a stick, and even people selling "witch hair" cut from the Black Witch's head (or so the black robe wearing vendor swore).

Gannon bought Kim a t-shirt that said "Witch-a-Paloosa 2016" on the front, and on the back it said, "I had one Hell of a time at Amen Hale!" She picked him a shirt that said, "Witch Buddy." They walked from vendor to vendor laughing and enjoying themselves.

Gannon stopped at a fortune teller's tent where a drunk "psychic" guy actually passed out in the tent during their fortune, right there in his chair. They quietly slipped around the tarot card table and leaned in on either side and took a few grinning group pictures with their cell phones; then Gannon held a finger in front of his lips to keep Kim quiet as he deftly lifted his five dollar bill back out of the glass offering bowl along with eight others that came along for the ride.

He and Kim tiptoed out of the tent and melted into the crowd, running until they came to one of the nicer food vendors where Gannon, now flush with unexpected cash, bought a ludicrously expensive spiced corn on a stick for himself. Kim chose a cone of deep fried peas of all things, and they both got a hot funnel cake and two large sweet teas for the god awful price of thirty-five dollars. There they were, at the fairground version of Ruth Chris *and* (with a five dollar tip) they scored great seats right by a fancy fan that sprayed out a fine mist of water keeping them cool while they sat there, ate, and laughed. They took a few minutes to email the pictures of the drunk fortune teller and pictures of their gourmet meal and some of each other to their friends.

The crowd in the grassy boulevard parted as a line of black cloaked figures passed through the boulevard carrying torches and chanting. They passed right by the happy couple.

Gannon flashed Kim a huge grin and grabbed her hand, hauling her from her chair. "Com'on! Time to go watch people be stupid."

They followed the ominously chanting, hooded group as they made their way to a big black tent erected on the edge of the field. Gannon, Kim, and a handful of other daring campers slipped under the edge of the big tent and watched from the shadows. The robed and hooded cultists were gathered in a ring at the center as their leader ranted and waved a black dagger over a squealing piglet.

A minute before Gannon gave in to Kim's pleading, soldiers and police came rushing in from all directions. Intimidating black robed cultists scattered like roaches fleeing a fogger. The Grand Pu-Bah dropped his knife and started crying like a baby when the police grabbed him. His right hand "woman" as it turned out, put on quite a show. When the cops got a hand on her black smock she wiggled out, completely naked, and ran around screaming like a banshee until they tackled her.

Kim had been scared to death and was begging to leave, but now they both laughed and laughed as the soldiers led the happily grunting pink piglet away on a leash like a camp mascot. Apparently it was against the law to chop up a piggy in public without a permit. After laughing at the Satanists, Gannon led them over to the bright lights of the holy rollers, to be fair about it he told her.

Ever the fount of surprising knowledge, Gannon informed Kim that this particular style of snorting and hollering used by the preacher currently holding court identified him as a *Tennessee Wind Sucker,* a well-known variety of Holy Roller. Unfortunately for the Wind Sucker, his sound system was going up against a ridiculously loud Molly Hatchet tribute band.

They walked over to where the concert was but Gannon stopped well away from the stage. The press of people was too thick to be safe, and he didn't want to take Kim into a place like that. They had a laugh when the amps blew and caught on fire, and a huge scare when the fire caused a stampede which ended with about twenty people getting hurt. Ambulances came in and took the injured people away.

When Kim said she was surprised that they weren't down there, trampled like the others, Gannon told her that he wasn't going to let anything hurt her. She stared up at him for a minute but didn't say a word. He thought she might be about to kiss him but she just gave his arm a squeeze and asked, "What's next, Gan?"

It was almost ten when they found a campfire that Gannon liked. It was a rich family of hippies. They'd packed in a lot of gear and looked like they planned to stay for a while. Gannon and Kim watched some TV on their host's portable set to catch up on the latest 'Amen Hale' news as Rupert happily shared the local camp gossip and welcomed them to their fire.

The Blanchard family were pagans from South Carolina. Rupert was in his early forties and his casual easy manner, solid tan, and shoulder-length hair made him look like a surfer who'd wandered away from the beach and ended up here by mistake. His wife Maria was tall and slim with long, luxurious black hair. She looked and sounded Mexican or possibly South American. Maria was seated in a chair reading a storybook to their three girls and three other camp children who were stretched out on a big quilt wide eyed as they listened.

Kim stayed with Gannon and Rupert watching the news with them for a few minutes, but then drifted over to the edge of the quilt, drawn in by Maria's animated reading. Maria noticed her, said something in Spanish, and her three girls moved over just enough to make a little space between them on the blanket. Kim didn't hesitate; she just smiled her thanks and wormed her way right in and made herself at home.

Rupert watched Gannon as he watched Kim. Her burst of pink and red hair was sandwiched between the other children's raven black as they all listened to Maria read a story about little fairy people who lived in a magic puddle and were being hunted by evil trolls. Kim laughed along with the girls and Rupert watched Gannon smile.

"Does she know you love her, Gannon?" Rupert asked.

Gannon shook his head no, not denying it. Though he hadn't admitted it even to himself until that instant.

Rupert watched him for another minute or two. "Is there anything we can do to help you two?"

Right then Maria was at a scary part of the story and Kim took the smallest girl into her arms, cuddling and whispering to her as they both listened to Maria, who was making scary faces, acting out the part of one of the trolls in the story.

"Trust me, you and Maria are helping already." Gannon tore his eyes away and looked back at Rupert. "But if you know of some place around here with good folk music and dancing, that would be perfect."

"Dancing you say?" Rupert gave him an appraising look that was not a compliment. "Gannon, you know that no real decisions come out of a night of mad dancing. Do you mean to take advantage of our young, burning beauty there, or do you really want her to fall in love with you?"

"Rupert, I'd never—" he began but stopped himself. "It's not like that with Kim."

Gannon gave the other man a hard look of his own but Rupert didn't show any signs of backing down. He was a father and he'd already picked up on the fact that Kim was totally out of her element here, and that she was trusting Gannon completely to take care of her. It looked like this father of three girls didn't know if that was such a good idea. Rupert may have been a hippie, but he was a father first. It made Gannon like, and trust him more.

"Then tell me how it is."

Rupert was pressing his host privileges pretty far but Gannon didn't fight it. It just showed that Rupert knew how it worked. When you set up at a place like this, if someone came to your fire it was understood that the host had certain privileges. You generally talked about what he wanted to talk about and if your host asked a direct question, you answered it or moved along.

"I'm not enough to keep her, Rupert. I'm just a poor kid from the sticks. I got no job, no family worth mentioning, and nothing to offer her except me, and that's not enough for a girl like Kim. Shit, I don't even own a car. We rode together with my friend Mike in his crappy ride. She's so far out of my league that she scares the hell out of me. I keep telling myself that she's just a girl and that the best I can hope for is that she spends a few days with me and then goes back to her real life."

"But—" Rupert prompted when Gannon went quiet.

"But I want it to be real." Gannon knew he couldn't keep her. He didn't have the money, the family, or any of the right magic it would take to keep a girl like

Kim, but his guts hurt with the want of it. The idea of "her" pulsed through his whole body like a fever he was trying to keep under control before it took over his whole mind and turned him into an idiot. Gannon started talking, soon forgetting that Rupert was even there as the words came out along with his memories and fears.

"When I was little, I used to visit my grandparents in North Carolina. There was this one magical night when the hillside became one enormous flashing light show, like a big Christmas tree, and I captured over fifty lightning bugs in a huge pickle jar. I was so happy when I came in for the night and set that huge jar by my bed. I poked some holes in the tin lid so the bugs had air to breathe and then I went to sleep with my whole room lit by their flickering light. It was the first night I ever slept without a nightlight or a teddy bear or worrying about what might be under my bed or even wanting a goodnight kiss from my parents. They were both still around back then. I didn't need anyone or anything else. I was safe with my jar."

A small bitter laugh colored his words. "It was like captured magic, I'd stolen it away from the night and kept it just for myself. What could possibly harm me when I had lightning in a jar, right beside my bed? I went to sleep so happy, only to wake up and find them all dead. That was the night I realized that there's some magic you can't keep. I stared at the pile of dead black bugs at the bottom of that jar and felt like a thief. *Greedy.* I was only eight but I felt greedy. I'd reached too far and taken too much, all for myself. Kim's that kind of magic, Rupert."

Gannon didn't look at the other man but he knew he was there, looking at him. Gannon couldn't stop wanting and dreaming about her, even if there was only one way this could end. If he tried to keep her he'd ruin her life, so he would keep her safe while he had her. He'd watch her close, and once her light started to dim and her wings slowed and her smile began to fade, he'd set her free.

"I'll take her home when she's ready to go, Rupert. I won't let anyone hurt her." *Even me,* Gannon thought to himself. He'd do it, but the thought made his mouth go dry. Gannon took another swig of his wine cooler.

"You know, there's a big bunch of gypsies camped at the end of the row." Rupert took a swallow from his own drink and added, "Gypsies always have music."

Gannon cocked a doubtful blue brow. "Real gypsies?" He'd met real gypsies before at the bluegrass festivals, and if they were real gypsies then they most certainly would have music.

"They sure looked real to me. I'll go down and see if they're in the mood for a little music tonight." With some groaning, Rupert heaved himself up out of his comfortable chair, and after a quick whispered word to Maria he merged with the crowd and trudged off down the dirt trail.

Rupert introduced Ferka and Harman, who each had mandolins, their sister Tsura, who had a violin, two younger girls dressed in long traditional gypsy dresses who carried tambourines with them, and an old man named Julian, who lugged a chair and a huge accordion. Whatever Rupert told them must have been impressive because they came looking serious and ready to play, but before they could pluck a string the shouting started.

Everyone began pointing up looking at the sky. Rising high over Amen Hale was a bright yellow light, growing brighter and brighter each second like a star on a dimmer switch. Yellow light bathed the campground. Every single man, woman, and child not already doing so looked up to see where the off color light was coming from. They stood, transfixed, and watched it grow brighter and climb higher—and then it stopped. It sat in the sky, anchored a few hundred yards above Amen Hale like a beacon. It wasn't distant and untouchable like stars in the night sky or even as high up as the planes that slipped in and out of the highest clouds. It was closer. Its radiance had also reached a stopping point, not wavering but remaining consistent. The night no longer looked like "true night" but more like a wild yellow dusk or an eerie pre-dawn on some alien world. The light wasn't hot white like the sun or the crisp reflected white given off by the moon. It was yellow. Common colors took on a strange cast. Kim's emerald green eyes looked a bright alien orange under the yellow rays.

There was some panic, but nothing too extreme. A few people ran for their lives, dropping everything to run in screaming circles or pulling up stakes on their stalls or tents in a wild rush to get away, but for every one that ran there were a hundred others that merely stared at the sky or talked calmly at their campfires with their neighbors.

The military activity intensified. The sound of planes and helicopters (an ever present background noise) became so loud that there was a period of forced silence until the rumbling noise calmed to a tolerable level and people could hear each other talk again.

The gypsies had stayed around the Blanchards' fire, all of them talking about the yellow star in the sky. Kim listened to the talk for a while, but then she pushed away from all of them and boldly declared to everyone at the Blanchards fire that she didn't care *what* it was or *who* made it but that it was beautiful and that she was glad to be there to see it. She said this as she looked right at Gannon, and that was when Tsura drew her bow across the strings of her violin.

All the gypsies went silent as the note hummed through the air like a spell riding the back of Kim's words. The men wordlessly went to their instruments. Tsura and Julian started singing and they started to play. It was beautiful. Mesmerized, Gannon stood there and watched for a few moments as Kim danced with Harnan's two young daughters. As they shook their tambourines Kim spun and danced, her slim body gliding around the two girls like sensuous living fire dancing around two spinning gypsy ravens. Kim matched the younger girls' movements quickly and easily, laughing and smiling.

The laugh brought him to his feet. Gannon went to her, drawn like a magnet to metal. By far, his favorite music at the folk festivals was the gypsy music. He didn't recognize the tune that Tsura started with but somehow he knew the steps and the rhythm that fit the beat and he took Kim and began the steps of the traditional folk dance as if he knew it by heart. As soon as the gypsies saw that Gannon knew the dance they all cried out happily.

"Haaa! You cannot hide what you are, little brother! You are nothing but a gypsy with BLUE HAIR!" Harman cried out as he laughed and played.

Ferka put his instrument down and joined in, dancing with his two daughters. Soon, the ten became twenty, and twenty became fifty, and then there were too many to count. Other musicians joined as well and their group took over the boulevard, spilling out into the street as they needed more space to fit the crowd. They were all spinning in circles like wheels around wheels, one ring going left, the next circling right, out and out, and at the center of it all danced Gannon and Kim, his burning star. His blue hair and her flaming red caught fire in the yellow light, making them look like fairy creatures spawned by the night itself to lead the magical dance.

They danced and danced, until sweat ran down Kim's face and Gannon's shirt was soaked through and stuck to his body, but she didn't care and laughed until her voice became rough from laughing—*and still they danced on!* The night took on a dreamlike quality bathed in sweat, music, and yellow light, the pulsing energy of hundreds of moving bodies, but to Gannon's eyes nothing was more amazing than Kim. She actually *glowed* in his arms as if her whole body burned and still they danced on.

The music built and built, the musicians being driven far beyond their natural limits by the same power that kept everyone dancing when they should have all collapsed long ago. They continued to spin when they should have been too dizzy to stand, some power keeping them upright and moving in ways that Gannon himself couldn't believe. Gannon had never danced like this in his life and Kim was utterly lost in whatever power had possessed them as she gave herself to the magic of the night, her whole body a beacon of magical fire. They couldn't stop and neither could the others; they were all captives to the gypsy band.

With a final shout, the music suddenly *stopped.*

Everyone collapsed where they stood as if the strings holding them upright had been cut. Panting and catching their breath, they struggled to their knees and looked to the sky and watched as the yellow star over Amen Hale grew dimmer and dimmer until it winked out of existence altogether. The night sky was once again reclaimed by darkness, the white light of a sickle moon, and a faint scattering of dots from envious distant stars.

Gannon rose to his feet on unsteady legs and lifted Kim from where she sat on the ground. He held her close and stared down into her face as she looked up.

"What am I to you now, Kim? Other than 'a thinker' and 'deep,'" he asked through panting breaths.

Her eyes searched his face in a way no other girl had ever looked at him before. Around them Gannon could see the others who'd danced were sitting, still arranged in their circles where they'd danced and dropped, but it seemed as if they were all watching the two of them. He put the crowd out of his mind and let Kim's eyes own him completely as he waited for her answer.

"An excellent tour guide," she began and had to stop to wet her dry lips and swallow to make her throat work.

"The best dancer—*ever*." Her eyes roved his face again like there was something there that only she saw.

"And everything I want."

Gannon's own heart was in his throat as she said it. He could hear the beat of his pulse in his ears.

"Gannon, I want to be with you forever. I love you." She sighed it out but then stopped as she felt Gannon stiffen, but those sitting nearby had heard her words but not felt his withdrawal; a wave of happy whispers carried her words to those farther away, passed back to others too distant to have heard.

"I will not ruin your life, Kim." Gannon's clear voice brought gasps of surprise. Silence returned and the crowd watched the drama unfold like theater in the round.

Gannon saw Kim as a magical creature, far too perfect to be put into his crap jar of a life. What could he possibly offer her? They could run off together, but where to? With no money, no future, no job, he was nothing but ruin for her. What would happen when the magic wore off? She would end up at the bottom of his jar, lifeless and ruined; and that, Gannon would not allow. He let his resolve fill his eyes as he stared at her.

"Why Gannon?" Kim asked, her eyes starting to fill with doubt and pain as she looked at him.

"Kim, you're wonderful. Beautiful. A princess. And you have a wonderful life ahead of you. But I'm just a penniless bum. A fool. And I will not hurt you by loving you."

"Then you do love me," Kim said.

"More than my own life. More than my own soul." He said it without a second of hesitation. He was surprised that she didn't scream or yell or cry. She didn't do any of that; she looked thoughtful, her eyes bright with the effort of her concentration. She appeared to reach some decision, but whatever it was, it did not bring a smile. It brought a look of fierce determination.

"Then I know exactly what to do," she announced.

Gannon became very aware that his arms were still around her and hers still around him. "What shall we do?" he asked, almost afraid.

"I'm not going to let my life become some idiot love story where I let you go and never find you again. Girls are only that stupid in movies and books. This is real life." Her grip around him tightened, pulling him closer against her body. He agreed. It definitely felt real. "I'm not going to let you go, Gannon. If I can't have you here, in this world, then we'll go to a world where I can have you. We'll go to a place where I'm not a princess and you're not a fool."

"Amen Hale," Gannon said it and there were a few muttered comments from the watching folk who hung on their every word. Gannon ignored them and stared into the face of a girl more beautiful than any he'd ever dared to dream of before. An angry line of determination was pinched between Kim's eyes as she stared back into his.

"Yes. Amen Hale," she confirmed. She meant it. She wanted it, and she wanted him, and it didn't look like she was going to change her mind. Her eyes softened as his hardened, but not in a bad way.

Gannon took one of her hands in his and turned to face the crowd. Over two hundred people were still gathered around, watching them expectantly, as if they were just waiting for the next song to begin so Gannon and Kim could lead the dance once again.

The beginning of an idea formed in Gannon's head as he looked at the people staring back at them. He opened his mouth and spoke, just going with it, not over thinking, just acting. "We need to get to Amen Hale. We do not belong here anymore. Please. Help us."

Surprised faces regarded him. Rupert, who was close by asked, "Are you sure about this, Gannon?"

"Kim and I will go to Amen Hale," Gannon said firmly.

"But how will you get past the gate?" asked a young man in the crowd.

"The soldiers won't let you pass." Another voice.

"It's impossible!" said another who was joined by others voicing the same or similar discouragements.

Gannon squared his shoulders and raised Kim's hand up high above his head with his own.

"Was she not chosen by the magic of the yellow star!?"

He shouted his words and the crowd blinked in surprise and then fell silent.

"Who here would dare deny the magic of the Fairy Dance!?" Gannon challenged loudly, and no one voiced an objection.

"How many of you danced a dance that they did not know before this night!?" Gannon demanded and a few raised hands while many others nodded.

"We danced and danced and kept on dancing when every one of us should have dropped!" More nods. People pushed closer.

"Was she not the queen of the fairy dance!?" Nods and murmurs of assent answered his challenge.

"Did we not stare in wonder as she burned before our eyes!?" he shouted and was answered even more firmly; a handful of fists even punched the air.

"Help us get to Amen Hale! The magic has chosen us! Now help us get there!"

Instead of letting the magic of the night slip away, doomed to become half remembered recollections by morning's light, people moved. They moved while the sweat of the dance was still wet on their brow and cool on their backs and the feel of whatever had touched them was still causing the hair to rise on their arms.

What Gannon started quickly took on a life of its own. Word spread from mouth to mouth and tales spread throughout the camp of the king and queen of the Fairy Dance. Those who'd been there and danced with them told others what they'd seen, like missionary prophets sharing the good news to all who would hear the tale. They told how they saw them at the center of the dance, Kim lit up like a living, orange flame while she danced with Gannon, whose body was wrapped in glowing blue flames, though he didn't notice this himself, too enraptured by the beauty in his arms to notice his own spectral light.

"Hail! Hail! To the lord and lady of the Fairy Dance!"

Voices shouted. Some long, wooden loading ramps from a nearby truck and a few pallets were quickly converted into a divan, and Gannon and Kim were shoved on top and hoisted into the air on the shoulders of strangers, who then paraded through the dirt boulevards as the cry went before them, "Make way for the chosen of Amen Hale! Make way for the lord and lady of the Fairy Dance! Open the gates and let them pass through! Open the gates! Open the gates! Open the gates!"

Down the muddy lanes they marched and cried out.

When the bearers grew tired, others stepped right in to take their place. There was no shortage of willing bearers. The crowds grew as people pressed in to ask what was happening. They passed through the camp like a comet, waking those asleep in their tents and collecting followers as they went by, adding their numbers to the comet's ever growing tail.

Gannon had no idea who drove the wheels of the beast on which they rode; all he and Kim could do was hold on for dear life as the crowd did as it wanted. In a way, it felt like the dance again, all these people spinning them around, this way and that; they were as powerless to stop it as they had been to stop the Dance. All they could do was hold on and let it take them where it wanted. So that was what they did.

It was an hour after dawn when their massive gathering finally ambled up the street heading toward the gates like some great, pregnant beast finally come to term and ready to be delivered. The military was prepared for trouble. They'd been watching for the past two hours as the group wound its way through the fairgrounds before turning up the street with more than four thousand chanting people at their backs.

"Open the gates! Open the gates! Open the gates!" The sound rang in the air over and over until they ground to a stop. A hundred soldiers stood directly in front of the gate, all holding guns at the ready but not yet pointing them at the crowd. On each side of the gate were rows of tanks and two vehicles that looked like tanker trucks with water cannons mounted on top. The soldiers who manned the water cannons did have the barrels pointed at the crowd and looked as if they were ready to cut loose at any minute and wash them all away.

One of the officers in charge stepped forward with a bullhorn.

"We've got rights! This road is public property!" a loud man up front challenged the soldier.

"Out of the way!" cried another.

The officer spoke into the bullhorn. "This is an unlawful assembly." His voice echoed and sounded mechanical and plastic. "This area is under martial law, which means you have no right of assembly here! You have no right to press this gate or to block this roadway. Your presence here has been tolerated up to this point, but if you give us a reason or fail to obey, we will remove or detain you by force. Now quit this gathering and go back to your tents immediately."

He lowered his bullhorn but not one single soul moved a muscle as the two groups eyed each other. Gannon felt Kim's hands squeeze tighter around his waist and he gripped the wiggly wooden rail of their makeshift float to keep them both steady. Down below them, one man stepped away from their crowd of followers and approached the soldier. Gannon recognized his surfer hairstyle even from the back—it was Rupert! He stopped in the middle of the patch of ground that separated the two groups and spoke to the officer.

"We don't expect you to let all of us pass the gate, and that's not what we're asking for, but these two," he pointed up at Gannon and Kim, "take these two to the gateway, and if they can get through then let them go to Amen Hale. And if Amen Hale doesn't want them, then send them back to us. It'll keep the peace and it won't cost you a damn thing. That's all we're asking for!"

Wild shouts and cries went up from the crowd at his back. Gannon and Kim stood there like a couple of statues on display as the soldiers and the crowd stared up at them. Rupert and the soldier kept talking back and forth but Gannon's attention was pulled to the area off to the side of the gate. He could see the tent they'd set up yesterday afternoon. Mike and Whip were standing there looking up at them. Having them see him up there made Gannon feel very foolish. The thought *what the hell am I doing*? rode through his head like a Harley without pipes but then he felt Kim squeezing his hand and he looked at her. She'd seen where he was looking.

"That's not your life anymore, Gan. You're mine now. Aren't you?" she asked him. Her amazing green eyes looked a little angry and the morning light brought each of her perfect freckles out. The delicate sprinkling of dots so perfect, the eyes so green, the girl so beautiful.

Gannon's throat closed up, which seemed to piss her off because she was waiting for an answer to her question. He tried to speak again, but she struck a pose and gave him a look that made it impossible for him to make his mouth work to speak as he stared at someone so beautiful, so instead of saying anything he went with body language instead.

Gannon leaned in and finally kissed her. He thought she was angry so her reaction surprised him. Kim kissed him back like she'd been dying for this moment, starving for it. Both her arms squeezed him like she planned to break him in half while she ate him from the head down like a giant hot-dog! It was the most passionate and certainly the most forceful kiss he'd ever had in his life and his own arms wrapped around her in response to her wildly passionate embrace as he tried to answer the challenge of her kiss.

Their unstable perch, however, forced them apart as they each gripped the rails on the contraption they rode. Gannon still didn't get a chance to organize any response to her question before a Hummer pulled up to the other side of the gate and the people who stepped out drew everyone's attention. The gate was nothing but two swinging metal arms that blocked the traffic so everyone saw who stepped out of the Hummer, and cheers went up like fireworks from the crowd

They were dressed in black leather and one very tall older man wore a suit. No one had seen him since early Wednesday morning, but stories of the mysterious "House Steward of Amen Hale" were told everywhere in the camp. They all knew that he was the one who did the interviews and chose who came in and who was turned away.

Byron spoke with the soldiers on the other side of the gate who quickly opened it for him. The steward and his five black clad guards came out to stand with the soldiers on their side of the gate while the crowd went completely wild. Two lines of soldiers bearing body length plastic shields marched out from each side of the road and formed a clear, see-through wall between the armed soldiers and the sea of people pressing in all around. Byron walked over to the officer who'd been addressing the crowd and motioned for him to give up his bullhorn, which he did, reluctantly.

The watching crowd was already going silent before Byron raised the device to his mouth. His gaze fixed on Gannon and Kim where they stood on the platform still held aloft on the shoulders of a dozen people beneath them.

"Was there, perhaps, a dance last night?" he asked, almost doubtfully.

The crowd went buck-ass wild, which surprised Byron so badly, he jumped, but then he laughed happily and whispered something to the guards he'd brought who were also smiling and laughing. He spoke again but this time looked up and spoke directly to Gannon and Kim.

"Are you the blue boy and the burning girl of the dance?" he asked.

Again the crowd erupted like a volcano of voices, cheering and shouting and hooping and hollering. Byron waited until it quieted enough for him to speak with the aid of the bullhorn, not waiting to be answered on his first inquiry as the crowd had already confirmed the identity of the two teens. That, along with the way they looked, who else could they possibly be? Blue hair and flame pinkish/red were not common toppings for human beings.

"Do you want to go to Amen Hale?" he asked. Again the crowd erupted and it took a minute for it to quiet enough for them to answer.

"Yes! We want to go!" Gannon shouted back.

Again the crowd erupted, but Byron waved them down. "And the young lady?" Bryon asked through the bullhorn.

"Yes! Please let us in!" she shouted back.

"Come with me," Byron said, motioning them down as the crowd cheered.

When they got on the ground, Rupert was there to shake Gannon's hand. He was smiling.

"Good fortune, my friend. And take good care of our burning beauty." He pulled Gannon closer and said, "Gannon, I don't think you give yourself enough credit. You deserve her. Never forget that." Rupert moved away as others crowded in, offering words of encouragement and quick hugs for both of them as Byron spoke to the crowd with his bullhorn again.

"I shall return if I am permitted." And with that uncertain promise he handed the bullhorn back to the officer and turned to greet Gannon and Kim, ignoring the soldier completely who was stuck speaking to his back.

"It is an honor to meet you both." Byron gave a slight bow from the waist toward the couple. "My name is Byron. I am the House Steward of Amen Hale."

Gannon and Kim returned a wobbly bow, attempting to copy Byron's own greeting.

"I'm Gannon The Grey, and this is Kim Ainsley." Gannon waited for the reaction his birth name always brought.

"Gannon The Grey?" Byron asked straight faced, but his eyes roved over the blue hair and blue eyebrows.

"Yes, sir. That's my name. It's on my birth certificate that way. I didn't do it, I just get to live with it," Gannon said stiffly.

A knowing smile found its way onto Byron's face. He turned to Kim.

"Miss Ainsley, what do you think of his name?"

"I *absolutely* love it," Kim said with passion.

"You *love* it!" Gannon popped, surprised and horrified. "How could you possibly love *that*?"

Kim didn't back down from his look of disgust; she stared right back, showing a fire of her own that burned with its own heat fueled by her own passion and reasons.

"I love it because it's you, Gan. And I love that it's not a normal name. You're definitely not normal, in case you hadn't noticed. I love your name."

"But you have a normal name," he countered back.

"And I don't like it at all." Kim frowned.

"Then you may change it when we enter Amen Hale. Think on what you wish your new name to be while we ride to the gateway." Byron ushered them toward the waiting Hummer.

"GANNON!" Mike's voice called from the line of people pressed up against the wall of soldiers. Whip was standing beside him looking frazzled and frightened.

"GANNON! What the hell are you doing, man! Don't do it, bro! Don't go!" Mike shouted.

"Do you need a moment?" Byron asked.

Gannon looked down into Kim's eyes and said "nope." He turned back and shouted to his best friend in the world.

"Have a nice life, buddy!" He raised his right hand and gave the "rock on" sign while he hit himself in the chest twice with his left and then waved goodbye.

"Bye, Whip! Take care of Mike for Gan!" Kim called.

Whip nodded numbly as she stared at them. She and Kim had actually become friends on the way down. They'd teamed up right away on a totally practical level before they even left the party with the guys. Together they tore Mike's car apart, going through all their stuff to make sure the guys had no guns, knives, duct tape, rope, or torture devices stashed in the car and weren't sickos planning on killing them or something. Kim and Whip had clicked together nicely on the way down and Kim actually felt a twinge of regret that she wouldn't get to know Whip better. She was a stoner, but she'd been fun.

The two teens climbed into the Hummer.

Byron and a woman in a grey pant suit that Byron introduced as "Agent Trisha" sat in the seat facing them. Agent Trisha said she was a representative from the government here to make sure their rights were not violated in any way and that they knew what they were getting themselves into.

"Is there anyone you would like to call and let know where you are and what you're doing before you do it?" Byron asked. "We will not be able to call when we reach Amen Hale. Phones do not work inside the Kingdom, so now is the time if you wish to speak to your family."

Kim looked at Gannon, asking him with her eyes if he needed to call.

"I'm good," he said. "My folks won't even notice I'm gone for a month of Sundays and Mike will tell them what happened eventually, but you should call your folks, Kim," Gannon urged.

Kim nodded and fished out her cell from her tiny purse and called. She pressed the phone to her ear and started to bite the nails on her free hand while she waited for someone to answer.

"Hi, Mom."

"I'm fine."

"No, I'm not on my way home. I'm staying here with Gannon."

"No. He didn't make me go with him. I went because I wanted to go. I—"

There was yelling on the other end of the phone. Kim held it away from her ear until it went quiet, then brought it back to her ear.

"Mom. I love you and Dad, but I won't be coming home again. I'm in love with Gan." Kim was fighting not to cry. Gannon, Byron, and Trisha watched the conversation play out on her face. There was no privacy for this call.

"Yes. His name is Gannon."

Kim smiled. "Yes, he has blue hair *and* blue eyebrows. I'll send you a picture of him."

Kim laughed at something and wiped at her eyes. "Yes, Mom, we're quite colorful together."

"Okay. Here he is." She scrunched up her face in warning and handed Gannon the phone.

He took it from her with two fingers like it might hurt him and scrunched up his face like she had as he held the phone to his ear. "Hello, Mrs. Ainsley." Gannon kept his eyes on Kim as he spoke on the phone.

"Forever." He said it and Kim nodded.

"I will never leave her, Mrs. Ainsley."

"Believe it or not, I did try that. But she wouldn't let me go, and I'm glad she didn't."

"No, ma'am. I won't try it again."

"Determined," he said as he looked into Kim's eyes. She smiled but then she heard the yelling start, so loud she could almost hear it herself. Gannon winced but didn't get upset; he just listened to the ranting and finally answered in a calm sure voice.

"Mrs. Ainsley, I'm only seventeen, so I don't have to worry about being charged with statutory rape or of being labeled as a sex offender. And I haven't raped your daughter. I've only kissed Kim once." Kim leaned toward him and pushed the phone down, away from his mouth, and kissed him again, a good long kiss that left her mother's voice speaking beneath their joined lips "*Is anyone there! Hello! Gannon! Kim! Answer Me!*"

Kim leaned back with a satisfied smile, happy with Gannon's dazed expression as he raised the phone back to his ear. "Sorry, Mrs. Ainsley. Make that twice that she's kissed me."

The yelling started again and Gannon held the phone to his chest and turned to Kim.

"Kim, will you marry me?" He asked her just like that.

"Of course, Gan," she answered just as quickly.

He looked to Byron who was watching it all with an odd expression, somewhere between amused fascination and expectation. "Is it possible for us to get married in Amen Hale, even if I'm seventeen and she's sixteen?"

A big satisfied smile appeared on Byron's face. "Astounding. She said you would want to be wed."

"Who?" asked Kim.

"Princess Emma. She's the White Witch. It seems she sees love coming a great ways off. I guess you would call it prophecy."

"She saw us yesterday?" Gannon asked, surprised.

Byron gave them both a wink. "Remember, magic is real in Amen Hale. The White Witch dreamed of you two last night, and of your fairy dance beneath the yellow star. She told me that your love for each other called to her while she slept. Princess Emma was the one who sent me to fetch you, but please, finish up your call. We must be off soon; there's much to do today." Byron turned to Kim. "Feel free to invite your immediate family to the wedding, my dear; they're welcome to attend if they can promise to control themselves and not interfere. Let your mother know to stay at her house and we will provide transportation for her and the rest of your family."

Kim and Gannon blinked, both looking as if they needed to lie down but Gannon managed to ask a question. "Byron, sir. What, time, or *when* is our wedding?"

"Your wedding is scheduled for eight thirty this evening, and the reception dinner will also be a celebration for Princess Bethany's birthday. It's going to be quiet a memorable day, as most days are in Amen Hale."

"That's for damn sure," said Trisha with lots of feeling as she watched the two startled teens juggle the phone between them, trying not to drop it onto the floorboard of the Hummer.

Ryan

My Kingdom for Some Privacy

I GROANED AND BLINKED, squinting into the bright morning light that poured through the window. Someone had opened the curtains and let the light in. But who would—the maid!

I sat up, quickly pulling the covers up over us both. Sky was lying face down on her stomach. She had a pillow pulled over her head like she was trying to hide from the harsh sunlight shining right onto our bed, but I could hear her under her pillow, breathing deeply, still asleep. I scanned the room. No sign of the maid, but she'd been in here, that much was certain.

Other than pulling our curtains open she'd left a tray on the table beside the bed. There were two tall crystal glasses of orange juice, some toast, and jam circled around with different fruit, cut into fancy shapes, snazzed up with little watermelon, honeydew, and other melons cut into the shapes of flowers. All of the flower melons were connected by little decorative vines arranged on the platter to make the edible flowers appear as part of some crazy melon flower plant. The whole spread was like a picture in a magazine or some over the top display you might see a fancy French chef on the food channel create. The platter, a tall gleaming carafe (probably holding more OJ), and all the silverware were gleaming silver, and the sunlight reflected off the polished metal so brightly that it was hard to stare directly at the food.

The crazy light show and the freakish food art made me take a morning reality check as the thought *Is this really for us?* slid through my head. I looked around the room again, this time seeing the "room" instead of searching for our overly intrusive maid. It was our bedroom, here in Amen Hale.

"Our room." The thought made me look down at the girl lying in the bed beside me. Golden blonde hair spilled out from under the pillow like a golden blanket running down her perfect back and then disappearing again under the sheet. I wanted to see more, but the sheet was covering most of her back now.

I played with the edge of the sheet as I looked down at her lying there beside me and was distracted by the sheet itself as I rubbed the fabric between my thumb and forefinger. It was so soft. I was surprised that I hadn't noticed it before. I wondered what on earth it was made out of or if it felt so different because the "thread count" was like a million or something. I had no idea what a good or bad thread count was but the sheets felt wonderful.

My eyes panned the room again, its high ceiling and all of its finery. I looked at the unbelievable breakfast again but it was a different hunger that made me look down at the girl lying under the "million thread count" sheet. The most beautiful thing in the room was not the gleaming silverware or the fancy food or the sheet or the room itself, it was her. By a hundred million miles it was all her. My hand pinched and rubbed the fabric as I thought about pulling down the sheet so I could see her. I wanted to see her.

She's mine. She's my wife, I reminded myself but I still hesitated a moment before finally pulling the sheet down her back. I paused for a moment at the perfect rise of her butt before pulling the sheet away entirely. I wanted to see all of her, and now I could. She was mine. My wife. The only part of her body that was hidden from my hungry eyes was her head, hidden under the pillow.

Just the fact that she wasn't awake to see me staring at her gave me the freedom to do exactly that. I tried not to shake the bed or wake her as I moved about on my knees, looking at every inch of her. Her legs were spread apart wide enough for me to see everything I wanted to see, and the morning light streaming through the window lit her body and revealed it to me in ways that seemed almost indecent. My throat went dry. I had to swallow. I was so hard and ready it hurt. If I didn't know that God had made the girl *and* the sunlight that showed her to me in such an absolutely revealing and personal way, I would have felt like a monster, staring at her while she slept, completely unaware of my eyes. But I didn't feel like a monster. God made her for me and the verses slipped into my head without my even really knowing why. Maybe to let myself know that it was OK to look. "*Rejoice with the wife of thy youth*" and "*He that findeth a wife findeth a good thing*" and "*Marriage is honorable in all and the bed undefiled.*"

I let myself drink in the sight of her perfection as I walked forward on my knees, up between her legs. I reached out to touch her legs but stopped, both hands just inches away, hovering over her beautiful flesh. I felt overwhelmed with how beautiful Sky was, how she was *human* and *loved God* and even more amazing *loved me* and was *mine*. I looked back to the wonderful breakfast and the room then back to Sky. I'd messed up in so many ways in the past few days but God had still been so good to me it just didn't make sense. Why would he bless me with her?

I hadn't prayed once since I found out that I was making things happen with powers given to me by the doctor's pills. I'd thought God was doing it, answering my prayers, and it turned out to be nothing but me answering my own prayers, and because of that, I'd simply stopped talking to God. I knew it was wrong not to pray. A sin not to spend time with him. God knew about the pills and I knew he wasn't surprised by what had happened. For me, it's not feeling conviction or shame that drives me to pray or turn back to God, and chastening and punishment usually didn't move me to turn back when I went astray. With me, repentance usually happened at some random moment when I realized (again) just how good He was to me, even when I didn't deserve it. "*It is the goodness of God that leadeth thee to repentance.*" The verse popped into my head. I closed my eyes and prayed silently.

Thank you, Lord, for my wife. I don't deserve her, and I don't know why you gave her to me, but what can I do but thank you for her and love her and rejoice in her. Please forgive me for not praying sooner, I know I should have and I know I've been a mess lately. Please forgive me. It seems weird to pray at a time like this, but I just couldn't touch her without saying thank you. So. O Lord God, with all my heart and soul, I thank you for what I am about to receive. Thank you. Thank you.

I opened my eyes and added one last "thank you" in a breathy whisper as my hands dropped down to touch both of her legs at the bend of her knees. My hands slid up her muscled legs, so toned and perfect. Her flesh wasn't super pale; it had just a hint of color but I could see quite clearly that the tan went everywhere so had to be natural. It couldn't have been from a tanning booth. Not once she started the drug study. I ran my hands up and down on her legs a couple of times and I heard her make a small sound under the pillow, but she didn't move anything except her back which arched and she raised her butt up into the air a little higher like a cat.

My eyes almost fell out of my head!

I leaned forward, my hands gliding up her legs on each side until I reached her butt, and I let my left hand glide across the perfect curve of her back while my right hand slid down, between her legs and held her, cupped in my hand.

"Hmm." Another sound escaped from under the pillow, and Sky spread her legs a little wider, giving me room to move closer to her. I rubbed in circles with my right hand while my left hand explored the perfect skin of her back and bottom, rubbing and feeling every inch of her. I let two fingers slip inside her and heard "yes" come from under the pillow, and she started to move with me as I moved my fingers in and out. I waited until she was making a steady stream of happy noises before I finally moved forward and pushed myself inside her.

"Good morning, Lord Ry—OH MY!"

My naked ass cheeks clenched tight as I froze—mid thrust—and turned my head and shoulders to look toward the door. The maid was just standing there with a hand slapped over her eyes! She'd walked right in on us!

"Sorry, m'lord! I just didn't expect you to be *up* so soon!" She reached out blindly behind her for the door but couldn't see where it was with her eyes covered.

"Ryan!" Sky growled and I looked down at her.

She lifted the pillow just enough to growl like some wild animal at me.

"Don't you dare stop! I don't care if the maid is here, Ryan! I don't care if she watches the whole show! Get busy!"

"Good Lord!" I cried, not sure what to do.

"I wish we were in my old room, at least my door locked!" I griped.

The world moved in a flash of colors and I blinked and looked down. Sky was still under me and she still held the same pillow pressed over her head but we were in my old room now. The bedspread under Sky's naked body was the spread in my old room; I could see the baseball patterns on the mostly teal spread.

I looked around for just a moment but then "Owhh!" I groaned as Sky gave me a squeeze with muscles in places I didn't know had muscles. That got me moving again in earnest.

"That's—better! Ryan! Ohh! Ohh! Yes! Yes!" Sky moaned as she matched my movement. Her head was still buried under her pillow and she didn't even know that we weren't in Amen Hale anymore, but I was sure that right at that moment she couldn't have cared less where we were or how we got there—and neither did I.

Emma

It All Comes Down to This

"THEY'RE DOWNSTAIRS NOW. Can you feel them?" Emma asked.

Mary sat up from her nest of pillows and crawled up behind Emma. She rested her chin on her shoulder and wrapped her arms around her middle and sighed a happy "Mary" sigh. "I'm touching you, Emms, so I know."

Emma was sitting on the edge of the bed pushing her toes down into the boots that Rain had made for her yesterday. She'd met with Byron over an hour ago, sending him out to pick up the young couple before getting into the shower. After a long shower, she spent almost forty minutes staring into a mirror, studying this new body and trying to come to know this creature she'd become before coming back into the bedroom, leaning on the bed to put her boots on.

Mary had still been spread out in the sheets, sleeping, and Emma knew why. She'd stayed up half the night playing in her dreams, sending out her own magic and dances she knew from someone she'd touched to the young couple who were in love. Emma didn't understand much of what had happened last night and wasn't all that troubled that she didn't understand. She trusted Mary, and she loved her, and Mary loved her too, so it didn't matter that she was playing in her head while she slept, *did it?*

And the young couple, they were happy, and in love, and they'd helped them—which was good—*wasn't it?*

Emma tried to concentrate and focus on things the way she used to and quickly gave up. Again. The well organized mind she seemed to remember having was gone. She tried to recall from her memories what she used to be like before the "change." All that she dredged up was a hopeless jumble of pieces. She remembered that lots of things had been so very, very important to her at one time, only she couldn't quite remember what those very important things were now. And what was even stranger was that she wasn't completely freaking out that she couldn't remember those very important things.

That was bad—*wasn't it?*

Emma was sad and worried about what she'd lost. She felt something wet on her cheek and turned her head to the side, surprised to find Mary awake, her face there beside her, her chin resting on her shoulder. Mary's butt length white hair was everywhere and the green stripe up front was all wet, stuck to the side of her face in the tears.

Emma had a warm feeling of deja vu as she remembered yesterday, when she'd woken the first time in Amen Hale—it had been exactly like this. Mary had been crying then too, with her chin on her shoulder in this same way and her hair wet with tears. Emma smiled for some reason and wondered why.

Why did I smile? What about this makes me feel good? She's crying—that's bad—isn't it? Shit. I must really be crazy.

"It's a witch thing, Emms," Mary spoke quietly, their faces close together. Emma was only thinking things in her heart and mind, but when Mary was touching you, she knew you and every single hope and dream inside you. Emma listened as Mary answered her thoughts like they were spoken words.

"We like things that are familiar, Emms. When something happens the same way twice or three times we like it for some reason. Even I don't know why. It's weird, almost like an OCD thing, but it shows up in lots of ways. We like things to balance, to match and to even out. It's not bad, it's just a witch thing we do. *And I'm sorry if I have morning breath.*" She spoke the last comment with her mouth held closed, mumbling the words.

Emma laughed and smiled for real, making Mary go starry eyed as she gazed at her perfect smile and Emma's amazing lips that looked wet and shiny and scrumptious without a touch of lip gloss. She watched those lips as Emma spoke.

"Mary, you could eat sardines straight out of a can and I still couldn't smell or taste anything on your breath other than how much you love me. It's too strong. Too yummy. You'll never have yuck mouth to me."

Mary's eyes got bigger as Emma closed the few inches that separated them and her mouth fell open. Emma closed her mouth around Mary's loose bottom lip and rolled it further into her mouth and *sucked.*

Someone started knocking on their door, but Emma had her eyes closed, sucking away. Mary knew (because she was touching her) that she'd never hear the door or open it even if she did. Emma tended to be a one thought at a time girl now, and right now it was all things that made Mary's heart race and other things tingle. The knocking continued. Louder.

"Mmmmm!" Mary made a noise and pulled away. Her lip escaped Emma's sucking clutches with a wet sounding "smack." The sound itself was XXX-rated as was the look on Emma's face.

"Someone's at the door, Emms!" Mary panted before Emma pounced.

Emma's amazing copper gold eyes squinted up and she cut an irritated glance toward the offending door.

"I'll go get rid of um!" she muttered like an Old West gunslinger as she marched toward the door. "And once they're gone we can do right now what we didn't do last night."

"Wait, Emms! I'm naked over here!" Mary squealed.

"Good! Stay that way!" Emma ordered and heard Mary squeal and dive under the pillows as Emma swung the door open with a "WHAT!"

Byron stood at the door blinking and startled. "Princess Emma. Forgive me for disturbing you, but you requested to be informed when our special guests arrived. They're out on the patio, taking a bit of breakfast. Princess, are you well?" Byron asked, concerned by the look on Emma's face which had transformed from squinty eyed anger when she'd opened the door to an odd, open eyed gaze that appeared to be seeing something other than what was right in front of her.

"I'm all right." She stepped out into the hall, closer to Byron than she'd been this morning when she had spoken to him. Emma reached out and ran her hand down the front of his suit, then turned her hand up, cupped, like she'd just gathered something in her hand. She brought her hand to her face, closed her eyes, and inhaled. Then she licked her palm.

"Hmm." She made a thoughtful sound of discovery, as if she'd learned something.

"What is it, Princess?" Byron asked, still eyeing her with cautious concern. Emma opened her eyes, looking in her right mind again, whatever that may be now. Byron was quite aware that she was "troubled" since her powers as a witch had awakened yesterday.

"Why do you love me like I'm your daughter, Byron? You just met me Wednesday night and now you love me. You really do. And I'm glad you do. But why? I'm not really your daughter—" her expression became lost and uncertain as she added, "*am I?*"

Byron stepped closer, intending to administer a respectful, standoffish hug, but Emma leaned in herself, completely without hesitation, turning his stiff attempt at comfort into a real embrace. She rested her head against his chest for a moment and sniffed. Then she started rubbing her face back and forth across on the front of his well-groomed suit like she was wallowing in the smell of him. Byron stood there stiffly, surprised and caught off guard by her odd need for contact and utter disregard for personal space.

Mary's maid had summoned Byron to their room early this morning when Emma had answered the door completely nude and wet from the shower. He had (of course) kept his distance while she ordered him to go to those people camped out beyond the gate and bring the "blue boy" and "burning girl" who had danced in the fairy dance to Amen Hale. "Bring them here, and get ready for their wedding," she'd said, then shut the door.

Byron disrupted his enormously busy morning schedule, grumbling as he headed out of the gate this morning thinking it exceedingly unlikely that he'd be able to locate a "blue boy" or a "burning girl" and certainly not a fairy dance. He'd gone as she requested, thinking at the time that she'd sent him off on a wild goose hunt brought on by a dream that had troubled her sleep. That she had power was beyond question because there most certainly had been a blue boy, a burning girl, and even a magical fairy dance. He had watched the proposal and acceptance from four feet away. There would be a wedding tonight.

"Hmm. Are you my daughter?" Byron's gentle voice mused thoughtfully as he answered her troubled gaze. "Well, that would be yes, and no. In our current situation you would be more of a *granddaughter* than a daughter I believe. Cathryn, your mother, I love as my daughter. You, my dear, I love as my granddaughter. I have never had a family of my own other than Cathryn and Cornelius, and for all these years Cathryn was childless. It was heartbreaking watching her go without a child to love. But now, finally, she has children. She has you and your Sisters." Byron gave her a smile and she smiled back at him adoringly.

"You do taste different from Cornelius. A father, but different." Her head tilted to the side as she looked up at him. "Pappa Byron," she put a name to his face with a nod, "what was I like before I became a witch? I can't remember."

Byron's lip quirked up at the corner at being called "Pappa Byron." He answered her question honestly, but very carefully. "You were quite complicated, Emma."

"Really?" Emma's eyebrows frowned for her, turning down. "I don't feel very complicated anymore. I feel almost simple. What kind of things did I do that seemed complicated?"

Now it was Byron's eyebrows that frowned as he worried about where this conversation might lead and what it might do to her fragile state of mind. He tiptoed ahead cautiously, vague in his answer. "Well. As you mentioned earlier, my dear, I only had one full day to see you as a regular girl before you changed. I did notice a few things that I can share with you. Little things. Things I'm sure you're already aware of."

"Oh please! Tell me!" Emma begged eagerly, excited to know more about her old "self." "Tell me all of it, even the small stuff will be great, Pappa, because I can't remember shit, it's all blurry and the pieces don't fit."

"Emma! I gotta pee!" Mary's voice bellowed from inside the bedroom. The door was still wide open.

Emma and Byron peeked back inside where a smiling Mary head regarded them, poking up from a mound of pillows in the middle of the bed.

"If you gotta pee, go pee!" Emma hollered back.

"But you told me to stay naked and stay in bed!" The head shouted back, louder than ever.

"You don't have to stay in bed just because I told you to!" Emma shouted back even louder.

A hand shot out of the pile of pillows pointing an accusing finger at Emma. "You're wearing the pants in this relationship, lady! And anyway, I *like* being the girl!" Mary's face pouted. "I *like it* when you tell me what to do!"

The bedroom door in the hall adjacent to Mary's flew open and Dana came stomping out with curlers still in her hair and still wearing a nightgown. She stomped up to Byron without noticing Emma, who'd hidden behind him.

"You want me to take care of this so it doesn't go on for another hour?" Dana asked flatly.

Byron eyed her, then took a step back and motioned her through the door. Dana stomped into Mary's room.

"You! Girl!" Dana shouted at Mary's pillow peeking head. "Go get in the shower!" Dana ordered.

"Mmm!" Mary made a frightened little sound and burrowed deeper, leaving only her eyes peeking out.

"But I gotta pee," came a squeaky voice from under the pile.

"Pee in the shower!" Dana barked and turned on her heels to leave but stopped cold at the doorway as she finally got a good look at the new Emma.

"What the *hell* happened to you!?" Dana said roughly as she ogled, looking up and down the length of her frame, then up and down again. Emma's once pale, scarecrow thin body had been transformed into a fantasy vision of long legs, sinful curves, and impossible beauty. The package was made even more shocking by the skin tight white, hip hugging pants that displayed her every feminine curve in pornographic detail. Her short-sleeved red and white top was nothing but cuffs around her upper arms and a choke collar around her neck with a square of fabric hanging down the front that left her midriff and sides exposed. Any sudden movements or just raising her arms the wrong way would expose her perfect breasts. Every inch of her once pale flesh was now a beautiful shade of sun-kissed gold, and she wore a belt made of square rubies the size of dominos with a gleaming black onyx clasp in the front. The glittering rubies flashed and sparkled, drawing the eye to the naked flesh of her flat muscled stomach above the band. The calf-high red boots she wore had three inch heels which took her already imposing 5'11" up to an amazonish 6'1" and with her short black hair spiked straight up as it was she looked even taller. The only reason she hadn't looked like a giant out in the hall when Dana marched by was because she was huddled behind Byron, who was a Lurch-like 6'7".

Emma's copper gold nails, her black lips, gleaming teeth, and the copper gold eyes were like the pieces of the puzzle that pushed the whole package over into fantasy land. *People are not built this way,* was the thought that spun through Dana's mind as she took it all in. It was too much. Even the clothes seemed designed, not to conceal, but to make it utterly impossible not to see her in a sexual way. See her—and want her.

"What–the hell–happened here?" Dana muttered as she gawked, like she was eyeing a horrific accident on the freeway.

Dana stiffened as Emma reached out a hand and ran it down the front of her bath robe. Emma put the tips of her fingers right into her mouth and sucked as she stared at Dana with her strange new eyes that were almost hypnotic in their beauty. Dana froze like a frightened mouse. Emma's eyes, long neck, and short spiky hair somehow reminded Dana of a hawk she'd seen at the zoo. She glanced back toward the safety of her own room where she knew David was probably still shaving at the sink.

"It's all right, Dana, there's nothing to fear." Byron tried to reassure her, though he didn't look too sure himself. "Emma did the same thing to me just a few moments ago. She is a little more, physical, now that she's become a witch. Mary is a hugger, and Emma is a—"

"Taster," Dana supplied with a frown.

"You taste good." Emma smiled at her, not bothered in the least by being called a "taster." "You taste much older than you sound though. And—" Emma reached out like she was about to go for another "taste," but Dana took a quick step back, out of her reach.

"You know," she said, looking from Emma to Byron, back and forth, "I'm gonna go finish getting dressed. See you later, Emma." She slipped past quickly and out into the hall, walking away, but stopped in front of her own door and spun to face Emma again.

"You and miss thing in there are a couple, *right*?" she asked/demanded as she looked Emma up and down again.

"Yes," Emma answered, somewhat possessively.

"Good." Dana punctuated that with a stiff nod. "Good, good, good," she muttered, disappearing into her room.

"It appears that Mary did as she was bid," Byron said as he peeked into Mary's room. The bed was empty and they could hear the water being turned on in the shower.

"Hey, is anyone over there!?" Mary's voice shouted from inside the shower.

A muffled male voice answered her through the wall. It sounded like David. "Yeah. I'm in here!"

"Are you in the shower too!?" Mary shouted back.

"No! I'm—"

"GIRL!" Dana's voice shouted back through the wall. "Leave my man alone!"

"But I want to talk! *I'm looonely*!" Mary lamented in a sing song way back through the wall.

The shouting conversation continued.

"Perhaps you should go and help Mary keep quiet," Byron suggested, but Emma's copper gold eyes went wide and she started shaking her head in a panicked NO.

"I can't go in there! Are you crazy!?" She hid behind Byron, latched to his back. Byron tried to turn around but she stayed behind him, moving as he moved. After a few moments of utter silliness, with Byron feeling like a dog chasing his own tail, he stopped trying to get Emma off his back and just talked to her while she was latched on.

"Why are you afraid to see Mary?"

"Because if I see her all naked and yummy I won't be able to think about anything but her. Which would be fine, *more than fine*, but right now I want to use my brain for myself and think about other things. You still need to tell me about the *me* I was! And I need to go see the blue boy and the burning girl. And Bethany's party is this afternoon. And I just got dressed, I want to keep my clothes on for a little while. And I'm really hungry." She put a hand to her flat stomach and squinted her beautiful eyes as if in pain as she looked toward the sound of Mary's shouting voice. She was still enjoying her "through the wall" dialogue with the neighbors.

"If I go in there I'll end up on the bathroom floor with Mary for hours. I just know it!" She seemed conflicted. Torn between wanting to go inside with Mary and wanting to go do other things. "She's so lonely," Emma said, weakening. She took a step toward Mary's voice.

"There, there now." Byron pulled her back before she walked in and lost herself. He walked her back out into the hall and hugged her, patting her back as he spoke. "There will be plenty of time for that later tonight. It's all right, Emma. You're already dressed and ready to start your day."

Emma began to rub herself on him while he spoke, wallowing in whatever it was she smelled or felt coming from him. Byron lifted his gaze as one of the maids walked down the hall, giving him and Emma a scandalized look, which made Byron look back down at the writhing girl with a dawning understanding that brought with it a flash of true worry. Dressed the way she was and with her challenged mental state, she could very easily be put in a bad situation. It could happen almost instantly. Even by well-meaning people. Byron was a fit and hale sixty-three year old man, not yet bent down by his years but old enough to be spared the tidal wave of hormones that a younger man would have raging through his body at the sight of her, let alone the touch of Emma's flesh.

The fact that Byron saw Emma as a granddaughter helped him keep things in their proper perspective as well, but he worried what would happen if one of the younger men touched her as she was now. A man who saw her as a woman. Byron doubted if she would even be able to control herself and if she'd even want to control herself if she encountered that kind of touch. Her new witch powers and mental condition seemed a recipe for disaster, but add in her new body and clothes and it was like a driving rain of lacquer thinner falling on a forest fire. If not watched very carefully, Emma would set ablaze anyone she touched.

She was, quite literally, too hot to handle by anyone who saw her as a potential sexual partner. Dana had interacted with Emma without difficulty, but Byron was quite certain that Dana was not attracted to women. He pondered the problem for a moment and decided that Emma could go *absolutely nowhere* without an acceptable chaperone. Someone would have to guard her constantly, from others and herself.

"Emma, do you trust me?" Byron asked her.

She stopped rubbing against him and looked up at his face with her copper gold eyes, so completely trusting. So utterly vulnerable. "Yes, Pappa. I love you."

Byron felt a tingle down his spine as he stared into her eyes. She truly loved him like a real grandchild. He swallowed at a lump that was suddenly in his throat and nodded. "Then let's go downstairs, my dear, and get you a bite to eat first, and you can meet your blue boy and burning girl. They are quite lovely. The wedding will be spectacular."

He took her hand and placed it on his arm and started walking her down the hall. Coming in their direction was Mary's maid, a very patient and perceptive woman named Hanna. Hanna had a gorgeous tray of breakfast things, and she stopped in front of Emma to let her browse the plate.

Byron watched Emma as she looked at the tray then back in the direction of the room then up to Byron. It was like watching a child. He saw that she was hungry, and she wanted the pretty food, but she was scared to go back into the room because of losing herself to Mary. She wanted him to help.

"Hanna, I'll take your tray for you." Byron lifted it from her hands. "Please stay with Princess Emma and guard her for just a moment. Do not let anyone other than the Queen or Black Rain herself touch her until I return."

"Yes sir." Hanna didn't ask questions, she just obeyed, stepping into a protective stance beside Emma as if she expected a fight.

Byron carried the tray back down the hall, but as he reached Mary's room Dana's door flew open again. She came charging out looking incensed.

"That freak just asked me to come over and wash her skanky back!" Dana shouted, taking a few more steps in his direction.

Byron balanced the tray easily in one hand as he opened Mary's door and spoke to Dana. "Lady Dana, you know that Mary means no harm. She's a witch, and she does not like to be alone." He turned and looked at her with calm, compassionate eyes that stopped her just before she launched into an angry rant.

"It's not something she can control, Lady Dana. Just as Bethany needs blood and sacrifice to live, Mary needs life. She needs other people to talk with and touch. She needs to be a part of other lives and other life to live."

Dana looked ashamed of herself. "Oh. Sorry." She turned and walked back into her room without another word.

Byron went inside and set the tray down on the table beside the bed.

"Princess Mary?" he called at the bathroom door.

"Yeah," Mary replied weakly. Byron stepped into the bathroom and quickly opened the shower door. Mary was sitting on the floor of the shower crying. "How bad is Emma?" she asked.

Byron reached in and turned off the water then stepped into the shower and lifted Mary up in his arms, not caring about how wet he got as he walked back into the bedroom with her and laid her gently on the bed. He propped her up, arranging some pillows behind her back, then brought her a well salted wedge of orange from the tray of food.

Mary sucked the orange then looked up at him. She already knew every word he and Emma had said as they spoke to each other and even the look on Emma's face when she gazed down the hall, scared to come back into the room. And all of the rest.

"You're right, Byron. We can't leave her alone for a second. It's not safe. And you have to be careful because she's doing things without even knowing that she's doing them. She's having accidents and doing magic all over the place. Take her downstairs and I'll be down as soon as I can. We'll enjoy the wedding and the party and the outside together and find other safe people to see and touch and taste together. And I'll do better for her. I promise, Byron. I promise." Mary started to cry again.

"Don't be unfair to yourself, Mary. You love her. We're all still learning how to take care of our Emma." Byron fixed a small plate with a few more pieces of fruit, handed it to her and kissed her forehead.

"Love you," Mary said as she sat up.

"And I you, Princess," Byron said then headed back out into the hall.

He almost swore when he looked down the hall and saw Emma and Hanna kissing each other. He quickly walked toward them, intending to separate them, but Emma stopped and stepped away from Hanna just as he reached them. Hanna seemed a little dazed by the encounter and Byron thought her eyes glowed a copper gold for just a second, but his attention was drawn back to Emma as she staggered and put a hand against the wall to steady herself.

"Give her that for me," Emma said breathlessly. "And comb her hair for me." She took another steadying breath or two before continuing her instructions. "She just got out of the shower and her hair's wet, use the detangler." Breath. "It's in the green bottle that's in the bathroom. That brush will snatch her bald if you don't use the detangler. And tell her I love her."

Hanna nodded, gave Byron a small curtsey, and headed off toward Mary's room like nothing strange had happened.

"Is Mary okay?" asked Emma, still recovering from the kiss.

Byron smiled. "Yes. Worried about you, but she's fine. She told me to take you downstairs and feed you and watch over you till she gets down to take care of you herself. And she promised to take *better* care of you."

Emma thought about that, then nodded and leaned against the wall. Byron offered her his arm which she took gratefully, still a bit wobbly. As they headed down the stairs they passed a few male servants who were walking up, and Byron held Emma safely away from them as they passed, but they were obviously enthralled just by the sight of her. They reached the bottom of the stairs and entered the Entry Hall and more people stopped to stare.

"Emma my dear, could I get you some different clothes to wear? Perhaps something a little less revealing?"

"I want to wear this."

"Why?" he asked.

"Because Rain thinks I looked beautiful in it. And it made her smile to see me wear this, so I'll wear it."

"You're wearing these clothes to make Rain notice you?"

"Yes, Pappa." Emma closed her eyes and took a deep breath.

"What about Mary?"

"Mary knows everything, Pappa." Emma opened her eyes and gave him a grin. "You know that."

"What about Believer?" Byron arched an eyebrow as he asked. "Will he not take exception to you sleeping with his wife."

"Why would he? I'm going to sleep with him too."

Byron stumbled and only Emma's hand on his arm kept him from falling and taking a tumble to the floor right in the middle of the Entry Hall.

"You okay?" She got him steady on his feet but was swaying herself now.

"Yes. Yes. Quite all right." Byron adjusted his suit (which was still wet) and put his arm back out for Emma to take again, reclaiming some of his lost dignity as they continued through to the Cathedral Hall. Byron stoically ignored the stares his tumble and Emma's clothes created.

"Does your sister know you plan on sleeping with her husband?" he asked in a conversational tone as he looked straight ahead.

"Yes. We're going to do him at the same time."

Byron couldn't help it. He stopped walking and looked at her, flabbergasted. "Why on earth would you do something like that?"

Emma's smile was beautiful and looked completely guileless and free of any sinister intent as she answered him. "Rain loves me, Pappa Byron, and I'm sure Believer will love me too, so what could possibly be wrong with us being together?"

"And what about Mary?" Byron asked.

"She can join us," Emma said weakly and then she rubbed herself on him right then and there, dropping the bottom jaws of those already staring at them. Byron's attention shifted to the crowd, and he didn't notice that Emma had lifted his hand to her face. She licked it.

"Emma?" Byron asked as she licked again.

"You taste good, Pappa." Her oral fixation and the wallowing didn't bother him but it was certainly turning a lot of heads in the hall.

Most of the four hundred and seventy-five souls who called Amen Hale home were working right now all over the campus at various tasks. Many were preparing meals, tending the grounds, watching prisoners, or preparing for Princess Bethany's birthday celebration and the impromptu wedding. But a fair number of those not working were right there in the Cathedral Hall. A group of thirty or so men, women, and children were listening to Mr. Pyle, the keeper of the Book of Shadows, read from the book, but most of those in the Cathedral Hall were "Royal Watching" for lack of a better term.

They were lounging around in groups, sitting on couches, leaning on walls, and hovering in doorways, waiting to see or possibly even talk to one of the Lords or Ladies or Princesses of Amen Hale. Having Emma on his arm, looking the way she looked and acting the way she was acting was chumming the water for the feeding frenzy of ravenous human eyeballs that circled like sharks, waiting to see some new wonder or some new horror.

Byron shot out a relieved "Blessed Be!" when he spotted Cathryn coming his way through the gawking crowd.

Emma didn't even look up as she switched to his other hand and was still licking away when Cathryn walked up to them. Cathryn watched for a moment without saying a word, and then placed her own hand on top of Byron's hand, and Emma licked her hand instead. She paused.

"Mmm," Emma made a satisfied noise and released Byron's hand and grabbed Cathryn's, allowing Byron to escape. Emma licked her way up Cathryn's arm while Cathryn stood there and calmly discussed the situation with Byron and his worries about a constant chaperone for Emma and her troubled mental state. Emma, for her part, seemed oblivious to anything they said as she rotated between licking and rubbing herself on Cathryn's body while every eye in the entry hall watched. Cathryn was as solid as a rock and Emma was oblivious; only Byron showed signs of squeamishness at what was happening and unease at the gallery of the staring eyes.

"Was she like this this morning?" Cathryn asked.

"No, my Queen. She was lucid and conversant."

"Did she do any magic that you noticed from then till now?"

"I'm not sure. She may have done something to Mary's maid, Hanna."

"Describe it," Cathryn ordered, and Byron did, down to the copper gold gleam he'd seen in Hanna's eyes.

"She sent Hanna in to give Mary her magic. She's starving to death," Cathryn concluded.

"Starving!" Byron looked shocked.

"Yes. Watch her, Byron. After she licks, she swallows."

Emma's eyes were still closed and she'd slid down Cathryn's frame and wrapped herself around one of her legs. She'd just been rubbing herself against the white fabric of Cathryn's dress, but Cathryn pulled up the cloth and even rolled down her hose to let Emma press her face against the flesh of her leg. Emma began to lick.

She made a long stroke up Cathryn's leg, from her knee up her thigh and they both watched as she stopped and swallowed.

"Did she eat anything this morning?" Cathryn asked.

"No," Byron answered.

"And I know she didn't eat anything yesterday. Not after her episode." Cathryn shook her head in frustration. Emma sat in the floor, still clinging to her leg and Cathryn's dress fell down to cover her which seemed even more scandalous than watching her lick the Queen's leg because now no one could see what was happening; they just knew that she was under there, licking.

"But there's nothing there, my Queen! She's swallowing but she's not eating anything!" Byron said, frustration in his voice.

Beneath the dress Cathryn felt Emma slip to the floor and lie on the ground, curled around her feet.

"We're not enough for her. We're her parents, Byron. We can't satisfy her in the way she needs."

"My Queen, just what do you intend to do?" Byron straightened, indignant, worried that he knew what Cathryn was about to do with his granddaughter and he didn't like it.

Cathryn recognized his reluctance and turned her eyes on him. It was not a friendly gaze and neither was her voice when she spoke to him. "Just because we can't see it, does not mean that it is not *there,* Byron!" she snapped. "There is no profit in denying what *is*! To do so would only kill her. Fish swim. Birds fly. Snakes crawl. Vampires drink blood. Bethany eats death. Mary eats life. Emma eats love. So mote it be."

A few of those in the crowd echoed the benediction, whispering "So mote it be." After a brief pause Byron assented as well, but he did not look pleased.

Cathryn closed her eyes and spoke to Amen Hale, not doubting for a moment that her words would be heard. "I need Jane," she said. She lifted her skirts to see Emma below her, curled into a fetal ball around her feet. She seemed to be asleep. Cathryn stepped out of her grasp and knelt down beside her and then heard a clear musical voice at the same time she heard the crowd of watching people gasp, surprised by Jane's appearance from thin air.

"What's wrong with Emma?" Jane asked.

"She's starving to death," Cathryn said and looked up into Jane's beautiful face and let her see all the things in her own face that Jane could without putting it all into words for everyone to hear. "Could you take her to Mary? Mary can help feed her what she needs." Cathryn's eyes asked more and Jane saw it.

Cathryn did not look away as Jane stared at her, but she added one last brick to the pile. "I love you both. And I would feed you if you needed my blood down to the last drop. And I would do this myself in a second because I love her, but I'm not the food she needs, Jane." Tears filled her eyes and Cathryn jumped when a cold hand touched her face. Jane was just suddenly there, closer, her hand touching her face.

"You are a good mother for her. And for me." Jane leaned forward and kissed Cathryn on her brow, and her long black hair fell across Cathryn's face as she moved by, and the smell of roses and Jane's magic almost made her swoon.

Jane scooped Emma up from the ground and then stood as if she weighed nothing. She leaned forward and breathed her breath into Emma's face.

"Jane." Emma breathed out her name and a smile formed on her black lips, but she didn't open her eyes.

They vanished.

Reeves

A Damned Decent Fellow

THE TWO BIG rental trucks drove into the warehouse through the open roll down doors, returning from picking up needed supplies for Amen Hale. As the guards beside the doors went to roll them down, French commandos made their move. Two men slipped around the corner and held each of the men at gunpoint, while at the same moment more soldiers poured out of the back of two trucks that had just entered. They quickly had the fifteen men in black leather lined up against the wall and disarmed.

A generator sitting outside the doors made a constant tap, tap, tapping, but there were no other sounds aside from breathing and shuffling of feet on the concrete floor. No music. No TV. A thick power cord ran to a power box. Feeding off the box were four sets of halogen lights on tripods which provided the only source of light in the warehouse. One white refrigerator stood sentinel beside three fold-out tables whereon was strewn a varied assortment of open and empty takeout boxes. The only other item in the warehouse was one stand-up, self-contained plastic portable toilet set against the wall on the far side of the warehouse, but other than a number of chairs around the tables the open space was bare.

The captive men in black didn't speak and neither did the French commandos, also in black. After a couple of minutes, five men in suits entered and approached the captive soldiers.

"Hello. My name is Arnaud Kassier. I am a representative of the French government. Who here wishes to speak for your group?" He spoke with an accent but his English was understandable and his voice friendly enough. He was a short man, with dark wiry hair, dark eyes, and a full mustache that sat atop a broad smile of coffee stained, crooked teeth. He was dressed in a plain grey suit and didn't wear a gun.

"I will," replied the only man among the captives with gray in his hair.

Arnaud said something in French and two guards quickly brought over a couple of chairs and set them up. Arnaud sat in one of the chairs and motioned to the other. "Please, if you would be so kind as to take a seat and we can speak for a moment. Yes?"

The man took a seat in the chair across from him. Arnaud studied him and the other men carefully. None of them looked worried or scared in the least. They weren't breathing hard and they didn't look stressed. They were all cooperative but utterly unafraid; the only emotions evident were on the faces of the younger men who actually looked annoyed, but *not* afraid. Arnaud spoke in French and mentioned this to the other men in suits who were standing nearby. They also thought it unusual and troubling.

"You are from Amen Hale," Arnaud began.

"Yes," answered the man.

"What is your name?" he asked.

"I will not tell you my name."

Arnaud pulled a little notepad from inside his suit jacket and flipped a few pages.

"Why are you here in France, Mr. Reeves?"

Reeves showed no outward signs of stress or surprise that they knew his name as he answered the question. "Food. Equipment. Supplies."

He offered no further information, even when Arnaud stared at him expectantly, as if waiting for more. Arnaud moved on. "You have entered our country unannounced and purchased a large quantity of weapons. Any government would be concerned as to what you plan on doing with these weapons, especially in this day and age in which we live. Terrorism and all that, you know."

"Hand held weapons and simple security gear is all we have purchased from your country."

"True, Mr. Reeves. And honestly, we are not concerned about the weapons, but we do insist on speaking with your government. It seems polite that we at least meet, face to face, if you will be, *shopping*, here for groceries and other items. When would be an appropriate time to meet with King Cornelius or perhaps Black Rain? We understand that she visited the market yesterday."

That drew a reaction from almost every man there including Reeves. They all looked angry. Furious.

"Sorry, I meant no offense. We were told that she had been assaulted. I *hope* she is well?"

"We have nothing further to say to you, Mr. Arnaud. Now I suggest you release us and allow us to go back to our place," Reeves said with heat in his voice.

Arnaud conferred with his colleagues for a moment before turning back to Reeves. As he spoke, the French commandos started to get the other men from Amen Hale onto their feet and moving toward the trucks.

"We request a meeting with your government in an official capacity. Either with your King and Queen or with the Black Witch. Please let them know that we will be glad to return your men when we meet." Arnaud stood and the soldiers who had filled the warehouse finished loading the men from Amen Hale into the backs of the two white rental trucks.

"It's not my place to speak to you, Mr. Arnaud, but either you are a fool or you are following orders that are foolish."

"Please, Mr. Reeves. We intend your men no harm. They will be treated as honored guests of our country until our official meeting." He pulled out a business card and handed it to Reeves. "This is my number." He motioned to one of the men in suits who stood nearby. "This is Ferrand Jacobs, an ambassador we wish you to take with you as our representative to Amen Hale. He can arrange the meeting time and place between our two countries."

One of the soldiers said something to Arnaud.

"Mr. Reeves," he gave a nod, "it has been a pleasure. I look forward to our next meeting." He gave Ferrand a quick word of instruction in French before turning and making a hasty retreat with the other suits. The two big trucks rumbled to life and drove out the doorway with the men from Amen Hale inside, leaving only Ferrand and Reeves standing in the empty warehouse.

Ferrand was a tall man with dark eyes and plain of face. He had ordinary, forgettable features and seemed an odd choice to send as the French representative.

"What do you think will happen, Mr. Reeves? How pissed do you think the Black Witch will be about all of this?"

His voice was a surprise, rich, resonant, and clear, by far the man's most memorable feature.

Reeves shrugged. "You tell me. If you pull a lion by its tail it may just turn and growl at you, but if you steal her cubs, what do you think will happen?"

Ferrand pressed a hand against his stomach like he was feeling ill. "We simply wish to meet her." He made it sound harmless. "There is a beautiful castle in the valley that is much more private and secure than this place you now reside. There are many other things that the French government is prepared to make available to your people. Things that the U.S. government cannot offer."

"Save it. I don't care and I doubt our Princess will either."

Ferrand nodded. "Sorry. Just doing my job." He pressed his hand to his stomach again, looking pained.

"You feeling all right?" Reeves said as he eyed the other man suspiciously.

"My wife is a horrible cook, but I try to eat what she fixes. Last night's dinner was disgusting." Ferrand grimaced.

"You need a dog," Reeves suggested.

"No, no." Ferrand shook his head. "It's not that simple for us, the way we eat dinner here is different from how you Americans do it. We really take our time, we drink wine, we talk, we smoke, *we flirt*. She's right there watching me the whole time. I watch her take a bite, she watches me take a drink of wine, I watch her pull a drag of her cigarette. Back and forth like a dance. Dinner can be a *very* sensual thing when done right." Ferrand had a faraway look in his eye and actually smiled as he patted his upset stomach.

Ferrand spent the next couple of minutes in small talk, mostly about his wife of three months, Leann, who had prepared the sickening meal he'd so willingly consumed.

Reeves tried not to like the man but he was finding it difficult. He appeared to be real and genuine, which most likely meant that every single word was nothing but artifice. Ferrand was most likely gay and hadn't touched a woman since he came out of his mother, and he probably came out complaining about that one brief encounter, but it was still a good story. And he told it well.

Reeves tried to keep the smile off his face as he walked over to the box by the refrigerator and dug through the medical supplies they had on hand. He pitched an unopened bottle of antacids at Ferrand, which he caught and then looked at the bottle. He looked back at Reeves with surprise.

"What?" Reeves challenged the look.

"Very decent of you, Mr. Reeves. Merci." Ferrand set to opening the bottle.

"By the way, in Amen Hale, we don't eat dinner like Americans do either. And I may speak English, but I am not American. I am a Child of Hale."

Ferrand heard the deep conviction in the other man's voice. It worried him.

"You must be very happy there?" He popped two chalky white wafers into his mouth and crunched.

"I am happy to serve my King and Queen and the Children of Hale," Reeves answered as he checked his watch; the Gateway would open in eleven minutes.

"If I may, Mr. Reeves," Ferrand stepped closer, still holding the bottle of antacids, "a quick question or two on formalities before we arrive. How should I *present myself* when I meet your King and Queen or your Princesses. Do they all require full obeisance?"

By his tightened facial expression Reeves could see Ferrand obviously hoped the answer was no. "Bow if you like, or don't bow. Greet them however you choose to, Ferrand," Reeves answered dismissively.

"Yes, but would you bow to them if you were me?" Ferrand pressed, his voice a little more strained and fearful, his eyes a little more desperate. Reeves realized that the man was wound tighter than he appeared.

"Yes, bow," Reeves told him.

Ferrand gave the bottle a fitful shake, dumping two more wafers into his hand. "But should I do a full prostration and spread myself on the floor or just to go to my knees with my head bowed or should I bow from the waist?" He demonstrated, bowing. "Or just a give a respectful bow of the head and—"

"Easy Ferrand!" Reeves snapped. "To your knees before the King and Queen, head bowed for a five count, as for the rest, let your aching guts make the decision for you, but don't be proud, if your guts say crawl, crawl."

Ferrand looked embarrassed at his lack of nerve. "Merci," he muttered then popped the wafers into his mouth and started to chew.

"Does it not get tedious, all that bowing?" Ferrand asked after the crunching ended.

"No," Reeves answered, again wondering if it was all a show, Ferrand nothing but an actor.

Ferrand pulled out a cigarette from his inside coat pocket. "Do you mind?" he asked.

"Go ahead," Reeves said, "but lose it before we go through the gate."

Ferrand was silent until he finished his cigarette.

"I think it would drive me mad after a while," he said as he ground his shoe on the discarded butt.

"What's that?" Reeves asked.

"All the bowing. I'd be all right for a while, but I think eventually it would drive me mad." Ferrand frowned.

Reeves checked his watch, only two minutes until the gate opened. He was tired of Ferrand. He'd decided he didn't like the man after all.

"Come on," Reeves ordered. They both walked over and stood before a blank section of warehouse wall where the gateway was about to appear. "Ferrand, why do you eat your wife's food?" Reeves asked as he stared straight ahead.

Ferrand's concentration was focused on the wall, watching for the second it would change into an archway, cutting through time and space connecting to some location within Amen Hale. It was an easy question to answer. "Because I love her."

"Why do you think I bow?" The words had a weight and a meaning behind them that made Ferrand turn to stare at the other man who still looked dead ahead, not returning his gaze.

For the first time Ferrand actually worried that he might not survive this trip. His thoughts went to his new young wife and her disastrous attempts at cooking. He truly hoped he'd have another opportunity to eat it and to pretend that each filthy forkful was the most wonderful thing he'd ever had in his mouth.

Dan

"This Situation"

I WAS ALREADY IN the hallway, standing in front of Mary's door waiting for them when Jane appeared carrying Emma in her arms, and I was surprised to hear in her head that for the first time *ever*, she wanted privacy. She didn't want me to see what was about to happen. I already knew what had happened downstairs and what she'd told Cathryn. I knew everything inside her mind and soul. But I was so surprised I thought my words to her without first considering how she'd react to it.

"*You really don't want me to see what you're about to do?*"

"I don't know," she thought back, fighting hard to think nothing. Parts of her mind became a blank white nothing.

She did know, and I knew it. She didn't want to admit it, even to herself. There were things like that inside her soul. I was sure it was like that in everyone's soul, but her soul was the one I lived in and loved and guarded. I watched her mind as it worked, each little piece of her personality, and all her desires and thoughts, all joined together like a magical machine to make the soul of this woman that I loved. Parts of her mind ran and hid from other parts that wanted them to see or know something that the rest of her didn't want to know, while other parts tried to lie to her because another part over here or there was scared or uncomfortable or wanted something it shouldn't.

I watched it all. I knew things about her that she didn't know about herself and I usually guarded her mind's secrets as jealously as each little shifting thought inside her. Her subconscious mind and I were like co-conspirators most of the time, doing whatever it took to make her feel better about who and what she was. I even let her lie to herself if that was what she needed, and sometimes she did.

But this time I didn't let her. I knew how she felt about what she was about to do. She didn't know what was going to happen inside the bedroom, and she was scared and embarrassed at having me see it and feel it and be a part of it as she fumbled about. I felt her trying not to think about me being there with her as she faced each new awkwardness, feeling each female hand as it touched and explored. Having me watch her hesitate or pull back or turn away scared her almost as much as the thought of me seeing her let go and find pleasure in what was happening. She knew I was hoping that she would find pleasure in it, but she was worried that she might freeze completely and that was another embarrassment.

She shifted her hold on Emma, one hand under her back and head and one under her legs as she held her very long body against her. I didn't take Emma from her hands. She didn't want me to touch her or her magic that seemed to spread like poison. She looked back into my eyes after shifting Emma about and I knew that she wanted this first time to be as private and unseen as possible, but at the same time, she knew that it couldn't happen. I felt the sadness of acceptance move through her. She wanted this to be like going into a dark room with the lights out, but she knew there was no way to turn the lights out in her mind. Or there hadn't been before. She didn't know. I was stronger now. More powerful. I could give her what she needed.

"*Jane, there is a way I can give you privacy—for this,*" I thought clearly to her as I stared into her eyes.

I told her "*for this*" because I didn't want "privacy" to become a pattern. With me inside her body, feeling everything she felt with her body, what she was about to do was not something I found a burden; other than the fact that it troubled Jane, I was fine with it. Connected as I was, our bodies and our pleasure were one and the same. I'd been enjoying her pleasure, a "female's pleasure," as we had sex because I was inside her soul feeling everything she felt, while at the same time I was inside myself feeling the pleasure of my own body in hers.

When I had explained this situation to Jane she'd laughed and jokingly told me to "go fuck myself" and then jumped my bones. *I*, of course, "fucked myself" and was glad to do so. With me inside her as I was, it was impossible for Jane to do anything that pleased her without it pleasing me as well, but I was still "guy" enough to be excited about what was about to happen between three of the most beautiful women on earth.

Watching the inner workings of Jane's soul had surely taught me that there were little pieces of my own male soul that were doing happy cartwheels inside me at the thought of being inside my wife's body while she was with Emma and Mary or Rain or whoever. And I also knew that there must be other parts of my mind that were enraged at those happy parts and were even now chasing them around inside my soul trying to kill those parts of me that might find pleasure in a situation that had brought so much distress and pain to the woman I loved and lived inside of.

The inner struggles of the darker side of my soul were there, but they were secondary to the needs and wants of the soul of my wife. Right now Jane needed privacy. I smashed the cartwheeling bastards inside me like roaches with a shoe and did what I had to do to make her more comfortable. Before I could think my words to Jane, a thought danced defiantly across my mind.

"It's hard to kill roaches."

It was odd moments like these than made me think I was insane.

"How can you give me privacy?" Jane spoke out loud. "You can't leave my mind, Dan. And I'm not really sure I'd want you to even if you could."

"I'm stronger now, Jane. I can do more. I can let that half of me that lives inside your soul fall inside just one part of you so completely that I won't see or hear or feel anything that happens in the rest of you until I came back from that one part of your soul."

She looked intrigued. I felt a trickle of relief and hope loosen the tightness inside her. She thought about me feeling her relief. She knew I knew. She didn't try to talk me out of it. She was finally doing less of that, which was good.

"What part of my mind would you stay in while I—" She didn't finish her words; even inside her mind, the thought ended like it had been cut with a knife.

"I'll just go to a day from your past. I'll live it with you, and that part of me that's inside you will be living that day while here and now you do what you have to do to help Emma."

She squinted her eyes at me and pressed her lips tight. "You don't mind any of this? I know you, Dan. I'm not in your head like you are mine but you still have eyes and a face and a body to read. I know you want to see it and be in me when I do this." She looked down at Emma again, seeing her body as I might.

We'd already discussed "*this situation*" and Jane had already agreed to sleep with Emma and Rain together to gain access for us to Rain's blood. That, Jane didn't mind. We both saw in Rain's eyes that she intended to feed us for the rest of eternity if need be and never once force her into her bed, and for that reason alone, Jane said she'd do it. If Rain loved her that much, Jane said she'd do whatever she wanted and I'd agreed. But I might have agreed to absolutely anything that won us more of Rain's blood, and I knew from seeing inside Jane's soul that she would have too.

We both agreed that we were lucky as hell or blessed beyond measure, or both, that someone who so *totally* owned us would be willing to give us what we wanted and needed and somehow demand absolutely nothing that she wanted in return. In some ways it made us feel like we owned her instead of the other way around. In a way we were an obligation, like a belt of more responsibilities tied around her waist. Two more mouths to feed.

We both hated the change but we knew that it wasn't Rain's fault; she didn't mean for this to happen. It was still frustrating, but trying to deny what had happened was pointless and there was nothing we could do to change it. Our vampire existence had been so simple before. There had been nothing in our universe of darkness except her to me and me to her. Jane and Dan. My life, inside her, around her, and through her, and her insane love for me were the limits of our existence.

Everything else had been so much less real that it couldn't be compared to what we were to each other. She was like the earth, hanging in the darkness of space and I was her moon, eternally moving about her, tied to her and living through her and in her. No other planets or stars clouded our perfect universe; it was just the two of us, together in the dark of our endless night.

But everything had changed; now Rain and her blood was a bright burning sun in the center of our universe around which we orbited. Our universe had changed. We changed with it. Constantly, inside myself and inside of Jane, a part of our vampire minds longed for Rain. And that was another problem. Rain's blood already owned us both completely. Jane did not want a second master.

We both knew that Emma had used her magic to bewitch Rain. She'd just become a witch and it seemed like her power was out of control. She'd bewitched Mary and Cathryn and who knew how many others as well. Jane was terrified that Emma's magic might find me, and that I'd fall in love with Emma just from being inside her soul while she was with her. And she was still terrified that Emma's magic might actually work on her and make her love her as much or even more than she loved me. Rain's blood already owned us and Jane did not want our world to change again.

As I listened, her fear turned toward a dark desire to destroy, to end the threat that lay right there in her arms. *Remove it*, she thought. *It's safer to kill her.* Another part of her soul whispered, *We can't risk losing more.*

She envisioned our universe with two bright burning suns with us spinning wildly around, this way and that while trying to hold onto each other. It was madness.

The darkest parts of her whispered seductions as she considered killing Emma right now and telling Cathryn and everyone else that she was "very sorry" and that she "just couldn't stop herself."

Around us, the air cooled. Two servants who'd been watching us from down the hall turned and left, chilled to the bone or moved by some will not of their own that Jane's magic had sent out. Some prelude to murder.

I didn't move. I knew that I wouldn't be able to stop her if she did decide to kill Emma. Jane was faster and stronger than I was. She stared down at Emma's face and eyes and watched the shallow rise and fall of her breathing and the sound of the blood running through her veins. She concentrated on the sound of Emma's beating heart.

I listened as she considered Emma's life, thinking about how this thudding sound, this beating heart, had hunted her *relentlessly* for years, always wanting more than she was willing to give. Year after year, Emma was there, and her heart was there, always asking for more. "Tha thump tha thump." She listened to the sound and thought how this organ (or whatever power moved it) still hunted her even now (even after she'd died), crawling always toward her, one relentless beat at a time, always asking for more. More love. More than she was willing to give.

Why did it choose me? Why did Emma's heart love *me* like this? She wanted to drop her and get away but she didn't, she couldn't. Here, at last, Emma's beating heart had found her. Jane was terrified. I chose that moment to speak because I was afraid not to speak.

"*Killing her would hurt you more than falling in love with her would. My love, if it happens, it happens.*"

Still she waited, truly undecided, balanced on the edge between killing her and "not."

I didn't know what to do.

The bedroom door began to open, and we both turned to face Mary. Once the door was open and she'd had a second of shocked surprise, she froze, staring at the three of us. Mary's eyes began to brighten and a pale green luminescence glowed from her skin. Jane and I could feel her draw magic around herself as she stepped out into the hall.

"What happened to Emma?" Mary asked crisply.

"She collapsed. She's starving," Jane answered emotionlessly, like the nightmare monster her glowing red eyes made her appear to be. Emma looked like a dead body already, hanging limp in Jane's arms.

Mary stared into Jane's red eyes for a moment longer then looked around, seeming to look at the air over Jane's head and walls and things unseen like she sometimes did. When she looked back at Jane, her face was enraged.

"What the hell are *you* holding her for? You don't even want her!" Mary spat hatefully as she stepped over to Emma and started to check on her, touching her face and chest. Making sure she was breathing. Mary looked up from where she worked on Emma, right into Jane's murderous red eyes and studied her face from less than a foot away with her own sparkling, emerald green glare.

"I wish I could just touch you and know what the hell's wrong with you. But just because I can't touch you and know what's in your head doesn't mean that I'm blind, you selfish bitch! You think I can't feel murder in the air! Tell me what the hell she ever did, other than love you, to make you want to kill her! TELL ME!" Mary shouted into Jane's face.

Jane growled, then said, "No," showing some teeth.

Mary gave her a spiteful smile and hissed out, 'Yesss." She stepped away from Emma and reached out toward my bare chest.

"Move!" Jane ordered.

I stayed put. Mary had never touched me before, and up until now I'd been careful not to let her. She'd touched Jane before and got absolutely nothing from her, and since then she'd never tried to touch me, but apparently she'd learned that magic that didn't work on Jane still worked on me. She probably learned that from touching Rain.

"Are you just going to stand there and let her touch you?" Jane thought to me.

"*Yes,*" I answered and felt her shocked surprise.

"But she'll know I was thinking about killing Emma! She'll know everything about us!" she shouted back to me in my head. Outraged.

"*Then decide right now, either kill Emma and tell Mary that you're* 'really sorry' *about it, or risk all our love to help save her,*" I told her calmly and listened to her panicked thoughts swarm like a kicked beehive, while Mary's outstretched hand drew closer to my bare chest and all the secrets that I held from both our hearts. I was freaking out but I didn't know what else to do.

"Why?! Why are you doing this, Dan?! I don't want to share our love with anyone! I don't want to love anyone the way I love you!" Jane's thoughts shouted into my head as loudly as she could and her eyes glowed even brighter as Mary's hand pushed closer.

"*I know your heart better than you do, Jane! If you knew what I knew, you wouldn't be afraid of loving Emma!*"

"WHY!?" she shouted so loudly in my mind I closed my eyes and winced as her power blasted inside me.

Mary touched me.

We both felt a little pop of energy as her palm touched my chest. Her power flowed into me and around me, slowly spreading down through my thoughts, each little part of my vampire mind, a section at a time. So many thoughts, feelings, smells, touches, sights, memories, and desires from both my mind and Jane's. I felt her power as it passed each part. It wasn't painful, but it was odd, like having someone reach into your flesh and run their hand down your spine, vertebra by vertebra, starting at the top of the neck at the base of your skull, all the way down to the tip of your tail bone. Each section, thoroughly explored.

When the feeling finally passed, I had to give myself a shake to chase off the creepy feeling of having all I was, from my beginning to this very moment, be known so completely by someone else. I looked over at Jane. Her glowing red eyes were watching us both, waiting to see what had happened to me and what Mary would do with her newfound knowledge.

"*Now I know how you always feel, my love.*" I pulled my lips back and showed some teeth, making a strained face.

She smiled.

"*That was—kinda creepy,*" I added.

"I like it just fine." Jane spoke the words out loud. "Usually," she added in her head.

Mary's green eyes regarded us both for a moment. We could both see that she was dazed and overwhelmed by whatever she'd gotten from touching me. And Jane through me. She didn't looked upset anymore, which was a good thing.

"Wow." Mary managed that one word after two, long, human minutes, during which she seemed to be sorting and arranging what she'd found, if I had to guess from watching her face.

She was about to speak when Emma's arm slid off her chest and fell dangling toward the ground. Mary watched the arm fall. She didn't look upset or afraid anymore. She pulled her hand away from my chest and touched Emma instead.

Emma made a soft moan when Mary touched her.

I looked, but I had no idea what Mary was thinking. Her eyes held far too much to read. It made her look more than human. And powerful. She reached up and swept one hand across her brow, drawing her long white and green hair to the side, then she bent down over Emma and kissed her on the lips. We felt magic.

It wasn't a long kiss, but when Mary pulled away we could see that Emma's eyes were open. She still hung completely limp in Jane's arms but her copper gold eyes were alert. She looked from Mary to Jane to me and back to Mary again.

"Emma, it's okay. Just rest," Mary told her. She held her hand to Emma's face. Emma licked her hand while she spoke to me.

"Dan, we both know Jane wants privacy for a while. Just pick a few memories to enjoy and we'll go feed Emma. Guard the door for us, Dano. No visitors."

"Dano?" I thought. That was the nickname my uncle Harold used for me. And the way Mary spoke to me now was different. No longer a stranger. She knew me.

"Dano?" Jane asked, giving Mary and me a look.

I shrugged.

"Dano," Mary confirmed with a nod; then she bent over Emma and started to kiss her right where she was in Jane's arms.

"Oh shit, here we go!" Jane thought frantically.

I felt her unease and embarrassment spike as she watched the action right in front of her face. She was close enough to join in if she wanted, I thought to myself, but then I got a grip and focused on Jane's desperate, panicked thoughts instead of the two beautiful girls kissing right in front of us.

"*What day do you want me to remember, my love? What memories?*" I thought to her to get her to think of something else for even a second.

She looked up at me, wide eyed and terrified. "Oh, I don't know! Something from when I was a kid!" she said quickly. "There was a slumber party when I was twelve. Maybe that. It was boring and stupid, but it was where I met Emma." The action in her arms was getting hard for her to hold; Emma's arms were wrapped around Mary and Mary's hands were all over Emma, pushing up her shirt.

"Get in the room, Mary," Jane ordered.

Mary lifted her face from Emma's clutches and walked into the room, reaching behind her back and pulling her dress up and over her head as she walked toward the bed. Emma was more awake now, her copper gold eyes glittering with magic as she raised her hand and touched Jane's face. She ran her fingertips across Jane's lips, even touching her teeth, before she pulled her hand back to her face and inhaled deeply.

"I always knew. Even when you didn't, Janers, I did." Emma stared into my wife's eyes and mine, as the part of me that lived in Jane looked into Emma's eyes as well, and I felt her power. I quickly fled and let that part of my soul slip out of Jane's conscious thoughts and down into her memories where we both hoped I'd be safe from Emma's power.

The body in front of me vanished from my awareness as inside my head the body of a twelve-year-old Jane came to life.

We were sitting in a Jeep Grand Cherokee with cracked beige leather seats. Jane and her mother had just pulled up to a huge brick house. Jane undid her seatbelt. It made a "swack" noise against the side door panel as it snapped back into place. She squinted as she peered though the tinted front glass of the truck. The landscape and porch lights were already on even though it wasn't full dark.

I still had my own body and my own eyes, and living two lives at once was normal to me, but seeing the other half of myself while feeling something else, somewhere else, was disorienting.

Jane looked up at me. "You didn't hear what I was thinking just now, did you?"

I walked up to her, still careful not to touch Emma, and wrote with my finger on the white flesh of her bare upper arm, printing the letters on her flesh like her arm was a piece of paper and my finger a pen, her sensitive skin feeling the words.

Y O U R E A T T H E S L U M B E R P A R T Y
B I G B R I C K H O U S E

"Mmm." Jane nodded and smiled, remembering something. I didn't know what. "That house was huge," she said. She still didn't move toward the door. She was stalling, I guessed.

I wrote again.

S E E Y O U I N A N H O U R
I L O V E Y O U

She nodded. "Just one hour, Dan, and if I'm not already out, then come join me in my head, and if I don't still love you more than her then drag me into some corner somewhere and make me forget everything except you!" She growled, then marched boldly into the room with Emma, but froze when she saw Mary.

Emma sat up straighter in her arms, both girls staring. Mary waited for them, standing on her knees in the middle of the bed, already naked and shiny with oil, her green eyes glowing like two, green emerald circles.

I reached a hand inside the room and turned off the lights.

"Thank you, Dan," I heard Jane say as I pulled the door shut and took up a position outside the door like a guard.

I wondered for a brief moment just how the hell "*this situation,*" as Jane and I had been calling it, had even come to be. First Rain's blood and now this. With so many people running around with powers, it did seem inevitable that we'd be rubbing up against each other and changing each other, but I didn't expect the rubbing and changing to happen quite this way. I let my body become as still as stone and set one part of my mind to the side, counting down—fifty-eight minutes and eighteen seconds left.

My body in the hall watched as servants and others walked by, but my attention was on the twelve-year-old girl whom I loved and lived inside of as she stood beside her mother and watched a bunch of older girls running wild through someone's very expensive looking living room.

Jane

Memories

"JANE HONEY, YOU call me if these girls get too wild. Most of them look a lot older than you. Are you sure you want to stay?" Mom eyed the gaggle of girls running wild in Maria Bianca's gargantuan living room with worry, and so did I.

This was Maria's slumber party, but her younger sister Enid had invited me to come so she'd have someone here her age to hang out with, but Enid had completely forgotten that it was her father's weekend to have her, and then she forgot to tell me not to come. So here I was, at a slumber party with thirty-six girls I did not know. Maria was sixteen (almost seventeen) and so were most of the girls here, so I'd be on the low end of the social food chain. I scanned the crowd, searching for a few other girls who looked twelve or younger. There weren't any.

Mom went and picked up my bag from where I'd dumped it by the wall with everyone else's stuff.

"Come on, Jane. We'll stop by Blockbuster and pick up a few movies and have another girls night together while your dad's out of town."

That shocked me into action. It was summer break and I was so bored I was becoming mental. If I walked into that stupid, blue Blockbuster building again, with the same stupid movies, I'd spew right there in the store. I grabbed my bag out of Mom's hands.

"I can't do another movie night, Mom," I growled.

Mom gave me the sad, poor, alone, "Daddy's out of town" mommy look.

I beamed back the flat, dead, lifeless gaze that only true boredom could create.

"Would another movie night with your mom be so bad?" she wheedled.

"I'd rather be tied up, have raw eggs dumped on me, be hauled down to the basement, thrown in a box, and be covered with roaches all night." My delivery was perfect. I kept the "bored out of my mind" face on until she started digging in her purse for her keys.

"Be careful what you wish for, Jane. These girls might just do it."

"Give me fear, torment, torture—but not more boredom. Please." I bumped my head against her chest as she hugged me. "I just," bump, "can't," bump, "take it," bump.

"Have fun. I'll see you at nine tomorrow. And keep your cell phone on you so you can call me from the roach box in the basement."

"Will do." Bump.

The first part of the evening was pretty standard. Most of the girls went out to the huge pool and swam. I lurked in the shadows and kept out of the way. Mrs. B. checked on me a few times as she ran past, cleaning up spilled drinks, sweeping up broken glass, breaking up fights, and making sure all the girls stayed "in the house" while Mr. B. was out in the yard with a big flashlight, circling the house like a cop, chasing teenage boys out of the bushes.

All in all, I was impressed; it was the coolest party I'd ever been to in my life. After an hour or so of being a homeless ghost, I found a spot where I thought I might fit in. Five girls were at the table in the breakfast nook playing cards. They were playing for real money. A pile of change and a few bills were in the pot, and each girl had her own little pile of bills and change in front of her. I dug the two twenties Mom had given me out of my pocket and sat in the open seat after they finished a hand.

Five heads turned and sized me up, giving me a range of looks that went from "the evil eye" to "yeah whatever."

I held up the two twenties. "Got change?"

"Got a name?" asked a tall, skinny, dark haired girl shuffling cards. She was flipping them around like she was trying to impress me.

"Jane."

The dealer grunted; she didn't give me her name, but she did give me change.

The girl sitting on my left side with caked on makeup so thick it looked super gross gave me a leer.

"You know, kiddo, if you run out of money you have to give up some clothes. One item, one buck. That's the way this game works."

"Bring it," I said stone faced, which won me a few laughs from the other girls but not Pancake Face. She gave me the truly evil eye.

"We'll see how you feel once you lose your shirt, little Miss Priss!" she spat at me.

I leaned back and put my foot right onto the table and rolled my jeans up high enough to show the top of my socks. The girls around the table watched as I rolled down the first sock to show a second sock. I rolled down the second sock to show a third. I rolled down the third to show a fourth and the other girls erupted in laughing hoots and hollers.

Except for Pancake Face. "Deal, Emma! Let's get busy taking the candy from this baby."

I smiled and let it go without poking back as the cards went round. I thought about how cool my mom really was as I watched the little pile of cards in front of me reach seven. Mom had suggested I wear four pairs of socks just in case there were boys here and we played Spin the Bottle. I'd told her she was nuts. And I'd been bored to tears all those times we played poker at the kitchen table with Dad for peanut M&Ms.

I was smiling and thinking about my mom as I gathered my cards and held them close to my face, fanned out to scope my hand, leaving just my eyes peeking over the top of my cards.

"No more change, ladies," the dealer said as she looked right at me and smiled. "Dollars only till Jane's down to one pair of socks. We wouldn't want her feet to sweat and stink up the place."

The other girls laughed and pitched in their bills.

I added my dough to the pile and looked back to my cards.

As we played I listened to these older girls talk about guys. Guys this, and guys that, and this guy's a scum bag, and that guy's hot, and this girl did it with that guy—on and on. They all pretty much ignored me except Pancake, who poked at me every chance she got, which just pissed her off even more because I gave back better than she dealt out. Pancake hated my guts and I was fine with that, but the other girls seemed to like me.

I was a little worried about Emma, the dealer. I kept catching her staring at me, which was weird, and she had some kind of mental problem. She didn't let anyone touch her. When she dealt, moved, or reached for something on the table, she always checked to make sure she wouldn't touch anyone. She said "don't touch me" every time someone came close and gave them the evil eye until they went away. Pancake I felt I could handle or at least outrun, but Emma scared me for some reason.

I reached down and felt the reassuring bulge of my cellphone in my pocket and kept playing. I lost more than I won and was down to my last three bucks at ten when Mr. and Mrs. B chased everyone out of the pool and upstairs to the huge loft. I knew the Biancas were rich, but I didn't realize how rich until I saw the enormous loft.

It was decked out with a theater at the far end and four huge couches in the middle that formed a circle around a table in the center that was covered with platters of junk food and snacks. Full sized arcade games lined the walls on both sides of the room, along with pinball machines, an air hockey table, a pool table, a foosball table, and other games I had no name for. In the last corner was a stage with flashing lights and huge speakers blaring music for the girls already dancing away.

For about an hour everyone played games, danced and ate on the steady stream of junk food brought in by a weary Mrs. B. Two new platters came in, two empty or otherwise desecrated trays went out. In and out.

I kept on the move. Not by choice, but because I was so scared I was about to pee myself. It seemed like Pancake Face had a new mission in life, to hover around me and try to make me cry or make me run away so she could follow me and make me run away again. Pancake leaned over the air hockey table and insulted me, while the black girl I was playing with looked at me like I was nuts each time I handed her insults back with more style and less words.

I waited an appropriate number of insults so I didn't *exactly* look like I was running away before I ran away. I walked to the other side of the room looking for some safe place to hide when I saw Emma, the tall girl I'd played cards with talking to another girl by the arcade games. I went to the game right beside them while they talked.

Emma had been walking around the room with a clipboard, talking to everyone, helping Maria get ready for the games they planned on playing later, but I'd caught her watching me a couple of times. The last time I caught her she'd been staring at Pancake, giving *her* the evil eye, which made me think she might not just stand by and watch if this psycho started slapping me around.

"Thanks, Mom!" I muttered under my breath as I pushed play on the full-sized Ms. Pac-Man arcade game. "Be careful what you ask for! Yeah. Right." Sometimes Mom being right all the time really sucked!

Pancake pushed in beside me while I was playing, crowding me at the controls.

I stared straight ahead and tried not to let how scared I was show on my face.

"So, Jane, where do you like to be hit the most? Would you like me to slap you in the face, or would you like to lie down and let me kick you like a dog?" Pancake asked sweetly.

I kept my eyes on my game, but my skin began to prickle like it was already getting ready for a blow.

She leaned in and whispered to me. "What's wrong, little Jane? Don't have a smart ass comment for me?"

I spun to get away, not even looking where I was going and crashed into Emma! She fell straight back and I landed right on top of her staring her right in the face. I lay there, eyeball to eyeball, waiting for her to say "Don't touch me!" but she just lay there under me like an ice cube and said nothing.

I rolled off and stood up. Emma was still in the floor, defreaking, but good ol' Pancake was right there smiling at me, enjoying how scared I was. Emma was the tallest girl in the room. And scary. I could tell Pancake hoped Emma would be pissed at me, but she wasn't. She just got up and brushed herself off.

"Are you girls okay?" Mrs. B. leaned in to check on us, putting a hand on Emma's shoulder.

Emma jumped away from her hand. "Don't touch me!" she snapped at her.

"Oh! Sorry, Emma! I forgot." Mrs. B. pulled her arms in to her chest and squinched up her face, obviously fighting her "mom" reflex to hug and make it all better.

"I saw you girls fall and wanted to make sure everyone was all right."

"I'm fine," I told Mrs. B.

"No you're not," Emma said, staring at me.

Mrs. B. and I both looked at her.

"Linda's been chasing Jane around the room for the past hour trying to scare her to death. She crashed into me trying to run away from her."

Mrs. B. looked at me and I looked down, embarrassed. What the hell was Emma doing!?

"Who's Linda?" Mrs. B. asked.

"She is." Emma pointed a long finger right at her.

Linda (aka Pancake Face) was standing there looking surprised at being ratted out. Especially at being ratted out by Emma. Over me!

"Linda, where do you live?" Mrs. B. asked in the "mother" voice.

"Orange Park, ma'am."

"That's way on the other side of town. It would be a long way for your parents to drive if they have to come and get you tonight."

Linda nodded, looking chastened.

Mrs. B. gave us all the "get along" pep talk, patted me on the head, and then took off to do more snack runs, which left me standing there with Emma. Linda had already shuffled off into the crowd trying to look harmless.

"You want to help me with this?" Emma asked, lifting the clipboard.

I nodded, and she showed me what she was doing with her "truth" questions for the Truth or Dare games tonight. She said she was helping out as a favor for Maria. I already knew from listening to her talk to the girls downstairs that Emma lived across the street from the Biancas but she hardly knew them. Her mother and Mrs. B. were friends so Emma got the invite. I also knew that Emma was home schooled. And with her issues, being home schooled was probably for the best.

As we went around the room, her piercing brown eyes watched where everyone walked like a hawk, and if anyone came too close she'd stop talking and give them her full attention until they were out of her "comfort zone." It made her weird to walk around the room with because she moved around groups of people but never through them (not wanting to get bumped accidentally). It was like watching a tall, skinny, shy lion bring down animals that strayed too close to the edge of the herd.

She gave me my own clipboard and I plunged into the thicker parts of the crowd where I knew Emma wouldn't go to finish the last girl or two so we could hand the stuff to Maria Bianca and her BFFs. They were somewhere private working on the "Dare Envelopes."

Pancake came for me as soon as she saw me on my own, and I ended up running back to Emma before she could lay her hands on me. Emma gave me a look, then looked out at where Linda leaned on a nearby couch eyeing me and didn't say anything as I followed her around, staying as close as I could get without popping her little magic bubble of personal space.

At eleven we started the games. There were six envelopes that people were competing for. Each envelope was a different color and had a different kind of dare in it. The people who answered the truth questions the best won the chance to give out the dares and won tokens they could use to either get out of taking a dare themselves or make someone else's dare into a double dare.

Emma and I didn't win an envelope, but we both cringed when Linda won one. She'd be able to use it later tonight on whomever she wanted, and Emma and I shared a look; we knew she'd be after us. Emma and I were almost frantic to win a token so we could escape her dare, but with thirty-six girls there, all of them desperate to win, it wasn't too surprising that neither of us won, but Emma and I both cussed up a storm when Linda won one. We watched Linda's celebration dance holding her token in one hand and her "Red Dare" envelope in the other.

"I'm doomed," I said.

Emma nodded.

"Might be me," she said.

I nodded.

Just after midnight, when the nonstop snack train from Mrs. B. officially shut down and our parental supervision retired for the night, they confiscated the cell phones and did the pat down for cameras. None of the other girls questioned it and I didn't ask why myself, but as I dropped my phone into a shoebox that already had my name on it I heard my mother's voice in my head saying, "Keep your cell with you." I nodded to myself and watched as they carried the shoe box away. It was that last bit of creepy coincidence that took the whole evening over the line, from normal weird and crazy to detached dreamlike freaky.

I actually relaxed some. I was off the reservation and totally on my own now. At least I knew Mom would check the basement if I turned up missing. Emma stayed with me and we talked as we waited for the rest of the girls to get patted down. I kept waiting for some other girl to come and steal her away and hijack the friend I seemed to have made but that didn't happen. As we talked I found out that Emma was actually a lot like me; the only person she really knew here was Maria and she'd only spoken to her a few times. They weren't really friends, just neighbors.

They had all of us gather around the couches and started the Dares. A girl named Kelly who had won the "Blue Dare" envelope ended up handing it to a girl she didn't even know after trying to give it to someone else who had secretly traded for a token and got out of it.

"Sorry. I don't know who you are but I hope you have fun," Kelly told the surprised girl and be-bopped her way happily back to her spot on one of the couches while the girl opened the blue envelope. She read it and actually smiled, looking relieved. She ended up pushing a penny around the toilet seat with her tongue.

The green envelope was a gross out food dare. Some girl had to eat a small pile of jellybeans that had been up other people's noses and a spoonful of chocolate covered ants and then drink a glass of raw eggs while they held her upside down. She did it all without barfing which surprised all of us.

The black envelope got deflected twice by people with tokens before it landed on a plain-looking girl named Sam. Some other girl who obviously didn't like Sam a whole lot walked up to her and handed her a token and smiled as she said, "Make that a double, *bitch*."

The girls went wild over the smack down, shouting and screaming with cruel delight. Emma and I laughed right along with them, enjoying ourselves with the rest of the girls. We watched Sam open her envelope. She blinked a few times then told us what it said.

"I'm supposed to lie down and let every girl here write a cuss word or something filthy on me and go home that way without washing it off. But how would this be a double dare?" she asked looking back at Maria Bianca.

Maria and her inner circle who were running the show decreed that she'd have to strip completely nude so she'd be embarrassed as hell, and, as a bonus, they'd all have more room to write. Her face went through a few shades of red as she stripped naked and stretched out on the table right in front of all of us.

"BITCH" went right across her forehead in great big letters and it got nastier from there. I watched as Emma ordered her to flip over then made a nice big X right between her shoulder blades and wrote "Stab Bitch Here" under the X to the delight of the room. I just wrote "Crack Ho" on the back of her neck where she couldn't see it and handed the pen to the next girl.

The white envelope was simple; someone had to crawl into a big pillow case and stay in there for an hour while we did whatever we wanted to the "bag." The girls carried her around the room once on their shoulders then carried her to the bathroom, turned on the water in the shower and left her tied up in there screaming.

The brown envelope was bad. The girl who finally got stuck with it cussed up a storm, called us all bitches, then stormed out without doing it. They ended up selling the brown envelope to a girl named Mina who'd begged and bartered for two tokens so she could top the others who only offered one. Mina took great delight in handing the brown envelope to a petite little blonde girl named Ann.

We already knew from the screaming fit the last girl threw what the dare was, but knowing it and seeing it were two different things. Pretty little Ann dropped her pants and panties then stepped up onto the table right in the middle of all the circular chairs, hunkered down, and started to push! Emma and I both screamed along with the rest of the girls as we watched not just one, but *two* good sized turds drop onto the table. Ann reached over to the nearby snack tray and grabbed some napkins and started to wipe her ass, and the half of the room still standing convulsed into laughing spasms and joined the rest of us already on the floor trying to breathe.

"You still got a mess back here, Ann, you ain't through yet, girlfriend," coached one black girl as she stared at Ann's back side with a critical eye from her seat that was dangerously close to the action.

Ann wiped again. We ALL screamed again!

The black girl gave the thumbs up and Ann descended the table like a little princess instead of the nasty gross freak we all now knew she really was, and then the three-girl-strong clean up crew moved in like the keystone cops, wearing yellow rubber gloves and spraying potpourri air freshener as they cleaned up the mess.

Linda stepped into the middle of the room while they were still cleaning up Ann's bio waste. We watched as she made some quick negotiations with all the people who had unused tokens. Hers was the last "Dare" of the night and they had no more use for the tokens so they probably just gave them to her so they wouldn't go to waste, but we watched with growing horror as she collected one after another.

"Emma, does this house have a basement?" I asked.

"Why?" She looked at me, raising an eyebrow.

"Because they're about to tie me up, pour raw eggs all over me, haul me down to the basement, drop me into a box, cover me with roaches, and then leave me down there till morning." I smiled. It had to be the roach box. It was like—*my destiny*. I could almost feel the little critters now.

"You're not scared of the roach treatment?" Emma looked surprised.

"No. I might be scared of freaky Linda, but I can handle roaches. They're not as creepy as that bitch." I couldn't hide the fear from my eyes as I said it. I'd never had someone really threaten to hurt me before and it had truly freaked me out. And now I didn't even have a cell phone to call my mom. Or 911.

"Little Jane. Little Jane," Linda called as she walked over and stopped right in front of me. She waved the red envelope back and forth in front of her, looking from me to Emma, who was giving her the totally evil eye. Voices egged her on as she waved the red envelope right in my face, but then she turned and waved it in Emma's face (which was too close) and Emma backed up a step.

"Don't touch me!" she snapped automatically.

Linda was surprised for just a second then looked at the red envelope and smiled at Emma. "It's time to make you run home to your momma, little *touch me not*. Put out your hand."

Emma held her hand out, palm up, and Linda dropped the red envelope into her hand. Then she dropped five tokens on top, one by one, as all the girls all around us started shouting for Emma to "Read the dare!"

Linda stood there gloating.

"Emma can't do it, Jane. And when she bails on you and goes home screaming 'Don't touch me! Don't touch me!' *I'm gonna kick your ass*." She mouthed the last part, not saying it out loud, then winked at me and walked back into the crowd. I didn't know what to do. The girls were all shouting and yelling and Emma looked wild eyed, like she might just do what Pancake said she would.

"Open it!"

"Read it, Emma!"

"Com'on, Emma! You can do it!"

"She cant do it!" screamed someone. "It's not fair!"

"Do! It! Do! It! Do! It!" The chant started.

Emma still held the letter and pile of tokens in her hand. She looked back toward the door out of the loft, then at me, then at the screaming crowd of girls. I realized that Pancake was right. She couldn't do this. It wasn't right to make her try. Emma had issues.

"Emma. You can go home. I'll be okay," I told her.

"Goodbye, Emma! I'll keep an eye on Jane for you!" Linda called and waved at her from the group of shouting girls.

Emma stiffened. She looked at Linda's evil smile then looked over at me. I know what she saw when she looked at me. I was scared out of my mind about being here alone with psycho Linda. I watched her as she looked back at me, then made her decision; not for herself, but for me, she opened the envelope. She sat up straight in surprise as she read it, her eyes huge white circles. She took a moment to get herself together, then read it to the shouting mob of teenage girls, already delighting in Emma's obvious distress.

"You need practice kissing boys." She read like a stiff machine and the girls screamed. Emma waited until it calmed down and started over.

"You need practice kissing boys. Pick one girl and kiss her for two minutes straight—non-stop—French kiss—open mouth—full tongue action—in the middle of the room. If it looks lame, the clock stops till it looks like a real kiss, so make sure you look like you're really enjoying it even if you're about to hurl."

Linda stood up and shouted over the ruckus, "But I put down five tokens! It should be an hour or at least thirty minutes! And she should have to strip! I put down five freakin' tokens, Maria! FIVE!"

The girls shouted and argued and even debated if it was fair to do this to Emma; every girl there knew she had serious "issues" with touching people. But the totally insane sum of five tokens was devastating. Maria and her little group agreed with most of what Linda wanted but said they had to take into consideration Emma's little problem. Ten nonstop minutes of completely naked French kissing in front of everyone was the final judgment. Maria whispered a quick apology to Emma and said it was the best she could do. I watched as Emma nodded.

"Who's she gonna kiss!?" The girls started to shout for Emma to choose but that caused a riot of pushing and shoving because no one wanted to be picked. They started to push one another toward her while the ones being pushed fought to get farther away, not wanting to be chosen and drug into Emma's disaster.

I was freaking out watching Emma as the mad throng of rowdy girls kept bumping into her while she tried to keep her little bubble of space, but it was useless, and each time someone touched her she twitched. I pulled my shirt off without thinking about what I was doing and tried not to think as the other girls started to shout and point at me making cat calls.

Emma turned around as I was unzipping my jeans, and the look of relief on her face made me glad some insane part of me had started moving my body around without really telling the rest of me what was going on. A girl gave her a shove from behind, pushing her toward me and Emma spun around with a vicious, "Don't touch me!" and a murderous glare.

The girls gave her some space like you would for a rabid dog that might bite. My God what have I gotten myself into!? I just hope she didn't bite me while we did this. And were we really going to do this!? Where were my damn roaches!? I looked down at my feet and tried hard not to think as I stepped on the heel of my shoe with my other foot and slid my foot free then worked my other shoe off. Still looking down I worked my jeans down to my hips, then hooked my underwear on each side with my thumbs and brought it all down at the same time and stepped out of my jeans and the rest, just wearing my four pair of socks and my bra.

I didn't look up until I had the bra off and had worked all the socks off with my toes which I did standing up. I did not bend over. I stood there with one hand covering my boobs and the other hand over what I could hide of me down below, but when I looked up I was surprised that Emma was gone.

"Where'd she go?" I asked a girl standing nearby.

"She's in the bathroom, getting undressed." She pointed the way.

I felt like an idiot. I wished I'd have thought of that too, instead of just getting naked out here in front of everyone like nasty Ann had.

Someone pinched my ass hard!

"Oww!" I yelled and spun around to find Linda standing there smiling at me, while I rubbed my ass where she had pinched the freakin' hell out of me.

The other girls thought it was funny, but I didn't. It hurt like hell and my eyes started to tear up. I tried to keep from crying as everyone laughed. Another girl reached out to do it too, but I jumped out of the way before she could pinch flesh, but then they all started trying to pinch me. All were laughing as I jumped around and spun in circles to keep them from getting behind me.

"Stop it!" I shouted as I got another pinch. I dropped both of my hands behind me to cover my butt as more girls rushed toward me, more arms reaching for me! All of them laughing; I even saw Maria laughing! Someone pinched my nipple, and I slapped her hand away but that left a cheek exposed and girls reached in and pinched.

"Stop it!" I shouted again and got pinched on my leg and someone else grabbed for my chest. I spun and tried to get away from their arms but I was surrounded by them!

"Leave me alone!" I screamed at them, just as someone pinched me again from behind on my leg hard!

Pinch! "Oww!" Pinch! "Oww!" Pinch! Pinch! "Stop it!" Pinch! Pinch! Pinch! Pinch! Pinch! Pinch! Pinch!

I pushed though them, still getting pinched, and ran crying for the door not even thinking about my clothes. The bathrooms were by the door out of the loft, and Emma was just coming out. I saw her standing there and somehow instead of running for the door I changed directions and ran straight to Emma and threw myself around her, crying.

I closed my eyes and cried! And cried. And cried.

I didn't even care that my head was pressed up against her naked chest or that I'd made a mess all over her with my tears and running nose. I didn't care. I wasn't thinking. I was crying, and it didn't seem like I could do both at the same time. I felt all the pinches like bee stings all over me. They hurt. I cried.

Emma said nothing as she stood there and held me to her chest and kept her arms around me.

When I finally settled into sniveling shakes, Emma turned me around and walked us back toward the crowd of girls at the couches. She kept her arm around my shoulder and held me tight against her as we walked, and I didn't even think about us being naked. I stared at the girls. They weren't laughing now; they were all sitting on or around the couches being quiet as they watched us walk toward them.

I couldn't stop shaking. They were all looking at me. Looking at my legs and where they'd pinched me all over.

I turned in toward Emma and closed my eyes. I didn't want to see them anymore. I hated them.

"Go get Tabitha out of the shower and put Linda inside the sack," Emma ordered.

"And why would we do that?" I heard Maria's voice say crisply.

"Because if you don't I'll walk Jane downstairs and show your mother and father what you let happen to her. And then I'll call the cops and tell them what *your parents* allowed to happen in *their* home to a twelve-year-old girl. And then I'll show my mother, *the lawyer,* and have her sue you, your five cronies that helped you, all the girls Jane can remember who hurt her, your whole family, your friends, and your fucking dog."

"You wouldn't dare!" some girl shouted.

Even in my shattered state of mind *that* seemed like a really poor choice of words.

They did everything Emma wanted. I opened my eyes to watch as they shoved Linda into the sopping wet, body-sized pillow case. She made them bring us our clothes and our stuff from the shoe boxes. She stepped away from me to pull her pants and shirt on and some of the girls stepped closer to help me get dressed. Emma spun and screamed, "Don't touch us!"

They left us alone. I didn't want the bra or underwear on. My chest hurt. Emma helped me step into my jeans and I made, "Owie! Owie! Owie!" noises as she pulled them up over my butt and then I started to cry again and she put her arms back around me.

"Put her shoes and underthings in the box with her cell phone and hand it to me."

Maria did it herself and handed the box to Emma.

"Sorry, Jane. We just got carried away. We're all really, reall—"

"Shut up!" Emma snapped.

Emma told Maria and her five friends that helped run the party to strip, pair up, and start kissing. "And Maria. It better be convincing."

They did it. There were no cat calls or shouts or jeering from the other girls though. We left while they were still naked and kissing. Emma kept her arm around me as she led me down the stairs and past Mr. B., who was asleep in a chair in the living room. We walked out the front door and out into the pouring rain.

I still hadn't said a single word and every minute or two I'd start shaking and the rain made the shaking worse. I wondered if I was in shock, but I kept walking where she led me. Emma's house was three houses down and we were soaked by the time we reached the small door by the garage. She took me inside and we stopped at the kitchen.

"Do you want to sit down?"

I shook my head no.

"You need to drink something. What do you want to drink?"

There was a tall fancy bottle of liquor with a couple of glasses there on the kitchen bar. I'd never had any alcohol before but for some reason I pointed to it. I think because it was there, and I could see it, while the milk was in the fridge and out of sight.

Emma poured me a glass. I took a sip. It burned on the way down and tasted a little like wood flavored mouthwash. I drank it. She made me drink a small glass of water and then led me upstairs to her room and got me out of my wet clothes and into one of her nightgowns. She did the same, then gathered up all our wet clothes.

"I'll be right back. I'm going to go put them in the dryer."

She left me standing in the middle of her room swaying unsteadily on my feet. My heart felt warm in my chest and I wasn't shaking anymore. I wondered if it was the drink or if I was feeling better now. Emma came back in and put a towel on my head to dry my hair. I closed my eyes and put my arms around her to steady myself while she worked.

I still had my eyes closed as she combed her fingers through my hair, pushing the damp strands out of my face and toward my back. She felt my brow, then her long fingers traced across my eyebrows, down my nose, down the sides of my face, and then she ran her fingers lightly around my mouth tracing my lips. Something about this touch reached deep inside me and mixed wonderfully with the warm feeling in my chest and made me tingle all over. I liked it. I liked this—I liked her—I liked her touching me.

Some internal warning bell sounded somewhere in my brain.

I opened my eyes and looked up at her face and into the brown eyes looking down into mine, and I finally realized—Emma's gay.

That frightened and shocked life back into me and got my brain working again. I broke the circle of her arms and backed up a step from her, blinking and startled. Emma pulled back from me as well, looking guilty and ashamed and sad and angry all at once. For some damn reason my mouth chose that moment to start working again.

"I'm not gay!" I said quickly.

Emma flinched like I'd hit her and took another step away from me.

"Once your clothes are dry I'll take you back to the Biancas," she said stiffly.

She wasn't looking at me now, she was looking away toward the wall. I wasn't sure but I thought Emma might be crying. I didn't want her to cry! I felt horrible! But I wasn't gay!

"I'll go see if the clothes are dry." Emma moved toward the door and I moved to stop her but she jumped back, like her magic bubble of space was back. "Don't you touch me!" she snapped, finally looking at me, her angry eyes filled with tears. She *was* crying!

My bottom lip started trembling and I cried, "But I want to touch you!"

"No, you don't!" Her voice croaked, it sounded like something had broken in her throat. The tears finally flew.

"Yes, I do!" I cried back, bewildered and confused as my own wild emotions and feelings and all the shock of the evening crashed around inside me.

"No, you don't!" she spat back again.

"Yes, I do!"

"Bullshit!"

"I dare you to kiss me!"

That made her eyes go wide for a shocked moment, but she quickly recovered her cynical sneer. "You don't want to kiss me. You're not *gay*."

I wasn't going to lie and say I was! But I had to say something. "I need practice!" I blurted. "For kissing boys!"

"Practice?" Emma frowned.

"My legs hurt, Emma. And I'm tired. Just kiss me and then let's go to bed," I said wearily.

"To sleep! To sleep! To bed to sleep!" I added quickly, raising my eyebrows and making a face as I realized how that might have sounded.

Emma couldn't help smiling.

I walked over to her like her bubble of space didn't exist to me and hugged her. She hugged me back.

Emma's hug led into Emma's kiss and I didn't pull away. I'd been ready to do this as a part of a stupid dare at a stupid slumber party in front of stupid mean girls so I could do it right here too. But this wasn't pretend, or practice, *this was real*, and I knew it. This was a real kiss. I felt it in the way Emma held me in her arms, in how she breathed and trembled and cried. I felt it in myself. In my heart and arms and legs. If this meant something to me I couldn't imagine how much this meant to Emma.

As we kissed I thought about how Emma didn't let anyone touch her—except me. Only me. It made me feel special. We'd only been kissing for maybe two minutes when I felt her start to pull away but I kept kissing her. I couldn't let her go yet! I'd been ready to do this for ten minutes straight as part of the dare.

I'd give Emma her ten minutes.

I'm not sure how long we kissed, I just gave myself to it. Emma stopped a couple of times, but I started again, and each time I pulled her back down to my lips she cried. Finally we stopped and Emma helped me crawl into the bed and I lay on my side. She crawled in with me and put her arms around me and I knew I had to say something.

We stared at each other in the dark bed. We were too close. It was too intimate. I felt too weird. Our lips were just inches apart. Something could happen. Something would happen if I didn't say something soon.

"Tomorrow we'll be friends, Emma. Just friends," I told her as we lay there.

She was quiet for a while as she looked into my eyes, but sleep was pulling at me now that I'd spoken. "Best friends?" she asked.

"Yes," I said and closed my eyes because I was sleepy and because of what I saw in her eyes.

"I love you." I heard the words whispered quietly beside me in the darkness on the other side of my closed eyes. I'd felt the breath of those words on my face as she said them.

I lay there and cried without making a sound or shaking the bed to let her know I'd heard. No sound. No movement. Only tears. Emma loved me. I so wanted to say it back, but I was afraid that if I did it would lead to other things. I wanted to say it back but I fought back the words that wanted out of my mouth. Tears leaked from my eyes and the weariness of my battered body drug me down. I wanted to say it back—

wanted to say—

wasn't suppose to say—

"I love you."

Bewitched

"MY LOVE. LITTLE One. You must wake." I heard Believer's rumbling voice and the warm clouds around me squeezed me in an embracing tightness that made me feel so safe and secure that I groaned in pleasure, and beside me I heard a sweet, little moan echo my own. I opened my eyes and looked beside me to see Bethany's bloody face hidden in a mad tangle of hair floating around her head. Her smiling white teeth peeked out of the red on her face that still looked sticky, not dried out. We were both soaked through, but it was a warm and wonderful dampness that was a part of being inside a living cloud.

"Hug me harder!" Bethany shouted, giggling wildly as white clouds gathered around her and did as she asked. The sound was so wonderful it made me smile.

Floating inside Believer's body was like floating weightless in space or like being inside a womb that was filled with warm, damp clouds instead of fluid. It left you feeling ephemeral and formless, but when Believer squeezed and hugged and the clouds closed in and pressed all the spread out pieces of what you were back together again and held you in one, tight, safe, solid form, that also felt wonderful.

Believer had not used his other abilities with Bethany here. He was being cautious. Which was like him. He was probably worried he would scare her or maybe even damage her if he had. Inside Believer's cloudy form were thousands and thousands of thin little white nerves that looked like luminescent veins hidden within his clouds. He could slip these tiny nerves through flesh and into to tight muscles and weary flesh without damaging the skin. It was so totally relaxing that the first time he did it, it frightened me to death, but it was worth it. All of it fit together into something *glorious.*

He would hold me tight on the outside with the warm weight of his enveloping clouds while at the same time that other, ghostly part of him filled me and held me tight and safe on the inside. It was like being hugged inside and outside at the same time. It was beyond wonderful. Being connected to him in that way made me feel like I was truly a part of his flesh, or more like I actually became "flesh" for him, as if my whole body were one big beating heart, pounding away in the center of his chest.

Believer was made of clouds and mist brought to life by Sky's magic, but his little white nerves actually had some substance, as did the only part of his entire body that was partly physical more than just cloud. It was white, made from millions of the little white nerves coming from his body to form that special part of himself. It was long and snakelike, but at the end that mattered it looked like what it was meant to be, other than the fact that it glowed like his little nerves and pulsed to the rhythm of his stormy body. It was the same as any man's, only it hung inside his body instead of outside. Believer had that *private part* of himself safely hidden away behind darker clouds within himself while we had Bethany here with us.

"Hug me again!" Bethany cried. The giggling continued.

I licked my lips and noticed that Believer's taste was off. I got a faint metallic taste in my mouth that made me think of licking a penny for some reason. I ran my tongue around my mouth and made the connection. It was the blood. Bethany had crawled inside Believer while she was still a bloody mess last night, clothes and all. I took a deep breath and smelled it floating around in his clouds. Blood wasn't a bad smell or a bad taste, but I didn't want to leave a mess that might not smell quite as good later.

With a thought I cleaned the blood and grime off Bethany and off myself and from wherever it had drifted inside my husband's body. Having magic made it easy to clean house, and inside my love was where I liked to live most of all. This was home.

"Good morning, my love," I said as I stretched.

"Happy birthday, honey," I told Bethany who reached over from where she floated and grabbed my hand, then walked herself down my arm, pulling herself closer until she wrapped herself around me like a monkey, causing us both to tumble in a flip like we were floating in space.

"Let's see what it feels like to have him hug us both together!" Bethany wiggled closer against me.

"Okay! Squeeze us again!" she called to my husband, who indulged the little monster attached to me. He squeezed, making us both laugh. Believer's deep happy rumble joined our happy sounds.

"Yes. They're awake now," Believer said, and I knew he was talking to someone outside. From in here we couldn't hear who it was or what they were saying, but we could hear Believer as he spoke to them. I was pretty sure it was our mother.

"Oh. I'm all clean." Bethany noticed that I'd done a little cleaning. "Good. You cleaned my dress too. Every time I take it off to get in the shower Penny steals it and washes it. It doesn't get that dirty that quickly," she complained.

"She's just trying to take care of you, honey."

"I know." Bethany sighed. "It's still kinda weird having people take care of me. *But it's nice,*" she added quickly.

"My love. It's time." Believer's voice rumbled, sounding more urgent. "You are needed. And our little one needs to eat some flesh to keep up her strength. They have prepared her a special breakfast in the royal dining room. Cathryn is out here waiting for you. It's time to come out."

"Can I come back tonight!?" Bethany asked, already wanting to come back again before she'd even left. She eyed me hopefully.

"Not tonight, honey. Another night soon, I promise."

She pouted a little, her eyebrows tilting down at the ends and up at the bridge of her delicate nose, but she nodded. Then she spoke to Believer herself like any child would do. If your mom says no, try Dad.

"*Believer.*" She used her sweetest little voice.

"Yes, my little one?" he rumbled back.

"During the day, when we're all just standing around sometimes, you know, waiting on stuff, would it be okay for me to come back? Even when we're not sleeping? I'm real tiny, you probably won't even notice me playing inside here."

Believer's laugh rumbled. It was a good laugh, more than just a polite little rumble, and I realized right then that Believer really did love Bethany. And he enjoyed having her here. Inside him. Playing. I could feel it in the clouds, the way the air pressure felt. I knew that he was happy and that made me happy.

"Yes, my little one. Even during the day, *if I'm able*, I'd love to have you come back and play inside me. I like to hear you laugh. It makes me very happy." He gave us both a last squeeze and Bethany laughed again for him. I just squeezed her too, adding my love to his as we both loved on my little sister with all of our hearts.

When we emerged from his happy clouds, we were met by grave faces. Our happy smiles vanished. Lucius and Cathryn were there, waiting in the room. They gave their brief 'good mornings', then led us out into the hall. Dan was standing like a magnificent statue in the hall just outside of Mary's room. I tried to stop but Cathryn pulled me by the hand and said, "No, child."

I looked at her for a moment then bowed my head and said, "Yes, mother," but I looked back. Dan's eyes watched me as she led me away.

Cathryn brought us downstairs, past the people of Amen Hale who followed us with their eyes until we disappeared from view, into the small private dining hall where breakfast was laid out and ready for us. Special food had been prepared for Bethany, little crackers with thinly shaved meat on top, lean strips of flesh that looked like peppered beef jerky, a brown soup, and a couple of other items along with one glass of red wine.

Bethany's maid was already there, sitting beside the seat meant for Bethany, clearly meaning to keep her company while she ate. Cathryn bid Bethany to sit and eat while the rest of us stepped into the small sitting room to the side that held a table, a couch, and two chairs.

Cornelius and Cathryn each took chairs so Believer and I sat on the couch, while Lucius hovered behind Cathryn's chair looking alert and ready. I realized that they were being very careful with me. Very, very careful.

I went deathly still.

They only did this when they were worried that I would react badly or lose control. What could it be!? I remembered Dan, standing in the hall and knew right away that he was part of it, but I couldn't think of what might have happened! My breaths started to become short and ragged as my worry began to change into panic, the first faint threads of power began slipping out of my flesh like sweat from my pores. Power ran over my body and down my hair bringing it to life, and I squeezed my eyes shut so tightly I saw blue and white and floating dots of light as I tried to hold it all inside. I thought about nothing but breathing. Breathing.

I heard the soothing words of Believer, Cathryn, and Cornelius as they assured me that all was well. We had some problems but nothing too grave. Believer held his hands over my face and all I could see when I opened my eyes were his clouds which cooled me. I couldn't even hear. Just my head was inside his cupped hands and the world and all the things in it were shut outside. My hair was damp when he removed his hands and let me see and hear again.

I noticed that the table between the chairs and couch had been removed from the little seating area. Taken away. Everyone was watching Cathryn who was standing in front of me. She pulled me up from the couch and had me kneel on the floor where the table had been, sitting me back on my heels while she knelt in front of me in exactly the same way. I had to tuck my dress in so that it wasn't all fanned out around me, but I got settled and Cathryn reached out and took my hands in hers.

She held her hands palm down over my wrists and I held her wrists with my hands palms up. We were sitting, knee to knee, holding wrists, facing each other. I'd never been in a position like this before with someone else, but I liked it. It was calming and personal and—*nice.*

I smiled and my mother smiled back at me.

"You like this."

"Yes. Much," I told her. I felt calm and ready for whatever crappy news I had to hear, but Cathryn gave me a serious look.

"Rain. Keep your eyes on my face. If you feel me use magic, don't worry, I'm just trying to keep you calm. We're being careful with you because your emotions may cause you to lose control of yourself. Just relax, breathe, and keep your eyes on my face. We'll start with the less emotional news."

Cathryn told me about the men working on the other side of the gateway who had been captured by the French government and were being held until we agreed to meet with them. I took this news calmly. She told me that we badly needed a few more gateways to go and pick up supplies now that the French connection wasn't safe to use. She told me about the needs for a prison to hold our new captives and about Lizzy killing herself and being raised by Bethany last night. She told me about the promise that Cornelius had made her give to not cut herself anymore and described the place we needed to make for her.

Her voice was calm and soft and sure and we were face to face. I saw her so well up close like this, and I felt like I heard her so much better than I normally did that I wondered why we didn't talk like this more often. It was easier, more natural to think of her as my mother like this. She told me about the young couple that was going to get married today which was nice—

"And this morning Emma collapsed. She was—"

My heart skipped a beat. I couldn't breathe. I tried to pull my hands away, but Cathryn held me tight, her hands gripped tightly around my wrists. My chest hurt and I kept struggling to get away.

"Breathe! Breathe, Rain!" Cathryn yelled and got me breathing the way she wanted, but the sense of calm I'd felt was shattered. Thankfully my power hadn't lashed out, but my heart was still pumping blood through my veins so fast that my hands shook in Cathryn's as she held me where I was.

"Why did Emma collapse!?" I demanded.

"Emma is like Bethany. She didn't even know she was hungry till she dropped, and we didn't know what she needed to eat until today."

"How bad was it!?"

Cathryn's face told me all I needed to know. I tried to get up again, but she pulled me back down by my wrists.

"She is being taken care of, Rain! And she will be fine," Cathryn said firmly.

"Taken care of? By whom!? How is she being taken care of!?" I demanded, wild eyed with worry. I fought the urge to get to my feet and run to her right that second.

"Look at me!" Cathryn ordered, raising her voice.

I looked at her, but she could tell I wanted to run; her hands and the odd position I was in were all that had held me here this long.

"Emma is being fed what she needs right now, Rain." She gave me a knowing look that made me shut up and think.

"By whom?" I asked.

"Jane and Mary."

"Both?" I asked, somehow not surprised.

"Yes."

"But is it enough?" I stared at Cathryn and hoped with all my heart that she'd say "no" so I could run and join them. But she didn't.

She tilted her head to the side, scrutinizing me carefully. Obviously seeing something that troubled her. She didn't answer my question but asked one of her own. "Are you bewitched by her? Did Emma do magic on you to make you fall in love with her?"

"Yes." A quick word.

I heard Believer rumble his worry from somewhere nearby. I knew his red eyes were watching me but somehow I didn't care at that moment.

Cornelius grunted. "You were right," he said to my mother softly.

Cathryn held my hands and stared into my eyes. I felt her magic and didn't resist as the warm feeling moved from her hands, up my arms, and into my chest. I calmed. She held my hands and stared into my eyes and asked her questions.

"Did you feel her when she was working magic on you?"

"Yes," I answered.

"But you didn't stop her," Cathryn said.

"No."

"How often has she used magic on you?"

"Many times."

"Many times!" Cornelius burst out loudly nearby.

Cathryn looked away to him and talked to him and the others. They spoke for a while. I heard Believer's confused and troubled voice, but the words slipped away as I stared straight ahead, waiting for her, waiting for my mother's eyes to meet mine again. I heard her speak to Believer.

"She's not harmed. I would never hurt her. And you may stop this at any time, Believer. You are her husband and her guardian, but we need to know what's happened." Believer's voice rumbled something. Unimportant. The only voice that seemed to matter was my mother's. She looked back into my eyes.

"Why didn't you try to stop Emma from bewitching you?" she asked.

"I didn't want to."

"Why?"

"Because I wanted to love her," I answered.

Believer's voice rumbled.

"There are different kids of love, my son," Cathryn said to someone. She looked back into my eyes.

"In what way do you love me, Rain?"

"Mother," I answered as I stared into her eyes.

"How do you love Bethany?"

"Daughter."

Believer's rumbling voice said something.

"How do you love Believer?"

"Husband."

She stopped and talked for a while. I heard Believer's rumbling voice. I didn't listen for some reason. I waited until Cathryn's eyes met mine.

"How do you love Emma?"

"Wife."

There were more questions. I answered them.

My mother lifted me up and led me to the couch and told me to take a nap.

I did.

Sky

Same Kind of Crazy

"RYAN, DID YOU want to pray for the food?" his father asked as we took our seats around the table for brunch. Ryan's smile disappeared but he nodded to his father.

"May I do it?" I asked.

Ryan looked at me, surprised and relieved. He smiled. I knew he was scared of what might happen if he prayed for the wrong thing.

"Of course, Sky, we'd love to have you pray for us," Ryan's mom answered me.

"I thank God for the food?" I asked.

She nodded, "And you can thank him for some of the blessings he's given you also. And ask him anything you want. Take your time, dear," she encouraged warmly.

I tried to pray like Ryan's father had yesterday when we all ate lunch together, like God was right here at the table and you could talk to him and tell him anything you wanted. It was *very* different from how the nuns prayed, but I liked this new way. I bowed my head and began.

"Father God, thank you for the food. And thank you for Ryan, and for letting me eat breakfast this morning with my new family. It was a nice surprise. And thank you for keeping everyone safe last night when the soldiers attacked Amen Hale. Thank you that Jane and Dan are alive again *even though they're really still dead.* And please help Dana to quit smoking. She says she wants to quit because it makes her stink, which is so strange because she likes fire, but not smoke. Oh! And thank you for how happy Believer was last night. He prayed to my soul and told me thank you, and that he was very, very happy with his life and how I made him and I want to pass that on to you. Believer says thanks. Amen."

I opened my eyes and looked around. Ryan was smiling, but his parents were staring at me like my hair was on fire. I knew the look they were giving me; I'd seen it all my life. "*You're crazy!*" People didn't say it out loud, but they said it with their faces all the same.

I looked at Ryan again, but he didn't seem surprised by my prayer at all. He flashed me his wonderful smile then started in on the food. Maybe my prayer sounded fine to him because he was crazy like me. I wondered if it sounded fine to God or if it sounded crazy to him too. But if it did sound fine to God then what did that mean? Did that mean God was crazy like me?

"Are you okay, honey?" Ryan's mom asked.

"Oh, I was just thinking." I looked at her. The "*You're crazy*" look was still there on her face, mixed with concern.

"You sure were concentrating hard on something. What were you thinking about, Sky?"

Wow, that was rude. My eyebrows raised in surprise. Maybe in America it wasn't rude to ask someone what they were thinking in front of other people. I wasn't really sure. I answered her question.

"I was wondering if God was crazy like me and Ryan or if he was more like you and Mr. Bryant."

Her face did what I thought it would do. Mr. Bryant's face was screaming "*Crazy!*" now too.

I looked back to my husband who was carefully picking up a blue mug from the table.

"Oh cool." He grinned as he peeked inside. "Mom even heated up the maple syrup." He looked at me. "What some?" he offered.

"UmHm." I nodded happily and reached for the pancakes.

Ryan talked to his parents while I talked to my parents on their phone. My father was staying home with my mother for now and taking care of her. He said that she was being mean as a snake and still struggling with withdrawal problems but that she already looked and sounded much better.

When I talked to her she was nice to me on the phone and even asked how Ryan was, which shocked me. She did sound different. Good different. I talked on the phone until my ear hurt while Ryan talked to his parents and answered their hundreds of questions. I finally told my mother goodbye and hung up, then walked to the window and peeked up at the sky.

It looked like a perfect day. There was a beautiful blue sky with only a few high wispy clouds and two crisscrossed lines where jets had left their trail through all that blue. I wanted to go flying, I decided as I looked out the window, and I was taking Ryan with me. But where would we go? I didn't want to visit my parents' house; there might be soldiers or someone waiting around in the bushes to grab us. We had to be careful, so it had to be some place where nobody would be looking for us. Some *normal* place where *normal people* went all the time doing *normal things* just for fun.

I realized with a happy thrill that I could actually go see a movie if I wanted to! I didn't have to ask my mother anymore. She'd always told me that the flashing lights would cause me to have a seizure, but I never believed her. She didn't want to take me. And if something did happen Ryan would be with me and he could take care of me. I wanted to do it.

"Ryan. I want to go to see a movie. And I want to go flying," I said when he and his parents took a second to breathe between talking and talking. Ryan looked at me, considering it, but then his face fell.

"Oh crap! We came here without anything. No wallet, no cash, no shoes." His frown became a wicked grin as he added "no clothes!"

I was wearing a pair of his drawstring gray sweats and a big white t-shirt that had a nice beach scene with the words, "Nassau Bahamas" on it. Ryan had sweats and a t-shirt too. We matched.

"*You* were naked! *I* had a pillow," I corrected with my own grin.

"Don't worry about cash, son," his father said. It turned out that Lucius had forced him to take forty thousand dollars in cash when he'd been here yesterday so they would stay home and stay safe instead of going to work where someone might try to grab them, or at the very least be mercilessly harassed by the media and paparazzi.

Mr. Bryant tried to talk us into going back to Amen Hale where it was safe, but Ryan said that he desperately needed a little "normal" and inside Amen Hale was not "normal."

Mrs. Bryant found me a shoulder bag to put one of her old money purses and our borrowed flip flops in. I slung the bag over my head and shoulder so I wouldn't lose it when we were flying. Ryan looked out the window beside the door, eyeing the soldiers who still guarded the house and the media and camera hounds who were camped all around.

"They're having Bethany's fourteenth birthday party today in Amen Hale and they plan on having a human sacrifice for her," Ryan said as he reached for the door handle. "It's one of the men who killed Rain in France and I'm totally okay with him dying, but I don't want to see it. Bethany's going to eat him after she kills him. I'd rather be somewhere else with Sky, doing something that does not involve blood or killing or death or little girls covered in blood. We both want to do something normal and just plain fun. Bye Mom, Dad. Love you. We'll be back soon."

Ryan pulled me out the door before they could start asking questions and trap us here for another hour. As soon as we stepped onto the porch the cameras started to flash and media people started to shout and come running from their cars and nearby trailers with their cameras. The four soldiers posted out front of the trailer were surprised by our appearance as well.

"You're sure all I need to do is hold your hand?" Ryan asked for the third time.

"I'm Sky," I told him. He kept his eyes on me as we started to rise straight up, into the air, while cameras flashed and people on the ground shouted at us. We stopped, hanging in the air, high above his trailer. Ryan's hand was squeezing mine really tightly.

"Easy, Ryan, you're squeezing too hard." He kept his eyes on my face but he stopped squeezing so hard.

"Are you scared of heights?" I asked.

"I didn't think I was," he answered back. "This is just weird, Sky. If I let go, what would happen?"

"Don't let go," I told him.

He nodded. Together we glided above the trailer park and Ryan pointed down to another trailer that had soldiers and media camped around it as well.

"That's Mary's house," he said. "And that's my friend Greg's house," he said as he pointed to another trailer.

In the distance we saw a helicopter flying toward us, and I flew us away from it and higher into the air. Ryan had told me not to say exactly where I wanted to go while we were in the house because it was probably bugged so I'd kept it to myself. I pictured in my mind the nice theater in Ormond Beach that I'd seen from the expressway so many times. I always looked at it as we drove by and dreamed of going to see a movie there.

The last movie I could remember seeing was when I was seven, before I got put on most of my medicines. I remember it was a Disney cartoon but couldn't recall which one. I pulled Ryan closer to me and thought about our destination and prepared a little bubble of warm comfortable air around us to fly in like a little ship, willing the air and everything else to go around our bubble us as we flew so we wouldn't arrive windblown and nasty or have a rough stop.

"Did you just make it warmer?" Ryan asked.

I nodded.

"In all of Jacksonville?" he asked, looking alarmed and I laughed.

"No. Just around us." He nodded and I asked, "Are you ready?"

"I guess," he said uncertainly.

I pulled him closer to me by his hand and kissed him.

"Let's go do something normal."

"Said the flying girl to the disappearing naked boy," Ryan said with a lopsided grin. "Any ideas for what you'd like to do after the movie?"

I touched his "Nassau Bahamas" t-shirt and whispered into his ear. "I want to swim naked on a beautiful tropical beach and make love in the water. Or on the beach. Or both."

"Will there be any maids on this beach?" Ryan asked, making a face.

I laughed.

The world below became a blur of colors as we flew through the air.

Black Rain

Heart Attack

I OPENED MY EYES to find I was on a couch in the alcove beside the dining room. I stayed still and tried to recall how I got here. I remembered waking up this morning inside Believer with Bethany and coming downstairs with Cathryn and Lucius, and I remembered getting upset because they were so careful. They'd been worried that I might lose control of myself.

I froze as my memories rushed back into my head, the missing pieces falling into places in slices. Cathryn holding my hands, the things she'd asked me, her magic holding me, keeping me still, keeping me calm, making me answer.

The questions she'd asked.

The answers I'd given.

About Emma. About Jane. About Mary. About Dan. About me.

All of it came back to me and I lay there, petrified with the horror of what I'd said. I remained perfectly still, my unblinking black eyes open but my mind did not use them, rendering them blacked out windows, unused and unwanted, while I thought on other things. What would my world be like now? Now that everyone knew what a freak I was!? And *why* had my mother done this to me!? Secrets inside my soul that I didn't even know about myself, all pulled out and laid naked before everyone to look at and see and talk about while I knelt there like a statue. Things that had been safely tucked away, forced out like pus from an infected wound.

Perhaps that was what my heart really was: an infected, pus-filled cavity that needed to be mashed, right here and now. Perhaps my mother did me a favor, as within so without. Perhaps Cathryn should have invited MORE people into the room before she stomach pumped the contents of my heart out onto the floor!

"She's awake." I heard Lucius's voice nearby.

"My lady," Believer's voice rumbled cautiously.

"Rain." Cathryn's voice. "Are you all right?"

I didn't move but others did, all around me they moved. Cathryn knelt by my head. Lucius hovered over her, looking down at me. Believer stood by the end of the couch looking down from high above, his red eyes burning down into me. Who knew what he was thinking, what he thought about me? What he'd do?

"Rain, are you all right? Please, don't be upset. We had to find out if Emma had hurt you in any other ways. Other than making you fall in love with her, I mean." Cathryn sounded nervous. Guilty. "I can feel that you're upset right now but please, don't be! Don't be embarrassed either. You have nothing to be embarrassed over. It's all right. Everything is all right, Rain."

Her voice urged me to be calm. I felt the first prickle of magic come from her and brush at my skin. I didn't stop it, but I studied it as it touched me. I willed my body to absorb it and break it down like a high tech magical forensic unit, searching for motive, purpose, power, flavor—and *sinister intent.*

I relaxed. It wasn't anything like what she'd done before; this was just her usual magic, filling her words and making them more than just words. I let her magic roll over me along with the rest of the ever present magic in Amen Hale, like a bouquet of flowers scenting the air in the room. Most of the smells were faint and innocuous but some were strong and demanding, asking me to change or come or do or be in some way or another. I'd never avoided magic before but always let it touch me as it wanted. I'd just *let it come.* Everyone's magic, touching me, shaping me, moving through me. I changed along with it. And now I'd changed again. Emma and Jane and Mary—and now I was bound to the vampires.

I bet they're hungry, I thought with a hot flash of concern.

"*Soon, my loves, soon,*" I sent my thought to Jane and Dan's mind. I knew that they heard me and didn't listen for a reply.

Beside me Cathryn was going on and on, rambling away, pushing her happy sauce at me with each breath she took; like a drunk who had beer on his breath, her magic didn't smell good to me right this instant because I was pissed at her! Before I opened my mouth and said something simply *vicious,* I thought about what she'd done, but I just couldn't see any reason for doing something so horrible to a daughter I loved. Maybe she knew something about mothering I didn't, but DAMN!

I gave myself a shake as I lay there, trying to let the excess angst ease out in a harmless way. I was still way too pissed for safety. I could feel the coiled tension through my whole body and I didn't trust myself to move without doing something unexpected. I was even trying hard not to think anything horrible. I didn't want to hurt anyone. Especially my mother.

"Believer. Pick me up," I said and watched his red burning eyes brighten at my words.

His huge form bent toward me and his arms lifted my stiff and rigid body from the couch. He settled me in his arms and I allowed my ice to shatter, letting my body be molded and shaped by his hands until I rested my head against his stormy chest. Soon my anger at my mother melted away and all I could think about was what I'd done to Believer.

For some reason, I couldn't find my tears.

"I love you," I said.

"I know," he rumbled.

"What are you thinking," I asked calmly.

"I am happy," he rumbled quietly. Calmly.

"How could you possibly be happy?" I asked, coming alive some as I frowned.

"Because my name was the first word that you spoke. My arms the ones you wanted. Because you said you loved me. Because you're awake and speaking to me here in my arms. I have much to be happy about, my lady."

"I'm sorry, Believer," I said.

"Why?" he asked.

"Because I changed again."

He moved me, holding me so that he could see my face and I his. I reached out with both hands and put one on each side of his beautiful, cloudy face.

"Am I still your husband?" he rumbled.

I nodded.

"Do you still love me?" The shadows over one eye darkened and reshaped, like he'd raised an eyebrow over just that one eye to get exactly the expression he wanted to show, and it made me smile. He must have been practicing in front of a mirror!

"Believer, you've learned how to do eyebrows so well!" I cheered and touched his one raised cloudy eyebrow as I spoke through my wide smile. "Yes. I love you and your fancy new eyebrow."

His rumbling laugh was wonderful to hear and cheered me more than my mother's nasty, spoon fed magic medicine.

"I am sorry that you have to share me now," I said sadly.

"Am I any different from Dan?" he asked me and I frowned, not understanding until Believer explained.

"He now has to share his mate because of Emma's power just as I do. He does not love her any more or less than I love you, and he has allowed it. I'm sure he did not want this or expect this to happen, and neither did I, but it has happened. Dan and I will both be fine, but how do you feel about what has happened? Are you angry at Emma?"

"No." I shook my head quickly, aghast at the suggestion.

The clouds around Believer's red coal fire eyes darkened. "You're in love with her," he grumbled. "I doubt you could be mad at her even if you wanted to." He gave me a "look" that matched well with his voice. He *had* been practicing his facial expressions. And he'd been thinking things through while I slept, it seemed. I hadn't even thought about Dan, standing out in the hall in front of Mary's room and what that meant. Sometimes I forgot just how smart Believer really was.

"Rain," Cathryn called again, and I looked down at her from my seat in Believer's arms. She had tears on her face but she seemed calm as she stared up at me. She was wearing a beautiful, light blue dress, but I didn't like the sleeves and it bunched at the middle. I played with her dress as I spoke to her, shaping and reshaping and moving this and that to make the fit more becoming.

"Yes, ma'am."

"Are you still angry with me?" she asked.

"I wish I could lie and say I wasn't, but—I can't," I said stiffly as I finished her dress.

"I'm sorry, Rain. I did not mean to—"

"Hey, wait a second!" I called to the servants. "Don't take that away yet! I'm starving!"

They were clearing the food from the table. Believer set me on my feet, and I dashed into the dining room and took a plate out of one of the gloved hands of a servant with a "thanks" and walked around the table, running my eyes over the little buns and other fancy breakfast fixings as I spoke to Cathryn who followed behind me.

"I love you, Mom, but you need to be more careful. There are places inside me that even Mary does not go because they will kill her. I've already killed my child and Rain Marie, and I don't want to kill you by accident. And on top of that, do you think you could have gotten more specific? You didn't even ask my favorite sexual position or what cuss words I like to scream when I cum!"

I grabbed a beautiful, little crystal bowl of cut and perfectly sectioned grapefruit and slammed it onto my plate and then angrily spooned too much sugar on top the way I liked it. My angry gaze fell on some curious looking crackers and a couple of long strips of meat, like funky bacon. I kept talking as I scavenged the remains of the fancy breakfast everyone had enjoyed while I'd recovered from my session of mind rape.

"I love you, and I'm trying to understand why you did it, and I'll get over it, but I'm still mad." I passed on the eggs; they looked as if they'd been on the table a while, but I went back and grabbed a piece of the funky bacon and plopped it onto my plate. There was only one more piece of the bacon and I grabbed the second piece as well. I didn't want it to go to waste. A servant pulled out a chair for me and seated me at the table, handing me a spoon for my grapefruit and placing a napkin in my lap while a second servant holding a silver pitcher spoke.

"Juice, milk, or something else to drink, Princess?"

"Whatever you have there is fine." I pointed businesslike to the silver pitcher he held.

He filled my glass. It was juice. The server who filled my glass was a middle-aged man with a lean, rugged face, dressed in full formal attire all the way down to the white gloves, slicked back hair, and the little towel draped *just so* over one arm. I didn't want to be brusque or mean to this man. He didn't deserve it. I took a deep calming breath.

"What's your name?" I asked the man as I spooned a sugary piece of grapefruit into my mouth.

"Randolf, Princess."

I spooned in another piece of grapefruit before I'd finished off the first and leaned back in my chair to chew as I looked at Randolf. I felt my mother's hands rest lightly on each of my shoulders from behind my chair. I didn't pull away from her as I watched Randolf. He seemed very professional, each movement crisp and exact. His eyes exactly where they needed to be and never lingering or uncertain.

My mother's hands slipped away as I leaned over my bowl and spooned in another two pieces and leaned back again. Cathryn's hands returned to my shoulders, silently begging my forgiveness, and I raised the hand not holding my spoon to touch hers as I chewed and continued my study of Randolf.

"How is your heart today, Randolf? Are you happy?"

Only his lips moved; they pursed for a moment before he spoke. "My heart is well, Princess, if a little troubled," he answered smoothly.

His simple and honest answer seemed perfect. It matched my own feelings exactly. *Well, but troubled*, I thought and nodded.

"Mine too, Randolf," I told him. "Mine too."

Gannon The Grey

This Could Work

THE YOUNG COUPLE enjoyed an unbelievable breakfast on a secluded, little patio while a dressed-up servant stood beside their table and waited on them hand and foot. Byron joined them at their table, encouraging them to continue eating as he spoke. He told them that their meeting with the White Witch had been delayed. He quickly suggested they walk the garden trails in the Prazo Maior until the gathering in the Hallow this afternoon, then bid them good day, dashing off to attend other pressing matters.

The servant, seeing their utterly lost expressions, explained that the Prazo Maior was the newly created trail and garden area on the south side of Amen Hale. Gannon shook the man's hand, not hiding his relief at the help. Merrik, at ease and laughing at Gannon's easy banter, guided the couple through the house, out the back patio, then pointed them in the right direction.

The wide-eyed pair weren't alone; others walked the trails with them, other couples, walking hand in hand and smiling, even stopping to kiss and hold each other. There were families with smiling children and a couple who picnicked together at one of the many stone tables placed along the trail.

The main attraction was the many themed garden areas, each one built around a statue. The first circled garden they passed featured a magnificent ring of fully grown cherry trees, the upper branches in full, white bloom while the lower limbs bore fully mature, ripe cherries, ready to pick and be enjoyed. The season and the sandy Florida soil were apparently not relevant factors in the trees' growth.

The nude statue's gleaming white marble matched the spotless blossoms except for the green vines that looked like inlaid jade which seemed shaped into the stone itself. The bright green vines of inlaid jade caught the eye, forcing a closer examination. The vibrantly colored, life-like vines wrapped around each ankle and ran up each leg, crossing at the small of her back and then around to her front where they crossed again between her breasts then up to the shoulders and down the arms to end in circles around each of her wrists like living manacles.

They'd seen the queen from a distance and Gannon felt uneasy staring at the statue that displayed her in such perfect detail, but there were others there admiring the statue; some even had children with them and they seemed fine with it. Kim seemed fine with it too, so he smiled and went with it. It was a small thing, but it reminded him that they weren't in Kansas anymore.

Next they entered a circular garden with white tile laid into the ground that was so bright the whole area gleamed in the sun. On the plinth in the center was a statue of a beautiful Oriental girl and a young man beside her holding her hand. They were both looking up toward heaven with contented smiles on their faces.

"Excuse me, ma'am, do you know who these people are?" Gannon asked an older woman in a brown robe who was standing beside them, looking at the same statue.

The woman seemed surprised at their lack of knowledge. She narrowed her eyes and did a double take of Gannon's blue hair and Kim's eye-popping flare pink/red before she spoke. Another couple admiring the statue who'd overheard the question was also giving them queer, questioning looks.

"Who *are* you two?" the lady asked.

"My name is Gannon The Grey and this is my fiancé, Alana Burning."

Gannon very deliberately used Kim's new name and watched her smile light up when he did. Before passing through the gateway Kim had chosen 'Alana Burning' as her new name. After entering Amen Hale, that name had been entered into the big book of names by Mr. Pyle, who hadn't batted an eye at hearing it or shown any surprise at all as he entered Gannon's own given name. After recording their names he'd taken their 'vows' of service, then welcomed them in, telling them they were now, 'Children of Hale'. The whole process had given Gannon chills down to the bone, but he'd put on a brave, confident face for his girl. This was what she wanted. This was where they needed to be.

"Gannon The Grey, aye?" The lady raised her eyebrows. "A bit *blue* to be grey aren't you?"

Alana glared at the woman. "It was his given name when he was born! It's on his birth certificate, and even more importantly, Mr. Pyle wrote it into the Book of Shadows just this morning. Along with mine. We are Children of Hale!" she finished fiercely and the suspicious woman retreated a step, putting her hands up defensively as she backed away.

"Forgive me—*Alana Burning*. I meant no offense." The strange woman gave her a small bow but kept her eyes on her, studying her and Gannon. Curious now. But not as if they were a thorn that did not belong.

"Did you say they just added your name to the book this morning?" asked the older man who'd been standing close enough to overhear. He and the woman on his arm both looked in their late fifties. They wore casual attire, he a white pullover shirt, slacks, and a wicker hat, she a blue sun dress with white flowers and a white hat, tied under her chin.

"Yes, sir. We arrived just this morning," Gannon answered politely.

"Welcome to Amen Hale then, Gannon, wasn't it? My name is Stan and this is my wife Beth." He shook Gannon's hand. "Alana." He greeted and shook her hand as well.

They all shared greetings and even the rude woman in her brown robe introduced herself as Velda Covengton. She was friendlier now but still eyed them curiously, especially their hair, as she wandered off down the trail.

"How many people did they let in this morning, Gannon?" Stan asked.

"Just us," he answered.

Stan nodded. "What do you know about Amen Hale?"

Alana answered him. "Mr. Pyle explained some things to us, but we haven't seen any of the Lords and Ladies in real life yet. Except for Cathryn; we saw her across the room as she walked through." She looked at the statue of the beautiful Oriental girl and the young man with her, holding her hand.

"Is this Sky and Ryan, the Black Witch's brother?" she guessed.

"Yes. This is Lord Ryan and the Lady Sky," Stan confirmed, with the correctly added honorifics.

"What's it like living here, Beth?" Alana asked the older woman.

Beth made a face. "Gracious, child, it's hard to say, everything is still getting settled. It's all so new. And magic makes everything change so fast." She put both arms out wide. "Just yesterday this new garden wasn't even here. Stan and I have been here since Wednesday evening, but it feels like we just arrived ourselves. People are still coming in most every day. And some of those who've been here from the very start are actually asking to leave."

"Why would anyone want to leave Amen Hale?" Gannon asked, somewhat alarmed. His grip on Alana's hand tightened.

Stan gave Beth a less than happy scowl but grunted and explained.

"It's not complicated. A few folks have decided that they want out. They're going to be asking the King today if they can leave from what I understand."

Beth flipped a hand through the air. "Good riddance I say. I hope he lets them go. I don't want anyone here who doesn't want to be here." She adjusted her hat primly, obviously piqued at those who would choose to leave.

"But why would anyone want to leave?" Gannon pressed.

"Amen Hale isn't for everyone," Stan answered. "Some folk are troubled by the bloodier parts of living here, with vampires who drink blood and with Princess Bethany who needs sacrifice to live. They're scared of where it all might be headed, and I can understand their concerns. And then there are others who are terrified that soldiers will attack us again and they want out before that happens."

"Complete idiots!" Beth labeled the lot, shaking her head and rolling her eyes.

"And then there are those who realize after being here a while that they don't much like having a King and a Queen telling them what to do and where to do it. And there are also some people who can't handle the lifestyle that we have here. You do *know* that we have no live TV and no phones here in Amen Hale, don't you?" Stan leaned in and stared hard at them until they both nodded.

"Good." Stan nodded as well.

"Stan, what do we do here?" Gannon glanced at Alana who was listening raptly to every word they said. "Do we work?" he asked. "We'll need our own place or an apartment or something. What do I do? I need to take care of Alana after we get married."

"And I need to take care of Gan," Alana said firmly.

Beth and Stan beamed at them, enjoying the young couple immensely. Stan motioned them over to a nearby bench where the four of them sat and Stan continued his educational discourse on life in Amen Hale.

"Gannon, I can see that you're worried about taking care of Alana and worried about keeping her safe and making a home for her, which is all very natural. But it's different here in Amen Hale where we have a King and Queen. It's the King and Queen's job to worry about making sure you and Alana are taken care of and that you're safe and happy and have a home. They take care of you and love you so you can take care of them and love them back."

"You're confusing them Stanly!" Beth fussed. "The boy asked about work—that's a J. O. B., old man! So explain how it works here."

Stan gave his wife a long-suffering patient look then said, "Yes, dear," and began again.

"A job. Yes, it's very important to have a good job. That's the way it works. We all work hard to get ahead, kicking butt and taking names and cutting deals to make a better life for ourselves and our loved ones. Or that's the way it happens *out there*," Stan pointed directionless out beyond the wall, "but not in Amen Hale. Here, we're a family, all of us working to serve and take care of each other, just like a family. Beth works in the laundry, washing and folding, while I work in the supply room keeping track of what we need and what we've used. In Amen Hale we work to make everyday life happen as it should, not to make money, because we don't need money. Before I came here I never would have been content to do what I'm doing now. I ran a good sized company. I had thirty-two employees."

"You were rich," Gannon guessed.

"Very," Beth added.

"Yes, we were," Stan said with a proud smile. "But now I keep track of how many rolls of toilet paper we've used and how much we need to order. What I do matters to every person here. Believe me." He laughed at his own humor and earned a slap on the arm from Beth.

"Are you both happy here?" Alana asked.

"Yes!" Stan and Beth both answered at the same time and then laughed at each other happily.

Gannon couldn't help smiling with them, this old couple, happy here in Amen Hale, laughing and smiling. Gannon looked to Alana. She was already staring at him, his thoughts mirrored perfectly in her eyes. It was as if she'd spoken every word.

Gannon felt goose bumps rise on his arms. They could be happy here, grow old together and be just like Stan and Beth. *This could work,* Gannon thought. He and Alana could be happy here. Suddenly his happy thoughts were assaulted like a dagger in the back by the unwelcome childhood memory about his jar of lightning bugs, all dead at the bottom of the jar.

But this time is different! Gannon thought fiercely. *This time, I've crawled into the jar with my firefly! If something goes wrong, I'll die with her.* As he stared at her, he realized that he would happily die with her, but that he would never be able to live without her. He became aware of the lack of voices and turned to find Stan and Beth both staring at them. Smiling.

Gannon blushed!

Alana laughed then kissed him.

"Yes, we're happy," Stan confirmed, starting again. "Cornelius and Cathryn are good people, we've know them for years and we trust them or we wouldn't be here. I trusted them enough to walk away from my company and bring my Beth to live in Amen Hale." He patted his wife's hand.

"You're going to love it here. I'm sure," Beth assured them warmly.

Stan and Beth talked about the past three days they'd spent in Amen Hale and what they thought life might be like once things got settled. They talked about some of the amazing things they'd seen done by the witches and Lords and Ladies of Hale. Alana and Gan told them about their upcoming wedding and about the fairy dance outside the walls and the White Witch sending for them.

The four of them rose from their bench and continued to explore the garden together as they talked. Beth and Stan were seeing the garden for the first time themselves so they were equally thrilled at what they found around each new bend in the trail. They passed under soaring arches and through magnificent statued gardens and explored hidden little grottos, tucked cunningly away to provide private and intimate places just off the trail.

The land rose and fell, shear rock rising up in places as high as fifty feet in the air while in other places the land sloped down almost like a depression or a bowl in the earth to hold a beautiful crystal clear spring filled with warm inviting water. The impossible landscape seemed utterly alien to the usual deadpan flat ground that was the norm for north Florida. It reminded Gannon of walking through Disney World where every tree and bush and boulder were placed just so, like pieces of art.

They were about to explore another narrow path leading off the trail when Alana found a lady's shirt lying on a bush, and then Beth found a pair of trousers on the ground. Their little party quietly backed away and returned to the main trail, leaving whoever was down there to whatever they were doing down there.

Stan and Beth acted as tour guides, sharing what they knew as they came upon each statue or monument until they heard the chiming bell calling Amen Hale to lunch, at eleven.

Gannon moved to follow but was pulled to a stop by Alana's hand as she stood in the path, rooted firmly in place.

"You and Beth go ahead. We're not hungry yet," Alana called to the older couple.

"Oh?" Stan said, looking back, then his eyebrows popped up. "Ooh!" he said with understanding. His eyes twinkled and his lips twitched fighting against a knowing smile.

"All right, you two," Beth said, giving them both a parental worthy glare, "but don't let the time get away from you. We're all supposed to be at The Hallow before noon, that's the big building down by the river that looks like a stadium. This is a meeting you can't be late for," Beth instructed.

"Yes, ma'am. We'll be there. We promise," Alana answered. "It's been nice speaking with you and Stan."

"We'll see you at the Hallow." Stan waved and he and his wife disappeared down the trail.

Once they were out of sight Alana started pulling Gannon back the way they'd already come. "Com'on, Gan, let's run!"

Alana took off and Gannon did his best to follow, running back down the path, passing others on their way out of the gardens, answering the summoning call of the lunch bell. Alana ran effortlessly, her training as a long distance runner showing as Gannon in his ratty, worn jeans and boots labored to keep pace while fighting a growing stitch in his side. Gannon was long and lean and athletic but Alana was a rail thin running machine with limitless energy.

"Where are we going!?" Gannon panted.

"Swimming!" Alana called back over her shoulder as she pulled ahead with a burst of blinding speed that Gannon couldn't hope to match. He watched her red and pink hair vanish around the bend and had to stop as he encountered a startled family recovering from a her passing. "Crazy girl!" the angry mother shouted at Alana's back.

"Excuse me! Sorry! Oops!" Gannon called out his apologies as he slalomed his own way through the stair step children, getting yelled at himself as he followed his Crazy Girl.

Gannon got to the turn off on the trail that led to the spring and started down the path but pulled up short as he noticed a t-shirt thrown on top of one of the bushes that said, "I had one HELL of a Time at AMEN HALE!"

He noticed Alana's green shorts, dropped onto the red brick path.

"Works for me," he panted and got busy adding a "Witch Buddy!" t-shirt, a pair of ratty jeans, some clunky boots, and a pair of BVDs to the Do Not Disturb! sign before heading around the bend to cool his burning body in the arms of his burning beauty.

Ferrand

The Laughing Witch

AFTER STEPPING THROUGH the gateway into an underground garage, Ferrand had been blindfolded. A voice he recognized as Lucius, the Captian of Amen Hales Guard, had him taken from the underground facility and deposited into a small room with nothing inside but one table and two chairs. They had him strip completely nude then a grim faced man gloved up and unapologetically searched his hair, inspected his open mouth, and his other orifices after which they provided him with a new set of brown clothing that resembled workman's attire.

Lucius entered his cell. He ordered the grim faced man to go burn his clothing, then he ordered Ferrand to take a seat. Lucius, with military crispness, asked only a handful of quick questions and then departed. It hadn't exactly been the welcome he'd hoped for, but Ferrand reminded himself, it could have been much worse.

Ferrand paced. Sat and waited. Got up and paced. More than an hour passed.

The door opened soundlessly and the Black Witch herself, dressed in her black dress, stepped through the door. No guards or security preceded her or followed her into the room, and the door behind her swung shut without hands touching it. Ferrand had seen pictures and video of Black Rain, but they were poor preparation for being in her presence.

She was young, and a beautiful girl, yet her nightmare eyes made her seemed older. It looked as if the natural orbs had been replaced with glass eyes, glossy and black as night. Her lips were a frightening shade of blue, similar to the coloring on a body after drowning or exposure to cold. Ferrand noticed with relief that her hair and dress were not waving about. From what was understood of her moods, this meant that she was in control of herself, for the moment at least.

The feel of the room changed as she entered. As Ferrand became intensely aware of her presence, his own breathing became something that required conscience thought instead of being an involuntary action. The room seemed to narrow, feeling smaller, as if her presence had crowded the space and filled it up and then had gone even farther, pushing at the walls and corners of the room, making them less firm and solid. *Less real?*

Without saying a word to him she sat down at the table.

He had not bowed to her, but such a display did not seem to be what she wanted and Ferrand trusted his guts as he joined her and slid into the chair on the opposite side of the table. She tilted her head to the side as she regarded him then raised her hand to take a small bite of a strip of browned meat she held. It appeared to be a piece of bacon.

"Would you like some?" Her voice was polite. She proffered the strip of meat.

"No, thank you, but—" He stopped as her face fell and watched with dismay as her glossy black hair began to move about her head, strands of black hair reaching out into the air around her head like roots digging through soil. He felt a prickle of power glide along his skin, causing the hair on his arms to rise.

"I insist," she ordered.

"Of course." Ferrand reached out and took the peculiar strip of meat from her hand. Its texture alarmed him the second he touched it. He feared he knew what it was even as he placed it in his mouth and tore off a bite and chewed.

As the taste hit his palate he began to struggle, the building pressure seeming to start at his bare feet under the table, where his toes curled. The feeling gained momentum as his panic grew—and then it charged upward. His already delicate stomach utterly betrayed him. He pitched to the side and spewed! He was blinded and choking, battling his heaving stomach for air.

Finding his mouth insufficient as an exit point, his body added the use of his nostrils as a secondary means of evacuation. Ferrand sputtered and choked and gagged and spat, but eventually he heard the laughing. The mad laughing of the Black Witch. He was still seated, bent over in his chair facing the floor as he pressed one thumb flat against the side of his nose, closing one barrel as he blew to clear the other side of vomit. He did the other side, then repeated the process again and again, trying to purge the horrid smell of vomit from his sinuses.

He had no towels or even a shirt to rip to shreds to make a rag, and the coarse brown clothing they'd put him in was useless and short sleeved so he used his hands to wipe at his face as best he could. He was panting and felt light headed and ill used when he finally sat up and looked at the girl on the other side of the table.

"Sorry for laughing." She smiled politely. "But you really should have seen your face. I've never seen *anyone* puke like that before."

As she started to laugh again, fury and outrage at the indignity filled Ferrand. He fought to stay calm as the stupid girl giggled. He tried to focus on his mission instead of his humiliation and the taste of human flesh in his mouth.

"Forgive me. It seems I have no stomach for human flesh." Ferrand fired back and gave a mockery of a smile. Instantly the girl's mirth vanished and was replaced by a quiet calm that made Ferrand wish the giggling would resume.

"You French bastard!" she growled. "You force yourself on top of me like a rape with clothes on and think you deserve a thank you for it. I ate flesh and sugared grapefruit for breakfast this morning and—I *liked it!"* she hissed. She stopped and glared at him and shook her head. "I don't have time for this shit," she said simply. "I want my people back *now*. Where are they?"

"They will return your people—"

"Shut up!" she screamed and stood abruptly from her seat, her black hair coming to life like a screeching alarm, but there was no place to flee. There was no escape. The light in the room dimmed and reddened while the girl glared at him in barely contained fury. She closed her eyes, taking slow steady breaths. Ferrand waited, his own outrage totally forgotten and replaced by a simple desire to get out of this room alive.

The witch opened her black eyes and spoke. "I will come to the warehouse at three o'clock and take my people, and then I will speak to your bastard government for five minutes. If any of them are missing, I will kill the President of France *and* his family because I intend to make it personal between us. It seems only fair as he has our children. Then I will kill the Prime Minister and his family, just in case this was all his idea. I will kill the French ass that sat in a seat and made the decision to touch the Children of Hale without cause. I will not kill the people of France, just the people who chose to do this."

The vomit and dried filth in his hair and on his hands and arms vanished and the clothes he wore shifted against his skin. He looked down to see that his top had transformed into a white sweater and his pants to a pair of perfectly fitted denim jeans. On his feet he felt socks and the wrapping of some type of footwear.

He was still marveling over the altered condition of his clothing when she ordered, "Get up!"

Ferrand rose to his feet and watched as the entire wall on the side of the room shimmered like a huge sheet of heated glass and then vanished altogether to reveal the warehouse in France. About a dozen scientists were staring at them from just four feet away. They had apparently been examining the area in the warehouse where the gateway usually opened when the eight by twelve foot section of metal vanished beneath their hands revealing a side view of the room in which he stood. There was nothing in that room but a table, two chairs, a very frightened Frenchman, and a terrifying Black Witch.

Soldiers standing behind the scientists pointed guns in her direction which she ignored as she watched Ferrand walk back to France in five steps before turning to look back at her.

"Ferrand. You need to know something about witches, it's something you may already know," she shrugged, "we cannot lie. I will do *exactly* what I said if my people are not returned, even if I weep while I do it. As above so below, as within so without. Black is my color and my name is Black Rain. So mote it be." The air shimmered and the tin metal sheeting reappeared, affixed to the metal above and below as if it had never been gone.

Soldiers, scientists, and others in the warehouse rushed to Ferrand, all talking at once.

"Silence!" he shouted. "Someone give me a phone! A PHONE!" He bellowed, wild eyed, turning in a circle, gesturing madly at the staring men gathered around him. Someone thrust a phone at him.

Ferrand snatched it up and started dialing.

Ryan and Sky

Oops

RYAN AND SKY emerged from the theater smiling and happy. He wore a Jacksonville Suns baseball cap and she had her long blond hair pinned up and tied back in a red scarf as part of their disguises. When they arrived, Ryan had Sky pick which movie they would see and had been delighted when she'd chosen an action movie instead of a chic flick. A new release showing on the theater's only I-Max screen. The film stared Sandra Bullock as a scientist; it had spies and bad guys fighting the good guys complete with lots of chases and explosions with the mandatory dash of romance somehow inserted into the mix.

Everything went smoothly. They didn't even have a hard time using their hundred dollar bill at the ticket counter; the girl dabbed at the bill with her marker to see if it was fake and then dealt out a pile of change which they used at the snack bar, loading up on junk to take into the theater.

"How on earth does anyone drink this much soda, Ryan!?" Sky asked as she dropped her "large" Diet Coke still three quarters full into the trash with a wet sounding "gloosh!" Ryan dropped his trash in the can and together they walked out of the theater.

No one pointed at them. No one yelled, "It's Sky and Ryan!" or "Get 'em!" or "There they are!" No cops, no soldiers, no Feds, no nothing.

He and Sky walked out, hand in hand, same as the rest of the people catching an afternoon flick, blinking as they emerged into the bright afternoon sun of Ormond Beach.

"That was fun!" Sky said, followed by an enthusiastic, "Are you ready to go to the beach now?"

"Sure."

They were already holding hands and without warning they began to rise into the air gliding up and over the cars in the parking lot and then higher up into the air above the theater as people below pointed and stared. Ryan's grip tightened a little, but he was getting more adjusted to being "Lois Lane" to Sky's "Superman," holding her hand and letting her power flow down his arm and into his body. He could feel it as a tingling sensation feeding in and spreading out and through his limbs as they rose higher into the air. The air around them warmed as Sky prepared for another of her super fast flights that left everything a blinding blur. They took off and the mix of colors beneath them quickly gave way to blue water.

After two minutes of blinding fast flight they came to a stop. Far below was a tropical island with hundreds of people stretched out along the beach, swimming in what looked like a carefully sculpted man-made lagoon. There were volleyball nets and tennis courts. Hammocks were hung here and there in the shaded areas along with row upon row of white folding chairs where the sun worshipers lay soaking in the rays as they gazed out at the blue green water. Further up the beach were long buildings where people were eating and other buildings that looked like bars where people were dancing to Carribean music. The tinny sound of the steal drums reached up to where we hung, high in the air. Off to the side of the island in deeper, darker waters were two enormous cruise ships with smaller boats shuttling passengers back and forth from the island's dock to the ships.

"We won't stay here, Ryan, but we need to fly down and get masks and snorkels and dive vests so we can really enjoy ourselves."

Ryan gave her a surprised look. "I didn't even think about a mask. Or a snorkel. Sometimes I forget that you're a lot smarter than me." He gave Sky a well-deserved nod as she blushed uncomfortably at his praise. "A good mask and snorkel would definitely be nice," he confirmed, then did a double take, looking at the scene below again and shaking his head.

There it was down below, but it happened so fast it was hard to believe that they were really somewhere in the Bahamas. Sky kept talking while he tried to get his head around his whole changing world.

"I haven't been here since I was fourteen but it was nice the last time I came." She pointed to an area close to the pier that had lots of shops and huts selling souvenirs. "We need to stop in down there. We need towels and suntan lotion and maybe some new swimsuits, and you don't have any rubber things. And we need the things or I'm going to get pregnant, Ryan. You know you didn't use one this morning. I could tell." She gave him a grin.

Ryan made a face. "Owh! Yeah. You're right. Sorry about that." He stared at her looking sheepish with guilt.

"It's okay," Sky said, then pulled him in and kissed him. "If it happens, we'll have a little me or a little you to love. But if we keep doing it like that we'll definitely have a little person growing inside me, but I'm okay with that if you are."

Ryan could tell by the look on Sky's face and the happy ring in her voice that she was *way* more than okay with it, she wanted it! She wanted to get pregnant. She wanted a little person to love. The girl did like making people to love. Every way she could make them. And Ryan had to admit from watching the way she dealt with Believer and Sky Dragon that she would make a great mother. She was firm but fair and loving to her cloud kids. She'd be wonderful with a flesh and blood baby too.

"Do you think your mom would watch the baby for us?" Ryan cocked an eyebrow.

Sky nodded, her smile huge.

Ryan grinned. "And we could get the maid to watch the baby too."

Sky nodded again, smiling so wide she looked like she was about to hurt herself.

"It felt better without a rubber anyway," Ryan said.

Sky nodded, smiling as wide as ever.

Ryan cleared his throat. "Let's go shopping, but give me a second to get decent."

Sky giggled and watched as Ryan awkwardly "adjusted" himself one handed into a more presentable placement to walk around in public. Things had grown some during their talk.

Ryan examined the island, trying to choose the best approach point and finally had Sky fly off and then approach from the far side of the island, flying low to the waves until they got to the beach where they flew just over the trees until they were in the palms behind the shops. Sky set them down on a well-worn trail where they merged into the flood of passengers coming up from the dock. They blended in like they belonged and began shopping, just like any other pair of happy vacationers.

They went into one of the nicer shops where Sky picked out a pair of swim trunks for him, and though they were not Speedos, they were definitely form fitting and eye popping. The suit she picked for herself made Ryan have an apoplectic fit until Sky told him that she'd modeled in suits even skimpier. Then he frowned and asked if she'd modeled nude.

"No!" she yelled and gave him a whack on the arm.

They stopped at another hut where Ryan paid three hundred dollars to have the best three hair stylists on the island work on Sky's hair at the same time, braiding it in long golden locks that ran clear down to her butt. Woven into the braids were jeweled beads, which cost another two hundred dollars. It took the three stylists over an hour to do her hair while Ryan watched and tried to find new ways to pamper her and spend Lucius's cash. Ryan brought in a girl who did Sky's feet and nails while the hair stylists worked on her braids.

After Sky's hair was finished, she dragged him to an open-sided cabana where they got a couple's massage as they stared out at the ocean and were oiled up from head to toe. They took a short nap right there before walking out to the beach.

Ryan noticed the stares more than Sky. Everyone they passed stared. Ryan could understand why they ogled at his wife; she was a walking goddess to whom all men should bow down and grovel like worms, but it wasn't just her they were staring at. Some girls actually tripped as they walked by, falling into the sand because they were staring at him, while the guys just blatantly drooled as their eyes followed Sky's bikini. But even older couples stared.

Together they made a picture that was too beautiful to walk by without taking that second or third glance, and it was that third one that made you fall, and it was that third look that made them fall, crash, spill or get slapped by their significant other. *If*, that is, they didn't trip first. Ryan looked down at his chest and his stomach. The oil made his washboard stomach look even more impressive than it usually did. He couldn't quite remember being this lean and ripped before and wondered if his sister had toned and tightened a few things the last time she messed with his clothes and hair.

By the time they reached the rental hut by the lagoon where the masks, snorkels, vests, and flippers were, Ryan was more than ready to leave the crowd and get to a nice private beach with less hungry eyes staring at his wife.

"Sir, I need your cruise pass ID to rent you all this equipment."

"How much to buy it outright, cash?" Ryan asked. "All of this that we have here including the bag it's in." He waved at the gear for him and Sky. The kid behind the counter looked surprised but came back with the sum of three seventy-five which Ryan paid, and he and Sky turned to find that they were completely surrounded by staring wide-eyed people.

"You're Sky and Ryan, right?" asked a man wearing sunglasses and holding a camera. "I heard you call her Sky. You two *are* the kids from that drug study aren't you?" he asked, pressing closer while raising the camera and pointing it at them. Too close.

Ryan shoved him in the chest and he fell back into the sand, then Ryan felt himself being lifted into the air. Sky had placed her hand on his shoulder and Ryan reached up and took her hand in his.

"No! Our bag and your purse are down there!" Ryan shouted.

Sky looked down to where someone was holding her purse open and looking inside.

"Hey!" she shouted.

The purse jumped out of the woman's hands as if it were alive and then flew up to her. The bag of swimming gear that they'd just bought took flight as well and Ryan grabbed it. They hovered a mere twenty feet above the ground, playing a strange version of aerial Twister as they tried to get all their bags repositioned and still keep in constant contact with each other so Ryan didn't fall.

They were both laughing by the time they were situated and ready to fly as below them the cameras clicked and flashed, watching for the world as they disappeared, flying off into the Caribbean sunset. A couple of human birds holding hands.

Memory and Me

I WALKED OUT OF the room in a foul mood, the door slamming behind me as I left. My meeting with the French Ambassador had gone about how I thought it would, although I hadn't expected him to go nuclear just from tasting human flesh. I thought it tasted great, but then I guess I was too much of a monster now to know what was what.

"Bastard!" I growled. But I felt a twinge of guilt over making him taste flesh.

Lucius was watching me, as were thirty men from our security teams, standing around me in their black outfits. A few were dressed in casual attire, dressed to blend in with the natives of wherever I would send them.

"How did it go?" Lucius asked.

"They'll have them ready to return at three o'clock. I sent Ferrand home with the "or else" portion of my terms."

"What did you say you'd do if they didn't deliver?" he asked.

"That I'd kill the President and Prime Minister of France along with their families. I told him that it didn't seem fair to kill innocent people in his country that didn't have anything to do with what happened. I also agreed to meet with them for five minutes once our people are safely returned."

I waited for Lucius to yell and tell me that I'd lost my mind but he nodded. "Seems simple enough, and it's not something that they'll ignore. They'll give our people back, and it will be a good example to other countries. But be careful this afternoon when you meet with them. Don't give them anything, Mistress. If we give them anything at all people will try to grab us wherever we turn up, like looking for leprechauns to catch and hold onto till they get the gold at the end of the rainbow."

I nodded, feeling a little better. It was nice not to be yelled at for doing something horrible. "I won't give them anything," I promised.

"Will you let some of our men go with you?"

"No," I answered.

He nodded, not arguing with me, but behind him Believer rumbled, looking less than pleased. His red eyes began glowing brighter.

"Mistress. We need another gateway for supplies," Lucius said. "Someplace secluded. Rural. A place we can take the trucks in and out of without being seen or attracting notice would be best. And some place where we might be able to acquire livestock. Feeding almost five hundred people is easier when we can buy the whole cow."

I walked over to one of the unused arches that I'd constructed in the garage and thought about where I wanted it to open. I hadn't traveled much in the life I'd shared with Rain Marie; mostly we'd stayed home or gone to the theme parks in Florida. We traveled once to the Grand Canyon and Tucson, Arizona, and we went to visit our uncle in New York City one summer. And I'd been to North Carolina. I went there after Rain Marie was gone. I pictured in my mind the neglected old cemetery behind a tiny, white church building, and I willed two trees, any two trees, growing along the dirt road beside the graves to lean toward each other and merge at the top, forming an arch big enough and broad enough to drive our trucks through.

The gateway shimmered and the black stone vanished revealing a weed- and shrub-ridden dirt road cut in beside a sun-dappled cemetery edged by a weather beaten white picket fence. I walked through the gateway followed by Lucius and Believer and felt the difference in the mountain air right away. Less humidity and cooler. The air smelled clear and clean, but flying bugs, bits of pollen, and glowing specks of who knew what drifted in the air above the graves catching the light.

Nature's own version of smog filled the air while at our feet grasshoppers bounded away with each step we took through the tall grass, taking flight in short noisy bursts. Lizards ran before us, leaping from the white stones so ideal for warming their cold-blooded bodies on.

The place was in even worse shape than I remembered and I saw that the old white church up by the road had burnt to the ground; only blackened sticks and rubble remained. Weeds and saplings were growing up between the stones themselves. With the church gone, it seemed that no one was here to tend the graves. The paved road was a good two hundred yards away, down the weedy, dirt road.

After taking a quick survey of the area, two of our white rental trucks rambled through the portal and down the dusty road, off to find groceries and needed supplies and hopefully some livestock as well. Lucius, Believer, and five of our men walked behind me as I walked between the graves.

I felt the wind on my face, and I let my power out to join with the comforting breeze. My flesh began to grow brighter and the air in the cemetery took on the smell of my magic.

The crickets and the sounds of nature went suddenly silent, and I raised my head, looking all around us, as did Believer and the men with us.

"No, no. All is well. Sing and dance and love and play," I told the frightened earth. The sounds of life returned, louder than ever for a moment, but it soon settled to what it had been before.

"Please tell the men that this place is special to me, Lucius."

"Yes, Mistress," he replied. "We'll have to leave soon to go to The Hollow. We only have about thirty minutes."

"Then we will be here until it's time for me to leave. Come and get us then," I told him.

Lucius left me and Believer alone, taking the other men with him. Believer followed me wordlessly as I walked the graves, searching for the one I wanted until I stood before it. The earth around the grave was wild with weeds and ants had moved in and set up shop, excavating an ugly hole in the ground instead of erecting a mound. Big red ants marched in and out of the penny-sized hole, busy trying to live.

I willed every ant for twenty feet around the grave to lie still and die. The bustling red army dropped and died, and I willed the soil to shift and smooth until it swallowed the ants, the penny-sized hole, and every other blemish around the grave, leaving the earth smooth and ready. I willed the weeds and shrubs to wither away and then had grass grow for fifteen feet around. I lay down in front of the tombstone and crossed my arms upon my chest.

"What are you doing, my love?" Believer asked.

"I'm going to remember for a while. Watch over me."

I closed my eyes and let my memories of that day come back, willing them into perfect, crystal clarity.

Our parents went on a trip to Branson for a church function and on the way back home they stopped at this graveyard to visit the graves of my mother's grandparents and great grandparents. The cemetery was way up in the hills at the North Carolina/Tennessee border where the Tennessee valley flattened out from the Blue Ridge mountains.

I looked out at the beautiful view with eyes that were glazed and hollow and barely alive. It was just four weeks after I'd had the abortion and killed Brendon. Four weeks since I'd pushed Rain Marie out and taken her place in her body. I was practically the walking dead myself as I ghosted between the worn and faded markers. I looked at the white stones jutting up from the soil with longing and curiosity. I actually felt more at home here in the cemetery than I had since that horrible day.

Our family dug and gardened around the graves of relatives long past as I walked apart on my own, stopping at places, lying down in front of this tombstone or that marker to feel the earth on my back and imagine what it would be like to finally lay this body down. I lay in the grass and stared at the sky and wondered if Rain Marie was happy right that very moment and if Brendon was all right.

I went from grave to grave like I was shopping, searching for the right fit, looking for a place to receive my stolen body so I could become shadows and scraps and dreams again. As I went from grave to grave, I glanced over a couple of times to our family who was sitting together, patiently watching me. They'd stopped digging, their flowers lay on the ground, forgotten as they watched me. I finally lay on one that felt right.

"Are you all right, baby?" my mother had asked me while I lay with my eyes closed on the grave that felt so welcoming and ready to hold the bones in which I dwelt. Or if not hold them, at least hold me, whatever I was.

I spoke. I used her mouth to talk.

"I like this one, Mom. This one feels right."

I heard her gasp in surprise. I heard as she fought back tears to speak again. "Did you read the stone?"

I opened my eyes and looked up at her, her face silhouetted by the puffy white clouds in the sky behind her. "No. I didn't. I should though," I said.

She pressed a hand over her mouth, eyes wide as she nodded.

I sat up and looked at the tombstone—and read it. It was the first thing I'd read since I took Rain Marie's body and slept that first night in her bed. When I woke the next morning I'd been little more than a zombie. I would eat, bathe, go to the bathroom and clean myself, but I did not speak, read, watch TV, or do anything on my own. Our parents took me to doctors and psychiatrists who asked if I'd hit my head or overdosed or almost drowned or undergone some kind of trauma. They tested blood, they did an MRI, they held me over the weekend to observe me away from my parents. Finally they suggested placing me in a home or an institution for the mentally insane, but my parents refused.

They took me home and watched me themselves. This exact place and time was the first time I did something for myself, for whatever "I" was, floating around inside this body. I sat up and looked at the faded marker, not because of Rain Marie or to keep this body alive for her and her parents, I did it for me and me alone. I read the worn writing on the stone.

Alison Driggs - Born 1890 - Died 1905

Survived by her infant daughter Amelia Rose Driggs

I studied the marker. I thought about the dates and used my mind to add up the numbers. I thought for myself. Then I spoke for myself.

"She died when she was fifteen, just like Rain Marie."

"Honey, you're Rain Marie," she said, fighting her tears. "What was her name?" Mom asked me, though she could see the stone herself. And she knew it was a her.

"Alison," I said.

"That's a pretty name," she said.

I looked back at her. "Is it?" I asked.

She looked into my face, crying now, so sad and so happy at the same time. "Yes. It's a very pretty name."

I glanced at Ryan and our dad; they'd come closer and were watching us silently. I looked back at the stone and reached out and touched the faded words "Survived by" cut into the white stone, feeling them with the tips of the fingers. *Of my fingers—*

Brendon should have survived. Our child should have survived, then our grave could have read "Survived by Brendon Rain Bryant" and I could have stayed with my Rain Marie. I missed her. She was alive, fun, wilful, wonderful, sad, angry, and desperate and-I missed her.

"Honey, you're Rain Marie." Our mother's voice spoke again as I stared at the faded letters etched in the white stone.

"You're Rain Marie," she insisted.

I looked up at her. I didn't speak but I thought to myself, whatever I was, *No, they're both gone. I'm what survived.*

They talked for a few minutes trying to get me to say something else, but when I didn't they led me to the car. Dad turned on the radio, tuned to his gospel music. I hated the music. Not Rain Marie. Me. *I* hated it. It wasn't the words so much as the melodies, echoing in the quiet space within and disturbing my stillness. I used her mouth again for my own purposes, forming the words as I had earlier.

"I hate the music."

They all turned to stare at me.

Dad turned off the radio.

I let the memory of their faces fade away and opened my eyes to see branches passing by, then bright sun, then branches again. My moment of confusion passed as I realized that Believer was carrying me in his arms. Believer held me, so I knew I was fine. Safe. I lifted my head to find that we were in Amen Hale, on the path that led to The Hollow.

People were on the trail in front of us. Sky Dragon walked beside Bethany, holding her hand. Penny, Bethany's little maid walked beside them. Closer, on either side of Believer, walked the vampires. I sat up in Believer's arms and got my knees under me and stood high enough off his curved arm to reach Believer's head and wrapped an arm around his neck. I peeked over his shoulder and looked behind us.

More people followed us. Hundreds of people. Mary and Emma were walking hand in hand following behind us. Emma was wearing her clothes that I'd made for her and she was beautiful. Tall and magnificent and so alive. She was talking to Mary and holding her hand as they walked together, but Mary's green eyes were looking right into my own.

She whispered to Emma and her head snapped up, looking at me and I shook in Believer's arms. He wrapped his arms around me as if to comfort me from a chill, but it wasn't cold that made me tremble, it was heat.

I willed the wind to whisper in Emma's ear, the softest of voices that only she could hear, "Hello, Beautiful."

She smiled for me and so did Mary. Mary was holding Emma's hand so she heard too. I smiled back at both of them as I peeked over Believer's shoulder. Behind Emma and Mary walked David and Dana and Dr. Burgis, talking as they walked together. The doctor looked happy but David and Dana looked somber and serious. Beyond them I saw Mr. and Mrs. Miller, Jane's parents walking beside a girl with short cropped hair that I didn't recognize, but who looked strangely familiar, like I should know her.

With a thought I let my eyes see her more clearly and I saw the resemblance right away; there was some of her mother in her, but the chiseled features of her father were too strong for her to be anyone other than Lucius's child. Lucius's face was all planes and angles, like Captain America. This girl had to be one of his daughters. I wondered if she was just visiting or if she was going to stay. Either way, I was glad she was here. She kept tugging at her hair with her hand and she was frowning. I could see why. Her hair was rough. I willed it to grow back out to the middle of her back and lightened it to a dishwater blond. She changed from being so-so to stunning, just like that.

"Welcome, daughter of Lucius, you look like your father," the wind whispered to her. She spun and looked behind her searching for the source of the voice and her hair fanned out around her. I stayed low and watched with mischievous delight as she had a small cow of discovery. She started showing the Millers her new hair. The girl was smiling and not crying, which was always a good sign. She seemed happy with what I'd done.

I thought about the men in France and that I should say a quick word to them also. I willed my voice to carry to our people who were captives.

"Children of Hale. You'll be home shortly. Since you're not here to join us, I'll tell you what's happening right now. We're all walking down the new pathway toward The Hallow where Princess Bethany is about to sacrifice the man who killed me yesterday when I went to France. As you watch your French jailers, I thought you might like to know that Amen Hale is also watching the French. Keep heart and be faithful, Children of Hale."

I hoped that would be a comfort to them. The French were probably trying to sway our men with beautiful women, cash, and kindness. They were probably being treated like kings right this moment. I hoped so.

I turned back around just before we entered The Hallow and looked at what I'd built. I'd made this place with Trisha's help, picking thoughts out of her talented mind and making what she thought come to life along with my own ideas, blending the two into what now stood. The Hallow was a Greco Roman styled, half circle structure that rose as high as a three-story building out of the ground. We'd built it from gray/black granite stone with a massive portico entry complete with giant soaring pillars. The structure resembled an ancient theater on the outside, but its inside and seating were much more modern and unique to our needs.

Believer didn't set me down when we arrived as I thought he would. He held me in his arms as we passed through the entry and down a high arched hall where attendants waited to direct the citizenry to their seating. On the right and left sides, steps ascended to rows of tiered seating, but Believer followed Bethany and Sky Dragon down the main hall that ended in a permanent gateway arch that connected to the wall on the opposite side of The Hallow in a hall that ran behind the seating area for the Lords and Ladies of Amen Hale.

Believer carried me in his arms to the far side of the gallery of individual thrones, out of everyone's way. He turned and faced the wall and held me, red eyed and greedy, hiding me from view until the others passed by and took their seats on their thrones.

I felt his arms tighten around me possessively and knew that he did not want to put me down. He was hurting.

"I love you, Believer," I said, though it was poor comfort after what I'd done this morning. I leaned back and tilted my head up so I could see his face and eyes.

His face was closed to me.

"What are you thinking," I asked.

A frown finally bent his straight line of a mouth down. “I am worried for you. You are bewitched, my love. You are not in control of your feelings or your body. I think you may embarrass yourself before all Amen Hale when you touch her.”

He moved to the side so I could see out to the platform. Mary, Bethany, and Emma were on the divan I’d made at Cathryn and Cornelius’s feet. Emma seemed confused and troubled as she gazed out at the still noisy hall filled with people settling into their seats. Mary and Bethany had a tight hold on her. Beyond them Jane and Dan sat on their own thrones looking like two perfect statues. *My Wives,* I thought with a sudden chill as to what that meant. What the hell was I going to do!?

“I’m a mess, Believer.” I turned back to him. “A mess!” I yelled at him as if it were all his fault. “And you know all of it! You know that Emma’s not the only one here I want to kiss and touch. Or *feed.* I can feel how hungry they are.” I studied the ground at my feet, avoiding his eyes.

“Does it hurt you to feel their hunger?” he asked me.

“No. But it makes me so sad. They didn’t mean for this to happen. They were so happy with it just being the two of them, and now they’re tied to me and dependent on me for their whole life. Their happiness. I’m so powerful, all it took was one taste of my blood and now they’re mine. Completely and totally mine. I can *feel* it.”

I started to cry.

“Cathryn asked you many questions about Jane and Dan this morning. I understand your obligations to them,” his rumbling voice assured me.

“I’m a monster,” I said and pressed my head against his chest and closed my eyes, not wanting to look at anyone.

“Is Emma a monster?” Believer asked.

I straightened instantly. “No!” I said, almost angrily as I glared up at him.

Believer smiled, and then I did get angry! With a flash of clarity I realized he was smiling because of my instant wild reaction to him calling Emma a monster. Another burst of insight blazed through the fog inside my mind as I realized that Emma had turned me into a love sick idiot. I blushed so fully my face felt hot. Very hot. Embarrassed half to death I looked at either the wall or the ground at my feet, too freaked out to meet his eyes.

Believer was watching me the whole time, studying my every reaction.

“Emma did not mean to bind you to herself as she did.” His voice was almost comforting. I didn’t feel I deserved comfort. I was a monster.

“Cathryn told me that you and Mary and Bethany all had accidents when you first came into your power as witches. What Emma did was an accident, my love, but that will not change what has happened. She has taken you with her power. You do not hate her for it. You love her. In the same way you did not mean to bind the vampires to yourself. It was an accident that happened because of your magic. It wasn't something you did intentionally or with malice. Jane and Dan will not hate you, they will love you. You are the same as Emma, so do not hate yourself."

He stared at me, his eyes so wise and understanding, forgiving things I hadn't even done yet. He was saying and doing all the right things, but I knew he was hurting.

This morning Cathryn had used her own magic on me and forced me to answer a series of brutally intrusive and personal questions. She had started off quite innocently with questions about Emma—but it didn't end there. At the time the words had no weight. She asked and I spoke. But Cathryn's magic pushed me toward one word or very simple answers without explanations and that led to a few huge misunderstandings on everyone's part.

Misunderstandings that I hadn't corrected.

"How do you love Emma?" she'd asked.

"Wife." They weren't surprised by the answer.

"How do you love Jane?"

"Wife," I answered again. I know that she'd been expecting some reasonable, sane response. She'd meant it as a test question. Like a cop asking someone taking a polygraph if her name was Mike when it was really Alice. But instead of a normal, sane response she got blindsided with FREAK! And then Cathryn seemed to lose it herself and kept asking question after crazy question.

"How do you love Mary?"

I answered "mine" which confused them and brought the inevitable follow-up question.

"Do you intend to take Mary to your bed for sex?"

I answered "yes" which surprised the holy hell out of me, but not them for some reason, which made me wonder *why* they weren't surprised? What was up with that!?

"How do you love Dan?"

Again I said "wife" which totally confused everyone, including me. I still didn't understand it, and I'd said it!

"Have you kissed Jane?"

"Yes."

"Have you kissed Dan?"

I answered with "yes" without explaining that I'd kissed Jane's body while Dan had been in control of her body because she was too freaked out to kiss me herself at first.

They asked me what would happen to the vampires if I didn't have any further contact with them or let them drink my blood again.

"Go mad or die," I answered.

So Believer thought that I not only planned to give Jane *and* Dan my blood but my body as well. And he thought that they would die if I didn't do it. And he knew I planned to be with Mary which I didn't even know myself until I heard the words come out of my own mouth. And I can't lie so it had to be the truth—didn't it?

They gave up asking about individuals and finally went with the shotgun approach and asked if I planned on inviting other people to my bed and for some insane reason I'd answered, "Not this minute," like in the next five minutes I might add a few more people to the list.

Sky Dragon stepped up to where we were huddled against the wall discussing what a mess I was.

"Believer. My brother, it's time to get started. We need to take our seats and Rain needs to go to her place." He pointed with his head toward his and Believer's own thrones to the right of Sky and Ryan's vacant seats. "Come on," he urged, then left to take his seat.

I looked out across the open courtyard where the people of Amen Hale were now all seated. Waiting and watching.

Believer eased me to the ground and I hugged him.

"May I ask you something horrible?" I asked.

"An unusual question. Ask." Believer's rumbling laugh surprised me and I looked up at his face, wondering if a Cloud Man could go mad. He smiled at me but it seemed the kind of smile that hid something worse behind it.

I took one steadying breath and asked my horrible question, putting all the frustration and emotion I was feeling into each word as I spoke. "If I kiss someone, forgive me, if I touch them, forgive me, if they touch me, forgive me, and if I let them bite all over me and enjoy it while they do, *please, please!* my love, forgive me! Forgive me for all of it right now," I begged. "But if I start to take off my clothes in front of all these people, please pick me up and whoever I'm getting naked with and take us some place private. You're right, I'm not in control of myself."

I closed my eyes and waited for him to yell at me. His cloudy hand reached under my chin, his thumb and fingers cupping my head and forcing me to stare up into his eyes while his other arm tightened around me painfully, pulling me up and holding me closer to his face where I couldn't look away. Believer's eyes became blazing red spheres and his voice, though still quiet, rumbled so deeply that it vibrated my bones as he spoke.

"Yes, my love! TO ALL OF IT!" he rumbled.

"Do what you must do. Do all during the day that pleases you. But you will come to me each night! And all their lips and touches and bites will not matter once I hold you. It will be my voice that makes you tremble, and my embrace that gives you pleasure, my air that fills your lungs, and my eyes that make you smile!"

His huge hand held me still as he stared down into my face and I trembled as I stared back, amazed and frightened half out of my mind.

Angry clouds boiled and crashed inside while human emotions raged wildly in his eyes. Passion! Anger! Pain! I saw the pain in his eyes. It was there in the way the clouds gathered around his face and in my own body because he held me so tight.

"Yes, my love!" I whimpered with pain, with desire, and with all my heart. "Yes to all of it!"

Cathryn

The Bloody Queen of Amen Hale

CATHRYN SAT IN her beautiful black throne beside Cornelius, hating herself and feeling miserable. She noticed that a number of those who entered were carrying suitcases. She didn't think it would be so many, but it couldn't be changed now. The bomb had already gone off. Every problem she tried to fix since rising from bed had exploded in her face. One by one, she'd transformed the difficulties of the day into disasters and coaxed disasters into becoming nightmares.

After watching the sun rise this morning with Jane and Dan, Cathryn had returned to her bed for a final hour of sleep only to have Jane knock on her door shortly after her head hit the pillow. The vampires had been walking the grounds and had discovered a group of disgruntled citizens meeting in secret. Curious, they stayed hidden and listened in.

Recent events, it seemed, had pushed a number of people beyond the breaking point. Jane told Cathryn what was said with perfect recall. The worst of their venom was directed at Bethany. Some people openly called her a "twisted little monster," saying that Amen Hale would be a far better place with her gone.

"Go back to each of them," Cathryn had ordered coldly. "If they work, find them where they are and tell them. If they sleep, rouse them from their bed and tell them. If they bathe, go to them there. Tell them to come to The Hallow this afternoon with their bags packed and formally make their request to leave Amen Hale. Cornelius and I will hear them in front of everyone, not in secret."

Jane and Dan had vanished, going to deliver her words.

Only an hour later, when faced with the crisis of Emma starving to death and dying at her feet, Cathryn had asked Jane to sacrifice her own body to save Emma's life. It was a horrible thing to ask but she simply couldn't think of what else to do.

She had followed that horrible experience with her disastrous attempt to help Rain, after which she went and vomited for thirty minutes straight and cried herself dry while two of her maids held her hair and then labored valiantly to put her back together again before she came to The Hallow.

When Jane and Dan had arrived to take their seats, Cathryn had asked Jane if she was all right. Jane's beautiful face regarded her for a moment in an oddly detached way, as if she were trying to decide whether to kill her then and there or answer her question. She appeared stable, but the stiffness of her body and the red glow in her eyes betrayed her damaged and dangerous condition.

"She's taken both of us, Mother," Jane answered calmly and politely with her beautiful voice. "We thought Dan would be safe if he hid down inside me, buried in my memories, but he wasn't. He fell in love with her in the past while I fell in love with her in the present. We both love her now. And we both love Rain, thanks to her blood. If there is anyone else you'd like Dan and me to sleep with, just point them out. I'm sure we'll love them too." She and Dan turned to go to their seats.

Cathryn was so shocked she almost fainted, but Dan appeared beside her, holding her arm and keeping her on her feet. Without making a scene, he guided her to her throne and seated her—then vanished again, appearing in his own seat beside his murderously enraged wife.

Cathryn sat in her throne thinking herself a total disaster as a mother and miserable failure as a Queen when she felt rumbling vibrations in the air and looked toward the far side of the royal seating gallery where Believer had Rain pushed tight against the wall. One enormous hand gripped her head roughly, forcing her to look up into his frightening, baleful glare. Cathryn couldn't make out the deep rumbling words but he was angry, angry at Rain, and it was all her fault.

Just thinking about what she'd done made her stomach roil again. She managed to fight off the nausea without embarrassing herself in front of all Amen Hale. Cathryn stayed seated, her heart in her throat as she listened to the angry rumble. She forced herself to face forward and watched them from the corner of her eye. She saw Cornelius doing the same. He sat stiffly in his seat, looking only forward.

The first questions she'd asked Rain this morning had been about Emma, to find out if she'd been bewitched, but when she'd asked about Jane (expecting a very different answer from the one she had received) things got out of hand. She wished she had some excuse or reason for what happened next, but she didn't. It was like eating potato chips; she couldn't seem to stop herself. She just kept asking questions because each answer seemed more unbelievable than the last, its discovery creating more questions. If she'd had any idea as to where things were going before she began she wouldn't have gone there.

But done was done. The bomb had exploded. It was all out there now, even the stuff Rain would *never* have admitted even to herself. All the deeply hidden and repressed sexual secrets in her heart, paraded out in front of her husband's red burning eyes as she knelt there, utterly helpless to resist.

Cathryn watched as Believer stepped away and set Rain on her feet but she was too shaken up to stand on her own. He picked her up and carried her to the platform. She was pale, wide eyed, and shaking. Tears streaked her face. Believer's red eyes blazed as his powerful arms extended, delivering Rain to her sisters. Rain's body was obviously a loan he meant to collect on shortly.

The three girls rushed forward to claim her, but as soon as Mary touched Rain she let out a yelp and jumped like she'd been shocked. Mary spun about and faced the two high thrones, her eyes two green daggers thrust right at Cathryn's heart, giving her a knowing look that mirrored Rain's own hurt anger from this morning, along with an odd mixture of shocked surprise.

"Goddess, not her as well," Cathryn whispered to herself.

Cornelius rose from his throne and stepped forward on the padded platform, and the girls crawled to him and curled around his legs and each other like human snakes. Rain, Bethany, and Emma held onto Cornelius, but Cathryn was surprised to find that Mary had crawled to her and snuggled between her legs with her back pressed up against Cathryn's throne. Cathryn cried soundlessly at the kindness and stroked Mary's snow white hair affectionately as Cornelius began to speak.

"Children of Amen Hale." His words were carried powerfully through all parts of The Hallow. Rain had set magic on the platform, wiring it and the words spoken from that spot with a magical sound system.

"We call you Children of Hale, and the Queen and I think of you as our children as well. But simply put, some of you do not see us in kind. You do not see us as a mother and a father and not as a King and Queen. Some of you see us as *strange* and *strangers*. This morning a group of you gathered in secret and called the Queen and me *murderers* and our children *monsters*."

Shocked gasps filled the hall followed quickly by angry voices. Cornelius raised his hand and soon the hall quieted, but a humming tension hung in the air, and everyone saw the reactions of the witches; they all looked dangerously alert. Rain's skin had taken on a faint white glow and her hair had begun to move about as if alive. Those in The Hallow watched as Emma and Bethany labored to keep her calm while Cornelius continued speaking.

"Three days ago, Kendal Flame was on her way home from Amen Hale. Evil men followed her when she left our home. They caught her at a gas station about four miles from here. They abducted her, carried her to a secluded wood where they brutalized her in unspeakable ways before they crucified her, upside down, and then burned her alive. *They* are murderers.

"Two days ago I stood in the path of an evil man to protect an innocent thirteen-year-old girl. My Bethany. A man named Yanosh and his mother stood before Cathryn and me and told us to our faces that he planned to rape Bethany and then sell her into slavery in Russia to be used as a whore. After he shared those vile words with us, he killed me when I tried to stop him. *Yanosh and his mother* were murderers.

"Two days ago, Black Rain hid her friends and family while she herself stepped into a black limo, knowing that it was a trap. She gave up her own life to keep her family safe. Soldiers from other countries destroyed that limo and killed her. *Those evil men* were murderers.

"Yesterday afternoon when Rain and Byron were out providing for Amen Hale, evil men attacked and almost killed Byron, and they did kill Rain. You saw her. After he punched her and knocked her down the stairs they shot her in the head. They shot her while she lay on the ground, not even trying to defend herself in any way. *They* are murderers.

"Yesterday evening U.S. soldiers attacked Amen Hale. They were following false orders at the time, given to them by a secret organization called The Order, but it was still the United States who attacked us and broke into the vampires' crypt where Jane and Dan slept. They stole Jane away, but most of you don't know what they did to Dan." Cornelius paused and looked over to where Dan sat in his throne, unmoving and beautiful. A perfect statue.

When Cornelius spoke again his voice was angrier, filled with outrage. "They took an axe to him and cut him into pieces! *Tiny! Little! Pieces!* And then they gathered those pieces and bits of flesh and dropped them into a vat of acid to melt him away! *They* were murders!

When Rain went to save Jane from the soldiers who'd stolen her away from us, she found that the American soldiers who'd been duped into stealing her were already dead, killed by The Order. The same group responsible for the rocket attack on the limo the day before which killed almost two hundred people, and now we find them trying to kill Jane and Dan. Do not be simple minded, thinking that The Order was a group of misguided religious zealots motivated by some noble 'godly' purpose. We know that this is not the case. The Order did not move against the vampires because of religious convictions! NO!" Cornelius shouted. "They were willing to kill and murder and destroy because *they themselves* wanted to be *immortal!* These men and women we have captured are butchers. Terrorists. Traitors. Bloody men, who are willing to do anything to have what they want." He paused for a moment and added the words, "*Murderers. And monsters.*"

The Hallow was silent. Cornelius's oration and the dire subject matter merged with the skin prickling feel of power that came whenever Rain entered a room. Having the vampires and the other witches added to the strangeness so that the atmosphere within the open space seemed alive with brooding power and menace.

"This is Amen Hale. I am Cornelius Amen Hale, and I am King here." He made it a statement of fact, not shouting. He spread his arms. "All of you chose to be here. Many of you begged to be here, and you agreed to submit yourselves to our rule. You have given me your vow of service, your solemn oaths, which I accepted in good faith. But there are those among us who feel that they can no longer stay in Amen Hale. Some say that our kingdom has become too bloody and that Cathryn and I have gone mad—and perhaps they're right." Cornelius didn't say it in a discounting way, but nodded, as if it were a valid argument.

"Others have other reasons, but all reasons, whatever they may be, lead out of Amen Hale. If you desire to leave us *now is the time.* I will release you from your vows. Choose now, choose well, and live with that choice. Those who wish to leave Amen Hale, come down to the courtyard without fear; you will not be harmed, insulted, or belittled for your choice, but you will be cast out forever. Your name will be removed from the Book of Shadows as if it had never been written within its pages."

Cornelius went back and sat down in his chair as people stood and moved, working their way down the rows of chairs, past others still seated and down to the gleaming white circular court in the middle of The Hallow. There was movement all over, and Cathryn watched as almost thirty men, women, and children assembled in the center of the room and stood before them.

Mary stood up and took Cathryn's hand to help her rise from her throne. Cathryn was about to try to stand, and she'd been worried that she wouldn't have the strength to leave her chair, and Mary knew, so she'd helped her. As Mary held her hand, Cathryn felt magic, power, and life flowing into her and she felt stronger, no longer weak or about to fall over and faint. Mary walked her to the same spot where Cornelius had stood and given his oration and then slid down her body to sit at her feet.

Bethany had stayed with Cornelius and sat with him in his throne, but Rain and Emma sat on the platform a few feet away, holding onto each other as they watched people gather in the courtyard. Cathryn looked up into the seats at those who would remain and not at those who stood in the courtyard directly in front of her, though many of them tried to catch her eye. All her attention was focused on those faces staring at her. The ones who still mattered. Mary's magic strengthened her body and The Hallow's magic carried her voice as she addressed the hall.

"I would like to talk to you about the wonderful plans and amazing dreams that I have for Amen Hale, but before we can dream about the beauty, we must have a reckoning *here and now*," she began ominously. "Three days ago I knelt in a pool of my husband's blood and held his dead, lifeless head in my lap. Bethany knelt beside me and told me that she *might—might,"* Cathryn whispered the words, "be able to bring him back—*if* she had enough blood. I offered her my own wrist instantly but she was worried that it would take more than I could give. *I*," Cathryn jabbed an angry finger at herself, "suggested we use Yanosh's horrid mother as a human sacrifice, and that was what we did. *I* pressed the sacrificial blade into a thirteen-year-old girl's tiny innocent hands. *I* held that horrid, old, murdering bitch as Bethany bled her and danced in her blood, and then *I* gave her my own wrist and let my own blood fall upon Cornelius's lifeless body to help bring him back. *I* started this, even though Bethany's magic brought it to life. If you must think of someone as a bloody, murdering monster, then let it be me. I name myself so! The Bloody Queen of Amen Hale!"

Her voice broke on the word "Hale" and she coughed and wiped at her eyes for a moment. The hall was absolutely silent while she gathered herself. As she looked down, Cathryn found that she'd grown two new witches around her legs some time while she spoke. Rain and Emma had joined Mary. Cathryn raised her head back to the crowd before her and finished what she wanted to say.

"In just a few moments we will have a human sacrifice, right here in The Hallow. Bethany will sacrifice the man who murdered her sister, and then we will send his body to the kitchens to be prepared for this evening's feast. I'm sure that some of you are telling yourselves that this is a one time horror, a spectacle that won't be repeated." Cathryn paused, and in one of those horror movie moments she said, "You're wrong."

She let the words echo around the hall before she spoke again. "This Kingdom was born in blood and by a blade thrust through a beating human heart. As within, so without. I know that this is not the Wiccan way, but it is the way in which we will live. It does no good to deny what we are or what we have become. You know that Cornelius and I are good people, and you have seen our children. They are loving and kind and of a sweet spirit. There will never be a day when we purposefully take an innocent human life, but those who attack us will feed us."

Cathryn sighed. "I have made my choice and I am happy in it. Now it is time for you to make your choice. Do what will make you happy, whatever that may be. So mote it be."

After a bit of effort she managed to free herself of Rain and Emma, but Mary walked her back to her seat and sat at her feet again. Cathryn watched as people talked, argued, and begged one another this way or that. Parents, husbands, friends, making choices for themselves as individuals that the group or their partner did not want and did not like. Desperate voices and outright arguing grew as minutes wore on and decisions were made.

In the end Cathryn was actually relieved to see that only fifty-three people chose to leave Amen Hale. It seemed a clear division, those standing in the central courtyard frowning and uncomfortable while those in their seats seemed at ease, if saddened, but content with their lot. With a few final words of discharge the milling mass of disaffected people were escorted from The Hallow.

Cathryn listened as her King spoke to those who choose to remain with them in Amen Hale and plant their hopes and dreams alongside her own. She stroked Mary's white hair and listened to Cornelius's strong, confident voice as he reassured, encouraged, and finally concluded.

"Everything has a beginning. And beginnings are usually difficult things. Messy. Changeable. Confusing. Look around us." Cornelius pointed to the empty seats. The three hundred and sixty people remaining looked a sparse crowd in a structure built to hold over two thousand. "As we add new people and fill this hall, you who sit here this day will be different from all those who come after you. Five or ten or fifty years from now you'll be able to tell a wide-eyed newcomer, '*I was there at the beginning!*' Wonderful and magical things are in our future, but so are challenges as we face the lust of greedy and envious men. We have magic and power," Cornelius eyed those who remained to drive home his next words, "and know this, the world wants what we have. But tomorrow's troubles we will deal with tomorrow. And tonight we will have a joyous wedding for two of our children, and then we will have a wonderful feast to celebrate Bethany's birthday. Everything has a proper time and a season. We have endured our time of decision and sorrow and sending away. Tonight is a time to wed and love and to celebrate life. But here and now the time has come for blood and death and sacrifice. So mote it be."

Jane

The Sleeping Lamb

TO EVERYONE ELSE it had been ten minutes, to Dan and me it felt like forever. We watched Bethany as she paced around the guy for the thirteenth time, stalling. She'd already dropped the knife twice, its metallic clang echoing loudly on the white glass floor of the circular courtyard. Bethany was so innocent and open, even the humans could see what she was thinking. She was blaming herself for the people who had just left Amen Hale and hating herself and her own little inner demon that liked blood and death and nasty things.

"*Like I said, she's not gonna do it,*" Dan said in my head.

When he had told me earlier that she wasn't going to kill the guy they'd hauled in for the human sacrifice, I'd broken my "silent treatment" just long enough to think, "*He's toast,*" as I watched Bethany's eyes glaze over when her little maid put the knife into her hand. Now I was pissed on top of everything else. How the hell did Dan know!? What could he have possibly seen that I missed? He was such a smart ass.

"*Harsh*," Dan's thought to me. I saw him raise one eyebrow. I ignored him, silent treatment in place.

"Please, have mercy! I've got a family for Christ's sake! Please! Don't do this! MERCY! PLEASE!" The man's pathetic begging had gone on nonstop since he was drug out to the courtyard and handed over to Sky Dragon who now held him in his iron grip, his arms wrapped around the man's shoulders and his hands clasped behind his head and neck, patiently waiting for Bethany to do her thing.

They'd cleaned the guy up and put a green pair of baggie pants on him that looked like hospital scrubs. I could see the outline of the adult-sized diaper they'd put on him so he wouldn't soil the blood when he died. He had no shirt and no shoes and he was sweating profusely. I could smell him.

"*Maybe all French guys smell that way? Or maybe he just needs a new diaper?*"

I fought off the smile that almost came to my face. "*Stop it, Dan. I don't want to smile right now.*"

I'd been giving him the cold shoulder, the silent treatment, and the evil eye since we had talked about what had happened in the room with Emma and Mary and what had happened in the past while I was here in the present. I didn't understand how that simple, stupid memory could have affected him the way it did. I stopped thinking about Emma and what she'd done to us and focused on Rain and what she was about to do for us. She sat on the platform right in front of us wrapped in Mary's and Emma's arms. I watched as she turned to face Emma and leaned in toward her.

"I have to go help Bethany. Stay here, beautiful girl," she whispered and Mary's arms released her and tightened around Emma.

Rain vanished from the platform and appeared in the courtyard standing beside Bethany, without walking, just there. To everyone else I knew it looked like what Dan and I did. But it wasn't. Not even close. Rain turned her angry black eyes on the screaming Frenchman and shouted, "Shut up!" His mouth clamped shut instantly, but he continued to struggle in Sky Dragon's grip.

"What is it, Bethany? What's wrong?" Rain asked her.

I could see muscles tighten in Bethany's neck as she tried to keep herself from shaking, and I heard the effort she put into keeping her voice from sounding like a child's. She'd made up her mind and she wanted to sound firm about it.

"I just want to kill animals from now on, Rain. I don't want to do people anymore." She watched as Rain's head tilted to the side. "You're not mad at me, are you? You can still kill him if you want, but—" Bethany shot a furtive glance at the crowd of staring and listening people and then to the struggling man and swallowed. She wanted to do it but didn't want to be a monster in everyone's eyes. She didn't want to rock the apple cart and ruin our little Kingdom for everyone else. I could see her fighting the *need* in her tiny body that cried out for *food!*

My own eyes focused in on Rain as my own hunger surged and my whole mouth went dry. It wasn't just a burning in my throat like before, when I'd been thirsty for human blood; this was more, just like Rain's blood was more. I wanted to coat the inside of my mouth with her blood and hold that glorious golden power in my mouth without swallowing and letting it go away. I wanted to hold it so long it would just become a part of me so I would *taste it* forever. What I burned for was right there, in her body, and I was dying to drink from her. But I couldn't.

"*She promised it would be soon.*"

I ignored Dan's soothing, comforting words and kept my own futile version of the silent treatment in place. In the human stream of time, flowing so much slower than Dan and me, Bethany was finally ready to speak again.

"Here." She held out the knife to Rain. I could see that she wanted to get the blade out of her hands. She thought if it wasn't in her hands she could think straight, she hoped anyway. I doubted it. The little monster was hungry.

Rain didn't say a word; she just reached out and took the blade from Bethany. There was silence in the hall; even the struggling man ceased his thrashing.

"Sorry, Rain. Let's just throw him out." Bethany pressed a hand to her stomach and closed her eyes. "Can I please have a goat instead? Just a goat." Her hands twitched at her sides as she fought the monster inside her that wanted to snatch the knife back out of Rain's hand and plunge it into the man's heart.

Sure enough, her eyes glazed over and she reached out and took the blade out of Rain's hand. Bethany's hand tightened on the blade and she blinked and looked down at her hand, her face showing how shocked she was to find the blade back in her hand.

"Ahh!" she cried and dropped it as if it were a snake. She skittered away a few steps, staring at it angrily as it lay on the floor. She cast a suspicious eye at Rain.

"Stop playing around!" she shouted at her.

"I didn't do anything," Rain said.

"Bethame, I can get you a goat," Sky Dragon said. "I'll be glad to get you a goat!"

He sent an imploring look to Rain. "Do you want to kill this man, my sister, or should I just put him back with the others?" His long, serpent-like neck was extended, allowing him to stare at them from over the top of his captive's head.

"Just hold him for me a little longer please," Rain said.

She and Bethany and Sky Dragon kept arguing. I watched the scene, but I also noticed the crowd of staring eyes around The Hallow. Sky Dragon sticking his neck out was convenient, and it let him see who he was talking to over the top of the man he was holding, but it also made him look very inhuman and monstrous. I saw the faces, the concern and fear growing on many that they'd made the wrong choice and that they should have left with the others while they had the chance.

I nodded grimly as I watched. It made sense. Two terrifying witches bickering over a sacrificial knife while a dragon monster held a begging thrashing man and waited for the blood to fly was a tough pill to swallow, even after being warned repeatedly that the nasty medicine was coming.

"I said I don't want to do people anymore!" Bethany said angrily. She stood a good ten steps away from the blade on the floor, but she kept her eyes on it. The knife was shining brightly in the sunlight as it lay on the too white floor. Bethany closed her eyes, fighting herself and her hunger. Sure enough, she walked back over and picked it up with her eyes closed tight. She opened her eyes to find herself kneeling with the blade in her hand again.

"What the!" She hurled it away from her and it clattered and slid across the floor, then she turned on Rain. "I said NO MORE!" she shouted. "Why do you keep putting that *thing* in my hand!"

"I didn't," Rain answered, surprised. "Honest, Beth, you just went all witchy and walked over there and picked it up again. I didn't do a thing. You know I can't lie!"

"You did too!" Bethany insisted; she was on that fine edge before tears began. I left my seat and "appeared" beside Rain down in the courtyard.

"Bethany, Rain didn't do it. You did it, honey." I tried to help.

The rows of seats around The Hallow and the Royal seating gallery had an overhanging lip of stone that shaded the seating areas from direct sunlight, but the center of the circular courtyard was bare and naked to the sky. I stood in sunlight, its brightness magnified by the white glass floor at my feet. My white skin sparkled and shimmered more brilliantly than I'd ever seen before. I looked like an angel or some kind of Fairy Queen stepped from the pages of a book, which was frighteningly close to the truth.

I heard the "ooohs" and "ahhs" from the watching humans around us, and Rain and Bethany looked utterly spellbound as they stared at me. Rain's lips parted and her breathing sped up as she gazed at all I was in the bright light of day. My own heart sped up as I thought about where her attentions might lead, my body tingling with anticipation of golden blood.

I realized that I really wanted her attention, I wanted her to notice me, to look at me, to want me, and the thought sickened me. Not that she wanted me or that I wanted her to want me but at how much my world had changed. Even sickened, I struck a pose and looked at her over my shoulder. I could see that she was smitten, but right then Bethany bent double in hunger, making Rain and me both look her way.

Apparently Bethany's monster within was not impressed that I looked pretty. It wanted what it wanted and I wasn't *it*. Thank God! Or Rain! Or the Muffin Man! Thank who the hell ever, but she didn't want *me*. She didn't want to eat *me* or love me in a way that would screw me over any more than I already was. I was just sweet Aunty Jane to Bethany. I watched as her angry words finally hit her mouth.

"You're both lying!" she shouted. I let my head turn and look at her so I would match the others who only now saw and heard what she said, then I looked over to Rain.

Rain lifted one eyebrow as if to say "got any ideas here?"

I shrugged. I had lots of ideas, but they were all fantasies about her blood. Or Emma's body. Or Dan. Or various X-rated and bloody combinations of the three.

"I'm putting this guy away; Bethany doesn't want him!" Sky Dragon said and started to haul the guy off.

"No! He dies now," Rain said. "Jane can kill him. She and Dan need to eat anyway."

"My whole body went rigid with shock, hurt, rage and fear! Mostly *fear*. Sickening, crushing *fear*."

"She promised us HER blood, Dan! Not some disgusting, stinking, Frenchman!" I screamed to him in my head.

Dan appeared beside me and wrapped his arms around me, holding me tight and pinning my arms against my sides to keep me from doing anything rash. He crushed me against his chest as I shook and started to cry.

"*It's all right, my love! Rain will do the right thing,*" his voice promised.

"I don't want to drink human blood EVER again!" I shouted back inside my panic stricken mind. "I won't do it, Dan! I'd rather starve! I'd rather die than have that human filth inside me again! She promised us, SHE PROMISED! She said—"

Dan's eyes went white, his gaze and magic making my own voice inside my head become quiet so I could hear his thoughts again as he shouted to me in my head.

"JANE! *She just doesn't know how bad it is. Rain thinks we still like human blood or that we can tolerate it. It's all right. Just wait. I promise with all my heart that it will be all right. There! There! It's happening right now. See, just turn you head, my love, and see for yourself. Look at her face. It's coming.*"

I did as Dan asked. I watched in slow motion as Rain took in my reaction. Her eyes widened. Her hands slowly flew to her mouth as she realized how I'd reacted to her suggestion and what it must mean. And what I must think. I kept the hurt and frightened look on my face, not wiping it away but letting her see what I truly felt and watched her face crumble completely into distressed horror. And then she was running to me. To both of us.

I was so happy! The tears I was crying kept coming, but now I was crying because I was happy.

"Oh Jane! Dan! I'm so sorry!" Rain threw her arms around Dan and me and started to cry herself.

I didn't think about anything for a second. I just soaked in the feel of her arms around us. She really did love us both, not just me, but both of us. And not for sex, she loved us just because she did. I saw it in her face as plain as day. She was going to take care of us and be good to us and give us her blood. I saw it all in her face just as if she'd told me herself. I looked up to see that Dan was crying too, bloody tears running from his eyes. We were going to be all right.

"Guys? Y'all okay?" Bethany asked uncertainly, her irrational anger forgotten. "What's up?" her sweet little voice asked.

Cathryn had descended the platform and arrived beside us.

"Jane. What's happened?" she asked me.

"We can't drink human blood anymore, Mother. We tried again before we came to The Hallow. We didn't want to be hungry with a human sacrifice going on. Dan and I couldn't force it down. We both tried."

Bethany was clueless, but Cathryn looked from us and then to Rain. She nodded grimly.

"I'm putting this guy back with the others," Sky Dragon said firmly.

"No!" Rain shouted.

"Why not?" Sky Dragon whined, perplexed. "Bethany doesn't want to kill humans anymore, Rain, and the vampires don't eat human blood anymore either." He leaned hard on the word "human" as he looked at Rain.

"He dies here," Rain insisted.

"No more people dying, Rain," Bethany said firmly, her eyes on Cathryn and then flicking toward the people seated around us. "Just throw him out of Amen Hale along with the others or give them to the government and let them lock them up somewhere. I can live with goats and bulls and bunnies if I have to. I don't have to eat people."

Sky Dragon started to walk off with the man again.

"No!" Rain shouted at him again.

"Rain!" Sky Dragon growled back. "I'm sick of holding this foul smelling bastard! His stinking sweat is absorbing into my body. It's more than disgusting. I know you're angry with him, Sis, but just let it go already! This is important to Bethany."

Rain sat up from holding Dan and me, wiping tears from her eyes.

"I finished Bethany's breakfast." She made it a statement. Like it should mean something.

Confused looks passed all around. I added my own confused face into the mix and so did Dan, shoulders shrugging as we took our proper place and carried our share of the non-verbal communication in our little group.

"What's the deal with Bethany's breakfast?" Sky Dragon asked, putting everyone's thoughts into words.

"Her *special* breakfast," Rain added with a frown.

"You really finished my breakfast?" Bethany asked, her eyes widening. "The peoplie parts?"

"You did, didn't you?" Cathryn mused, looking thoughtful herself.

"Did you like it?" Bethany asked, making a face somewhere between grossed out and hopeful. Hopeful that she wasn't the only one that big of a monster. Hoping that someone else shared her particular strain of ugliness.

"I loved it," Rain told her. While not proud of it, she wasn't hiding from it either. The tightness at the corner of her eyes told me she was still grossed out, though she didn't want to show it to Bethany.

"I don't think I have to eat human flesh to live, but it tasted wonderful. From now on, Chef Andre will be cooking for two. For me and for you." Rain gave her a smile.

Bethany smiled for just a second, then frowned and shook her head as she looked out at the people in The Hallow. Rain followed her gaze and looked with her as Bethany spoke. Her voice was hushed.

"I liked it too, Rain, but come on, we can't keep eating people. It's *bad.* And anyway, it's gonna freak everyone out and make them all want to leave us." They both looked out at the three hundred fifty-two faces staring down at them, every last one tuned in, trying to hear the conversation and follow along with whatever was happening here in the courtyard.

"Eating people is bad, Rain," Bethany said quietly, almost a whisper. A whisper that carried.

Rain looked back at her and stroked a hand down Bethany's head then placed a gentle kiss on her forehead.

"Is it?" she asked her. Rain's hair and her black dress began to wave gently and her skin began to glow. The air in The Hallow, which had been a little hot and stuffy for the humans, became cool, and the soured, potent stench of the Frenchman held in Sky Dragon's arms vanished and was replaced with a crisp almost wintery smell. At the same time the room began to darken and heads lifted to see the open ceiling high above us closing, the stone moving in from all sides, creating a shrinking circle of sunlight pouring in from above until the last laser like ray of golden light was cut, leaving the hall in shadowed darkness except for Rain's glowing body and the crowns of fire on David's and Dana's heads until those too winked out, leaving only Rain's glow.

The quiet rustle of whispers from the frightened people seated all around us quickly went silent as Rain began to speak. Her voice sounded almost happy as her magic carried it to every corner of the hall as she looked out at the shadowed forms sitting in the seats surrounding us.

"I have a story I'd like to tell you," she said. "It's just a made up story, and it probably won't be wonderful, but I hope you'll listen and maybe even like it. I like to listen to stories in the dark, so I made it dark. Sometimes a made up story is the best way to tell a thing that's hard to tell. Or hard to hear. Give me just a minute and then I'll start."

She gave Bethany another quick kiss on the forehead and then was kissed on her forehead by Cathryn. Cathryn pulled Bethany down to the floor and they sat on the ground together, holding each other, and Dan and I did the same, sitting on the white floor that was still warm from the sun. This felt strangely familiar, it reminded me of telling scary stories around a bonfire with Stacy and Emma during summer camp. This was like that, but our bonfire was Rain's glowing body and the story was probably going to be scary as hell. I nodded to myself.

"*Should you kiss her forehead too or let her kiss yours?*" Dan suggested, snapping me out of my musings.

"*I don't know? Do you really think I should?*"

I looked at Rain and growled to Dan, "*Dammit, she's about to start any minute. I missed it!*"

"*Damn, sorry, I should have said something before we sat down.*" For some reason my Dan being angry at himself for not helping me grovel better broke my heart.

"*Dan, I'm so—*"

"*I know, Jane. I know and I love you. And this may sound weird, but I'm not sad this has happened. I'm glad I won't be drinking human blood ever again. I'd rather spend the rest of my eternity with you, feeding off of someone we both know and love, who even loves us back, than feeding off strangers we don't know or like and who fear us and hate us.*"

Dan slipped behind me and wrapped his arms around me, holding me as we both looked up at Rain's glowing face. We looked at the black eyes and blue lips of our master's face and waited for our story like two happy children. Content and waiting.

"Once upon a time," she began innocently, "a Black Lion and her cub went on a journey. As they traveled, they came upon a beautiful valley that was filled with little white lambs, all grazing happily in the sun. But the valley belonged to the magnificent White Lion, the greatest and wisest and most wonderful of all Lions. The Black Lion hoped that if she was respectful and very, very careful, the White Lion would let them stay and live in the valley too. But make no mistake," Rain paused and looked around, her voice serious and darkly warning, "the White

Lion owns the valley, the hills, the streams, the air, and the rocks, but his most dear and precious possessions were the little white lambs that grazed on the hills. The Black Lion and her cub picked an out-of-the-way spot down by the river where they could lie in the sun and rest and be at peace. And that was what they did. But something strange happened.

A dozen white lambs came to the Black Lion and her cub.

"May we stay with you?' they asked.

"Why?' asked the Black Lion. "You have the White Lion, and he is better than me in every way."

But they stayed. The lambs lay down with the lion and played with her cub and loved her. And soon the Black Lion loved them too. And soon the little white lambs became little black lambs because the Black Lion loved them and wanted them and claimed them as her own. But then the other lambs in the valley came to see this strange sight because word had spread far and wide of the Black Lion and her strange flock of black lambs. Some of the white lambs were frightened. And some were angry. And some were jealous.

"And there came a day that one of the little black lambs fell into a deep sleep and a group of white lambs came at night and stole her away and were set to kill her, but the Black Lion ROARED!" Rain's voice filled the hall sounding like a lion's roar. "And she chased them down, and she saved her little sleeping lamb! Because she loved her, she loves her *so much*!" Her voice broke and she stopped to fight back tears.

Dan tightened his grip around me. I knew that I was the sleeping lamb, and I remembered when she came for me and her face when she found me. I felt tears on my own face. Bloody tears.

"The Black Lion captured the evil white lambs who tried to kill her precious black lamb, and she brought them back to her place by the river."

Rain changed her voice with the introduction of a new character, an arrogant haughty voice.

'*What are you doing with those white lambs?*' asked one of the black lambs who lived with her.

"'I'm going to kill them and eat them,' she answered, 'and I am going to feed them to my cub.'

"'*But why?*' asked the little black lamb.

"'Because. I'm a lion,' answered the Black Lion.

"'*But it's wrong to eat lambs!*' insisted her one angry black lamb. '*It's not right! I can't stay here if you do this!*'

"He found another that felt the same and together the two black lambs turned and marched away from the Black Lion and her eight remaining black lambs and her little black lion cub. And as the two marched away, they changed color and became white lambs again, because the Black Lion no longer loved them, and they did not love her."

Rain added a new voice, sounding younger and sweeter, more like Bethany.

"'*But will the White Lion be angry if we eat his little white lambs?*' asked the cub of her mother.

"Her mother answered, 'Remember that these evil lambs tried to kill our precious little lamb while she slept. Should they not reap what they have sown?'

"'*But the lambs that are left will see us eating the flesh of lamb and see our teeth bite and our claws tear and they will all run away and hate us!*' cried the little lion to her mother.

"'If they run away and hate us because we are lions, then they never truly loved us, my little one. We are lions. We have teeth and claws and a hunger for meat. We are what we are. Rise my beautiful child. Rise, slay, and eat.'"

The ceiling opened just enough to illuminate Rain, standing in a brilliant white shaft of light. In her hand was Bethany's sacrificial blade, somehow just suddenly there. Sunlight reflected off the polished metal of the blade in a fantastic way that made me wonder if it was done with magic or just a freak happening of light and angles and shining metal.

Amazed. Dreamlike. Surreal. I had no word for what I felt. Rain's story seemed to start so simply but it became so much more in the telling. I'd never experienced a moment quite like it and I was still aglow with wonder.

Dan and I watched as Bethany rose to her feet, walked to Rain, and wrapped her hands around the handle of the blade that Rain held out to her. Once Bethany's hands were firm on the handle, Rain drew her hands up, drawing both palms up each side of the blade slicing them open. Golden blood flowed down the blade and onto Bethany's hands.

"Slay. And be satisfied, my Little One," Rain told her.

Bethany was there but gone, moving in a glassy-eyed trance as she walked toward Sky Dragon and the man he held. Rain closed her eyes and held her hands out at waist level to each side of her body, and Dan and I appeared at her sides, on our knees. We each took one of her cupped, upturned hands in ours and watched as she called her power into the blood already pooled there in her palm. The color brightened until she held two pools of shining molten gold.

"I love you both," she said to us. "Drink me. Kiss me. Bite me. I want to feel your teeth in my neck."

We drank golden blood and she never ran dry no matter how much we took. We drank and drank and drank. Then Dan bit her neck while I kissed her and she reacted as she had yesterday in the field, screaming her pleasure into my mouth while Dan's venom filled her. Then I bit the other side of her neck and gave her my venom and all that I was while Dan kissed her and she screamed again, her body, still clothed in her black dress, shaking with pleasure and not pain.

And then Dan and I both lay down on the white stone floor, so full, sated, satisfied, and happy that we just couldn't stand or move. We lay down and pulled her down with us and laid her between us. Dan and I slept. What happened next I do not know, for I was at peace, asleep, and dreaming that I was a little black lamb, asleep by a river, while a sleeping Black Lion who loved me *so much* purred at my back and made me smile.

Hillary

Things That Make Me Crazy

"THANK YOU MR. and Mrs. Dae. If you'll go with Agent Vasches, please." Hillary watched the bedraggled couple gather their sparse collection of belongings and follow the female agent through the door. Together, Hillary and Governor Daniels had been interviewing the cast outs who'd just exited the gateway and walked right into their arms.

The expatriated citizens of Amen Hale certainly had some disturbing things to say. They told them about Emma Tate and her *new* sex-toy body and her morning exploits under the Queen's dress before being handed off to the vampires, already unconscious. They told her about the Queen's plan to "cut" the suicidal girl Lizzy herself. The men and women they interviewed told them about the human sacrifice that was about to take place (or had already taken place). And that all those who'd chosen to stay in Amen Hale were being forced to watch it happen.

The public sentiments over the human sacrifice of the terrorists responsible for the rocket attack was (somewhat understandably) a sadistic gung ho thumbs up, but Hillary knew that the American public wouldn't stand for the sexual abuse and child abductions. Those were the things that would make people crazy. It made Hillary want to do something crazy herself when she thought about Lizzy being in there with Cathryn cutting on her with a knife.

When she'd met Cathryn, Hillary hadn't thought she was criminally insane, just a manipulative monster, but she was reconsidering. If the testimony of those who had just left Amen Hale was to be believed, Cathryn was a homicidal psychopath, a sexual sadist, and for what it was worth, *a witch*! Just the kind of person you didn't want your daughter to cuddle up to and call "Mom."

"Human sacrifice!" exclaimed Daniels. "That old mansion is not some *Aztec temple* where cutting someone's heart out is business as usual! And the sexual abuse! I'm sure it's on the news right now. The public will be calling for us to send troops over the damn wall. They won't let it stand, especially with these people continuing to take in new children. Some kids trapped in a horrible spot they may endure, but people won't be able to sit by and watch new kids get thrown to the dogs. That's the kind of thing that makes good, moral people into wild-eyed nuts willing to do bad things for what they see as good reasons."

Hillary nodded because Daniels' thoughts echoed her own. Rob Daniels, the new Governor of Florida, had arrived at her command tent almost two hours ago, sent to help her "manage" the situation. Daniels was of average height, about five ten. As for his appearance, add six inches to the man and he'd look almost exactly like the last governor of Florida, as if the State didn't really want a change, merely a smaller version of the same man to match their shrinking tourism-based economy. Hillary knew that the President wanted someone else involved and he was already friends with Daniels. So Daniels was part of her team. He seemed capable and so far was taking his lead from her, which was what she wanted.

"The President has ordered a complete closing of the borders," Hillary said. "And he's drafting an official declaration to King Cornelius stating that no U.S.-born minors will be allowed to enter Amen Hale for *any* reason, even with parental consent. In his letter he's demanded, quite firmly, that Kim Ainsley be returned to her parents. I can't believe they let those two through this morning. I wasn't here at the time or I would have prevented it."

Daniels frowned. "There's over a million people in Jacksonville. Can we ask them to move somewhere less populated? Somewhere rural, like the Midwest."

"No." Hillary stared at Daniels as if he were an idiot. "The President wants them to stay right where they are. They're settled and he wants them to stay that way. And we're forty minutes away from the city here, Daniels; this is about as rural as Florida gets."

"Dammit," he rubbed at his face, "whatever happened to the crazies staying in California?" he complained weakly. "May I at least share that I *asked* if we could relocate?" he asked "oh so casually."

"Hell no!" Hillary shot back immediately. "Don't say a single word about it, *Governor*." She colored his title darkly. "And don't even dream about playing politics with anything that goes on here," Hillary warned, reevaluating her opinion of the man. Daniels was already wilting, but she still got into his face to make her point crystal clear.

"You can tell the press that the President is relieved that Jacksonville is a military town and well equipped to handle a crisis like this, score some points that way, but everything else stays *here*. You asked to be included in this because it was happening in your state, but if I feel for one second that you're less than trustworthy you'll be out on your ass. And in case you haven't noticed, Washington is not running on the 'business as usual' model right now. What the President wants, he gets, and for right now at least, he doesn't even have to explain why."

Governor Daniels nodded, completely cowed.

What Hillary said was true. Washington was reeling and struggling to figure itself out. Soldiers were all over the Capital and Federal agents and police were chasing down lists of names who were connected to The Order in various ways. Wealthy business owners, CEOs, senators, appellate judges, and congressmen shredded files and ran like common criminals. The middle-aged, pot-bellied professionals were providing the media with an orgasmic display of high-speed car chases, crashes, armed standoffs, and exciting videotaped raids with police and soldiers busting into hotel rooms to drag the once distinguished and powerful gentlemen off to jail.

The President was using every trick at his disposal to appear as the vindictive, righteously searching hand of an outraged America, determined to clean house and clean it well. The people no longer trusted Congress or the Senate, and every hour more and more power found its way to the President, and oddly enough, to her as the crisis deepened. The fact that The Order only inducted males cleared Hillary of any suspicion, even with her extensive political background. As the reputations of well known political figures imploded all around Washington, Hillary wasn't too proud to wave around her '*get out of suspicion free*' card, even if it was printed on the recycled paper of sexual discrimination.

As if everything happening in Washington weren't enough, there was still Amen Hale to deal with. And no matter which country you happen to live in, the news was the same. It was as if the entire world were tuned in and watching TV but with only two channels to choose from, the Washington Meltdown Network or Amen Hale Horror Theater. And as bad as things were in Washington, Hillary knew the news media would sensationalize each sick and sadistic detail these people leaving Amen Hale offered up until the place made Dante's Inferno sound like a summer camp.

"He's ordering them to give up the Ainsley girl and her boyfriend. That's good news," Rob piped up, forcing a smile and changing the subject. "Maybe we'll get those kids back some time this afternoon, before everyone tunes into the evening news to see the latest madness."

"I doubt it," Hillary said sadly, thinking about Emma Tate. "Once these people get someone's child, they don't like to let go." From the descriptions she'd heard, Emma wasn't even recognizable as the same human being. Hillary shuddered, thinking about her own daughter and what she'd do if she were stuck in Amen Hale.

"What?" asked Daniels.

"Just thinking," Hillary said.

"About the kids?"

"About all of it," Hillary answered.

There were a great many things she needed to think about. And most of it was ugly.

Gannon and Alana

Fascinated or Terrified?

GANNON AND ALANA watched from their seats in the first row of the balcony as Princess Bethany slit the prisoner's throat while at the same Princess Rain let the two vampires drink her blood. The vampires drank cleanly, making no mess as they pressed their faces to her cut palms, while at the same time Princess Bethany made a nightmare mess, letting blood shower down and cover her from head to toe.

After the throat, she stabbed her victim straight in the heart and everyone in the hall felt her frightening magic as she ran her hands over the body and used her magic to draw out every last stubborn drop in a final spray of red. And then the Princess lay down on the blood-soaked floor and rolled in the thick red muck, soaking it up with her dress and her long black hair and covering every inch of herself with thick sticky red until she finally flopped back onto her back and laughed and laughed while she made blood angels on the floor.

Gannon was very glad they hadn't eaten lunch; his stomach felt like it was in his chest, not upset, but in the wrong place. Crowding his heart. He felt weird, and strangely enlightened in a horrifying way, as if by watching this man die he now appreciated all life more. His life, Alana's life, the dead man's life, *everyone's.*

He wondered if he was in shock just from seeing what he'd seen. Sounds seemed off as they came into his head, and everything looked a little strange, but the lighting in The Hallow was strange to begin with. And sound in the place carried oddly. He didn't know how much of the weirdness was the place and how much was him.

Gannon looked at Alana to see how she was holding up. She was pale, but she didn't look away from what was happening and her grip on his hand was firm. He thought about last night, when he'd drug her along with him as they followed that chanting line of Satan worshipers for fun out on the fairgrounds. She'd been so terrified that she'd begged to leave, not wanting to see the hooded men do harm to a piglet, *an animal*, but here she'd just watched a human sacrifice without running or screaming. He didn't know what to think about that or what thoughts were going through her head. He didn't dare ask her how she was doing, afraid he might ruin her control by making her speak.

Princess Bethany was still lying on the bloody floor when Cathryn stood and spoke from the platform. She ordered that the sacrificed man be removed and prepared for tonight's feast. She excused those who wished to go, but Alana made no move to rise and Gannon stayed beside her. He was surprised to see that most of the people remained in their seats, determined to see it through to the end, too fascinated to leave or to terrified to move. He didn't know if Alana was fascinated—or terrified. Again, he didn't ask, he just stayed in his seat and held her hand.

They watched as the vampires stopped drinking from Princess Rain's hands and took turns biting and kissing her. It looked like a passionate dance the way the two glittering white bodies moved; one held her and bit her neck while the other kissed her passionately. It would have been more frightening, but the Princess obviously enjoyed what they did.

It was difficult to watch for a completely different reason. Seeing her writhe and hearing her scream in pleasure made Alana blush like mad and made Gannon break out in a sweat. They had clothes on, but it was still so raw, sexual, and exposing watching the three of them together as they "fed" and then afterward as they touched affectionately before slumping onto the floor in a clinging pile. The vampires seemed drunk on her blood and Black Rain was reduced to a boneless smile, so whited with pleasure she was blind to everyone other than the two vampires as they pulled her down between them onto the floor and went to sleep, right there in front of everyone.

Asleep was how they all ended. Princess Bethany asleep on the floor, lying in a pool of drying blood while fifteen feet away her sister slept, lying between two vampires.

Once everyone was down, Byron stepped onto the platform and in a hushed voice made a few announcements, calling out job assignments and duties and things to be done and who he wanted to do each task. He called for Gannon and Alana and for two girls named Izzy and Lizzy, telling them to go to the Royal Dining Hall before excusing everyone from The Hallow.

"How are you?" Gannon asked Alana.

She looked pale and tired, but she smiled. "I like it here," she said.

Gannon couldn't hide his horrified surprise and Alana frowned. "What's wrong, Gan?"

"Last night you almost had a heart attack over that pig that *almost* got sacrificed and now you're not freaked over watching this man get sacrificed?" He leaned closer to her. "I'm just trying to understand what's going on in here." He tapped her forehead with a finger.

"It was so honest," Alana said. "They just say it like it is here. Even if the truth is horrible."

"Honest?" He made it a question.

"Yes. I like honest. It's why I liked you the second I met you." She smiled when Gannon looked confused.

"You didn't tell me that you wouldn't take some other girl if I didn't go, but you did say that no one else would be as good as me. That was honest. And when I asked you why you let Mitch hit you, you told me you were trying to win a girl, not a fight. That was honest. And after the dance, when I asked you if you loved me you said that you did, but that you loved me too much to let me ruin my life with a fool like you. That was insanely honest."

Gannon sobered, frowning as he remembered that particular bit of madness. "That was horrible," he said.

Alana's smile faded, still there, but only in her eyes. "It was horrible. But it was honest." She looked back down at the courtyard.

The giant one called Believer who looked like a storm cloud pressed into a giant man stood protectively over Black Rain and the two vampires while the one who looked like a dragon man knelt beside the sleeping form of Princess Bethany who was almost invisible, just a red lump on the red floor. She watched as he draped a white cloth over her face to keep the sunlight from her eyes. The girl with pink and red hair watched this small kindness and remembered it.

Gannon reached out to the salt shaker at the same time as Princess Emma, and she snatched her hand back.

"Don't touch me," she warned quickly.

Gannon and Alana shared a glance between them. Their light brunch seemed to be going well up until now, with the King and Queen asking the questions they needed to ask in order to prepare for the wedding, as well as questions about their likes and dislikes to determine a proper "*place of service*," as they called it. The twins, Izzy and Lizzy, were weird but fun. They kept doing the usual weird twin things, like finishing each other's sentences and other strangeness that made it clear they were two peas from the same alien pod.

"Sorry, my Lady," Gannon offered an awkward apology to Emma.

"I'm not mad or anything, I just don't want you to get hurt. I'm very, very poisonous." she warned. Gannon leaned back in his chair as she pinned him with her hawkish copper gold eyes. He kept his hands well away from the Princess.

"Poisonous is an odd way to describe it," said Cornelius. He sat at the head of the table enjoying the spread of cut fruits, thin broth, and other fare that was appropriate for hungry, yet traumatized stomachs.

"Poison me," Mary said.

Emma leaned over to the girl seated beside her, gave her a quick kiss, and pulled back and licked her shiny black lips. She went back for more. The longer kiss began to stretch out into a long, long, long kiss.

"It's almost like being back in lockup," Lizzy said as she eyed the two girls sucking face without shock or surprise.

"It was all girls and," she shrugged, "you know." She speared a piece of cut and sectioned watermelon from her bowl and popped it into her mouth.

"We like boys," said Izzy as she stole a piece of watermelon from Lizzy's bowl. She'd already finished hers.

"Never did go for the girl thing," said Lizzy around a mouthful of melon.

"Is she really poisonous?" Alana asked Cathryn, who was resting in her chair, nursing a glass of wine, watching all of them.

Cathryn asked, "Alana, what would you do if Gannon fell in love with Emma?"

Alana was startled by the question, but Cathryn looked serious. She looked from Cathryn to Gannon then to Emma (who was still kissing Mary) and frowned, considering it. "Die, I guess."

"It's what I'd do," said Izzy casually, then stopped suddenly and shot a guilty look to Cathryn and Cornelius.

"You're right," Lizzy seconded her twin sadly. "If we really were in love with a guy and he dumped us, we'd die. I'm still you inside. You know I couldn't handle us losing our guy if we really loved him." Her twin nodded, reassured and happier. Strange conversation concluded, Izzy went back to stealing her sister's watermelon.

"I just hope we can find one as cool as your *blue*. He's cute." Lizzy eyed Gannon and gave him a wink.

"He is, isn't he?" Alana smiled as she looked at her man with a proud eye. "He's a keeper."

The twins giggled, sounding just like each other.

Cathryn was smiling too; she motioned with her wine glass toward Emma and Mary (who were still kissing). "Alana, what would you do if *you* fell in love with Emma?"

"Ow!" Gannon made a noise and a stricken face to match.

Alana smiled big as if it were a joke. "I don't know? Kiss her, I guess." She laughed as she said it, looking at the two girls still lip locked and liking it.

"Now what if you both loved her?" Cathryn asked. "What then?"

Alana and Gannon stiffened, suddenly worried about where this was headed. Gannon pulled Alana up and out of her chair and drew her into his lap protectively. Alana wrapped her arms around him, wanting to be protected. They were both alert and worried.

"Princess Emma's beautiful, but I'm happy with my firefly," Gannon said respectfully.

Cathryn nodded. "And that's the reason Emma didn't want you to touch her. You know the stories of King Midas and what happened when he touched something?"

"Whatever he touched turned to gold," Alana said, putting the pieces together. "So if Princess Emma touches us, we would fall in love with her. Just like that."

Cathryn hedged, "It might not happen from a casual touch over a salt shaker, but any contact is dangerous. It's as she said, she's poisonous. We have to be exceedingly careful who we let get close to her."

Mary and Emma finally stopped kissing and settled back into their chairs.

"Sorry, Mom. She's just so—*wonderful.* It's hard to stop kissing her." Emma sounded breathy. She gave Mary another smoldering look, and Mary's eyes unfocused and she started to lean back in for more.

"Emma, come here, child. You need some distance from Mary, and we have guests you wanted to meet and talk to."

Emma looked confused, her head going from Cathryn to Mary, like she was trying to decide between ice cream or chocolate.

Cathryn put her arms out. "Come."

Emma came to her and sat in her lap, then rubbed her face against Cathryn's and took another long deep breath with her face buried in Cathryn's hair. She held the breath, then blew out. She kept her arms around Cathryn's waist but looked sensible and mentally functional again as she ran her eyes around the table.

"Thanks, Mom. I've got my brain back."

Cathryn laughed. "You're welcome, my child."

"Are we going to be able to keep them?" Emma asked as she looked at Gannon and Alana.

Cornelius grunted. "It's going to be much harder than we thought. The President of the United States has made it clear that he wants these two returned." He drew a packet out from inside his coat and opened it. He sifted through the pages, and then held one out, offering it to Emma.

Emma took it and raised the page of thick parchment paper to her face. The images on the presidential letterhead she recognized and she noticed the raised seal with the embossed image of an eagle, but the letters in the writing seemed to squirm under her eyes as if alive. She blinked and rubbed at her eyes and held the paper so close it almost touched the tip of her nose as she concentrated, focusing on one word at time, but each word she read seemed disconnected from the word before and after it, and she kept losing her place.

Emma put the paper down on the table. "I can't read anymore. It's been taken." She said it without emotion or feeling.

Cathryn and Mary gathered around her and hugged her but she didn't cry.

"What does it say, Father?" she asked.

"They want them back, my dear," Cornelius said.

Emma nodded and looked at Gannon and Alana, then took the paper and very carefully handed it to them and watched as they read it together, their faces becoming grimmer as they read, their grip on one another tightening. Alana was crying when they finally set the paper down on the table. Gannon was already mentally making plans on what they'd do after they left Amen Hale, his eyes distant, but Alana hadn't given up. She was desperate to find some solution to the problem in the room in which they sat, directing her tear-filled angry eyes at Cathryn, Cornelius, Emma, and Mary.

Emma asked Alana, "What do you think would happen if you went back to your parents?"

"I will not 'go' back! I'm not 'going' anywhere. My name is in the Book of Shadows," she said firmly.

"Take it easy, Alana," Gannon cautioned, but his efforts to calm her just made her angrier and more determined.

"They can't lie, Gannon!" she whisper/yelled at him. "They invited us in and let us write our name in the book! They won't throw us out because they *can't* throw us out! They're witches, and they can't lie. They have to be honest!" She turned her angry eyes back to the witches and crumpled the President's paper in her fist, dropping it onto the table. She glared, challenging them to keep their word while Gannon reluctantly backed her play.

Cathryn smiled. "You're right about all of it, Alana. We cannot lie, and we cannot cast you out without a cause."

"Burning girl," Emma said. "What would you do if the government came and took you away from us?"

Alana stared at the faces looking back at her across the table wondering how they could even say such things. She and Gannon hadn't left with those *other* people. She'd stayed. She'd watched every drop of blood hit the floor! She *belonged* here! After what they'd just seen, she wondered how they could be thinking she'd leave!

"What would happen if soldiers came and took you away, Alana?" Emma asked again, firmer, her tone demanding an answer.

"The Black Lion would roar!" Alana shouted her angry answer as she glared at them through a curtain of tears. "She would come for me *herself!* She would bring me home!"

Everyone at the table seemed stunned and sat there staring at her like she'd totally flipped out except Princess Emma; she smiled like a *witch* and asked Alana another question.

"Are you her lamb?"

Black Rain

Fantasy and Reality

I STRUGGLED TO SIT up, but arms were around me, holding me as emotions pounded up from the ground beneath me as if the earth itself were trying to cry out or speak to me.

"Save me!"

"Roar for me! Come for me!"

"Save me! Roar for me! Come for me!"

My heart was racing as I struggled to lift Dan's arms off. He was behind me, his body spooned up around me and Jane was in front of me, asleep on her side pressed up against me with one of her arms over me as well.

"My love, are you well?" Believer asked as I freed my upper half and sat up, blinking and disoriented, heart still pounding from the strange message from the ground and waking in a strange place in a strange position.

The last thing I truly remembered was being bitten and kissed and the feel of teeth in my neck and lips on my mouth before letting myself be carried away by pleasure while they shared me. I didn't feel naked, but I couldn't stop from looking down just to make sure. The dress was intact and on me.

Feeling a bit more in control and settled, I took in my surroundings. I was lying on the floor of The Hallow, sandwiched tight from the waist down between two unconscious vampires. Just fifteen feet away, Sky Dragon was standing with a tall muscle-bound black man, each of them holding large umbrellas over their heads to block the sun that poured in from the opening in the center of the roof high above us. Between their feet and under the shade of the umbrella was a red splat of *yuck!* on the floor. I looked at the dragon and the man and their banana yellow and hot pink umbrellas that were lit so beautifully from above, casting colors onto the disgusting floor.

"Why the umbrellas?" and "What *is* that bloody gunk?" My daydreams were always so weird. I waited for the rest of it, looking around. No white rabbit ran by. The midgets didn't charge in. No marching band or monsters. No fairies and no music for the dancing, I thought for sure that Sky Dragon and the other man would do a Gene Kelly number with the umbrellas.

I looked again at the blob of red on the floor under the umbrellas and something about the size and shape made me freeze. I could make out strands of hair running out, glued and matted onto the floor, and then I recognized the blood-covered contours of an upturned face, the white teeth peeking through the red mask. A chill ran through my whole body. It was Bethany.

"Bethany is well. Don't get worked up. She's just sleeping," Sky Dragon told me from where he stood, holding his pink umbrella.

I saw the slow rise and fall of her breathing and felt myself start breathing again. Then I noticed that the corner of her mouth was turned up in a smile like a happy corpse. I stared at her for a minute longer just to see what we'd become. It was bloody, but for some insane reason it wasn't ugly to me. And she wasn't ugly either.

"Even covered with blood she looks like an angel, beautiful and precious," I said.

Sky Dragon wiggled his umbrella. "Rain." He pointed up at the ceiling with his pink sunlit turtle shell. "Could you fix the ceiling, Sis? I didn't want to move her, but I didn't want her roasting in the sun either."

I looked up. Above me, the hole in the ceiling closed as I wanted, and before we fell into total darkness I called for light to be in the room and a soft glow that came from nowhere and everywhere took the place of the harsh sunlight. The dim glow provided enough illumination to see by while leaving the room in comfortable shadow, ideal for sleeping vampires and bloody little girls.

Pink and yellow umbrellas snapped shut and dipped to the floor at the same time, and I found myself staring at the umbrellas, frowning. Still no dancing. I laughed as I realized that I'd still been waiting for the music to start. My real world and my dream world were so close together now. How strange.

Sky Dragon and the big black man looked at me like I'd gone mad. I thought that was a bit unfair and judgmental. I wasn't the one holding a bright pink or yellow umbrella indoors.

"Rain?" Believer called.

Using just my first name gave me enough of a jolt to make me look up at him and into his worried red eyes.

"Did you hear it?" I asked him.

He frowned. "Did I hear what woke you from your sleep?" He shook his head. "No. I did not."

"I heard a voice calling to me from the ground."

"The ground spoke to you?" he asked, frowning. He and Sky Dragon were both watching me as if I were broken, both trying to determine how "bad" the damage was.

"Yes!" I insisted. "A voice came straight from the ground or the floor. It said that one of my people needed me."

I wanted to reach over and touch the floor but my lower half was still pinned under Dan's legs and one of Jane's arms. "Someone needs me. The ground told me so," I affirmed stubbornly, pooching my lips out.

"Perhaps it was a dream," Believer suggested. He was using his deep, mellow, "talk the jumper down off the cliff" voice. "It's almost time to go. We need to travel to France to retrieve our men they have taken from us."

"*Believer!*" I whined his name. "Stop using verbal kung-fu!"

"What do you mean?" he asked innocently.

Yeah right! "First, you tell me it was all just a dream, then you hit me with a tight timetable, and follow up with the smack down of a subject change!" I frowned at him. "I did hear the floor talking. It wasn't a dream!"

His rumbling laugh made me look up. He was smiling at me. I raised my arms over my head and he reached down without having to be told or asked and lifted me free from my prison of undead arms and legs and stood me on my feet, balancing me until I could stand on my own.

I felt my neck. There were no marks left, but I remembered that they'd bitten me on both sides. I looked down at my vampire lovers, asleep on the floor. There was a foot and a half wide gap between them where my body had been. The empty space bothered me deeply. I felt a strong urge to crawl back in and fill that void with my life and love and human flesh, but someone needed me somewhere. The ground itself had told me so and for some reason I didn't think the ground would lie. I knelt down and pressed my palms and cheek flat against the dirty floor and closed my eyes.

"Where?" I asked it.

"*Royal dining hall*," a whisper answered me, and my black eyes snapped open as wide as they'd go.

I hadn't really expected an answer! It was not quite a voice and yet still a voice, but one thing was for sure, it was not a dream! This was definitely going onto the list of weird things. I turned my head and looked at the white floor and thought, "Oh come on! I mean, who *really* talks to floors? And of those *few* sad people, like me, who *did* talk to their floors, how many of those floors actually talked back?' Again I thought that my fantasy world and my reality were connected in some pretty strange and obscene ways.

But my eye caught a glimpse of Bethany on the floor in her bed of blood, and I felt bad for thinking what I was thinking because it seemed so judgmental. Who was I to call anything obscene or strange or ugly? I leaned down and gave the blood-spattered floor a good kiss.

"Thank you," I told it sincerely and stood up.

Believer was staring at me, his fancy new eyebrows both locked in the arched and incredulous position. I ignored him and his eyebrows. I believed the floor. And I thought the floor deserved the kiss I'd given him or her (if it was a girl floor). I laughed again and watched my cloud men stare at me like I was bat shit nuts, which was like staring at a glass of spilt milk and worrying about it spilling. *Sanity* was a fine ship that sailed from my port two years ago with me begging to get aboard but told to stay behind.

The thought chilled and sobered me as I walked over to Bethany. First, I willed her to stay asleep while I worked on her and then I cleaned her up. The blood vanished off her body, her dress, and her hair, and all the blood that was on the floor of The Hallow vanished as well. I used my power to soothe Bethany's skin and her muscles that may have been cramped from sleeping on the hard floor. I did her hair and a touch of makeup and created a pillow for her head to rest on and some new soft little shoes for her feet and I made her a new silver bracelet with a bloodstone charm. I held the charm up to my lips and spoke my will into it.

"*Each kiss I give unto this stone, remain and live for her alone. From time to time throughout the day, let kisses come out in surprising ways. I want you to make her laugh in delight and give her my love when not in my sight. And if there should come a dangerous day that threatens to take my dear one away. Give up your life and the magic you hold to save this sweet life now fourteen years old.*"

I kissed the charm ten times, thinking of how much I loved her each time, and then I placed the bracelet around her wrist and touched the new little shoes on her feet. Bethany liked to go barefoot, but I thought that maybe she'd like the shoes. Even if she only wore them for an hour I'd be happy with that.

I knelt down and, without using magic, pushed Jane back up against Dan's body. I took the extra effort to lift his arm and place it over her, repositioning them as best as I could, then stood and stepped away from the two of them. I could feel them inside me. They'd filled me with their venom and magic and a part of what they were. I knew I was changed by what they'd done, but I didn't know how or how much.

Now that I was thinking about it, I felt my skin tingling. I held my left hand out in front of me. My dress had long sleeves with lace cuffs and I wanted to see my wrist. With a thought I changed my dress; both black sleeves vanished leaving my shoulders and arms bare. I pressed the long black nail on my index finger against the flesh of my wrist and it pierced the skin easily, making me jump.

"Ow! That hurt!" I was surprised at how much it hurt. "Freakin' ow!"

"Not now!" Sky Dragon whined. "You just cleaned up in here, Sis, don't make another mess." He tried to make a joke of it, but I knew he was truly worried about me now. Believer was a silent brooding mass of dark clouds beside Sky Dragon, his face nothing but pent up worry and frustration.

"Relax guys. I was just making sure I'm still mortal in this body after being bitten by the vampires." I held up the evidence of mortality, my bleeding wrist. "See. Still flesh and blood. Still human," I announced happily with a smile as blood trickled down my bare forearm.

Believer and Sky Dragon shared a look that took my smile away.

"Why are you guys staring at me like that?" I waved my bleeding appendage at them. "If I was vampire I wouldn't bleed, my skin would be hard like theirs. And I'd be moving fast like them. And my heart wouldn't be beating anymore. Not that a dead heart could kill me, but you know what I'm saying." I studied their faces but all that did was convince me that something really was wrong.

Sky Dragon's eye ridges came up and he looked over to Believer, handing off the bad news to his older brother.

"There are a few changes that we can see, my love." He spoke to me in his "jumper" voice again. Not a good sign. "Your skin is paler than it was before, though not as pale as the vampires, and your teeth and hair have changed as well. And your eyes are still solid black but there is a hint of red in their depths that is new."

I could feel the blood as it trailed down my bare skin. I could feel it as it pooled at my elbow and even feel the shimmy when a drop of blood fell away to start its journey toward the floor below.

"Are you experiencing blood lust?" Believer asked me.

I blinked up at him in surprise. I looked at my arm and the red drops on the white floor and shook my head. "No," I said, somewhat surprised. "Not at all. But my skin feels weird."

Now that I was looking and could see my arms I could see the difference. My skin *was* paler. I ran a hand down my arm and noticed that the touch of hand to flesh was strange as well. I ran one more experiment, giving myself another tiny cut. It hurt. More than it should have. It seemed I felt everything more strongly.

I moved on. "How bad are the eyes, Bro?" I asked Sky Dragon.

He stepped over and took my face in his cool hands. I could feel each of his cloudy fingers with such detail. He leaned in, scoping out the damage, his own red eyes staring hard into my eyes. "They're almost the same as before, but I must say," he squinted, peering down deeper, "that faint red glow, deep down in there is a little disturbing."

"Disturbing?" I made it a question and pulled back from his hands enough so I could see all of his face.

"Just a little," he said innocently and shrugged.

"Sky Dragon!" I fussed. "How the hell can it be 'a little' disturbing? It's one of those things that either is or isn't, you dweeb." I gave him a whack on the arm. My hand stung just from whacking him.

"What's different about my teeth!?" I griped.

"Just use your tongue, Sis," Sky Dragon suggested. "But be careful about it."

"Huh," I grunted. I explored carefully as suggested, and sure enough, things had moved around in my mouth. My teeth were straighter and sharper, but I was shocked to find that my canines were still their regular size and I didn't have little holes in the back of each canine tooth like Jane and Dan for injecting venom. My teeth were just like my skin, only vampire on the surface but all human underneath.

I reached up and touched my hair. It was smooth and glossy like Jane's. I pulled the hair up to my face and sniffed. A hint of roses. I could smell their magic. Mary said she never went too deep into me when she touched me with her power, and it seemed like the vampires had done the same and just redecorated my outside with their magic. Pale sensitive skin. Sweet smelling hair. Disturbing eyes. I really could have done without the disturbing eyes.

"Weird," I said. I made a face and gave myself a good shake.

Sky Dragon laughed, earning a dark look from Believer, but I joined him and we both laughed and shared Believer's frustrated frown together.

"We need to be at the warehouse in France in less than twelve minutes, my love," Believer said quite firmly.

I stopped laughing and so did Sky Dragon, but he still snickered quietly, his mirth leaking out in a cute little snake-like "hiss hiss hiss" that made me smile and made his brother grumble like a complaining parent with two unruly kids.

"Take Bethany up to her bed," I told Sky Dragon, "and have some more guards come to watch over Jane and Dan for me while I'm away."

Believer said, "I am going with you. You are not yourself, and I will not allow you to go as you are without me there to watch over you." He stared hard at me and I stared hard back. We'd already discussed this.

"You are a mess, Sis," Sky Dragon snuck in his jab, and I shot him a dirty look which earned me a "hiss hiss hiss" laugh of my own from the tickled dragon.

"You are still changing even as we speak," Believer argued. "Your skin is lightening further and your eyes are still changing. Perhaps other changes are taking place that we are not even aware of." He knelt down and wrapped his huge arms around me and looked me in the face. "You are not yourself, my love. I am afraid for you."

"But it's too dangerous for—" I started.

"You will not go there without me!" he thundered, his red eyes burning so brightly they lit my face like two bright red lamps.

I was calm as I reached up and touched his troubled cloudy face with my hand. His face was so lovely. He was beautiful. I forgot the world and all that was in it for a moment and watched the clouds swirl and churn beneath my hand. Who on earth could tell me no? To whom would I bow and submit myself in anything? I obeyed my mother and father, should I not obey my husband as well? He just agreed to horrible, horrible things because I wanted them. Could I not obey even in this? He was right anyway, but I was scared for him. Things were getting strange.

I bowed my head. "All right," I said.

The rumbling tension I felt within his clouds calmed.

"You're right anyway," I confessed reluctantly. "About all of it. I do feel odd, and it's not just my skin. I feel—something. I've never felt like this before, I don't know what it means. It's not death I feel, it's something else, something bigger." I ran my hands through my hair and gave myself a shake, trying to free myself of the strange feeling that clung to me like a second skin.

"Come and watch over me, Believer. I need you."

"Then let us do this quickly," he said. "We will go, take our people, and leave five minutes later."

"Sounds good to me," I said and hugged him, then pulled back enough to give him a smile that was his alone, and he smiled back at me, his eyes now bright with a different kind of glow.

I turned and walked a few steps away (for safety) and then let power slip out of my body. My hair and dress billowed around me wildly while white light shone from my flesh. The black guard was crawling away on his hands and knees, trying to get some distance between himself and my power. I didn't worry over him, I'd be gone soon enough. A slender rope of white glass rose up from the floor forming an arch which became a gateway opening to the large silver mirror on the wall in the Cathedral Hall. I could see people in the wide hall scattering as my power and light spilled out into the room with a force strong enough to move small objects too close to my power.

"Come, my husband. We need to make one quick stop before we go to France."

Alana Burning

The Reluctant Lamb

THE TWINS WERE chattering away with Mary about inane teen crap that they'd missed out on while they were in some kind of institution and Gannon was beside me talking with King Cornelius about the wedding and our potential place of service and where we would live after the wedding. All very important stuff, but I couldn't stop thinking about Emma's last question after my meltdown.

"Are you her lamb?" she had asked me.

Cathryn and Cornelius had stepped in before I had a chance to answer, giving a dozen assurances that Gan and I were not only welcome but wanted and safe here in Amen Hale. That was ten minutes ago and everyone had moved on to other things. Everyone that is, except me.

I sat huddled in Gan's lap, curled into myself with his arms wrapped around me like a caterpillar in my own little embarrassed cocoon. My freaky religious fervor (or psychotic break) had fizzled out completely. Okay, so I'd flipped out. Maybe what I'd seen earlier had done more to me than I thought. Yelling at them about the rules of this place. Good one. Like *I* was going to tell *them* what could or couldn't happen here. Like I was the one in charge. I blame my mother!

Am I her lamb? Yeah right!

Princess Rain didn't know me or even know my name. She didn't know my old plain name or my fancy new one. She didn't know me or Gan or anything about us, and I'd shouted like some kind of religious maniac that she would "ROAR!" for me. Like her story was real. She'd even said it was just a made-up story. Just thinking about how I'd acted made me cringe. I was an idiot. God, I was an I-D-I-O-T! If she did roar anything that's what she'd roar. "IDIOT!"

I'd just been so mad at that moment and the story about the lambs kept going thorough my head. It seemed the right thing to say. I didn't really think she would come for me. I came here for me, not for her. I wanted to be honest about it. The only reason we'd come here was so Gan and I could be together. This was the only place where that could happen. I wondered if you had to love her to be one of—

"Alana? Alana?" Gannon asked.

"What's that? Sorry, I didn't hear," I said.

King Cornelius was looking at me and waiting.

"Sorry, sir. I was just thinking," I said lamely as I tried to catch up.

"It's all right, Alana." He was studying me like a doctor eyeing a patient, concern pinching crows' feet into the corners of his eyes but his smile stayed the same. He had a nice face, kind and fatherly, even if he did have long silver hippie hair.

"It's been a long night and a trying day. And you and Gannon have the wedding tonight."

He called a servant over and gave some instructions. I heard something about a room before he turned back to us. "You and Gannon need a few hours of sleep before the ladies of Amen Hale descend upon the both of you to get you ready for the wedding. And you'll want to be rested and ready for when you meet your family."

My heart jumped and started to race like a floored engine. "You won't let them take us, will you?" I asked quickly. I hadn't yelled but I'd spoken so fast I wasn't sure he'd heard me.

King Cornelius blinked but then he smiled and said. "No."

Just the one word. Spoken very much on purpose. It sounded solid. *Kingly,* if that was a word. Like his "no" really meant something. I felt a huge smile take over my face. It was my first smile since my meltdown.

"Good." I gave one word back.

"I will be expecting your betrothed to save me a dance," Queen Cathryn told me and looked at Gannon.

I watched Gannon's eyes go wide with surprise, but he recovered quickly. He gave her a smile and a debonair dip of his head. My Gan was very quick. "I would be honored to dance with you, Queen Cathryn," he said, which sent the twins into a giggling fit and started both saying "Me too! Me too!" which made us all laugh.

And that was when we all felt it coming.

Servants around the table froze in mid motion and every one of us fell silent. Heads turned toward the doorway behind us.

"This is so NOT GOOD!" Princess Mary yelled as she jumped up from her seat. "She's coming in power, Mother! She's going to be dangerous! Very dangerous!"

Every head in the room turned to stare at me! AT ME! Like it was all my fault! There was a mad scramble of movement as King Cornelius started giving orders and telling everyone where to go and what to do and where to stand and everyone did exactly what he said. The servants moved to the back of the room and flattened themselves against the walls, and the rest of us got to our feet and moved to face the doorway except Cathryn. She remained seated and kept Emma in her lap, getting a firm grip on her. King Cornelius and Princess Mary stood in front of us to either side like bookends and we all faced the doorway together like some sort of crazy firing line, ready to be shot!

My heart was trying to abandon ship and jump right out of my throat and run away screaming as the white glow filled the outer hall then spilled around the corner before Black Rain stepped into the open doorway. She stood there and stared into the room like some radiant alien creature from another world. Her long black hair moved about her head like a huge floating halo, fanning out in all directions and waving about as if she were surrounded by water instead of air. It struck me right then that her hair was like a lion's mane. Her dress blew about her body, but the sleeves were gone now, showing her white arms.

It was hard to look at her but almost impossible not to at the same time. I squinted my eyes and Gannon used a hand to shield his eyes and so did the twins and King Cornelius. The room felt too small to hold her and her light if she stepped the rest of the way into the room. Everyone was still and waiting.

She couldn't be here for me! Just because I said she'd come. She didn't even know my name.

She looked into the room, studying who was here, looking at faces. She looked at the twins and smiled at them. She looked past us, I guessed to Cathryn and Emma but I didn't turn to see, and then she looked at Gannon and studied him for a moment before looking at me. Her black eyes stared at me and I watched as her blue lips turned up in a smile.

"Roar."

She said the one word while she stared at me, then she turned on her heels and left, taking her light and blinding power with her.

It was quiet for a minute.

"She came for me," I heard myself say, and then I had to sit down.

I wasn't the only one.

There was some talk and then Gan picked me up. We followed a servant upstairs. Gan carried me in his arms and soon we were lying down in the bed and he was holding me tight, running his hand through my hair.

"Are you all right, Alana?" he asked. He asked a few more times then he used my old name. "Kim! Talk to me!" He was holding me by my shoulders, shaking me, staring down at me. So worried and afraid. Crying.

"I'm so sorry I brought us here! God, Kim, I'm sorry! I was supposed to protect you. I didn't know it would be like this. We can still leave. We can go back with your parents when they get here. You *should* go back with your parents! You should go home where it's safe. You should go home."

He ranted on and on for another five minutes until I summoned the strength I needed to open my eyes. I reached up and pulled his worried, anguished face down to mine and held him.

"Come to bed, Gan."

I closed my eyes.

Anna Lee

Old Dad vs. New Dad

ANNA LEE REACHED her hand down into the icy water of the red cooler at her feet and fished out a cold can of regular Coke and handed it to her father. Her father used to drink Diet Coke. Her father used to complain if she watched an R-rated slasher movie. Her "old" father never would have let her within a thousand miles of anything like what she'd just witnessed. But her "old" father was gone and her "new" father was different. She hadn't decided if she liked him more or less, but she had decided that he was still her Dad, no matter what. She still claimed him as hers.

"So, about the hair?" He touched it and raised his eyebrows. "This isn't a wig, it feels real. Did one of the Princesses make your hair grow back out?" he asked.

"Princess Rain," Anna Lee answered.

"Do you like it?" he asked, not surprised at all that someone had magicked her ugly hair long again.

She gave him a look like he was a complete and total idiot. Like he had to ask. Her hair was *totally* awesome!

He smiled easily and laughed easily, two things which her old robot dad never did, then tilted back to finish off his can of *regular* Coke. Anna's mind was like a computer that kept tabulating all the anomalies between "old" dad and "new" dad, trying to make it into some kind of math problem that would add up to better or worse.

Her father bent down, searching under the table for a garbage bag and Anna Lee looked at his hair. It was cut in the same military burr that spiked at the top, but now his hair was solid black and he didn't have a bald spot at the top where it used to be.

She realized she was doing it again. It was annoying.

One of the men came running into the Archway room and straight up to her father. "She's coming, sir. Lord Believer is with her. But you might want to give your new sunglasses a try; she's shining like a shooting star," he panted.

"Stay right here," her father told her then went to do his job and greet Princess Rain.

Anna wasn't really surprised that these people took her dad and made him one of them. And she wasn't surprised that he was almost in charge. She'd always been proud of him, but seeing that other people valued him this much reminded her just how special he really was. She watched as he directed people where to go and what to do and thought it was strange how some things stayed the same—no matter how much other things changed.

Her father stood at attention with fifteen men lined up behind him, all of them wearing super dark sunglasses.

Princess Rain and her giant monster of a husband came walking down the sloped driveway. She was shining so brightly that it was hard to look at her. She'd been glowing earlier when she told her story in The Hallow but it was nothing like this. She looked amazing! Anna watched as a few of the men behind her father dropped to their knees, but it didn't look like it was something they did because they were about to fall over, it looked like they did it because they wanted to do it.

"Does she like her hair, Lucius?"

Anna's eyes snapped from looking at the kneeling guards to Black Rain who now stood in front of her father. They were both staring right at her.

"I believe she's very happy with it, Mistress."

"She's beautiful." Black Rain smiled at her. "I knew she was yours the moment I saw her. She is welcome to come and go from Amen Hale as she likes. You have no choice so she shall have every choice. I'm glad she's here for you. Make sure you take some time to spend with her," she told her father.

"We should go, my love," Believer's big voice rumbled. "It's already a few minutes past three."

"Are you going with her then, Lord Believer?" her father asked.

"Yes," he said firmly. "She's been acting peculiar since being bitten. She must have supervision."

Princess Rain nodded. "He's right." She looked up at her husband. "Keep an eye on me, but please, my love, if something strange happens, concentrate on saving yourself and not this flesh and blood in which I walk. This," she held her arms out, "is replaceable." She placed her open palms on Believer's chest. "But this is not replaceable. Which would hurt me more to lose, my love?" She stared up at him.

Believer frowned. "I do not like leaving home. It's always so dangerous, and I do not like it," he complained.

Black Rain ran her hands over her arms as if chilled. She looked back to Lucius.

"Perhaps you and a few men as well. Not too many. And let me smell each of you first to make sure you'll be okay."

Anna watched as she sniffed at each of the five men and her father. She seemed reassured and a little confused by whatever she'd smelled, but she shrugged it off and opened the gateway to France. Anna watched as her father and the other men marched through the open gateway portal.

"Something is wrong. You are acting strange, my love," Believer rumbled.

"It'll be okay. Five minutes and we're out of there," she told him. "Let's go get our lost sheep."

They stepped through the gateway together and into France.

Black Rain

What Should Not Be

I WAS FIGHTING THE queer, prickling feeling that danced on my new, pale skin as I stepped into the warehouse with Believer at my side. In front of us stood two men and one woman and behind them stood our men, lined up and ready to go. As soon as they saw me, they fell to their knees. All of them.

I turned my attention to the three people in front of us. One of the men was Ferrand. He was wearing a pained smile and holding a fancy box in his hands, some gift from the French government no doubt. The other man was an ugly balding man with a huge bristly mustache and a too wide smile on his face, and beside him was an attractive older woman who looked like she was about to pass out.

The sound of many voices made me stop and look to the right side of the warehouse where a massive crowd of people were all staring at me. The French had roped off a section of the warehouse and set up tiered, bleacher style seats like in a high school gym. There must have been well over three hundred well-dressed people there, a few dozen already causing problems, calling out to me, trying to gain my attention. Handlers were trying to regain order but it was a complete fiasco.

Strangers! Hundreds of gawking strangers.

I felt as if a vaudevillian with a mustache, cane, and a black top hat had sold tickets for a show.

Come one! Come all! Take a peek at the freak!

I was nothing but a side show attraction to these people. They'd forced me to come here so they could have a damned show! I was like a puppet with a stick shoved up its ass and forced to perform on their stage! They'd captured my people to make me dance for them, so they could *see the witch!*

My temper soared and my power raged. I squeezed my eyes shut and began to shake to keep some control lest I kill everyone around me. People screamed from every direction. I heard Believer's rumbling voice yelling something at me that I couldn't make out over the roar in my ears and the queer feeling riding my body.

I felt as if I were about to rip apart as I shouted back, "Get my black lambs home now!"

All I wanted were my stolen lambs. They'd stolen my lambs! These bastards thought they were stealing from a witch, but they weren't stealing from a witch, they were stealing from a LION!

"I am a lion." The words came out of my mouth, and as soon as I heard them I knew it was true.

"I am a Lion!" I shouted. The rightness of it hummed through my entire being.

"I AM THE BLACK LION!" I screamed and my vision went red—and then I fell.

Pain flared through my forehead first and then engulfed my whole body as if every cell within me were being scorched to ashes and then reborn one at a time. I thrashed and writhed. I didn't know if it lasted seconds, minutes, hours, or years. I only know that it stopped.

I hung limp in Believer's arms. I wasn't hurting anymore but I felt disjointed and awkward, nothing was working right. Even breathing was different. Everything was new. I felt odd inside and out. It was the same feeling I got when I first came into a new body after dying except I felt changed on the inside as well. I knew that something had changed in my soul and that couldn't be good.

I pushed that thought from my mind and concentrated on using my eyes. I tried to focus and move my hands, but my hands weren't going where I wanted and my vision was blurry. My dress pinched horribly all over. It was tight on me like a child's dress. I could feel that the dress had split up the side, as if I'd grown bigger and busted out of it! Had every single part of me changed!? I hadn't even finished changing from the vampires' bites and now this!

I heard shouting and screams and people speaking in French and Believer and Lucius shouting orders and yelling. A mad riot of noise. It was all too much happening at once for me to make any sense of it. It was all just screaming and noise.

Are we still in France? I thought in total amazement. Had it only been minutes and not years? I twitched trying to get my neck to point in the right direction to see what was happening but I couldn't get my eyes to focus yet.

And then suddenly, there was less noise. No more shouting and yelling in French. That had to be a good sign.

Lucius began yelling, sending someone to fetch my mother.

What have I done to myself now?

My eyes finally focused on Believer's face. He was holding me, frowning fiercely as he stared down into my face and eyes. Believer was always so good at hiding how horrible things were, but this time his face was nakedly grim. If I didn't know better I'd think he was scared.

I stopped looking at his face and stared at the ceiling above me. I managed to reach across myself and touch my arm. My skin felt great before but now it felt even smoother than silk and it was even more sensitive, insanely sensitive.

I heard Lucius's daughter's voice asking if I was hurt. She sounded so concerned about me even though she'd never met me face to face. Did she love me because I did her hair or was her empathy because I cared about her father or because her father cared for me? Or was it just because, no more or less than she'd show for anyone else. Why *did* anyone care about anyone else?

"Believer," I slurred, struggling to get the words out of my new mouth. "Take me someplace private, I need to take my dress off. Take me to the walled garden." I felt the dress cutting into me, tight against my flesh, and I felt other things. Strange things.

"Why do you need to take your dress off?" he asked, his red eyes growing brighter with this new unsettling worry, but he was already walking, taking huge steps and moving us quickly where I wished to go.

"Just take me there," I told him, my voice sounding tired and bitter. I felt it, but I didn't believe it myself yet. I'd have to see it to believe it. Believer walked and I heard the movement of people rushing to follow.

"What's happened!" I heard my mother's anxious voice call out.

"Much," was Believer's vague answer given as he walked. "Please follow us, Mother."

In a minute we were through the back doors off the Cathedral Hall and headed down the main trail that led to a raised circular hill of land in the center of the walled garden. The wedding and birthday celebration were being arranged in the

South Grounds off the new dining hall but the inside Walled Garden wasn't empty either. A small group of ladies were tucked in at the monstrous metal table where my mother and father liked to have tea.

"I will ask them to leave us," Believer said in a soft spoken rumble as we neared the frightened women.

"No love. They're all women, let them stay. Just lay me on the table and you can chase the men away."

He nodded. It was a task he'd gladly do.

I heard the women clucking like a bunch of mother hens and I closed my eyes as Believer laid me down gently onto the metal table then left to order the men following behind us to leave. As soon as I was on the table I felt my mother's hands on my face. Just the feel of her hands made me catch my breath. I kept my eyes closed as I listened to the chattering, horrified voices of the women, all lamenting my condition as if I were a dead body laid on a slab at a morgue.

"O Goddess!" a high shrill voice cried out.

"Www-w*hat?*" Breath. "What happened!? What caused this?"

What? What? What? I'd have to call her "Suup."

"She's been cursed, Cathryn! There's no hope for her. She's demon possessed!" A different voice. Older and gravely. "The Prophet of Doom," I dubbed the voice.

"She's not cursed! Don't say that!" cried the voice of—"Reason."

"Blessed Be! This is terrible!" Some more high-pitched commentary from "Shrilly."

"Is she asleep, my Queen?" Reason asked.

"I don't know." Cathryn sounded as if she were trying hard not to cry.

"Oh, my Queen, I'm so sorry." Sympathy for the mother. "Sympathy" had a sweet quavering voice like a sweet old lady. I bet she looked like a grandmother. I envisioned a silver beehive bun.

"She's even more beautiful now, my Queen." I couldn't help smiling. *Someone out there needs glasses*, I thought. But that was kind of her. I'd call that one "Mercy."

"Should we wake her?" A young voice. I couldn't tell—

"No! No! Don't wake it. Quick. Take my blade! Kill it before it wakes!"

My mother's hands left my face.

Smack! Gasps.

"She's possessed, Cathryn Ann!" A voice spoke from lower, somewhere on the ground. The Prophet of Doom again. "It will be the end of us! You must kill it!"

"Silence!" My mother's voice cracked like a whip. "Hold your fool tongues!" she hissed at all of them.

"Rain. What's happened?"

I opened my eyes and she pulled back in surprise. I saw fear in her eyes. My eyes must be a complete nightmare now. She mastered her fear and leaned over my face again, looking down into my eyes, stroking my cheek.

"What happened, Rain?" she asked gently.

"How bad is it, Mom?" I asked wearily.

"I can't lie. It's bad, my child, but not in the way you think. Now tell me what happened?"

I sat up and looked around the table. The faces of the women staring back at me told me that I was a monster straight from the pit of hell. I'd never seen such fear on the faces of our people. It wasn't just fear, it was terror. I wondered which one was Mercy and which one was Reason because every face held the same expression. It seemed Reason had fled and Mercy had run dry and poor old Sympathy probably just peed her grannie panties. The Prophet was easy to pick out; she was the old witch with a busted lip, lying on the ground.

Believer walked back up to the table, and I turned my eyes on him and saw him frown. Not him too, I thought.

"What happened, Rain?" Cathryn pressed. "Tell me what caused this."

I looked back at her. "I'm not sure, it happened so fast it's hard to know for sure, but I know that I'm not a witch anymore." My voice still sounded the same, if a bit larger. At least there was that.

"How do you know you're not a witch?"

I shrugged. "Is my coven mark still there?" I asked.

"No. The coven mark is gone." She was staring hard at my forehead.

"She's dead then," I said simply. "She must have burned to death. I felt fire go through me when I changed."

"Who's dead, Rain?"

"The Black Witch is dead, and the girl I was along with her."

I watched her raise trembling hands to her mouth and I finally started to get scared. She wished the old me were back and not this monster I'd become. I had to be hideous! Why had Mercy called me beautiful?

"How did the Black Witch die?" Cathryn asked.

For some reason I laughed. What was I supposed to say? I went with the closest thing to the truth I could think to say.

"She was eaten by a Lion."

I saw Believer's eyes staring down at me from behind Cathryn, his intelligent sharp mind studying me and all that I was. I forced myself to smile at him though I wanted to cry.

"Do you still want me?" I asked him.

"Yes, my love. I do," he said and smiled at me.

I felt a pressure in my lungs and around my heart release that I hadn't even know was there and took a full breath of air into my new lungs. I felt acclimated to my new body enough to stand and I rose unsteadily to my feet, standing on the table top. I turned and faced my mother then willed my torn and shredded dress to vanish. I heard the other women around the table gasp but my mother didn't seem too surprised by the tail.

"Well. Turn around girl and let me see it," she said.

"Oh," I said, feeling silly. "Yes ma'am."

My new tail snapped this way and that and moved around like it had a mind of its own. It seemed I could still easily throw it into manual pilot and drive the thing myself if I choose to, but it was doing fine, so I let it be.

"What's it look like, Mom?" I asked.

"You're beautiful," she said simply. "You have a fine line of short hair that follows your spine, from your neck all the way to the tail, but that's the only hair on your body. Just the hair on your head, the line down your spine, and the tail. And you're taller now, your body seems to have changed to match your new form."

I held my arms out and looked at myself in the afternoon sun. I was sparkling faintly, somewhat like Jane and Dan. My vampire-hybrid skin was pale but had a distinctive pale silver cast to it that shimmered mysteriously in the sunlight. It was beautiful all by itself. Everyone's reaction didn't make sense if this was all there was, and they hadn't seen the tail until just now, so why the hell was everyone freaking out the way they were? I spun around to face my mother, my tail cutting back and forth in an agitated "S" pattern behind me as I faced my mother with my hands on my hips.

"What else, Mom? What has everyone so freaked out the second they see me? And why did that old bitch," I jabbed a finger at The Prophet of Doom who was huddled on the ground, "want to push a stake through my heart? What the hell's wrong with me?"

Cathryn frowned and nodded. "All right, Rain, but first promise me you'll stay calm. You need to control yourself better. No more charging around ripping the paint off the walls with your power and scaring our people to death like you did in the dining hall!" She actually yelled at me. She was mad. She stood there and glared at me, with *her* hands on *her* hips, giving *me* the evil eye. She was going totally "Mom" on me.

I felt the uncertainty as it slipped onto my face. Maybe I had gone a bit overboard when I crashed the dining room party. My tail circled around me once and half way again, protectively. I dropped my head. The tip of my tail rubbed under my chin like it was worried about me.

I liked my tail. It was already growing on me.

"Sorry, Mother. Is everyone all right?" I asked, my voice contrite. Submissive.

"Mary doesn't know. The twins are fine, they had a blast, but our two new guests fared far worse than the girls. Mary said that Gannon, the boy with the blue hair, was almost broken. He was already on edge from watching the sacrifice."

"I did not mean to hurt them."

"You're going to have to be more careful, Rain. You're too powerful to act out this way, even if one of your lambs cries out. No more flying off the handle. It's time to grow up. As you said, the Black Witch is dead, the Black Lion has come. So mote it be. Think and act with wisdom." She looked at me and shook her head, like she was still trying to understand what I was while at the same time telling me how to be what I'd become. Weird, but there it was.

"Is this your final form, Rain, or will you continue to change every day for the rest of your life?" she asked wearily.

"I honestly don't know," I answered. "Now please tell me why everyone is looking at me like I'm a nightmare?"

"Promise you won't overreact first."

My tail uncoiled and snapped a few times behind me, expressing my angst, and I took a couple of calming breaths and centered myself.

"I promise with all my heart and soul that I'll do my best to stay calm, Mother. Even if my eyes look like the maggot ridden sockets of the crypt keeper himself. Now what gives?"

"Your eyes are red. And you have horns."

I raised my eyebrows. Then I looked at Believer for some reason, like I didn't quite believe her. He nodded.

I frowned. I hadn't felt horns before when I touched my hair, but I hadn't felt the front of my head. I slowly raised my hands to the side of my head and felt my way up until I found them; above my temples at the top of my hairline on each side of my forehead were horns. They went out about two inches and turned forward and then swept upward about six inches ending in wicked sharp points. Now that I was looking for them I could see them at the upper edges of my periphery vision.

"They're not red or bone white," my mother said. "They're a glossy black at the base and fade to a beautiful shade of blue at the tips. Like your lips. And that's not the only thing that's blue now, my child."

She pointed to my chest and I looked down. My tail stiffened, snapping straight as a board out behind me, as shocked as I was! My nipples were bright blue.

"S-SHIT!" I shouted, staring at the two blue circles of flesh in total disbelief. What the hell had I been thinking!? Then I remembered that Emma liked my blue lips. And so did Jane.

"Oh," I said, much calmer. I studied myself. My legs, my arms. My body did look longer, leaner, and more muscular in a predatory, animal kind of way. And I was curvier. I walked down the length of the table and back toward my mother a few times experimentally, getting a feel for my new form and how it wanted to move. It seemed I swayed a lot more as I walked, and I wondered if it was the "cat" part of what I'd become doing the extra hip action or if it was the vampire part making me more graceful and sensual or if it was some other part—whatever part the horns came from.

I looked down at my mother. She was smiling at me.

"Do you like it?" she asked.

I thought about it. My tail gave me a light jealous slap up side my head and I squinted my eyes at it.

"Fine. I like the tail," I said. It went back behind me cutting happy shapes in the air, and I turned back to my mother. "But the horns!" I whined, then pointed to the ground. "People will react like The Prophet of Doom there when they see me." She was still on the ground looking up at me and Cathryn.

"Forgive me, Princess," she groveled.

"Why the hell would I do that, you old bitch!?" I snapped. "What if Bethany wakes up with horns or a third eye in her forehead or a second set of arms or a mouth on her back with a thousand teeth complete with the voices of the damned echoing up from down inside the bottomless pit of its throat? *What then?*" I demanded. "Would you dare to lay a hand on her as you just dared to kill me?" I glared down at her. She started to open her mouth and I cut her off before she spoke.

"Stop! If you lie to me you will dig your own grave in this garden and pull the earth in on top of yourself, so speak carefully, old woman."

Her grey eyes seemed alert as she tongued her busted lip. "I was surprised, my lady. I beg you, please have mercy on a foolish old woman."

"No," Cathryn said, stepping between us and facing the surprised old woman. "You spoke from your heart. I'm sorry I brought you here, Mother. It was a mistake."

The old woman looked shocked. I was shocked. The Prophet of Doom was Cathryn's mother! And Cathryn had slapped her own mother in the face! For me! And now she was kicking her out of Amen Hale.

I was about to say something when the old woman lurched angrily to her feet. "You ungrateful, horrid girl!" She pressed her mouth together, turning it into an ugly white circle like a dry water hole with a mass of wrinkled gullies running toward it.

Cathryn spoke kindly to the angry old woman. "You still have your condo at Riverbrook Towers, but we no longer have the accounts set up to pay your monthly stipend. I'll have Lucius provide you with enough cash to last till you die, but don't spend it all, Mother. You will not be back, and there will be no more money."

The old woman seethed. She turned away from Cathryn and toward me. "You've stolen my child from me! Now give me back the life that you've taken. Make me beautiful again!" she screeched, spittle flying. Her busted lip ripped further, the yelling straining her paper thin flesh further than it was want to go. Blood ran from her mouth making her look mad and deranged.

"Make me beautiful again and you can *have my daughter!*" she spat the words at me. "But take her and cast me out and I'll curse you till the day I die with all the power I have. I was born on a blackened eve and I've been a witch for eighty-seven years, girl, I know how to make a curse come to pass!" She stared at me like a monster herself, blood dripping from her chin as she gritted her dentures together.

I bent my knees and jumped off the table and SOARED! I must have gone fifteen feet through the air before landing on the other side of them without a sound. Cathryn and her mother didn't move as I stalked up to them, but three of the women at the table broke and ran away.

"Pay my price, demon, and you can have her! I swear I will curse you and that bloody little monster you claim as your child if you don't pay me my price." Her mouth turned up in a wicked smile.

"Oh, Mother." Cathryn started shaking her head and walked away with her face in her hands to be comforted by the other women still at the table. Believer's eyes glowed brightly and a low rumble came from his body.

"You would curse me and my little one?" I asked.

"Yes!" she growled.

"By whose power would you call the curse, mother of my mother?" I asked seriously. "Even you would not dare to voice so vain a prayer to the Almighty White Lion? His curse I fear greatly. If not him, who would you ask then? Would you ask Satan, the Red Dragon, to avenge you?" I paused but she made no reply so I continued with my conjecture. "Perhaps you know of a god of the forest or field that will carry your curse and make war against the Black Lion for the injustice you've endured. Perhaps the Great White Stag or the mighty Golden Eagle or perhaps one of the old gods like Odin or Zeus, Radien or Ra, will they hear your plea for wrath?"

I came closer and noticed that I really was taller now. I stared down into the old woman's eyes from what had to be well over six feet, but the old witch stared right back at me without batting an eye. She *was* evil. Holy shit! She gave *me* the creeps.

"Bargain struck!" I said and let power carry my voice outward and echo it around the garden.

Bargain Struck. Bargain Struck. Bargain Struck. Bargain Struck.

I threw in some wind and a small peal of thunder for effect.

The old monster smiled up at me like a freaking demon. I felt so sorry for Cathryn growing up with her as a mother.

I called my power into her and willed the skeleton of the old hag to straighten and become young and strong and straight and willed the muscles and tissue to stretch along with her spine. The old woman cried out and fell to the ground as the changes came. I filled out her skin and the flesh and even had her real teeth grow back in again. I fleshed her out in every way and made her new and beautiful again, about the age of a twenty-one year old woman. But I did keep some things the same.

She rose to her feet and looked at herself in fascinated glee, and I added the final touch of a beautiful white dress and I put her long golden blonde hair up in an elaborate weave that made her look like a queen. I even gave her matching shoes.

"Acceptable?" I asked as she ran her hands over her face and teeth and touched her breasts.

She gave me a shrewd look and reached her hand up her dress and inspected her personal areas and then bent down and touched her toes twice. After another minute or two of poking and prodding and stretching she looked at me, grinning like the cat that swallowed the canary. "Yes. Acceptable. Bargain struck. My daughter is your mother and nothing to me. Have the bitch," she said as she looked at Cathryn.

"Get out!" Cathryn screamed at her from where she stood with the other women. She was crying.

"And since you have traded me for beauty, take beauty and nothing more!" she cried.

Her mother stalked toward her as if she were the queen of Amen Hale and not Cathryn. "You cannot lie, Cathryn." Her beautiful young face smiled. "Thanks to these girls you've tied yourself to, you truly, truly cannot lie. You promised to give me money. So keep your promise, and give me my money. You said it would be enough cash for me to live until I died."

She smiled and put her arms out and turned in a circle. "As you can see, girl, I will live for a very long time. So make the money you give me be enough to last me the rest of my very long life."

Cathryn laughed hysterically; the other women were all that held her upright. "You traded me, you old fool!" she shouted. "I'm not your child anymore. Don't you remember? I'm nothing to you! I don't owe you anything!"

She started laughing again and her mother balled up her fist like she was about to hit her when Believer rumbled and leaned down, putting his huge head beside Cathryn's.

"Do not touch my mother!" he rumbled, his red eyes blazing.

The young hag stumbled back a step in surprise, looking from Believer to Cathryn then back to me.

Cathryn shouted, "Take your young body and go live on your back like a whore! You've done it before. It's the family business, you know. That's what you told me." Cathryn took a deep breath and straightened. "Just go, you evil monster, go and never come back."

I called an arch of stone to spring up from the ground about ten feet behind Cathryn's mother. A gateway opened to the arch just beyond the wall of Amen Hale, and through the open portal we could see two very surprised soldiers standing guard, looking in on our ugly family drama.

The young hag looked at Cathryn and me, and I could see that she regretted not playing her cards better than she had, but a smile spread across the pretty face. She certainly was beautiful. That Cathryn's looks came from her mother was obvious. She threw her head back and laughed but then stopped, coughing and wheezing for a moment. She doubled over, trying to catch her breath. When she rose up she looked at me with murderous eyes.

"You bitch! You didn't give me young lungs, did you!?" she seethed.

"You asked for beauty, not youth. I gave as I was asked. Payment *was accepted*," I reminded her. "Your lungs, your heart, and your poor eighty-six year old brain will not last too long, but enjoy the beauty of the flesh while you can. And thank you for your daughter. I will love her every day with all my heart and soul, like you should have."

She stood there and seethed for a moment then turned and started toward the arch, but she ranted as she walked. "You'll pay for this!" she shouted then coughed. "Try to trick me! I'll curse that bloody monster you call your child and she'll be dead in ten days. She'll rot before your eyes and it will be all your—"

She was already through the arch and ten steps past the soldiers when she froze. She turned, her eyes wide and staring. One lurching, zombie-like step at a time she moved back toward the gateway.

"Help me, Please!" she begged of the soldier on the right, reaching for him, but he backed away from her like she had the plague.

"Someone help me! I don't want to go back in there! I don't want to go! They're going to kill me!" She wept toward the other soldier on the other side, but he ignored her, smiling as he looked past her and back to us on our side. He waved at us.

I saw that he was looking at me and I saw his eyes go wide when he finally got through looking at my body and met my eyes that were staring at him. He took a step back. Then took two more steps. And then he turned and ran.

As the pleading, begging, beautiful zombie of Cathryn's mother walked onto our side I let the stone arch fade back into the ground again. Cathryn's mother shuffled off into the garden and stopped in an open patch of soil within sight of where we stood. She knelt down and started digging with her bare hands into the wet earth, crying and begging as she dug.

I walked over to my mother and knelt in front of her, wrapping my arms around her waist. I kept my head tilted back so I didn't accidentally gore her, but it was such a pain. I wanted to push my face into her chest and cry but I couldn't. My tail wrapped around Cathryn for me, making it a little better because I could feel with the tail so it was almost like holding her with my arms.

"I'm so sorry, Mom. I'm sorry she was your mother. I'm sorry she didn't love you more. I'm sorry I killed her. I'm sorry I wasn't more careful with my magic. I warned her not to lie to me. I'm so sorry."

She touched my head and pressed it up against her, carefully. I let her guide me and I cried.

"I'm not sorry, my child. It was an honest bargain, truly struck and paid in full. Although she was a fool to accept payment based on a couple of toe touches."

I snickered and so did Cathryn. And then we both laughed out loud together, as twenty feet away, her mother and my mother's mother dug her own grave and wept for mercy that would only come from the cold wet earth.

Ferrand

Over Cooked Fish

FERRAND WAS SHUTTING his phone as he walked up.

"How are they?" asked Kaisser.

Another man vacated the seat beside Kaisser, making room, and Ferrand dropped into the chair with a muttered "merci." They were facing a huge bank of monitors displaying video of the encounter with Black Rain. Arnaud Kaisser's hair was snow white, as were his eyebrows, mustache, ear, nose, and arm hair. Ferrand's hair was the same, blasted white. Most of the people in the warehouse had the same color changes, but the ones who'd been the closest to Black Rain were completely whited out.

Ferrand had just finished speaking to the hospital, receiving the latest update on the two dozen people who had passed out when the warehouse was flooded with blinding, white light from Black Rain as she collapsed, shaking and thrashing about on the floor.

"Everyone is now awake except for Miss Dupair, and the doctors seem to think she will be fine. So far there seems to be no lasting health problems other than the change in hair color and eye color. They are doing tests on those who were the closest and they want both of us to come in as soon as possible."

Kaisser looked away from the monitor to stare at Ferrand's eyes, which were still brown.

"I don't understand how your eyes are fine and you were with her more than the rest of us."

Ferrand looked at Mr. Kaisser's unnatural whited out irises. An hour ago they were coal black and now a pale round wafer of gray was all that kept him from being nothing but a black pupil floating in a big white field.

"I kept my eyes closed and looked away when she began to shine like the sun."

Arnaud Kaisser grunted. "Well, take a look and see what you missed, Ferrand." He pointed to the monitor in front of him. It showed an image of Black Rain, screaming in horrible pain, her eyes squeezed tight, and on her head were a set of what appeared to be horns.

"That's not all." Kaisser spoke to one of the nearby computer technicians who cued up the video he wanted. "Watch this. This was taken with a thermal imaging camera. Her temperature was human when she walked in but watch the video."

He motioned to the tech who hit a key to start the video. Ferrand watched the gateway open and the outline of two shapes walk out of the opening. One was human sized and the other a much larger shape and cooler, with less red and more blue, Believer, her cloud man husband. They stepped into the room and then as he watched the shape of Black Rain became warmer as she looked toward the gathered spectators.

Then she grew even hotter and the camera outline of her body went completely red and she collapsed. The red shape thrashed about on the ground, squirming and writhing. He hadn't seen this himself at the time, but he could see himself in the field of the camera now, the outline of his blue and red image off to one side crawling away on his hands and knees.

It lasted only a minute and then the red image cooled to an image that resembled the normal blue and red of a human shape and then the large shape of the cloud man scooped up the limp form off the floor. The video played for a little longer and then stopped, showing a side shot of the cloud man carrying the body in his arms.

"Zoom in on the tail," Kaisser directed the techs, and an outlined section expanded to fill the screen. "Do you see it?" Kaisser asked Ferrand.

"Yes." Ferrand could see the red line from her butt running down to her feet. "Horns and a tail. Did she survive whatever happened?" Ferrand asked.

"We believe that she did," Kaisser said. "There are a hundred different theories going around about what this might mean, but some people are thinking that this was her true form all along, and when she lost her temper she lost her disguise along with it. A demon hiding inside a girl?" Kaisser raised his bushy eyebrows.

Ferrand laughed. "Simple minded idiots." He looked at Kaisser. "You don't believe that foolishness, do you?"

"No, I don't believe it," Kaisser said calmly. "But tell me why you think they are the idiots."

"Because they are scared little children!" he answered the older man angrily. "Because they are religious fools who want to forget all the facts. This," he pointed at the monitor, "is a young girl who took some pills that gave her and a group of other mentally disturbed teens the ability to use parts of their minds in ways the rest of us cannot. That is a fact Arnaud. A fact is not open for debate. There are no gray edges to consider. It is simple. This young girl thought she was a witch so she changed herself into a witch. Obviously she thinks she's this creature now so she changed herself again. It's the same as the girl who can fly and the two who turned themselves into vampires and the boy who starts fires. You've seen the girl Arnaud, she's insane, just like all the children in the drug study. Remember the report we have from Wednesday at the doctor's office. When this first started, she burned right there in the doctor's office and made herself a new body. And then she made herself into a pillar of fire after the limo was destroyed. So even this is not new. Her shape is new but what she's done is not."

Kaisser seemed impressed with the logic of it. "So you don't think she's a demon?" he asked, but this time it had the sound of a question he asked for himself and not for his job.

"Of course not, Arnaud. I spent time with the girl and spoke to her. She might be the most frightening and powerful person on the planet, but she's just a young woman. A teenage girl. Nothing more. When I met her she was frustrated and angry and worried about her people, and worried about having to kill our people if we did not give her people back. I don't think she wanted to hurt anyone; she just wanted this sorry business done with."

Kaisser eyed Ferrand with an odd expression. "You seem to be quite an outspoken advocate for the young lady now. Are you taken by her power in some way? The same has happened to other men who have met her and the others there in Amen Hale. Do you feel any lingering feelings toward the girl?"

Ferrand laughed at the suggestion. His voice was bitter when he spoke. "I assure you, the ten minutes I spent alone with Black Rain were not pleasant and I do not want to ever see her again if I can help it. I've given my report about what happened there, Kaisser."

Kaisser smiled under his bushy white mustache. "You understand that I had to ask."

Ferrand ignored the weak apology. "What happens now, sir? Is the time for rational decisions ruled by logic behind us? Does one plus one now equal a fish? Will the ministry go mad with stories of demons and begin the kind of religious debate that will only make a mess into a disaster?"

Kaisser shook his head. "I don't know. I told them it was madness to let that crowd of people into the room. Some of them saw her horns and they are already talking, Ferrand. We've already had a call from the Vatican. The Pope himself has asked to see the video." Arnaud Kaiser sat back in his chair beside the younger man and sighed.

"I wish we'd simply left them alone and not troubled them. This is a mess that I would rather watch on TV as it happened in another country. We are French, dammit!" he declared indignantly. "We avoid the messes the rest of the world likes to play in. We try to get along not *cause* the problems," Kaisser concluded.

Ferrand gave one weary regretful nod. He certainly wished they'd left the men from Amen Hale alone to buy their groceries in peace.

"Do you think she will be angry? Perhaps blame us for this disaster?"

Ferrand nodded.

"Do you think she will attack us or perhaps make good on her threats against the President or the Prime Minister or their families?" Kaisser sat up, his voice growing alarmed, but when Ferrand answered his voice was flat, tired, and certain.

"No, sir. She has her men back and that was what she wanted."

Kaisser gave him a doubtful look. "How can you be so certain she will not return for a little payback?"

"She seemed a simple girl and she wanted simple things," Ferrand said then went a little further to help make his point. "Sir. I think if the whole world went to hell and the last glass of water on earth were in France she would not come here to drink it. I believe she is done with France. We have been very poor hosts, sir." He met the other man's bleached out gaze. "I think we should delete the video, burn the pictures, and deny the meeting ever took place and pray that she does not come back." That said, Ferrand stood up.

"Have a good evening, Mr. Kaisser. My wife is cooking dinner. Her email described some horrible seafood creation. I'm going home to enjoy it." He began to walk away.

"You can't leave now! Are you mad!?" Kaisser yelled at the man's departing back. "We have work to do here, Ferrand! Ferrand!"

Ferrand ignored him and kept walking, his mind on which wine to buy on the way home. He'd have to ask the proprietor what went well with overcooked fish.

The Powers That Be

Where is Superman?

THE PRESIDENT WATCHED as the old woman pulled the earth in on top of herself. Techs had already edited the video and the scene jumped to the last few handfuls of soil, drug in by one arm that jutted up out of the ground. The six people in the room watched as the arm kept moving in jerky twitches, covering the face of the woman until it stiffened and went still. The fingers of the hand pointed down to where the body lay beneath the ground.

"That's got to be the most horrible thing I've ever seen," he said as he stared at the monitor.

Satellites, spy planes, and drones constantly aimed their powerful cameras at Amen Hale and this afternoon their ever watchful eyes had recorded the happenings in the garden. The video of Black Rain walking up and down the length of the table completely nude, showing her horns and tail and everything else, had certainly made for interesting viewing. Lip readers and multiple camera angles had made it possible for them to put together the conversation, and they knew the why's, what's, and basic reasons behind what they'd seen happen between Queen Cathryn, Cathryn's elderly mother, and Black Rain, but that didn't change the horror of watching it on the screen even if it seemed somewhat justified, or at the very least self inflicted.

There were only six people in the room, the President, Samuel Fisk, Cheryl Watson, David Lansing, General Gates, and Samuel Appontas, the newly appointed head of the FBI.

"Who in their right mind even tries to cut a deal with something that has horns?" Fisk asked. There was not enough air in the room for levity after what they'd just watched, and Fisk wasn't trying to make a joke. He was serious.

"What now?" Fisk asked the President.

"Seal the damn place off, that's what we do!" Gates suggested gruffly. "Just don't let anyone else in there. And if anyone comes out we hold them so they don't go to the press."

Cheryl Watson, one of his inside circle of advisors and his chief speech writer and spin doctor, spoke up. "What we just saw can't get out. We have to be certain that every scrap of this video is accounted for and every copy hidden away. You saw what she did for that old woman. If people think they can get a new young body or maybe even eternal life from this girl, the chaos would be impossible to contain. Just watching that old woman go from a withered crone to the plumb of youth sent shivers down my spine."

Cheryl was an old woman herself and looked like someone's grandmother, silver haired and somewhat wizened with age even though she was as tough as nails with a mind sharp as a razor. She looked back to the monitor with its frozen image of the dead hand thrust up out of the ground and experienced a very different kind of shiver. "But Fisk hit the nail on the head. You don't cut deals with anyone who has horns." She gave Fisk a grim faced nod.

"Hopefully she'll take the Queen's advice," David Lansing said, "and keep a better handle on her temper in the future. Cathryn really laid into her hard."

Fisk laughed. "You think crazy Cathryn's going to help keep her in line? Why did she yell at her, David?" He gave the other man a condescending glare, calling him an idiot with the look on his face. Fisk was well on his way toward one of his temperamental rants. "The lady was angry because she frightened the two new kids, not for the rest of the shit the girl did. Mommy Dearest was fine with the human sacrifice this afternoon and putting fifty people in France into the hospital and letting her daughter prance around naked on a table like a stripper before the two of them watched 'young' granny bury herself alive. Oh! And momma's little girl looks like a demon from hell now which she seemed to be quite happy about!" Fisk reached full volume as he got to his last sentences. "Shit! If I thought it would work, I'd say kill the lot of them! Bomb it, burn it, nuke the whole damn place into a sea of glass!"

"Give it a rest, Sam!" The President said firmly. "We are not attacking these people, and that's final! It doesn't do any good to drop bombs on people who don't die. Attacking them is not an option."

"I agree, Mr. President," General Gates concurred quickly. "And if we can't kill them and we can't get them to move, then the only other option is to live with them as best we can. We need to start thinking long term and do our best to get along with these crazy kids. And that's *exactly* what they are, a bunch of kids playing make believe. If all this shit had happened twenty years ago, before our standards went to hell, we'd have Wonder Woman and Superman and Captain America running around instead of monsters. You'd have some nice young man wearing a pair of stupid blue tights with a red cape standing in your office right now, asking real respectfully what he could do to serve his country instead of a bunch of witches starting their own country and eating people alive."

"Damn, Gates," Cheryl said, flipping out her note pad and scribbling away, "that was actually a keen observation. These days with kids living on nothing but horror movies, vampire books, and occult garbage, trashy music, and internet porn. I can use that. And the Superman's dead angle is beautiful. Teen idols are disgusting these days. Little whores or rapper thugs that act like animals." She was scribbling away as she spoke. "Blame everyone *but* the kids. We blame society, blame degrading values, blame the pills that these kids took without knowing what they were, villainize Dr. Burgis and paint the kids as struggling victims." She raised her head and looked around the table.

"Any other ideas, gentlemen, or has Gates got all the brains today?"

The General chuckled.

Lansing spoke up. "Nothing we say will matter once people get to see Black Rain with her horns and tail. We could parade a team of priests and doctors out and have them swear up one side and down the other that she's just a girl, but the second the public laid their eyes on some video like what we just watched they'd pitch it all and go wild. Hell, I'm trying real hard to keep it together right now after seeing all that. You heard what she said, this girl thinks she's a god now! She's calling herself the 'Black Lion' and comparing herself to Odin and Zeus. And if she thinks she's a god then what does that really mean? Let's just think about that for a second. Shit!" Lansing stood and started to pace while the others in the room watched him and shared concerned looks between them until Cheryl chipped in.

"Actually, David, you make a damn good point. Well done, you get a star. You have brains today as well." She started scribbling in her pad again.

"What damn good point did I make?!" David snapped, thinking he was being calmed or placated. He stopped his pacing to glare at Cheryl as she scribbled in her pad.

She spoke while she scribbled without looking up. "What you said is spot on, David. We need to minimize Black Rain as much as we possibly can and try to move her into the background. And we need to water down the whole 'god' angle as quickly as possible. We can cue up that old Fox news video she shot on the front porch of her trailer and play that part again where she tells everyone she doesn't want people lighting candles or bowing down to her and the part where she says she's just a girl. She doesn't look like that anymore, but that's hardly common knowledge yet, and if it becomes common knowledge and some video gets out with her new form it will make people doubt what they're seeing. They'll think the video is faked. We need to focus on the others and talk about them, perhaps focus more on Queen Cathryn and King Cornelius. Play up the historical angle and the fact that he's a descendent of Nathan Hale. He and Cathryn look very good on camera and they are human faces we can use instead of Black Rain and her new look." Cheryl shuddered.

David smiled and jumped in, instantly won over and excited to have some productive direction and even a crumb of what seemed honest praise.

"And there's Sky and Ryan out there flying around today, making news." He smiled at Cheryl. "Those two look fantastic, and they can draw some of the attention away from the ugly ones. And David and Dana have a fantastic back story; we can focus on those two as well." He dropped back into his seat, ready to rejoin the effort and add his two cents.

"Excuse me." Appontas piped up. "I know the political spin is an important part of keeping people calm, but what are we going to do about the wedding? Remember, there's a wedding tonight in Amen Hale for those two kids they took in this morning, and we need to decide what to do. Do we let the parents and the rest of the guests go to Amen Hale or not? And what happens if the witches insist? Do we resist with force or not? Right now there are nearly fifty people gathered at the Ainsley residence waiting for some magical portal to open so they can go to their daughter's wedding."

They talked and agonized but settled on a course of action. The guests would be searched and stripped of all cameras and recording devices before going and only those with a close and valid connection to the bride and groom would be allowed to go. An FBI photographer would take the wedding photos and other agents would go in to make sure the "American citizens" returned home safely and didn't get lost in the garden.

With the crises of government, the President was meeting with the press off and on throughout the day, but he'd dodged, deflected, and danced around almost every question concerning the situation in Amen Hale. All day and most of yesterday he'd given out nothing more than the most basic information and reassurances, but that would end tonight at 9 p.m.

His press secretary had already made the announcement earlier that day and Cheryl and her speech writers were busy, turning the seeds of General Gates' ideas into the heart of an hour-long special Presidential Address to the Nation. The people of the United States and most of the world would be tuned in and listening, ready to hear what the leader of the free world had to say about witches, flying girls, magic pills, rumors of human sacrifices and sexual abuse, gods and demons, and everything in between.

"Where is Superman?"

The first three words in the speech would set the tone.

Blame society, blame declining values, blame poor role models, blame the doctor and the pills, but don't blame the kids—that was the plan. Containment was the destination. Spin was the engine. The world was the vehicle. And the President of the United States of America was the man behind the wheel.

Bethany Grave

Kickin' My Own Ass!

BETHANY OPENED HER eyes, happy to find that she was in her own bed. She stretched and snuggled down into the sheets and pillows for a second, enjoying the feel of her warm, comfortable bed and the super soft sheets for a moment. She reached up and rubbed her face and ran a hand up and through her hair, *all clean*. She wasn't surprised. Rain had cleaned her up and put her in bed. Good! She hated showers.

She felt good. She noticed her pretty new bracelet and wondered why it was put on her when she was asleep and if it were a birthday gift. With a happy groan, Bethany rolled out of bed and trudged into the bathroom and then into the smaller toilet room. She hiked her dress up and sat down and started to pee when she saw something black, like the end of a velvety rope, dangling down from right above her head.

She reached up and grabbed it and felt her own hand around the thing. It was a weird sensation. She grabbed it with both hands which felt even weirder; she could feel her own hands around the velvet rope.

The rope twitched. Like it was alive.

"That is *so* weird," she pronounced. She squinted at the thing, set her arms, and gave it a good hard yank.

Her butt came off the seat and she pitched face first onto the floor where she sprawled in a heap, butt in the air.

Bethany screamed in pain and surprise, felt behind herself and wrapped both hands around the thing, right at the base where it connected. She wrenched hard at it and screamed and the tip of the tail whacked her upside the head.

Bethany pulled again, screamed again, got whacked again. Twice, right upside the head.

Bethany tugged and twisted again, screamed again, got whacked again. Three times.

Bethany paused before she yanked, pulled, tugged, or twisted again. She lay there on the floor sniffling with her butt in the air, both hands still wrapped about the base of her tail. She hurt! Her butt hurt! And—her poor *tail* hurt! She looked at it as it quivered in anticipatory dread in the air above her, waiting for the next painful yank.

She was still eyeing the thing, panting and freaked as Sky Dragon burst into the bathroom.

"Bethame!" he shouted and rushed to where she lay on the bathroom floor but stopped and stared down at her and her "tail" in shocked surprise.

Bethany looked up at him then realized she was exposed and rushed to pull her dress down so she wasn't showing her bottom. The tail cooperated and dropped down so the dress would cover her butt, but it was long enough that the end still stuck out from the bottom of her dress and waved about down by her feet.

Sky Dragon reached down and helped her up to her feet.

Bethany stood there for a moment then said very matter of factly, "I got a tail."

"I saw that," he replied calmly.

"I need a minute," she said.

Sky Dragon backed up three steps out of the little toilet room and Bethany shut the door.

Sky Dragon listened outside the door anxiously. He heard some sniffling.

"Weird," he heard Bethany say.

"Oh man, that's just freaky," she said after another minute.

"Oh."

"Hey! Careful."

"Hehehe." A sweet little giggle.

After another four minutes of odd "Princess to tail" dialogue the door opened again.

"My Dragon, could you bring me my knife?" she asked.

Sky Dragon's eye ridges shot up in alarm. "Bethame! I really don't know if you should cut your tail off. It would probably hurt. A whole lot!"

"I'm not cutting my tail off. Silly Dragon!" She laughed and it seemed as if her tail laughed with her, flailing about merrily.

He watched as her tail reached up and stroked the side of her face affectionately and Bethany tilted her head to the side and trapped it between her face and her shoulder in a hug of sorts before it squirmed out and away. Bethany noticed Sky Dragon staring at her and frowned.

"What?" she asked self-consciously.

"I didn't think you liked the tail," Sky Dragon said cautiously.

Bethany rolled her eyes. "Oh! That was before I knew it was *my* tail," she said, like that explained everything.

"I need my knife. I'm gonna cut a hole in my dress," she explained again. "For my tail." The tail waved at him as if it were saying "hi" and Bethany looked at it and smiled like a proud momma. It wrapped around her middle with the tip coming up her back and down over her shoulder and resting across her chest. It was as if her tail was giving her a hug.

"Now this is a really cool birthday present," she said as she stroked the tail and smiled.

Sky Dragon noticed something change on the dress while she spoke. He pointed to Bethany's dress. "Bethame, I think your dress already has a place for your tail. Look at your dress, my Princess."

"What?" Bethany grabbed at her dress and pulled it around until she saw the perfectly formed opening that looked like it was custom made for her brand new tail.

"How the heck did that happen!?" she exclaimed. "That wasn't there before! It wasn't like that when I woke up. Did you do magic on it, My Dragon?" She looked at him and he shook his dragon head no.

"Well, I know Rain couldn't have done it, she didn't even know I needed my dress fixed."

Bethany's tail dipped down and came up inside the dress and peeked out the hole and Bethany tugged and shimmied it into place with a big happy smile.

"It's perfect!" Bethany chirped.

Sky Dragon was smiling but his eyes were on the bracelet on Bethany's wrist. He was pretty sure it only held eight kisses now. If the tail was a kiss, that is. He wondered what would happen next.

Mary and Emma

Easy Listening

EMMA HAD TAKEN one of the maids with her power earlier that morning and now the woman loved her, only there was a problem—she was married. Hanna already told Emma that she intended to leave her husband to serve her in *every* possible way, and that she hadn't been happily married anyway, but Cathryn insisted on meeting with her and her husband before she would allow it.

Minutes before the couple arrived to meet with her in the Green Room, Cathryn had to leave to take care of an emergency and a servant told Mary that Cathryn placed her in charge of the meeting and the judgment that would come of it. Mary didn't want to go downstairs and meet the couple in the Green Room or the Writing Parlor with everyone milling about because of how dangerous it would be for

Emma. And she didn't want to use Cathryn's room with her gone, so she had both of them come up to her bedroom of all places.

"Please! Just let me hide in the bathroom, Mary!" Emma begged.

"Hell no. That would be like saying you did something *wrong* and you didn't. I want you out here in the room to hear every word that these two say. If this woman is going to be sleeping with the woman I love, then the woman I love needs to know who she's sleeping with. You can't just touch her and know her like me, you need to hear it, so that is what you'll do. Now sit!" Mary insisted.

Emma ended up sitting in the middle of the bed looking like a big sexy spider in the middle of her web.

Once Hanna and Frank arrived, Emma apologized to Frank over and over until Mary finally told her that she loved her but to shut up and be silent. So she sat on the bed and watched as Mary, Frank, and Hanna sat at the one little table in their bedroom while Mary played the part of all-knowing, all-seeing, mystical, magical, white haired witch marriage counselor. It was wild because neither of them could lie while Mary held their hands, and Mary knew all the junk in both their trunks and wasn't shy about sharing.

Frank and Hanna's relationship had grown distant over the past few years, arguing and becoming cold and mean to each other and Mary made them face some of their larger issues honestly. Despite their problems it was obvious that Hanna and Frank still loved each other and wanted to stay together.

Emma was more than impressed as she listened to Mary speak to this older couple with total confidence, understanding concepts and problems she shouldn't have had any knowledge of as a seventeen-year-old girl. Emma was sure Mary was calling on the collected wisdom of the other people she'd touched as she dealt with the Dantzs' issues.

The whole face-to-face meeting only lasted about twenty minutes and then Mary had Hanna and Emma wait out in the hall while she spoke with Frank inside the room. Mary made Frank write down a list of ten things he was to never do again and five things he was to start doing right away. This bit of instruction—hard, solid, and actionable (*and on a list*) was exactly what Frank needed. Many times he'd spoken with his wife about their problems, but like many women, Hanna wouldn't tell him what she really wanted or what pleased her or what displeased her—she expected him to "know" and snatch the answers out of thin air or be smart enough to figure it out. The advice he received from friends was never acted upon because he either did not consider the source reliable or he did not transfer the information to an actionable list.

Mary knew Frank Dantz. She knew the way his mind worked as well as her own. Frank was a list man. He made lists and worked his list and lived his life based on his lists of things to do. Mary knew exactly what to say to Frank, how to say it, and how to package the instructions for the way Frank's mind worked. After spending fifteen minutes alone with Frank she left the room and walked out into the hallway where Emma and Hanna waited for her.

"How'd it go, Princess Mary?" Hanna asked right away.

"Good," Mary answered. "And in short order you'll be a very happy wife. But now it's your turn to make Frank into a happy husband. There are some things that you will change in how you treat me." Mary shook her head. "I mean treat Frank—Frank. Sorry." She closed her eyes and reached over and touched Emma, taking calming breaths with her eyes closed.

"You okay, Mary?" Emma asked, worried for her.

Mary straightened up. "Yeah, Emms, I'm fine. Frank's shit was involved and lengthy; Hanna's will be simple."

She looked at Hanna. "Just two very simple things, both easily done, but neither are things that are natural for your nature."

Mary put on her "scary witch" face as she walked over and gripped Hanna's chin with her hand and looked into her surprised face. "But we will change your nature, Hanna Dantz," Mary told her firmly. "Only two things need be done but they must be done well. First, you will tell Frank you love him at least three times each day."

"But why? Frank knows that I love him," Hanna argued instantly, her back stiffening as if she'd been asked to do something unconscionable. Irrational. Illogical. Something about the word was caught in her mind. A mental hang-up.

Mary knew that Hanna could easily tell Frank he was lazy or call him a sorry bastard a hundred times a day without batting an eye, but telling him she loved him (and she did) was either too frightening or redundant to her for some reason.

"Hanna," Mary said sternly, "I gave Frank a huge list of things to do but I know he's going to try like hell to do everything on that list. I'm touching you right now and I know that you have absolutely no intention of telling him that you love him three times each day." Mary's skin began to glow with a soft green luminescence and her eyes shone brightly, her fingers tightening their hold on Hanna's frightened face and her voice filling with power as she spoke.

"Emma loves you, Hanna, and so do I, but I love all of our people, including Frank. I'm going to go right back in there and tell him you want to stay a frigid bitch and I'll have him leave your ass if you don't do exactly as I say because it would be a kindness to the both of you. A kindness. Do you understand me, Child of Amen Hale?"

Emma wanted to scream, but she forced herself to stay quiet and stand still and watch.

"Please don't!" Hanna managed to say while Emma held tight onto her bottom jaw. "I hear and I will obey!"

"Three times a day," Mary repeated and Hanna nodded. "Second, you will touch him five times each day when he does not expect you to touch him. You will count these touches because you will lie to yourself and tell yourself that one is two and two is five." Mary held out a string that looked like it had been cut from the bottom of the blinds in their room. Which it had.

"Keep this with you at all times and make a knot each time you touch him. If you fall behind, catch up the next day, but one way or another, come the end of the week, come the end of every week," Mary added firmly, "I want thirty-five knots in this cord. Each touch doesn't have to be sex, but it does have to be something intimate. Walk up behind him and touch him on the back of his neck, Frank likes that. Or walk up behind him and rub his back while he's doing the dishes, cuddle with him on the couch while he reads his stupid cookbooks, or hold his hand as you wait in line together to eat a meal or just lean upon him in an intimate way. Or go ahead and make it sexual and give him a kiss when he least expects it or surprise him and step into the shower with him. He fantasizes about *that* every damn time he steps into the shower."

Mary's face was filled with overflowing frustration as if Frank's emotions had seeped into her bones. As she spoke she even mimed the motions as if they were forever burned into her memory.

"He always asks if you want to join him as he walks to the shower. You usually don't reply, and if you do it's not nice, so he goes in alone. He reaches in and turns the water on and undresses while the water warms up. He steps in. He turns and faces the shower door and says the same sad words *every single time*. 'Maybe tonight,' he says and stares at the door. But 'tonight' never comes, does it, Hanna? You always wait till he's done and then you take *your* shower—*alone*." Mary growled angrily.

Hanna broke away from Mary's hand and rushed into the room where they'd left Frank, working and refining his to do list.

Mary let out a big sigh of relief and took Emma's hand in hers, as if she wanted to follow her own advice, and the two of them sat down there in the hall beside Mary's bedroom door and leaned their backs against the wall. Inside the room they could hear the faint noises of the maid and her husband having passionate "make up" sex in their bedroom—probably on their bed.

"Thank you, Mary," Emma told her.

Mary stifled a giggle and Emma's smile widened as the noise level in the bedroom increased. The last of the clothes were off, the sounds clearly telling the state of things between Hanna and Frank. They both pressed their ears to the door, listening to the sounds of the couple's pleasure with happy smiles.

Sky

Curiosity

IT WAS A perfect day. Our little private island had been wonderful with a nice breeze blowing off the ocean the whole time to keep us cool, and we had no waves, the sea on our side of the island was crystal clear and glassy flat. Ryan loved snorkeling and we swam for hours. We were so wiped out that we didn't even make love when we got back to the beach.

We laid out our towels under a couple of palms and went to sleep in the warm sun, and then when we got up we just cuddled and talked. We talked and talked. Ryan wanted to know all about me and he asked questions and laughed at my stories and told me stories too about his school and his family and friends and his church.

Ryan told me he wanted us to go to church this Sunday and that it was time for us to start worshiping God together and I liked that too. He said that a lot of what he thought he knew about God he wasn't totally sure about anymore, but he said he was sure that he loved God and that he wanted to serve and worship him. I did too. We'd taken one last dip in the ocean to get the sand off before grabbing our stuff and flying home.

We landed on our little balcony, but the door was locked from the inside so we flew down and walked up to the front door.

"Greetings, Lord Ryan, Lady Sky. It's so very good to have you home again." The doorman's broad smile and warm welcome seemed perfect. The doorman was dressed in a snappy grey suit and he had a younger boy, about ten years old, who stood at attention beside him dressed the same. The boy was staring at us with huge, amazed blue eyes. He was so cute in his little man suit.

I reached out and pushed his blond hair back into place, and he smiled for me.

"What's your name?" I asked him.

He blushed and seemed tongue tied and the other man helped him.

"His name is Jasper, my lady, he's my boy," he said proudly.

"You're so handsome," I told the blue-eyed boy. He made me wonder what our little boy or girl would look like. The big doorman and little doorman held both doors wide for us as Ryan and I went inside.

"Lord Ryan, Lady Sky," a woman in the foyer greeted.

She curtsied as we passed by and walked into the crowded entry hall that was filled with people sitting in chairs and lounging on the couches talking and even playing some board games, but as soon as we came in everyone turned and WOW did they STARE! Eyes were popping out as Ryan and I walked in. We were still in our swimsuits and I had my long hair in braids and we both had our golden tans.

"My Lady, may I ask where you and Lord Ryan went?" a girl my age asked as we came close to her and her group of friends.

"We flew to the Bahamas. It was great," I told her with a smile.

Ryan dug into the little bag he carried and came out with a beautiful conch shell and handed it to her with his own smile, and she practically melted onto the floor, but other people were already asking questions, lots of questions. Ryan didn't try to answer them; he took my hand in his and kept us moving past everyone crowding around to the stairs.

"Shower," he said as we mounted the stairs.

"Yes, please," I agreed. I was beached out and tired the way only swimming in the ocean can make you. I was ready for a shower and somehow I didn't really feel like talking to all those people who wanted so badly to talk to me.

It was strange. Before I had Ryan, I would have been happy to talk myself to death with anyone who would talk to me that didn't work for my mother or father.

A cook, a gardener, a garbage man, even the girl at the drive-through window at McDonalds. But now, not so much. I wondered if I was getting stuck up now that I had my handsome husband and constantly having all this bowing and the "My Ladies" everyone kept saying every time I walked by.

Maybe I was getting stuck up? Probably. *Yuck!* I didn't want to be stuck up like my mother and father. But I didn't think Ryan had a stuck up bone in his body and he hadn't talked to them either.

So maybe I wasn't stuck up after all—maybe?

I didn't feel stuck up. But if I became stuck up, would I know that I was stuck up when I became stuck up or would it just sneak up on me and get me? I didn't know.

We turned the corner at the top of the stairs where the Royal Bedrooms were and saw Mary and a girl with short, spiky black hair and tight white pants sitting in the hall outside one of the rooms.

"Hey, Mary, what's up, girl?" Ryan called to her.

"Shit!" Mary shouted as soon as she saw us, then rushed to cover the other girl's eyes with her hands. She whispered into her ear.

Ryan pulled us to a stop, watching the two cautiously.

"Mary. You okay?" he asked.

"Yeah!" she shouted. "Just be careful as you walk by and *don't touch Emma.* You and Sky can't touch her. EVER!"

"Why?" I asked.

"And what the heck happened to her?" Ryan asked as he looked at her. "You okay over there, Emma?"

Emma turned her head in Ryan's direction, but Mary kept her eyes covered.

"No way, Emma, don't look at them," Mary cautioned her. "They just got back from the beach and they're in their swimsuits and they look way too yummy. So very yummy!" Mary's green eyes stared at us and sparkled like two green jewels filled with sparkly glowing neon. It was scary.

"Mary, you and Emma stay put, right there, and we'll just—*ease* on by," Ryan said.

"Kay," Mary replied with a smile, but her irises were still electric green circles.

We flattened ourselves up against the wall and began to scoot by. Mary kept her hand over Emma's eyes.

"You're so damn lucky you're gay," Mary told Emma as she eyed us both.

"And why's that?" Emma laughed under Mary's hand.

Wow! Emma had some fantastic teeth now. And black lips! Her whole body was changed!

Mary followed us with her eyes. "Because right now you'd only be having seizures over Sky in her little stringy bikini, but I'm being tortured by both of them.

And Ryan's wearing a Speedo! Damn! They even smell like the ocean. I bet if we licked them they'd taste like *salt!*"

"Let's run!" Ryan shouted and we ran for our hot, salty, little lives down the hallway and into our room where we both slammed the door shut behind us. Ryan and I went to lock the door, but there were no locks on these doors!

"Lean on it!" he suggested and I joined him as we pressed our backs up against the bedroom door as if we expected them to bust the door down, charge in, and lick the salt right off us. And other stuff.

Ryan was leaning on the door, staring off into space, his face confused and worried by what had just happened, but I was curious.

I leaned over and—*licked* his shoulder.

"Hey! What was that?" Ryan asked with a small surprised and half worried smile on his face.

I licked my lips and considered for a moment, then nodded in happy surprise. "She was right, I can taste the salt!" I smiled at him.

Ryan looked at me for a second with the "you crazy girl" look on his face and I frowned. He wasn't supposed to look at me that way.

I felt him pull the tie string on the side of my bikini.

"My turn to see if you taste like salt," he said with a voice that made my breath catch.

I think I misread that last look—

Black Rain

Sweat of the Brow

MY OLD BODY was completely gone. The last few times I died I'd managed to either save some of me or find a scrap of my flesh I could use to make myself a new body with, but this time there was nothing left. I could dig up a piece of an old body buried somewhere here in the garden to create an older version of myself, but I did not want the old body back. I wasn't "her" anymore. What I'd become was more than what she had been.

Mary needed me to be more. Jane and Dan needed me to be more. My little Red Lamb needed me to be more. So many people here in Amen Hale needed me to be more than a witch. The Black Witch was dead, but I was alive. Standing flat footed I was now six feet ten inches tall, but if you added in the two extra inches that my horns extended beyond the crown of my head I was exactly seven feet tall from tip to toe.

Apart from the horns and tail I didn't look deformed or awkward in any way. I was proportioned so beautifully that I didn't even look big until I stood next to someone else. The vampire-like skin was amazing, the tail I adored, the horns were a pain in the ass and were always in the way, but I accepted them stoically as a part of what I was, but the eyes were absolutely horrible.

Two red glowing dots hung suspended in the middle of my pitch black eyes. Believer and Sky Dragon had eyes that resembled two smoldering red coals that glowed brighter when they were angry or stressed. My two red glowing dots floated in the middle of midnight voids and the effect was apparently a great deal more than "disturbing." I kept thinking of the soldier who looked through the gateway at me. He liked the view until he saw my eyes, and then the rest of the package didn't matter at all.

I felt like a beautiful Medusa. I seriously considered adding a hood to my "native wear" ensemble that I'd made for myself until an image of a girl with a brown paper bag over her head popped into my brain. I decided that I'd rather make everyone who saw me shit their pants than have to live like that. No hood! No cape!

As far as clothing went I wasn't wearing much of anything actually. My jeans and t-shirt days were behind me and I was not going back into formalwear like my old black dress no matter how much Believer complained about me going "native." Covering my breasts were two black strips of cloth creating an X across my chest, and for my bottom all I had was a black loincloth up front that hung from a silver chain wrapped around my waist that followed the rise of my hips. The three foot long strip of black cloth hid the important part from view but was still narrow enough to swing between my legs as I walked or sat down. My back side I left exposed for all to see so my tail was free. There was no way I was covering my tail for anyone and the rest just fit my mood.

Cathryn and Lucius walked ahead of us, and Believer and I followed a short distance behind. We were headed toward a large outbuilding down by the river where they'd chosen to store the prisoners. Cathryn told me that of all the problems facing Amen Hale, this was the one that needed to be addressed immediately, so that was where we were headed. I people watched as we went, taking note of how everyone reacted to my new body and my eyes. So far I'd seen good, bad, indifferent, and one young boy who cried and ran away.

On the trail ahead of us I saw a group of women pushing carts mounded high with laundry. I watched as the group of ladies formed a line and curtsied smartly as Cathryn and Lucius marched by but then looked down the path and met my eyes. I saw the shock on their faces. After a quick whispered conversation the women quickly moved to the other side of their laundry carts as if they wanted to put something between themselves and me as I passed.

One young girl was trying to break away from the others. I watched as one of the women gave her arm a vicious yank. I heard the threats of a beating, but the girl ignored the woman and the others with her and pulled away and marched purposefully around to the front of the laundry carts and then went to her knees beside the path as she rubbed her hurt arm. She kept her head down and didn't look up until she saw my bare feet stop in front of her.

I was already smiling at her when she did look up at me, and she didn't flinch when she met my eyes, although she did frown as she looked at the top of my head, staring at the horns. The other women stayed on their side of the baskets, and I didn't look at them as I knelt down on the path, knee to knee in front of this girl almost like Cathryn had done with me this morning.

She looked to be about fifteen while the other women behind the laundry carts were older, in their forties or fifties. The girl was a little overweight, frumpy and disheveled, but she seemed like a bright young girl. Determined and purposeful. She wore a blue work smock and looked up at me, unafraid, studying my horns through a pair of thick glasses. I noticed that the eyes behind the lenses were red and puffy from crying which reminded me of the woman who pulled her arm. Perhaps she was her mother.

"What's your name?" I asked.

"I'm Shelly Odonell." She answered well, without adding "princess" or "lady" or "whatever."

"Why were you crying, Shelly?" I thought she might be upset about the threat of a beating but it turned out she was upset for a very different reason.

"Some of the prisoners cry a lot, Princess," she said sincerely. "It's sad in there, listening to them scream and beg."

Shelly seemed a bit young to work with the prisoners, but that was not my place to decide, that was Byron and Lucius's stuff. I resisted the strong urge to heal the hurt arm which she petted. It was not my place to criticize that lady for yanking her arm if she was the girl's mother, unless it became abuse. But this girl had gone to her knees for me and done so on purpose, and that had cost her and might end up costing her even more if that lady made good on her promise. I would not send Shelly away empty. I willed her eyes to adjust and her vision to become human perfect.

She squinted her eyes, trying to see me through glasses which she no longer needed. She kept squinting away for a minute, trying varying degrees of "squint" until she finally took off the glasses and looked around in wide-eyed amazement. I already had a finger pressed over my smiling lips telling her to "hush" when she looked up at me with her happy smile. She nodded silently like a confidant.

I held my arms out and Shelly rose to her feet and came to me without hesitation, and I hugged her. Shelly hadn't looked away from my frightening eyes, she did not care that I had horns, and she did not scream when my tail wrapped around her ankles. Her hug warmed parts of me that I did not know were cold. I spoke to her as I enjoyed her wonderful, honest affection.

"I know it's sad to work with the prisoners, but remember, they tried to kill us. And don't worry, Shelly, I'll have Mary touch the prisoners and she'll know if any of them deserve mercy."

I pulled back enough to look at her. She was smiling, happy tears making dirty little trails down her face. She'd been working hard and sweating hard. I needed to get up and go do the same. Work hard, sweat, and take care of our people like they were trying to take care of me.

I kissed Shelly's dirty, sweaty forehead and got back to my feet and walked past the gawking clutch of older women who no longer seemed quite so terrified. Believer had been waiting for me and he fell into step beside me wordlessly with a small smile on his face as we headed down the trail, off to make a better, cleaner, safer, and more humane place to hold my dinner.

Mary and Emma

Coven Mark

GANNON LINGERED IN the doorway, his eyes fixed on Alana who sat in a chair beside the bed smiling at him as the women worked on her hair and feet at the same time.

"I'll be back as soon as they have me in my tux," Gannon said firmly to the room.

He looked to the far corner and gave Princess Emma a final warning glare before leaving with the two male servants and the tailor who waited out in the hall holding a black tuxedo still on the hanger in its garment bag.

Emma sat in a chair placed in the far corner of the room with Mary sitting in her lap. Emma had promised that she would stay in her corner in the back of the room unless Mary moved her, but Gannon was still worried about her being in the same room with Alana. Gannon was worried about almost everything he'd seen since coming to Amen Hale.

Alana had already selected a wedding dress from the ones they had on hand, and the seamstress had taken the dress back to her sewing parlor to make some alterations but had left behind her body length mirror propped up against the wall. Alana stared at herself in the mirror and the brave smile she'd put on for Gannon melted away. She started to cry. Willomena, the older woman who was combing her wet hair made a "tsking" noise.

"Now, now. What's all this about?" she asked.

"Gannon is freaked out. He thinks we should leave with my mother when she comes for the wedding," she said.

Now that Gannon was gone she spoke her mind and fears plainly.

Willomena grunted. "Does he still want to marry you?"

"Yes," she said, sniffling, still staring at herself in the mirror.

"I see," she said, still working on her hair. Willomena's waist length braid of silver hair looked like such bounty next to the short red and pink locks.

Mary left Emma in her chair and sat on the floor beside the black woman who was doing Alana's pedicure.

"May I help you, Latrice?" she asked. "I could do the other foot with you if you don't mind."

Latrice moved over and moved her box of grooming tools between the two of them, and Mary scooted in and took Alana's left foot into her lap while the other woman worked on the right. She reached over and touched Latrice's hand, nodded to herself, then set to work.

"What has your young man so upset, my dear?" Willomena asked.

"He thinks I've lost my mind. And that I'll get worse if we stay here. He's worried about me."

"Have you lost your mind?" Willomena asked as she picked up a basket full of headdresses, veils, and tiaras, searching for something that would work for a girl with so little to work with.

"I'm pretty sure I have," Alana said sadly as she stared into the mirror.

Willomena held one of the headdresses up to her head and Alana looked at it in the mirror and made a face. After four more she said, "Maybe that one, but please let me see the rest."

"Of course, dear." Willomena grabbed a second container filled with wedding paraphernalia. "What makes you so sure you've lost your mind?" she asked as she pried the lid off the big plastic tub. "Ah ha! This is the one I wanted."

"I'm seeing things," Alana sighed. "Willomena, what do you see when you look in the mirror?"

Willomena stopped what she was doing and put her face next to Alana's and stared into the mirror, cheek to cheek with the beautiful young girl and smiled. "I see nothing but a beautiful young girl."

"I see my mother's angry face telling me to come home," Alana said wearily.

"Do you want to go home?" Willomena asked, looking at her in the mirror.

"No, ma'am. I want to stay," she said sadly. "Oh! I like that one." She perked up as she noticed what Willomena held in her hands.

Willomena positioned the simple lacy tiara on her head and moved it about. They eyed it together.

"You don't think Gannon will stay here with you? Is that it?" Willomena asked as the door opened and the seamstress came in with the gown she'd altered. She'd taken it in a good two inches from its already waspish measurements to accommodate Alana's unusually thin frame.

"Stay seated, sweetie," Latrice spoke up as the foot she was working on wiggled excitedly. "The Princess and I need another five minutes down here and then you'll need at least five more for your toes to dry."

"Yes, ma'am."

"Well?" Willomena prompted. "You were talking about your blue boy. Will he stay here with you since you have your heart set on living here?"

"I don't know what he'll do. I want him to stay here with me and be happy, but he's crazy to get me out of here, Willomena. You've seen him, he thinks you're all out to get us. But I won't leave Amen Hale," she said firmly.

The seamstress tip-toed, wide eyed, around the group and began to spread out the different pieces of the wedding gown on the bed. It was quiet for a few minutes while hair, gown, and toes were worked on, but once Mary finished her foot she came around and sat on the floor beside Alana's chair and looked into the long mirror. Alana's face stared into the mirror just above hers, and Mary talked to the face in the mirror instead of the girl in the chair right above her head.

"Hello, Mirror Alana, you look almost as sad as our Alana out here," Mary said to the mirror.

The Alana in the mirror smiled weakly. "Hello, Mirror Mary. Is it okay to call you Mary or must I call you Mirror Mary or Princess Mirror Mary?" she asked the Mary in the Mirror.

Mary's reflection smiled and seemed to consider what to say for a moment, but then she leaned closer to the mirror staring hard at her own face, looking more and more troubled by something she saw in her own reflection.

"I'm sorry, Princess Mary." Alana thought she may have upset her with questions about her name.

Mary was still looking at her face in the mirror as she spoke to Alana.

"Alana, you may call me Mary, or stupid or idiot or whatever you want to call me. Call me friend or even Sister if it feels right. And don't feel bad about losing your mind, I lost mine days ago."

She leaned in closer to the mirror to get a better look at herself, but the door opened and a servant entered, struggling along with a huge, heavy box-like black case. Mary scooted back out of the way to let her by and the woman set the huge thing on the dresser with a loud thud, undid some clasps, and opened the contraption to reveal a salon in a box, complete with everything imaginable to get a bride's hair and face in proper runway condition. Box in place, the woman turned and greeted the room.

"Greetings, Princes Mary, Princess Emma, I'm Romanda Mave. I'm to do the bride's hair and makeup." She greeted them and was about to speak to Alana but stopped and turned back to Mary.

"Princess Mary," Romanda licked her lips and met Mary's green-eyed gaze. "I don't know if this is my place, but I think you should go check on your sister. Something horrible has happened."

Emma stood. A dropped pin would have been loud at that instant.

"What has happened?" Mary said firmly.

"They say that she had some kind of fit when she went to France to bring back our men. That she fell to the floor twitching and thrashing and—" She seemed hesitant to spit out the words. "Well, they say that she has changed into a demon." Romanda's face looked troubled as she said this, one hand covering her mouth and chin.

"A demon?" Mary said, confused.

"An enormous demon!" Romanda shouted, all pretense of reluctance gone as she shared her tale with wild-eyed arm waving vigor. "With horns *and* a tail!" Romanda frowned at the doubtful faces that stared at her. "I'd not lie to you, my lady. It's horrible!" She waited a moment longer to gauge their response then shrugged. "I just thought you'd want to know is all."

"Where is Rain right now, Mave!?" Emma demanded from where she stood in her corner of the room.

Romanda's attention snapped to the dangerous witch in the corner looking at her with her teeth gritted together and copper gold eyes shining with power.

"One of the servants told me that she's walking around the yard!" Romanda said quickly and pointed in the general direction. "Out where they're getting ready for the wedding."

"I can't move dammit!" Emma shouted and looked down at her feet. "I promised that I would not move so you have to come and get me, Mary, because I promised and I can't move from this damned spot!" She seethed where she stood in captive frustration.

Mary rose very calmly, forcing herself to move slowly as she stepped up to Romanda. She reached out and touched the side of her face. After a moment she took her hand away and gave the other woman a hard look.

"Romanda, I know you. You are a life long bearer of tales and a hopeless gossip, a shrew and a braggart and a sower of discord. From now on, if you have a tale to tell in my presence, kneel before me and put out your hand and if it pleases me to know what you know *then* I will touch you. You will not be punished this time." She looked over to Willomena who nodded unhappily.

Romanda went to her knees.

"Forgive me, Princess!" she begged.

"I forgive you, Romanda, learn from this mistake and try to be a better witch," Mary said as she crossed the room and collected Emma, wrapping an arm around the taller girl like she was the smaller of the two and Emma the one who needed protection.

"No one move as we pass by," Mary cautioned. The other women in the room stood clear as the two walked, arm in arm, out the door.

"What's happened to Rain!?" Alana shouted at them before Mary closed the door behind them.

Mary and Emma both looked back at Alana, but now their eyes were glittering with magic and Mary's skin even glowed with a pale green luminescence.

"We don't know but we're going to go find out," Mary said firmly then took a step back into the room with Emma and they both regarded Alana for a silent moment before Mary spoke to her.

"In just a few minutes your Blue is going to walk through this door. When he sees you, you need to be calm and happy and confident." She leaned closer. "He does not need to see you all freaked out. We both know he'd shit a brick, so suck it up, girl! It's time to fight for what you want. *Right now!*" Mary snapped.

Alana was nodding rapidly. "Right! Right! You're right, Mary. I'm sorry." She wiped at her nose and eyes, still nodding her head.

"Latrice, fetch a cool rag," Willomena ordered, "let's wipe her face and cool her down and everyone make sure it's all smiles and good cheer when our groom arrives." Her voice was not a request and the other women in the room replied with "yes ma'ams."

Mary pulled the door shut and started down the hall with Emma close by her side.

"What *the hell* has happened, Mary?" Emma stood still and pulled Mary around to face her. "I don't know by touch like you! And it wouldn't do me any damn good if you spelled it out for me because I can't read anymore! So just say what you learned from Romanda and keep it simple because that's how I need it now, dammit." Emma quivered with angst and worry and frustration at her own condition.

"Stay calm," Mary said patiently. "Now look at my Coven Mark."

Emma did as instructed and frowned. Then frowned some more as she considered what it might mean.

"Yes. Rain's star is missing. But she must be okay because she's up and walking around."

Mary stopped for a second, watching Emma's face, then continued. "I didn't learn much of anything useful from Romanda, nothing but hearsay, but people told her that Rain's outside with Cathryn right now, walking around half naked. So on the bright side, Rain's naked."

She waited another minute, watching Emma's face, before moving on. "They did say she was big and scary with horns and a tail. Let's go out there and see what the hell happened. Okay?"

Emma thought for a minute then nodded. "Thank you, Mary."

Mary knew that Emma was thanking her for doing exactly as she had asked and using small, simple sentences, easily understood and acted upon. Mary leaned in to kiss her, but a hand pressed over her lips stopped her.

"No. Let's go see Rain," Emma said firmly.

Mary shook off her haze of desire and nodded. "Yeah. Thanks. Let's."

Together, the girls headed downstairs to see what had happened to Rain and why there were only three witches in their coven.

Black Rain

Sex Ed

I WALKED THROUGH THE midst of beautifully adorned tables. Antique crystal punch bowls glittered in the sunlight, most still empty and waiting to be filled. Several contraptions on carts were parked by the tables, the devices ready to heat or cool the appetizers that would be brought out later. Fortunately for me, not all the bowls were empty. I stole a strawberry from the chilled bowl beside the table where two servants were assembling the chocolate fountain. The servants bustled all around us, adding the final touches to the wedding preparations, rushing now as it was almost time to bring the guests to Amen Hale.

It was odd to stand in the middle of everyone almost completely naked, but I was forcing them to see me in this new body and be near me. I'd been walking around them as they worked at tasks that they could not flee from for the past fifteen minutes and they were finally starting to settle down and not go nuts whenever I came near, feigning interest in whatever it was they were working on. I unsettled the women because of my horns and eyes, but the poor men also had to deal with my body. The children seemed to be the least troubled by me, but the protective parents wouldn't let them anywhere near me, even when they asked.

"It was a very good idea. They seem to be doing much better, my love," Believer complimented my mother's ploy.

"Yeah. But I wonder how the wedding guests will react to me. And the bride and groom will probably die when they see me, my beautiful, red lamb and her poor, blue guy." I shook my head, disgusted at myself for hurting them. Especially for hurting my beautiful, little, red lamb. She'd called me and I'd come, but I'd hurt her in doing as she asked because I was walking around wildly out of control like a monster.

"Be optimistic," Believer suggested with a positive, encouraging tone. "Perhaps the bride and groom are doing better already, and the wedding guests will have more than just you to look at when they arrive; they will also have me and Sky Dragon. You are not the only one who looks frightening around here." Believer stretched up to his full height that was still a foot taller than me and puffed his chest out and sucked in his middle impressively.

The hurt, upset face I'd been nurturing gave way to a smile as he hammed it up. I looked at him as he posed for me and had to admit that he was right. Believer's arms and legs made mine look like little sticks and the trunk of his body was huge. At first glance anyone who saw him was confused and baffled simply because what they were seeing did not make sense. Believer was an enigma. His body an impossible contradiction that pretty much baked everyone's noodle the first time they saw him as they tried to puzzle out why he didn't come apart and fly out in every direction.

He was a magnificent, eight foot tall mass of living, rolling clouds held together in the shape of a man by the power of Sky's magic. Believer's head was the size of a bucket sitting on top of his blocky body and his cloudy arms and legs were as thick as tree limbs. Two red, glowing eyes and a slit of a mouth that split his face were his only facial features, but the clouds that made up his face could lighten or darken to form shadows and add lines around his eyes and mouth and even take the place of eyebrows to give him a broad range of facial expressions.

Although he looked like clouds, the surface of his skin was warm and spongy soft to the touch but solid further in. His arms and legs were impossibly strong, and he had only three large thick fingers and a thumb on each hand, but I'd never been bothered by it. They were his hands and they worked perfectly. The outside of his body that the world saw was only the beginning because he was even more wonderful on the inside where he took me.

Believer was right, as long as I didn't call my power and make a nuisance of myself he would be the bigger monster, until people met my eyes at least.

We were walking hand in hand and Believer stopped where a woman was tying flowers onto seat backs at the ends of each row of chairs set up for the wedding guests.

"Mrs. Richards, may I ask you a question?" Believer spoke very respectfully to the woman. I wasn't surprised that he knew her name because Believer never forgot anything or anyone he met.

Mrs. Richards eyed the two of us cautiously. She was wearing a black robe, the hems and collar lined with frightening runes and symbols, but her face was average and friendly. She was in her forties with shoulder length brown hair and the few extra pounds she carried looked right for her frame.

"Gladly, Prince Believer, if I can I will answer your question. Let's hear it then." She spoke carefully and kept her wary eyes on me though she spoke to him.

"I need your honest opinion, Mrs. Richards. Could you judge which one of us is more frightening?"

He struck an intimidating pose while I stood beside him and smiled at her as harmlessly as I could, my tail even wrapped around me, and tried to appear sweet and innocent as I attempted to channel Bambi. Her eyes went from Believer's puffed up man monster pose to me until she finally smiled and shook her head at the silliness.

"All men are fools, even if made of clouds and magic." She chuckled and Believer frowned. "All the people in Amen Hale know you have a kindhearted soul, my Prince, and they know that you would not willingly hurt a fly. You are not frightening to any who know you," she concluded with a nod.

I laughed but Believer frowned hugely. "But why would I want to harm a fly?" his deep rumbling voice complained.

"Thank you, Mrs. Richards," I thanked her, laughing even harder as I pulled my frowning and confused husband along with me.

Our posing and posturing had drawn a lot of attention from those around us. I hoped our laughter would be like magic medicine spread out on all the fears and worries of our people as they saw that I could laugh and be happy and smile and have fun and that I was not a demon from hell that only found pleasure in blood and death. I noticed the other servants who quickly converged on Mrs. Richards asking her about the odd exchange.

Believer gave me a confident smug smile. "Our people are accustomed to me but these guests are not. I assure you that I will be more disturbing than you."

"You know just what to say to a girl to make her feel special." I gave him my sarcastic compliment, but my words and tone told him plainly that I loved him and that I really meant it.

"I like your new size," he said out of the blue.

I nodded. "It is kinda nice to walk with you and hold your hand without having to reach up. We match now, except for how big you are in the middle."

"Would you like me to slim down so I more closely resemble a human form like Sky Dragon?" he asked seriously.

"Hell no!" I said, shocked at the suggestion. "I need you to stay big enough to hold me and our company when we have guests over."

Believer arched his one fancy eyebrow he employed when he wanted to say that something was bullshit.

"What?" I tried to ask innocently.

"You mean someone other than Bethany?" Believer accused.

I squirmed under the scrutiny of his knowing gaze and finally stepped closer and pressed my head into his chest to hide my face, embarrassed at the situation and bothered that it had somehow come up in our conversation. I hoped he'd just drop it. I wondered what my face looked like. Did my new skin still blush?

His arms wrapped around me and my tail wrapped around one of his legs, squeezing and caressing up and down.

"Emma?" he asked. He wasn't going to drop it.

"Yes," I fessed, still hiding myself in his cloudy chest.

"And?" he asked.

"And maybe Mary." I squirmed in his arms like he'd poked me with something sharp! We're so not having this conversation! "Believer—"

"No," he rumbled and moved me so he could see me.

I looked into his eyes. It made him angry when I did not meet his eyes so I looked into his face as he spoke to me.

"Do not hide what is in your heart from me. I will not call on your mother's magic to see what is inside your heart, so I ask that you simply be forthcoming. I know that you are embarrassed and feel ashamed and uncomfortable about your desire to be with others, but you do not need to feel this way. Just tell me all your heart. If there is something that you say that I find bothersome or cannot handle I will let you know and we will discuss it together. Now who, other than Emma and Mary, were you wanting to bring to our bed within my body?"

It felt wrong to be talking about things that were so private out here in the middle of a field surrounded by so may people. Even though our words were quiet and I didn't think anyone could hear us I was still self-conscious and still getting used to being basically naked. I spotted a couple of men staring at my bare ass and my tail reached up and wrapped around Believer's wrist and pulled his hand from the small of my back down lower so that it covered my butt. Both of their heads moved up as their eyes went from my ass to my eyes, only to find them staring back right into them and they both jumped. One man turned and quickly walked away while the other just dropped to his knees on the spot and looked at the ground.

But that made other people stop what they were doing to stare and that made me want to scream. My tail thrashed about behind me, as angry as I was, and I closed my eyes and took deep breaths. Believer was patient and gave me a moment or two to settle down. He was always patient with me. And kind. And he wanted to know who else I wanted to be with. What the hell was wrong with me? What the hell *wasn't* wrong with me? I was what I was.

"It would be nice to have Jane with us, but I don't think she would be with someone other than me, Emma, or Dan. I wouldn't invite Dan inside you unless you told me it was all right ." I didn't know what to say after that so I just said, "Pick me up."

He bent down and carefully scooped me off my feet and lifted me easily into his arms, but I no longer fit as I once did. I used to be so small that the crook of his arm felt like a little apartment with room for a mini fridge. Now it felt much more like a man holding a woman instead of a monster holding a child-sized doll. I stared up into my husband's eyes and felt more a woman with him than a plaything or a lovely toy. Again, it felt like we matched now.

He smiled at me. It was a good smile, and I thought that he must have seen something in me at that moment that he liked. I wanted to keep him smiling like that but I had some questions that I needed to ask. Questions that I was scared to ask but had to ask.

"Believer, what is sex like for you? When Sky made your—penis," I forced myself to say penis instead of "thing," "did she make it so you could feel pleasure like a flesh and blood man or is sex something that you do just to make me happy? Does it feel good for you when you're in me? Does sex give you pleasure?" I asked honestly. It was the kind of thing I should have already known but there had never been time or the right moment to ask. Until now.

Believer was looking down at me, studying my face and my every move. I couldn't imagine what was going through his mind right now but I kept my eyes on his face, watching him while he watched me.

"When I went to Sky and asked her to remake me so that I could be a man, she was still a virgin, and having never been with a man, she had no idea what a man's pleasure was like. She understood the male anatomy but she did not feel comfortable making me as other men, so she made me different. She improvised. The penis she made for me is the most sensitive part of my body and, yes, it does give me pleasure to be inside you, but my real pleasure comes from your flesh itself. The little white nerves inside my body that sink down into your flesh and bind me to you also connect me to your every sensation and feeling. When we are connected in that way, your pleasure *is* my pleasure. When you have your orgasm, I also experience it as my own."

I thought about what he said. Sky changed Believer and made him "able to perform" before she'd been with Ryan. So she had done the best she could, and from my side of the experience at least, her best was pretty damn good.

"So, you like it?" I asked again. "Sex?"

"Yes." He leaned a little closer to me, studying my face. "You look doubtful." He smiled as he said this.

Did I look doubtful? I must. I made a helpless face and shrugged.

"Shall I describe my experience?" he asked, still smiling.

"I'm sorry," I said for some reason.

Believer was quiet for a minute, studying me like he always did.

"You do not share your fears or doubts with me easily, Rain, but I know that you worry that I am less man than other men. You think that I am limited by my nature or by the manner of my creation and you worry that I do not have the same hungers and desires as other men. I think you worry that I lack the capacity to appreciate how beautiful you are. Again. You are wrong, my love, about all of it." He looked down the length of me, his eyes drinking in the sight of me as he spoke.

"It's true that I fell in love with the woman inside this body, but I think that of all men, or women it would seem, be they humans or clouds or monsters, I am most fortunate." His eyes met mine again and I saw in them some of what I'd seen earlier: passion, hunger, and desire for me, living in his eyes.

"I do enjoy sex. When you worry about me, you often ask me what I am thinking, and I have been struggling with my thoughts of late. Sometimes as I watch you, you will stand or walk or move in a certain way and I suddenly find myself remembering the way your body felt when you were inside me and we were making love. For a while I tried to stop this from happening as it seemed somehow improper and undisciplined that my thoughts would abandon the moment and what was happening here before me. It was as if I had no control over my own mind." A small rumble of a laugh came from him. "I have had many arguments with myself on the logic of allowing myself these diversions and fantasies. But I am more human than saint it seems because I have given up trying to discipline my mind and I now let my thoughts go where they want as I look at you."

He moved me enough to free a hand so that he could reach my face, and one huge finger traced along a smile I hadn't know was there. Believer's cloudy hand played over my face and neck as he stared into my eyes, and my heart raced as he spoke and touched me. My new vampire flesh made each touch of his hands so much more than I'd ever felt with human flesh. I listened to his voice as I stared up into his eyes and I knew with all my heart that he not only loved me, he wanted me and he enjoyed me.

"Right now I am thinking about being with you again. About what we will do together tonight. I want to feel the heat of your passion build through your flesh like a spreading fire, burning hotter and deeper each moment we are together. I want to feel the movement of your body and the pull and tightness of your flesh. And to feel each thrust as I push myself inside you, bringing us pleasure as I touch you and cause every part of your body to sing with growing anticipation, climbing higher and higher until it reaches the point of release when your whole—"

"Okay! Stop! Please stop!" I begged, trying to keep my voice low as I grabbed his hand that rested on my bare stomach. "Stop! Stop! Stop!" I whimpered stop but my tail wrapped around his wrist and pulled his hand lower! I sucked in a deep stuttering breath and Believer's rumbling laugh shook my body as I closed my eyes and tried not to lose my mind as conflicting desires waged war inside me. I was suddenly very much aware that I was practically naked in his arms, my bare bottom pressed up against his chest. He was so close to me!

"Tonight, my love. Not here. Not now." His deep voice rumbled softly for my ears alone.

He was pulling his hand away (over my tail's continued objections) and I agreed with him even if my tail didn't.

I'd be with him tonight, but not right here, and not right now.

"Not here. Not right now," I managed to say.

I closed my eyes and took deep calming breaths. Tonight, I promised myself as I calmed. I kept my eyes closed as Believer walked around with me in his arms. I heard him tell someone I was resting. I felt him lower me so someone could see my face and wondered who it was because I did not recognize the voice. Believer walked and spoke to others, following Cathryn's advice even with me in my "not sleep," playing possum in his arms.

Angel

Nightcap

ANGEL WAS BESIDE herself with worry. She pounded even harder on David and Dana's door and thought about going for help, but then the door opened a crack and Dana's bleary eyes peeked out.

"Get in here!" Dana ordered in a rough scratchy voice, and Angel slipped into the room.

Dana didn't yell at her for pounding on the door for the past five minutes; she knew that Angel was crazy with worry because she'd wedged something under the door and in a sense locked the door in this crazy house that had no locks on doors.

"So what's going on out there in crazy town?" Dana asked her strange little maid as she staggered her way back to the bed where David lay butt naked and out cold. He was lying face down so she didn't mind Angel seeing his nice backside, but she still grabbed a sheet and pulled it over him.

Couldn't be too careful. Especially when you're drunk and stupid.

They'd both been shaken up after The Hallow. David had been the one to grab a bottle of Crown from the kitchen and take her straight to the room where they killed the bottle and passed out in bed trying to forget everything they'd just seen. Dana was far better at holding her liquor than David so she'd heard Angel's repeated knocking and woke up to answer the door.

"You won't believe what's happened now, Lady Dana," Angel began with more emotion than she usually showed.

"Okay. Let's hear it," Dana slurred.

"Princess Rain has grown horns and a tail, and she's a giant now." She delivered this in her usual quiet voice.

"How big is she this time?" Dana asked.

Angel stared at her in blank faced surprise, then frowned in concentration.

"Almost as big as Believer."

"Weird," Dana said, then snorted. "I've seen her change into a pillar of fire a hundred feet tall. A seven foot tall freak is no big deal. She'll change back to her old self soon enough." Dana rubbed at her face sleepily.

Angel nodded, totally confused by Dana's calm while at the same time oddly reassured.

"Are you coming to the wedding, Lady Dana? They're going to start soon. And they have the feast tonight for Bethany's birthday." Angel asked the question though she already knew the answer.

Dana smiled at her. "No to the first, and *hell no* to the second. I'm going to stay as drunk as I can all night long and wake up tomorrow not even remembering what happened today." She stood up and started to look for her glass and spotted it on the table beside the totally empty bottle of Crown.

"Damn, I'm almost awake now and I'm out of Crown," Dana lamented.

The little blonde ghost of a girl walked over and picked up her glass and walked into the bathroom. Dana listened as the water ran for a minute. She guessed she was rinsing out the glass. Angel returned and set the glass down and reached into her pocket and produced a small bottle of whisky, enough to fill one glass.

"I told them I was coming and this was what they gave me. I hope it's okay. They only gave me this tiny bottle." She poured it into Dana's glass and brought it to her, but she pulled her hand back at the last minute, giving Dana an oddly concerned look.

Dana watched the glass cleaning and drink pouring in a drunken stupor as she sat on the edge of the bed, but now she frowned.

"What the hell?" she asked.

"Let me help you get up and go to the bathroom first." Angel set the drink down on the table.

"If you're going to sleep till tomorrow then you need to go pee before you go to bed, my Lady." She grabbed Dana by the arm and walked her toward the bathroom.

"You know, I do need to pee. Really, really, really need to pee," Dana said as she staggered along on Angel's arm.

"Not yet, Lady Dana, wait till we get to the toilet," Angel urged.

She helped her on and off, wet a rag, and cleaned her face and other places before helping her back out to the bed and pressing the glass into her hand. She watched as Dana finished the hard liquor then took the glass from her. She pulled back the sheets and had her lie down naked beside her David then covered them up after putting a pillow under David's head. Angel took one of the extra pillows off the bed and put it on the floor at the foot of the bed, then she wrapped herself in Dana's white bath robe and curled up right there and went to sleep.

Ryan

Another Good Soldier

I OPENED THE SHOWER door a crack to see who the heck was in our bathroom. Three smiling maids stared back at me as they rolled in a rack of clothes set on casters. Sky peeked out of the crack beneath me, waving at them with a big smile. They waved back, giggling.

Sky leaned her head back and looked up at me. “Ryan, it really is okay if they see us naked. They’re maids. It’s their job to take care of us and this is part of taking care of us. And I really do like having help with my hair and clothes and stuff because I’ve never done those things myself. I’ve always had a maid. I need them.”

“Good grief, Sky, one of them was bad enough, now there’s an army of them out there!” I whined.

"Look at the clothes on the rack, Ryan. It's formalwear! We're going to need lots of help getting dressed." I heard the excitement in Sky's voice. She wanted to dress up and go meet people and I couldn't blame her; the two of us had been together all day so she must be ready to interact with other life forms. Female ones.

"Please, Ryan." She was blinking as she looked up at me, water dripping off my chin onto her face. "Get used to having servants," she said. "I want them to take care of us, but I can help. Here." She moved behind me and covered my eyes with her hands.

"Now just pretend nobody's there. Push the door open and walk outside."

"Naked and wet and blind, in front of three women that aren't my wife?" I asked. "You're not worried that they'll do something? So far everyone we've seen today has tried to jump our bones."

She laughed. "I think they would only jump your bones if you asked them to. Did you want them to jump your bones?" she teased.

"No!" I said seriously. "You've wore my poor bones out, woman! It's all I can do just to stand up."

She gave me a kiss on the back of the neck.

"You're going to have to get used to this because I'm not giving up our maids. Now move it!" she ordered.

I wondered if there was an old Chinese proverb that said, "Only *fool* come between woman and her maid!"

"Yes, my Sky." I reached out blindly, pushed the door open, and carefully walked out of the shower with Sky's body pressed up against mine as she walked behind me and kept me in the dark. My sister has told me a few times about her running mental list of weird things. My wife held her hands over my eyes and laughed along with the three giggling women who toweled me dry, and I decided right then that I would begin a list of my own, starting with this.

Savanah was a little younger than my mom, but she acted like a mom and not a girl, so I didn't mind her helping me get dressed while the two younger girls worked on Sky. She gave my impressive silk tie a final adjustment. She'd dressed me in some insanely expensive blue suit with a white shirt and red tie. Either the suit made me look good or I made the suit look good but one way or another, we looked good together, the suit and I. As I stared into the mirror, I did not recognize myself as myself—who was I? *Where was I?*

"Lord Ryan, eat a few more finger sandwiches. You're looking a bit woozy," Savanah suggested as she eyed me with what looked like worry. I tried to argue, but she went to the plate of little square sandwiches and came back with three in her hand.

"Now stop being difficult. I'm trying to take care of you and you will do what is right and obey me. Now open."

I opened and she shoved the little square, baby-sized ham sandwich in while Sky and the other maids laughed at me.

This morning we'd taken off and left our pills behind when I accidentally and unexpectedly transported us to my old bedroom at my parents' house. Sky had hidden our last dose of pills under our mattress last night and we were supposed to take them at noon but we'd been off at the beach. She was worried over the pills, but I'd promised her we would take them as soon as we got back, so before the maids had gotten too serious we downed one blue pill and six white pills each. The servants brought us food to settle our stomachs and we ate while they worked on us and dressed us up the way they wanted for the wedding, but the pills also made us a little doped up and fuzzy. I was worried that Sky and I might fall asleep and start snoring as the "I do's" were being exchanged.

"You've company in your parlor by the way, Lord Ryan," Julie said to me as she worked on Sky's hair.

"Who's out there?" I mumbled around a mouthful of sandwich before Savanah poked the third little sandwich into my pie hole with an evil grin.

"Princess Bethany, her maid, and Lord Dragon," Julie answered. "They're playing cards at your parlor table."

I chewed, swallowed, and said. "You hear that, Sky? Sky Dragon is now *Lord* Dragon."

Sky's hair was still in the fancy braids, but the girls were busy adjusting little things they saw as "off" or not perfect enough. Her big happy smile beamed at me from between the nest of arms working around her head, pulling and tugging and making each strand perfect.

Sky said, "Lord Sky Dragon is long. Lord Dragon sounds better."

It did sound better. I nodded, conceding the point. "Am I done, Mrs. Savanah?"

"You'll do for now, but you need a proper manicure and a proper—"

"Maybe tomorrow," I cut in cheerfully and walked over to Sky. She was making pained faces as the two women unwound one of the braids that had come partially undone, either at the beach or in the shower. I squeezed through the action and stole a kiss.

"I'm going to go join Lord Dragon's card game. See you after they're done torturing you."

"Okay. Go have fun," she said still wincing as the two women fought with her hair.

I walked out the bathroom, through our bedroom and into the small entry area that held a couch and a table with four chairs. Sky Dragon, Bethany, and her little black maid sat at the table. Sky Dragon was dealing cards as I pulled out the fourth chair and took a seat.

"Deal me in!" I said happily.

"Hello, Brother," Sky Dragon said thumbing cards in my direction with what passed for a smile on his dragon face. I didn't have a problem thinking of him as family. I liked him. He was a real decent guy. Weird to have a brother that was my wife's son though. But not as weird as being dried off by three maids.

I laughed.

Sky Dragon looked at me funny and raised one of his eye ridges at me.

"You really look nice!" Bethany gave me a big smile. "Are you and Sky ready to go?"

"I am. I think Sky's got another fifteen or twenty minutes before she's done cookin'. Were you guys waiting for me?" I asked as I gave Bethany's little maid sitting across from me a polite wave which she returned shyly.

"We were waiting for Sky," Bethany said honestly with a look in Sky Dragon's direction.

"I have not seen her all day and I was worried." He shifted in his seat and gave me an odd look.

"Where did you guys go today?" Bethany asked.

"We went to the movies. And then to an island out in the middle of nowhere. It was nice, but too dangerous."

"Dangerous?" Sky Dragon set the cards down and gave me a hard look, but I nodded. I deserved the look.

"The next time we go out I'd rather have you or Believer with us if you don't mind coming. Nothing happened today other than me shoving a pushy camera thug into the dirt, but it was still too risky."

"Are you planning to go anywhere tomorrow?" Sky Dragon leaned forward in his chair.

"We talked about possibly going to a concert tomorrow afternoon, but even if we skip the concert we are definitely going to church this Sunday."

"Would you like to get together after the wedding to plan it out with Lucius?" he asked.

"Yes, please. Thanks, Sky Dragon," I said sincerely.

He nodded and picked his cards back up.

"So how are you feelin', Sis?" I asked Bethany with a big smile.

"Great," she said eyeing me suspiciously. "You look like your feelin' pretty good yourself, Ryan."

I waved the comment away. "Yeah. Sky had us take our pills. We were supposed to take them at twelve but we were out and about. If I do or say something stupid, just forgive me in advance. But if you could keep a close eye on me and Sky tonight I would appreciate it. We might fall asleep during the wedding."

"How do the pills make you feel?" Sky Dragon asked.

"A little feverish and warm. Easily distracted and funky. And sleepy," I said.

"Sounds like pretty good stuff," Bethany said with a smile.

My face fell into a stern mask. "Listen to me, little sis. These pills are seriously bad news and dangerous as hell. They're poison to anyone not seventeen years old and some of the kids in the study have been put into the hospital or died taking them."

"Then why are you still taking them?" she asked, surprised and concerned.

"Today is our last day taking the damn things. We're done. Dr. Burgis told Sky that if she didn't take the pills for at least five days her powers would fade. I don't believe that but Sky does, so," I shrugged, "we took our pills."

Something waving around behind Bethany's chair caught my eye and I leaned to the side to get a better look.

"Yeah. I got a tail now," Bethany said happily as I stared at the long black tail emerging from an opening in the back of her dress and running out through the slats in the back of her chair. The "tail" lifted up and came to Bethany's outstretched hand. She held the end out to me.

"Do you want to touch my tail, Ryan?" she asked sweetly.

"It's *really* soft," said the little black maid, her huge eyes staring at me, telling me to touch it.

"The tail is cool," said Sky Dragon, and I heard the other part as well, that silent order to "LIKE THE TAIL!"

I lit up, snapping a happy face into position and getting with the program as I took the hint from troops already on the ground. I was drugged up but I could still take a hint.

"Yeah! Let me see that thing," I said like a madman.

A smiling Bethany held out a foot long section of black "tail" to me. As I reached out to touch it the tail wrapped around my palm and gave me a little squeeze, almost like a handshake.

"Whoa," I said, completely freaked out and woozy. I closed my hand gently around it and felt as the velvety black rope slid out of my hand and went back to Bethany, wrapping around her arm like it had a life of its own.

"Bethany. Do you mind telling me how you got your tail?" I asked with my smile still locked into position.

Bethany and Sky Dragon shared some eye contact.

"Sky Dragon thinks my bracelet gave me my tail, but I think it's because Rain told me a story about lions."

She held the bracelet up. "Rain put ten kisses inside my bracelet that are supposed to come out and surprise me. It fixed my dress for me and made me a place for my tail to poke out, and just a few minutes ago it helped me cheat at cards!"

She declared with a huge grin, like this was the greatest thing in the history of the world.

"I had the suckiest hand *ev-er,* and I said, 'My cards suck!' and then my cards switched with Sky Dragon's cards."

"They did suck," Sky Dragon confirmed the suckage, nodding his head as he studied his current collection of cards.

I laughed but I shouldn't have. Why was I laughing? This was so totally wrong! I forced myself to sober up. "Let me get this straight, one way or another, Rain made you grow a tail?" I confirmed seriously.

"A very *cool* tail," Sky Dragon said again. "Now let's play cards," he griped.

I took the hint and fell in like a good soldier and the card game and the topics of conversation stayed away from Bethany and her happy tail that was waving around behind her chair. I let myself blab about our trip. I talked about what Sky and I saw at the movies, what the beach was like, the fish we saw that looked big enough to eat us and seeing the cruise boats and the island packed with tourists. As I blabbed, Sky Dragon and I did our best to let Bethany and her maid win every hand as any good soldier would.

The bathroom door opened and the three maids came out. They were all dressed up and looked as if they planned to go to the wedding as well, but something must have happened in the bathroom because they were pale as sheets and clearly unsettled by something. Sky walked out in the tasteful but plain light green dress that she'd been told to wear by the maids so she didn't shame the bride on her big day, but what had all of us at our table staring like dumbstruck idiots was the floating piece of living cloth that looked like a glimmering cloud, somehow pressed flat and shaped into lace and crafted into a wedding train.

The cloth floated along in the air beside Sky like a ghostly apparition. A constant wavelike motion moved the material in gently undulating waves which somehow made me think of breathing. There was a long, white band of white material attached to the top of the cloud train and three foot long ribbon-like strips on each side moved around like arms. Centered at the top of the white material were two glowing blue eyes and just below that a smiling well-shaped mouth with human looking lips shaded a sunburnt red.

Sky was standing beside it with that far off, glazed look that the pills gave us when we took them. The floating cloud cloth wrapped the end of one of its arms around Sky's hand. It was holding her hand. Sky smiled at it then looked at all of us.

"This is my daughter. Her name is Niu. It means 'girl,'" she said proudly.

"Who are they, Mother?" The cloth's mouth moved and a sweet and curious voice came out.

Sky Dragon was already standing and Bethany, Penny, and I stood to our feet as Sky introduced us one at a time and explained what each of us were to her new daughter. Niu seemed respectful but strangely distracted.

"I want to honor Niu's request," Sky said, sounding composed and in control of herself, though I could see by the glassy mirror of her eyes she was blasted. "When Niu was just a little cloud with two blue eyes and a mouth she asked me why we were all dressed up and she thought our dresses were very pretty." Sky glanced over at the floating cloth and smiled.

"She likes dresses and girl stuff. I told her about the wedding and she wanted to be made into a wedding train so she could be in the wedding too."

Niu's white ribbon arm tugged on Sky's arm. "Mother. Please take me to the bride. I do not wish to be rude, but the maids said that we are late, and I still need to ask if she will even wear me." The end of her other little floating ribbon of an arm reached up and covered her mouth and her shining blue eyes rounded, looking surprised. "I don't even know if she's pretty. What does the bride look like?"

Sky shook her head. "I don't know, Niu, I haven't met her yet."

Savanah's emotional cup had overflown and tears were on her face as she spoke up from where the maids stood in a waiting line. "I saw her, Niu, and she is too beautiful for me to begin to describe."

The living cloth practically quivered. "Let's go! I want to see her!"

The group of happily weeping women gathered around Sky and Niu and walked out the door in a tight packed female herd. I stood there staring out the door in a daze until Bethany took my arm and slung it around her shoulder and started walking me forward with her tiny arm around my waist.

"Come on, you drugged up pill popper. Let's go to the wedding and watch Niu make this girl look pretty wrapped around her butt!" She laughed as we walked out the door and into the hallway.

"Her train tail is going to make your cat tail look pretty plain," Sky Dragon said.

Bethany's tail snapped out and whacked him right upside his dragon head!

Bethany laughed as Sky Dragon walked beside us with one hand covering an eye.

I looked at him and shook my head. Wounded soldier. Made a mistake and got popped for it. He needed to get with the program. I said the mantra.

"The tail is cool."

Karen Ainsley

Mother's Nightmare

MRS. AINSLEY SAT at her kitchen table with Agent Reed's big bulky Blackberry resting on the table top. She stared at the image on the screen, an aerial shot. The time stamp was fifteen minutes ago. The lawn was covered with servants in white busy with preparations, musicians, white tables, flowers, decorative torches lining the paths, and chairs already set up for the wedding. A wedding that could not be about to happen.

"Where are the rest of the pictures?" she asked, her voice clipped and angry. There had only been five images and none of them showed Alana or anyone important other than inconsequential servants.

"That's all they sent," Trisha told her.

She handed the phone to her husband and stood without another word, pushing her way through the throng of strangers and family out the glass doors to her back yard where there were even more strangers and people who had absolutely no business at her house or in her life. The boy's white trash mother, stepfather, and older sister were here. When they had arrived, they were in jeans and casual attire but the government handlers had changed them into what they would never be, proper humans.

Even in her new pink dress and styled hair, Karen Crumbacker still looked like a pathetic waste. She sat in one of the patio chairs, shoulders hunched forward, back bowed and belly resting on her knees. She looked haggard and slack jawed, and her eyes kept wandering the crowd of faces aimlessly like a lost sheep. As Karen watched, she reached up and dabbed at her eyes with a wadded up tissue that she'd already used to blow her nose. The fact that fate had given this lump the same first name she had was laughable; they were practically a different species. Whatever her son was, he was not fit to be in the same room with her daughter, let alone put a hand on her or marry her.

Karen walked away from the disturbing woman to whom she would be related by marriage within the hour and walked to the edge of the pool deck. As she stared out over the marsh, she noticed Gannon's older sister staring out at the view only a few steps away. The girl was young, early twenties, slim and lean, and though she doubted it would last with her mother's unfortunate genes to contend with, she was fetching. They'd dressed her in a white gown that showed her slim figure and styled her shoulder length dark hair. She wore a hard, almost angry expression on her face, not the slack, soft doughy expression of her mother.

Karen walked up to her.

"Hello," she said stiffly.

The girl looked at her and judged *her* unworthy of her time and looked back at the marsh.

"Are you Gannon's sister?" She tried a more direct approach.

"Yes."

"What is your brother like?" she asked now that the girl's mouth appeared to be working.

"What is your daughter like?" she countered, still looking out toward the marsh.

The older sister was as difficult as her brother it seemed. Karen knew the sister hadn't been spared their parents' penchant for the ridiculous. They'd named her Valaria Vale. Why a woman would name her children or allow her idiot husband to name their children "Gannon The Grey" and "Valaria Vale" she would never understand. Although, with a last name as unfortunate as "Crumbacker" *what do you do?*

Valaria opened her purse and took out a cigarette, lit it, and took a drag.

One of the FBI agents standing nearby for security walked over. "Miss, the grass in the marsh is very dry, please be careful with your cigarette butt," he suggested politely.

She gave him the finger, took another drag, then flicked the still glowing butt out into the tall dry grass.

Where did people like this even come from, she wondered as Valaria walked back over to her lump of a mother. Trailer parks? Dilapidated structures out in the woods? Ditches, rocks, holes in the ground? Filthy inbreed communes? *To hell with Gannon and his whole hillbilly, child stealing, family!* she thought fiercely. Gannon The Grey belonged in Hell. He fit. It would probably be a step up for him.

But Kimberly Ragene Ainsley did not belong in Amen Hale, she belonged at home, with her mother, not in some godforsaken, child abusing, sadistic hellhole! And these people had her daughter right now. Karen Ainsley reached into her pocket and pulled out a tissue (one that she'd already used on her nose and meant to throw away) and used it to wipe at her tears.

Black Rain

Family Reunion

"MY LOVE, MARY and Emma are coming," Believer said to me as I lay in his arms acting like I was asleep. "Your mother and father are with them, but your sisters seem to be quite upset."

I sighed. "Set me down," I said.

My modest husband first adjusted my loin cloth to make sure it hung properly and then set me on my feet. They were walking down the path right toward us. Mary and Emma stomped along in front, Cathryn, Cornelius, Lucius, and a group of fifteen or twenty of our men dressed in black outfits who stepped lively to keep pace.

When Mary and Emma saw me and met my eyes, they froze like statues, still twenty yards away. Cathryn spoke with them. I was sure she was reassuring them, telling them it wasn't as bad as it looked. Cathryn hadn't asked me any questions about what I was now and neither had Believer, but I knew that that was about to change. I could see the green glow in the air around Mary and I could feel the charge in the air as she closed the last of the distance between us. Emma stalked along beside her like a tall beautiful cat with its claws out and ready to scratch. I stepped away from Believer to meet them alone.

Mary stopped in front of me. "No way! What the hell is this?" she demanded as she looked me up and down.

Emma walked in a wide circle around me, giving my wildly swinging tail some wide clearance as she passed behind me. Cathryn, Cornelius, Lucius, Believer, and the people of Amen Hale gathered around us and watched as I faced my two sisters.

"Mary." I shook my head sadly, totally surprised by her hostile reaction since she'd wanted this to happen. "Don't you remember? You prayed. You needed me to be more than I was—*and now I am*. You prayed for rain, Mary Fae, and now you're angry that a flood came and killed the Black Witch? There is an old saying that you may appreciate now. Be careful what you pray for because you *just might get it*."

She shook her head looking me up and down. "I didn't pray for this!" she cried in distress, hands balled into fists at her sides. "This isn't what I wanted!"

Believer said, "Mary, do not be afraid. Rain is the same as before even though she has changed."

He tried to soothe her, but she just gave him a suspicious squint of glowing green eyes and I decided right then I'd do this the easy way.

"Mary, this will take all day if I let you freak out till hell freezes over, just come here and touch me, but be extra careful, Mary, because I'm not the Black Witch anymore, I'm the Black Lion now. I am a god."

Emma froze in mid stride. Mary blinked. Just a few steps behind Mary, Cornelius visibly paled but Cathryn didn't bat an eye and neither did Lucius, but his men did. Some of them began to whisper to their friends while a few began to quietly go to their knees. I watched one of the men urging another to kneel, pulling him by the shoulder. I didn't speak out loud but willed the wind to whisper my voice into the man's ears.

"Don't encourage anyone to bow to me. Let each man, woman, or child make that choice for themselves."

He looked up and stared at me open mouthed and I added.

"I have spoken to you, now tell the man you're holding my words if you would serve me."

I watched as he began speaking to the man he had his hands on, and I turned back to Mary and Emma.

"Promise me you won't hurt me on purpose. Before I touch you," Mary said with her eyes on my horns.

I frowned. "Shit, I'm still figuring myself out, Mar. I hope whatever you did before will still work, but you're going to have to find your own way to protect yourself because I do plan on touching you. I plan to touch every part of you." I stared at her and her eyes got bigger and bigger and bigger as I looked at her in a way I never had before.

"Oh my god," she said breathlessly.

"I'm right here, Mary." I smiled at her.

Cathryn laughed, surprising those around her so badly they jumped, but then she spoke to me.

"Rain. It's time to bring the guests here and let them mingle before the wedding. We don't have time for intimacy, we have work to do, my child." Cathryn was smiling as she said it.

"Yes, Mother," I answered. "But may I touch Mary first, and then she'll know what I am."

She nodded.

I went to my knees and put my arms out, waiting for Mary like a giant Venus fly trap waiting for a human fly. It was almost impossible for her to resist the urge to touch me, even if it was dangerous. All Mary had to do was touch someone to know them completely and know everything they'd ever done or thought or dreamed. But even as the Black Witch, she'd always stayed on the surface, never venturing deep inside what I was.

She could still see and know much from me though, just as someone with their face pressed against a window can see much of what goes on inside a house while still safely outside. What I said, what I did, what I saw, some of what I felt, and even thoughts she saw on the surface of my mind. I thought about these things and Mary being safe (outside of what I'd become) and kept that in the center of my mind as I waited with my eyes closed and arms open. I felt arms reach around my back and her head rested against my chest and I wrapped my arms around Mary. She shook and twitched in my grip, but not too violently, and after a minute she calmed.

"Are you all right, Mary?" I asked her gently.

"Yes." Her voice was strange. Soft and open and very un-Maryish.

"I don't know what to call you now because you're so many things to me," she said in the same odd voice.

I thought about all the things Mary was to me now. She had been my best friend for almost two years. And my sister in our coven. And now my lover though we hadn't even kissed. And more than that, she was one of my lambs now, and I was her Black Lion. She was mine.

"Yes. I am," Mary said, hearing my thoughts.

Time pressed at me annoyingly. I knew that we needed to get going, we had work to do. I wondered if Mary had met the bride and touched her and had her memories of where she lived so I could make a gateway and bring the guests for the wedding to Amen Hale.

"Yes," Mary answered having heard all I just thought. "Look in my mind, Rain, I've touched her and I have what you need." Mary said this, but she sounded so sad and frightened for some reason.

I willed Mary's thoughts about the bride to come into my mind and suddenly I had memories in my own head about a beautiful girl named "Alana" but her name used to be "Kim." I saw her huge white stucco home on the marsh and the living areas and rooms and the pool out back with its large open patio area for entertaining.

"Thanks, Mary." My tail had wrapped around her, the tip playing in her hair at the back of her neck, but I was surprised to see that Mary was crying now.

"Please forgive me, Rain."

"For what?" I asked.

"I knew you didn't want to be a god. I knew it, but I still did this to you."

She stared up at me. She was on the edge of a complete breakdown. I had no idea what was happening but she definitely had my attention now. We were still kneeling on the grass and I still held her loosely in the circle of my arms but she withdrew her arms from me and held them tight to herself, as if she didn't deserve to touch me.

"What do you mean? What did you do, Mary?"

"I took advantage of you, Rain. I manipulated you when you were weak and tired. I forced you to do it." She wiped at her eyes, then continued her confession. "I was selfish and greedy and evil. And scared. You were thinking about ending it all and taking away our powers and making us normal again, and I didn't want it to end, so I prayed to you. I knew exactly how to do it so that you would have to say yes. I knew you'd say yes. But I didn't think it would do this to you."

She stared up at my horns as her hands clenched and opened and moved around as if she were in the grips of an ADD fit; she couldn't seem to find a place to put them that felt right to her. "You didn't want this," Mary said. "I used you. I hurt you. I don't deserve you. I should have let you take it all away! You still can, Rain. Take it all away and make it end. Let it end and let me die for my sins alone."

She closed her eyes and looked down, too ashamed to look at me. Emma had been standing close enough to hear every word and her beautiful fear-filled eyes stared into mine, dreading what I might do.

I thought about last night, how completely worn down I'd been after saving Jane and what Mary did when I had collapsed on the lawn. She'd known exactly what to say and exactly how to say it because she knew my thoughts. She also must have known that I'd been thinking seriously about taking everyone's powers away, and watching the people of Amen Hale fall to their knees to worship me had pushed me over the line, toward a decision to end it all.

I didn't think Mary was power mad or evil, she just went nuts when she felt the end coming and she'd fought in the only way she could, by changing my mind. I wondered for a moment how far Mary would have gone to keep her power. If I wasn't immortal and a dagger through my heart would have done it, would she have killed me to keep her power?

"I don't know. Maybe. I'm sorry. I love you. Kill me."

Her answering voice to my thoughts was only a broken whisper spoken with her head still down, looking at my feet.

I loved her but I had to do something. I organized my terms carefully. I didn't bother telling her, Mary already knew. She nodded without saying a word, and I stood to my feet and Mary got even lower, kneeling down to the ground with her head at my feet.

"Rain?" Cathryn asked. "What are you going to do?"

Emma echoed Cathryn, "What are you going to do to her, Rain?"

"I will do what must be done," I answered them both.

"Let all Amen Hale know that I have sinned!" Mary shouted and her magic carried her words out across the lawn to all the servants in the field.

Everyone not already staring at us stopped whatever they were doing and gave us their full, frightened attention. Mary held my ankles and spoke with her face in the grass, her head between my feet.

"I have sinned against my friend! I have sinned against my sister! I have sinned against my lover! And I have sinned against my god!" she shouted.

I stood as still as a statue looking down at her and not out at the people around me. At my feet, Mary used my tail to wipe tears from her eyes and hugged it to herself. I loved her and I'd already forgiven her, but she shouted out, "She has forgiven me!" Her words rolled across the lawn like a warm soothing wind as her magic touched everyone. She told them so they would know what she already knew.

She kissed both my feet and finished with her promise. "I, Mary Fae, do swear and bind myself that I will never seek to make myself a god, or to make any other person or creature into a god, and that I will serve only The Black Lion all the days of my eternity. I give myself to her forever. So mote it be."

Only a handful of people echoed the benediction, "So mote it be." Cathryn's voice was clear and easy to hear but most of our people were silent, caught in a dazed open mouthed condition that was a mix of wonder/dread/confusion and apprehension about what was going to happen next.

Mary continued to cry herself out but when I next looked up I was shocked to see my brother Ryan looking right at me and my first thought was "OH SHIT!"

Bethany and Sky Dragon were beside him, but my attention was fixed on Ryan because I knew that this meeting was going to be ugly. Ryan didn't look horrified as he stared at me, but he did look upset. I knew he'd just heard all that Mary had said, and I threw my arms out and shrugged my shoulders in a helpless gesture.

"What could I do, Ryan? I couldn't very well let her do it again. Mary's sorry she did it, and she asked me to forgive her, and I did. And she promised not to do this," I pointed with both index fingers at my horns, "to anyone else."

Ryan walked closer, staring at me as if he were still trying to come to grips with what was standing in front of him. He looked on the ground to where Mary was curled around my feet, crying her eyes out, as my tail did its best to comfort her. He frowned grimly at Mary's weeping form.

"Don't be mad at her, Ryan. I'm the one she sinned against and I've already forgiven her," I said firmly.

"How did she even do this to you?" There was real anger in his voice.

"It wasn't just her. I made some stupid mistakes too, but what Mary did was bad." I nodded. "She used magic on me and prayed to me in such a way that I was compelled to answer, and the only way to answer her prayer was to become more than what I was, and the only thing more than what I was is what I now am. I am a god now, Ryan. I am the Black Lion."

His face fell and his eyes darkened dangerously as he stood there looking at me. "You told Mom and Dad and that reporter and everyone on TV that you didn't want people to bow down or pray to you. You're not supposed to be able to lie. You lied, Rain. You lied to everyone." He finished like judge, jury, and executioner. Guilty verdict delivered.

"The Black Witch made that promise, Ryan, and she died keeping it," I answered calmly. "I am still Rain, and I'm still your sister, but I am not the Black Witch anymore. I'm the Black Lion."

His face became a dark mask of righteous judgment. Standing behind him I saw Cathryn's and Cornelius's terrified faces looking on. They realized the danger we all faced. Lucius, Believer, and the others around us began looking at Ryan as if he were the one with horns and a tail.

Emma sensed the danger and came to me and wrapped herself around my leg beside Mary, and Bethany ran to me and fell on my other leg. Bethany's dark eyes stared up at me and her tail wrapped around her protectively, and I wept to see the face of my little lion staring up at me with such fear.

I looked back into the cold, angry eyes of my brother. He stared at me and the girls holding onto me. It felt as if all Amen Hale held its breath and waited to see what Ryan would do.

"I won't allow this, Rain. If you can't go back to being whatever it was you were before, then I'll end this myself."

"Will you end it, Ryan, or will you let God end it?" I asked.

His eyes narrowed further and his features hardened, setting himself to do whatever he meant to do.

I plunged ahead quickly, my words spoken without dignity but in a frightened rush. "Do you even care anymore that it's your power and not God's that you're throwing around!? Have you claimed the power for yourself that you thought was His? Will you answer your own prayers now, my brother?" I gave him a tilt of the head. "That's how it started with me." I finished well, finally getting my composure back.

A line ran across his brow like a crack in his mask of righteous indignation, and I quickly pressed on, not giving him time to think around what I'd just said. "All of this might end, Ryan, but it would not end in any way that you would like."

Ryan shook his head, fanning the flames of his outrage. "Someone has to put a stop to this!" he growled, then pointed to the men kneeling on the ground a few short yards away. "You think I don't know where this is heading!? I can see it, and I won't let it happen!"

"Do you think it's your place to judge me!?" I fired back.

"Someone has to!" he shouted. "God gave me the power to do it for a reason. He knew that I would need it!" he growled, staring me down as if he were ten feet tall to my puny seven.

"Will you also judge Bethany and Mary and Emma?" I asked.

He looked at them, clinging at my legs and feet and frowned, but not in anger.

"Is it your place to judge Believer and Sky Dragon and your beautiful Sky and all the rest? Are you the Lord now, Ryan? '*Judgment is mine, saith the Lord, I will repay.*'" I quoted a verse at him and gave him a sad mocking smile and watched his determination waver.

Behind him I saw the hopeful faces of Cathryn and Cornelius rooting me on as I tried to keep Ryan from unleashing his own personal brand of Holy Armageddon upon Amen Hale.

"I'm not the only one who can become a god, *Lord Ryan*." He winced as I colored his name. "A God I believe you know once said, '*Judge not that you be not judged.*' Although you seem willing to ignore his command while doling out judgment in his name, I actually think what he said was worth listening to. I will not judge you or try to stop you, so go ahead and judge me and all the rest of us if you want, Ryan, but consider the inconvenience factor."

I reached up with both hands, feeing the poky tips of my horns as I frowned. "If you're going to become a god of fire, brimstone, and judgment, you might grow a set of these things yourself, and they're a real bitch because they get in the way constantly. Your baseball cap wearing days would be done and you'd never be able to pull a t-shirt over your head again, but I actually think you'd like the tail."

I nodded and ended all the yelling and tension on a positive note and smiled at him. I waited along with everyone else, all our eyes focused on Ryan as he stood there, thinking.

One minute passed.

Two minutes passed.

"The tail is cool," he said finally, looking confused and dazed.

Sky Dragon stepped up beside Ryan and put an arm over his shoulder. "Ease up, Bro, those pills are making you crazy. Let's go get you a glass of wine and let you sit down."

Ryan let Sky Dragon lead him away and we all stared around in stunned relief as everyone attempted to "defreak" in their own individual ways.

"Someone! Anyone! Bring me a glass of wine!" Cathryn shouted with a tremble in her voice.

Cornelius was holding her arm to keep her on her feet. She looked shaken and her face was pale, her lips bloodless.

"Your brother is dangerous and unstable," Lucius complained, frowning.

Mary's voice drifted up from down at my feet. "You really thought we were about to become a big, greasy smudge." Mary had wrapped herself around my feet and she had her eyes closed, but she was touching me, so she was using my eyes and hearing my thoughts.

"Ryan's just drugged up on those pills," Bethany's sweet, little voice piped up in Ryan's defense. "He'll mellow out once he's done trippin'."

"What!? The Hell!? Was that!?" Emma burst out like a pent up explosion. She took one step away from my leg then turned and stared up at me like she was about to pick up where Ryan left off. "Here all our lives are on the line—and you bust out with '*the Inconvenience Factor*'?! That's what you use as your big closing argument to save our asses!" She threw her hands up in the air in exasperation. "What the hell were you thinking?! What kind of god busts out with some retarded ass nonsense like '*the Inconvenience Factor*'?! I almost—"

I reached out and grabbed her in a burst of speed that left her breathless. I held her up against myself as I stared down into her very surprised face.

"This kind of god," I said.

And then I kissed her.

Valaria Vale

Brother's Keeper

THE SCENE ON the other side of the gateway was amazing. Flower arrangements were everywhere. Chairs and tables decorated and ready for the wedding stood to one side along with a group of musicians all playing hauntingly beautiful music on stringed instruments. The wedding guests coming from the Ainsleys' patio merged with a crowd of people already there, all wearing beautiful gowns or tuxedos, milling about as white liveried servants roamed about with trays of drinks and hors d'oeuvres.

Valaria headed into the elegantly dressed mix with single-minded determination, searching the crowd for a head with blue hair.

All she spotted was the giant cloud man, who was standing off to the side of the gathering with a half naked girl with creepy, red eyes and horns sprouting out of her head. After all the cryptic warnings from the House Steward about what they may see, Valaria was actually a little disappointed, and then she almost got whacked by someone's tail. A young girl walking by had a long black tail happily swishing about behind her, poking through a hole in the back of her dress.

"All right. That's kinda weird," she mumbled, then marched ahead.

People she did not know greeted her politely, and she returned the greetings but kept searching until she spotted what she was looking for. Blue hair. He was sitting away from the main group on a stone bench, staring out at nothing. He looked good. But he also looked bad. He was extremely handsome in his well-tailored black tux, but the happy, carefree grace that he always wore like a warm glow seemed stripped away. Valaria knew that something was way wrong. She walked up, totally unseen, and sat on the bench right beside him.

"Val?" Gannon said, confused at first by the dress before he lit up and shouted "Val!" and threw his arms around her and hugged her for a brief moment before gripping her arms and pulling away, looking over her shoulder as if he expected trouble.

"What the hell are you doing here!" he hissed as his eyes tracked back and forth looking behind her.

"Me! What the hell are you doing here!?" she answered back. She couldn't help turning around to see if someone was coming for them. Her brother was acting so spooked it was catching.

Gannon let go of her arms and forced himself to calm down. He looked his sister up and down again. "You actually wore a dress. Have you *ever* worn a dress before?" he teased, giving her one of his old smiles.

"Shut up." She gave him a shove.

"Is it just you or did Mom come?"

"Me, Mom, and Ben," she answered, then had to explain for the next five minutes how they knew where he was, how they got here, and what it was like at the Ainsleys' as Gannon chattered away, asking questions before she could finish her answers.

Gannon could be quiet when he was happy or angry, but he was always overly chatty when he was scared, nervous, or sad. She was betting he was all three right now. This looked bad all the way around. If this girl were the right one he wouldn't be acting like this.

"Are you gonna tell me what's wrong or are you gonna make me ask?" she finally asked. They'd turned around on their stone bench and were people watching together.

"I love Alana," Gannon sighed out, "and I want to marry her, but this place is insane. They really do have human sacrifices here, Val. And they have real vampires and real witches. And be careful what you eat tonight because they'll be serving up the guy they sacrificed this afternoon."

"For real?" Valeria cut in, hoping he was kidding.

"It will probably be made to look like regular food. These people aren't for show, they're the real deal." He pointed to where Black Rain stood on the other side of the field with Believer beside her. "See the tall girl with horns and red glowing eyes? That used to be the Black Witch."

"What the hell happened to her?"

"She told us all some stupid story about lions, and then she turned into that thing." He waved an arm in Rain's direction.

"Screw this hell hole. Let's bolt!" Valaria was already searching the crowd, looking for their mom and Ben.

"It's not that easy, Val," Gannon said wearily.

She turned her gaze back to him. "What do ya mean, not that easy? We'll get Ben and Mom, walk through the gateway thing, and then run like hell."

"Val, that's not what I mean. I don't think Alana *will* leave," Gannon said sadly.

"Why not?"

Gannon seemed to struggle for words as he made a face that usually preceded throwing up. "It's impossible to explain. Unless you were there to see it and feel it. Really, Val."

Valaria pushed her glass of wine into her brother's hand. He took a drink and started speaking. Chatty.

"They had us all gathered together into a big building, built almost like a church, and made us watch as they did it. The guy was begging and screaming until they used magic to shut his mouth, but he kept on kicking and fighting—and then the knife, the little girl didn't want to do it but the Black Witch made her do it—and the blood and all the rest." Gannon put a hand over his stomach and had to take a few deep breaths to keep from throwing up.

Valaria felt shaken just from watching her brother. She looked out at the people in their fine clothes and listened on purpose for a second to the beautiful music. Every beautiful dress, smiling servant, the beautiful house and flowers, and even the music took on a sinister cast. Valaria felt goose bumps rise on her arms. They needed to get out!

"Did your girl watch all this with you?" she asked.

"She didn't even blink," he said sadly. "She watched every bit and even made me stay to watch shit we didn't even have to watch. I think Alana's in shock from watching all that sick shit, but I think she's also bought into the idea that the Black Witch is really a god now. Alana's losing it more and more each second we stay here."

Valaria was confused. "Alana, Alana, who the hell's Alana? I thought your girl's name was Kim."

Gannon rolled his eyes. "They let us change our names when we came here this morning. Kim hated her name so she changed it to 'Alana Burning,' but she begged me to keep mine the same." He laughed. "My stupid name actually fits here." He kept laughing and Valaria gave him an angry shake.

"Dammit, Gannon! You just got here this morning and they already changed her name, threw her ass into shock, brainwashed her, and now they want you to marry her so you'll stay and they can fry your blue brains along with hers." She threw a hand out at the scene in front of them. "They plan on doing this wedding in about thirty minutes. You're not really going to go through with this, are you?"

She watched in horror as he nodded.

"You just met these people!" she argued. "Hell, you just met this girl! You don't even know her, Gannon, let alone love her."

"I do love her. I brought her here and I won't leave her here alone!" Gannon said. His voice was fiercely determined but his face wasn't. "I can't leave her. Dammit, Val, she wouldn't even be here if it wasn't for me; she'd be safe at home with her mother and father and her stupid, rich, jock boyfriend. God knows what the witches will do to her if I leave. They're already circling around her like buzzards over road kill."

Valaria listened as her brother heaped guilt and responsibility on himself for this girl who sounded like, *well,* road kill.

"If she's getting worse each second, you better play all your cards now to see if you can save her." The crowd was getting thick and Valaria wanted some time alone with her brother. She needed to stiffen his weak spine.

"Come on, Gannon, let's go for a little walk and talk this through." She stood up, but he stayed on his bench.

"What are you talking about, Val? I'm marrying her. I'm staying here, and I'm keeping her safe." Gannon said it, but it was even weaker. He was practically begging her to do it.

Valaria pointed out into the crowd. "Hey, I think I see Kim's mother coming this way."

Gannon was up in an instant.

"Let's go!" he said as he followed his sister farther away from the wedding party and farther away from his bride.

Alana Burning

My Mean Mother

"KIM!" MY MOTHER'S angry voice shouted my name, and the air got squeezed out of me as Niu tightened around my waist in surprise.

The women around me reluctantly parted, opening a path to the doorway and my mother. She stood there glaring. Her face and eyes said that she was about to destroy me, but I didn't flinch, look down, or cringe. Niu's arms were around my waist, holding tight, and I knew Gannon was out there waiting for me. Princess Emma was on the couch right beside me, and all the women helping me get dressed gave me their warm support. And then there was Sky's reassuring smile as well. She'd told me about her own mother.

I looked back at mine, and somehow her outrage didn't reach my heart. She came into the room and stopped in front of me, staring at my face suspiciously, wondering why I wasn't quaking in my boots or frantically arguing my point.

I just smiled at her.

"Kimberly, do you intend to go through with this insanity?" she asked crisply. Not angry. It was the way she usually talked. To me, to Dad, to my two brothers, to the kid at the checkout line bagging the groceries.

I kept my voice polite as I answered, "Yes, I'm getting married. And you should also know that my name's not Kimberly anymore. I changed it when I came here. I'm Alana now."

"Alana." She said my name and made a face like she'd eaten something that shouldn't have been eaten.

"All right—*Alana.*" Her tone shifted to manipulative mother mode. "If you're determined to go through with this, what do you intend to do once you're married? Are you going to stay here in this *place*?" She raised her eyebrows at me. "What do you think your life here will be like?" She gave me an ugly smile as she looked, side to side, at the ladies around me. "Will you be a maid or work in the kitchens or do the laundry for the King and Queen?"

"Actually, we were discussing that when you walked in," Emma said as she stood up from the couch where she'd been sprawled out like a long sexy cat, talking to me while we waited for the wedding to start.

"Emma, I told you that I've made up my mind," I said firmly and she nodded, looking ashamed that she'd asked again.

I wasn't surprised to see my mother stare in gape mouthed surprise as she took in the whole sight of Emma because there was so much to see. She eyed her shocking clothes, the amazing glittering ruby belt around her waist, her black lips, her amazing eyes, the body that just screamed SEX! SEX! SEX! and the mark on her forehead.

Emma had fainted earlier and they'd brought her to the couch here in the Green Room to rest and recover. Hanna and Byron had carried her because they were the only two allowed to touch her. Hanna had stayed behind by Emma's couch like a guard dog, keeping everyone clear and well away. Hanna explained that she'd touched the Princess this morning, before they understood her condition, so it didn't matter if she touched her again because she already loved her.

Hanna seemed fine to all of us, although she did seem to enjoy touching Emma a bit more than was proper for a servant, and her touches seemed to linger longer than necessary. Emma seemed happy with her, giving Hanna little smiles and intentionally asking her for things that would bring her close. Hanna was a forty-year-old woman; though fit and far from ugly, she was still more than twice Emma's age and it seemed, not dirty, but awkward. Still, I was glad that there was at least one person in the room that Emma could touch because there were so many of us that she couldn't. I didn't want her to be alone.

"*A-la-na.*" My mother said my new name in three distinct pieces, her eyes still on Emma. "Please introduce me, and then explain what she's talking about. Is this about the wedding or some new insanity?"

"Mother, this is Princess Emma Hale. The White Witch. And she is talking about what I shall be here in Amen Hale." My mother looked from Emma to me.

"And—" She waited for more.

"And I have decided to be a servant and join these women." I gestured toward the servants. "Gannon and I will serve Amen Hale, King Cornelius, Queen Cathryn, the Princesses, and the Lords and Ladies of Amen Hale. We'll be servants. And we'll be happy."

My mother stiffened, her eyes two deep pits of disappointment and hurt, but the women standing quietly around the room gave me warm, welcoming smiles as if I were already one of them and was welcome among them.

"Was this your only choice?" my mother asked shrewdly, taking in Emma's sad face and the happy smiling maids.

I said it as simply as I could. "Princess Emma wanted me to become her sister and be the fifth Princess of Amen Hale."

My mother looked totally shocked for a second, but then her face fell again. "She offered to make you a Princess but you would rather do the dishes?" She sounded angry and confused. "Why?"

"The price is too high. I won't pay it," I said clearly without giving details, then smiled as I added, "Don't worry, I'll be happy here. I know you wanted a different life for me, and you had lots of plans, but it's not like I'm dead you know." I dared a little angst. "I may have a new name, a new home, a husband, and eventually a family, but I'll still be your daughter. We don't have phones but we'll be able to write letters back and forth and maybe even visit every once in a while."

I watched my mother as she considered everything I said very carefully. Nothing ever made her lose her cool and she always thought things through the same way she talked, quickly and crisply.

"Are you certain you thought this through carefully?" She paused and grimaced. "Alana, you're emotional right now. And in love." Her features and her voice softened as she added, "And being in love always melts your brains and makes you silly if it's the real thing." She sighed and looked at Emma reverting to her old crisp self.

"Why did you want Alana to be a Princess? Is it because she's beautiful?" she said, noticing once again at how Emma was dressed.

Emma shook her head. "Alana is *very* beautiful," she gave me an uncomfortable, shy glance, "but this isn't about beauty. It's about magic and power and the order of things. I'm part of a coven of four witches called Star Night. Tuesday night when one of the coven was taken and murdered by some religious nuts, the magic started to search for a replacement. A fourth witch. The first woman it tried to take refused the offer. And then the magic found another who accepted and paid the price. It found me." Emma took two steps closer and rested one glossy black nailed finger on her forehead. "There should be four stars on my Coven Mark, Mrs. Ainsley." We could all see that there were only three stars now. "A few hours ago we lost one of our sisters, and now the magic seeks a fourth witch, and the magic will continue to search until it finds a fourth."

Emma had already told me her own story as she lay on the couch. She told me how she became a witch and how she'd done it and what it had cost her to become a witch. She said that she'd gained her heart's desire (the love of the vampire girl Jane) but that she also lost much more than she ever planned to lose because she'd lost her mind. She explained the price. She explained what to do and exactly how to do it, and then she asked me if I wanted it.

The ladies in the room and Sky and Niu had all listened quietly to everything Emma had told me and I'd wondered why they were all treating me so oddly. I realized right then that they were already starting to treat me like a Princess and that frightened me. The whole thing sounded like a horrible trap and wildly unpredictable, like anything could happen. Any good you experienced seemed to be offset by some unexpected ugliness or unplanned costs.

I politely thanked her for the offer, told her that I was honored, but that I would rather be a servant of Amen Hale and simply live here with Gan and serve along with the others. Emma hadn't been surprised at my rejection. She even said that any sane person would make the same choice I made. Emma had wished us well, gave me a final longing look, then retreated to her couch as Savanah and the other servants had gathered around me, hugging me and handling me a little less like a princess and more like a friend or a new daughter.

My mother seemed pale and shaken. Either Princess Emma had frightened her or what the Princess had said about me and what I'd been offered had frightened her, but fear was not a look I was used to seeing on my mother's face.

"Alana, if you tell me that you thought this through carefully and you're sure that you made the right decision then I'll believe it," she said with feeling.

I blinked in total surprise.

Was this woman my mother?

"I made the right choice." I said with feeling as well.

Then Niu spoke, "It's the choice I would make too, Alana, if I were in your place." Niu's sweet, high pitched voice seemed to come from nowhere though I felt the small movements in the cloth in my waist as she opened and closed her mouth to speak the words. Her eyes and mouth were behind me at the top of the train.

Sky had made her that way so she could see the faces of the crowd as we walked down the aisle together and make sure she billowed and fanned out perfectly.

When Sky had come to me with her new daughter and told me that Niu had asked her to turn her into a wedding train so she could help me be more beautiful in my wedding, I'd been speechless, and after spending just five minutes with Niu I'd fallen in love with her. I could tell by some of her questions that she was new, and like a child, but in other ways she seemed so wise. Niu was wonderful and I was glad she'd be with me when I did this. It made me feel like I wasn't alone, and for some reason having her around me, occasionally giving me a squeeze, made me feel confident and like I belonged here. Like I'd always belonged here.

"Who said that?" My mother's head swiveled this way and that as she searched for the source of the voice.

"Mother, I want to introduce you to my best friend in the whole world," I said with a big grin.

Niu laughed behind me, the sweet merry sound so wonderful it made me laugh too.

"I thought your best friend was Sharon. Or that Gannon would have claimed the title by now," she said, still looking around for the source of the voice, mystified as to where it was coming from.

"Sharon was Kimberly Ainsley's best friend and Gannon will be my husband, but Niu is my best friend. You will be surprised when you see her, but remember, Niu is a person, with a soul and a spirit. She's new, so be nice."

The maids, Emma, and Sky put on big expectant smiles as they waited for the reveal and I turned around, facing the other direction craning my neck and looking back over my shoulder as best I could to see my mother's reaction. Niu let her gently billowing length settle to the ground so she wouldn't be so distracting as she spoke.

"Hello Mrs. Ainsley. I'm Niu."

My mother smiled, but she frowned with her eyes as she looked at Niu and I was glad that I'd cautioned her to be good, but when she finally spoke she didn't even sound like my mother. She was polite, respectful, and even sweet.

"Hello, Niu. I'm sure that I'm not the first to say it, but it simply must be said again, you are beautiful. And 'Niu' is such a lovely name. What does it mean?"

"Niu means girl in Chinese, Mrs. Ainsley," she said happily.

"Alana," Niu spoke to me in a voice that was almost a whisper yet still loud enough for everyone to hear, "I thought you said that your mother was mean."

"I thought she was!" I answered honestly in my own too loud whisper.

The ladies around us tried to stifle their laughs, clamping hands over mouths, but then my mother started to laugh and we all joined her, Princess Emma, Sky, Niu, and the ladies among whom I would be serving. We all laughed, and I was so happy I started to cry.

Alana Burning

Offerings and Sacrifice

EMMA STOOD BY the glass doors with Hanna, looking out at the lawn, watching the wedding guests. My mother had just left to take her seat with the others and my father now stood beside me, holding my arm, happily speaking to Sky and Niu, fascinated with their company as we waited for the wedding march to start.

"Do you want to see your Lion, Alana? She's standing at the back row of seats. I'll step away while you look if you want to come see," she offered kindly.

"Thank you, Princess Emma," my father answered for us, "we're good."

Emma shook her head and went back to looking out the window.

Dad gave me a curious look. "Why does she keep saying that, Kimmy?" My father refused to call me by my new name no matter how much I complained.

"Saying what?" I played stupid.

"Your Lion?" he asked.

"It's my business, Dad," I said defensively, not meeting his eyes.

"It sounds like a religious thing. Is it?" he pressed.

"It's my business."

"And sticking my nose in your business is *my business*. I'm your father," he said smugly.

I stared at the glass doors. I wanted to go look out at the lawn and see her. And see what she looked like now. Dad leaned close to my ear, keeping his voice low so the others wouldn't overhear.

"I know they are saying that this girl is a god now, but you don't believe that." He gave my hand a gentle squeeze where it rested on his arm and gave me one of his mocking little smiles. Dad always talked down to us like we were all idiots. He was smart and liked to remind everyone that he was smarter than they were.

"I met Princess Rain when I was out there. I talked to her for a while and she seems like a decent person. A bit theatrical with her outfit, but I guess having a tail would make clothes a bit hard to wear." He raised his eyebrows and laughed, shaking his head. "Once they get these drugs safe enough for a sane person to take it will change absolutely everything. But Kim, if you plan to live here you can't be weak minded. You'll have to keep your wits about you and be careful. Don't buy into these colorful fantasy lives they've built for themselves. Keep the facts fixed firmly in your head. Princess Rain is a seventeen-year-old girl who took pills and developed unused portions of her brain. Dr. Burgis, the man who engineered the pills is right out there," he pointed toward the glass doors, "and he lives here in Amen Hale with the kids, still keeping an eye on them, still working on his research. I met him. He's a delightful and brilliant man." He chuckled. "What these pills can do will make computers and the internet seem like Neanderthal paintings on the walls of caves. The future is going to be fantastic. It will be the dawn of a frightening new era of human civilization and it could be ugly if it's not handled correctly..."

My father continued to blather along, but I tuned him out. I ran my hand over the bow tied at my waist and Niu gave me a comforting squeeze in return. After a minute Dad realized that my lights were on but I'd abandoned ship and he turned and began to pester Sky. Dad loved to talk.

"Emma, would you mind moving?" I asked.

She and Hanna walked to the side leaving the glass doors open for me while Savanah and Sky kept my father busy.

I quickly snuck away to the doors and looked out across the lawn to where the chairs were all set up.

I saw her. She was standing about ten feet behind the last row of chairs. Princess Emma had told me that Rain looked different now, but I could hardly believe my eyes! Her long black tail swished about behind her and all she wore was a strip of cloth coving her front and the same over her breasts. Like my father said, it wasn't much. Her black hair ran down to the small of her back but it no longer waved about like she stood under water; now it simply looked like beautiful black hair. The blue tips of horns stuck up above her hair just a few inches, and I smiled and giggled as the thought struck me that they looked like blue antennas.

I watched her as she stood there, talking to Mary and I wondered what she was and what she was to me. Was this even the same girl who'd told the story in The Hallow and came for me when I called? Why did she come to me? Why was I so sure she would come? Why did I want her to come? What was I even doing? Was she a god or a girl? Was she my Lion?

Question after question tumbled through my mind as I stared at her, watching how she moved and laughed and how her tail played happily behind her. My attention moved to the stage as Gannon walked up the steps and took his place beside King Cornelius. I couldn't really see his face from this far away, but he looked handsome in his black tuxedo. His blue hair stood out so nicely, making him different from everyone else. He was my *Blue*. He stood straight and tall, waiting for me to come to him.

"Is it almost time?" asked Niu in her sweet voice.

"Yes. As soon as the music changes, it's time to go," I said. The door was open just a crack and the sound of violins and other stringed instruments could be heard playing softly along with the soft murmurs of the guests.

"The music is beautiful," Niu said.

"Thank you again, Niu. I still can't believe you had Sky make you into my wedding train. That's the nicest thing anyone's ever done for me." My voice started to break and my tears threatened to run and ruin my makeup. "I don't know what to say to you or how to thank you."

"Alana," Niu said, sounding emotional herself, "please forgive me."

"For what, Niu?" I asked, surprised.

"I misled you. I did not lie, but I let you think my actions were altruistic, which is the same as a lie because I did not choose this form for you. When my Sky first made me I saw that she and the ladies with her all had on such pretty dresses. I asked them why they were wearing such pretty dresses and they told me that there was going to be a wedding. I was so excited. I knew what a wedding was, and I knew that the bride is always the most beautiful person at a wedding and that everyone would be looking at her. So I asked my Sky to make me into a wedding train so I could be in the wedding and everyone could see how beautiful I was. I wanted everyone to see me and my beauty. I did it for me and not for you, Alana.

Forgive me, my friend. After having spent time with you, my first thoughts in life seem so petty and small now. I am vain and selfish," she finished sadly.

"But that's not how you feel now, is it?" I said.

"No," she answered softly.

"Niu, I'm alone in so many ways," I admitted to her and to myself. "I am scared in this place with all its magic, and I'm worried about Gannon and how freaked out he was earlier. I'm worried about my parents and family and what they will be thinking when I stand up there and get married to this boy they don't even know. And I'm worried I might faint or trip or get so nervous that I throw up as I stand up there in front of everyone. And I am scared of Rain, the Black Lion. Something about her is special to me and I don't understand it. And in just a few moments I will walk out this door and I will see all my family and Gannon and I will see my Lion and I am scared, Niu." I had to stop to take a breath.

"You're my only real friend. I don't care what you look like, I'd still have you tied around my waist if you looked like a dirty dish rag. I'm just glad you're with me and that I won't be alone. Even when I say my vows you will be holding me and that is what I need the most. I need a friend, Niu," I told her.

"I am your friend, Alana. You are not alone."

Before I went back to my father, I turned around and let Niu see the wedding party for a while and she asked questions about Gannon and King Cornelius and Black Rain. As Niu spoke, I watched the woman who had done my hair and make-up, off to the side, talking with Princess Emma.

She was on her knees, begging. Hanna pulled her to her feet and gave her a shove, propelling her toward the other servants and away from Emma. She'd been begging Emma to let her be the fourth witch since I'd refused the offer. Emma apparently didn't want her, but she wasn't taking the hint.

Niu gave me a hard squeeze around the middle, getting my attention.

"Oh. Sorry, Niu, I was watching Romanda go crazy. What'd I miss?"

"It's time!" she said loudly. "The MUSIC has changed!"

"Aaaa!" I screamed. "DaAAaaad! Come! Come! Come!" I yelled, bouncing on the toes of my snug white flats.

I heard Niu laughing as everyone gathered around, quickly getting into position. Niu had been holding back all this time but now she stretched out and began to billow and shimmer and glow and all the women around us oohed and ahhed as Niu and I stepped out with my father and started up the path. We were still a good ways away, but already I could see the staring eyes of everyone up ahead and the red eyes of my Lion, and on the stage Gannon was looking at me.

"Niu," I whispered to her.

"Yes," she whispered back.

"Forgive me for lying to you."

Beside me my Dad gave me a curious look and his smile dropped to half mast.

"What did you lie about?" Niu asked me.

"I'm glad you're not a dirty dish rag. I'm glad you're beautiful."

Niu giggled. "I'm glad I'm not a dirty dish rag either."

We both giggled.

"Hush, you two," Dad told us both, but he was smiling. Dad liked Niu.

We hushed and walked forward in silence to the sound of the music and my father's measured strides. My eyes locked on Rain and the broad smile she wore as we approached. I didn't care about the horns, the tail, or what she wore or didn't wear, or how tall she was—I focused on her smile.

As we drew closer I whispered to my father that I needed to stop and bow. He released my arm and I turned to face her and did the best curtsey I could manage with Niu stretched out behind me, but Rain was smiling when I came up from my curtsey, and I smiled back at her and ignored the eyes of the crowd who stood before their chairs and watched from not fifteen feet away. My father impatiently waited for me as I looked at—

"*My Lion*," I whispered.

"Hello, my little Red Lamb," she said.

Dad stepped over and took my arm again. "Princess." He gave her a stiff nod and pulled me away before I could say anything back. I walked down the aisle beside him in a dreamy daze.

My vision squeezed in like a funnel by the standing crowd of smiling people so that I looked ahead and upward, toward Gannon. He stood there looking down at me, so serious and grave and handsome beside King Cornelius's happy smiling face and I smiled at him. My father stopped at the foot of the platform, and Cornelius said a few words, addressing our friends and family before asking my father, "Who gives this woman to be married?"

Dad was quiet. I watched as his wild eyes went from me, up to Gannon, then he turned and looked at Mom in the front row. She nodded, clearly embarrassed by his delay.

"Her mother and I do," Dad said in a growl. He kissed me on the head and let me go and I walked up the four steps with Niu billowing out behind me to a fresh wave of oohs and ahhs as everyone got a better view of us together.

I came to stand before Gannon with King Cornelius standing between us. He started, speaking of love and commitment and sacrifice for each other's happiness. It wasn't the usual words I heard at a wedding but they were similar and they were beautiful. Gannon was staring into my eyes as Cornelius finally asked, "If any person objects to this union, let them speak now or forever hold their—"

"I have something I need to say to Alana before we get married," Gannon said abruptly.

Surprised noises rose from my family.

"Gannon?" I asked, confused and frightened by the look on his face.

Cornelius seemed surprised as well, but he nodded. "We will give you two a moment then." He looked out at the crowd. "Quiet please!" he ordered firmly, then he stepped back a few paces, watching us.

"Alana, I love you with all my heart, and I will marry you, but we can't stay here." He didn't whisper, he spoke loud enough for everyone to hear. He glanced at King Cornelius then back to me before he continued. "We can't stay with these people, Alana. I won't let you lose your mind as they hold their bloody human sacrifices every day! And their sick little sex show with the vampires! And I won't share you around with all these witches who stare at you like a piece of fresh meat!" His voice was loud and angry and I heard the murmur of voices from my family, agreeing with him, worried about his words. "We'll get married, we'll enjoy the reception, and even eat the food they serve. And then we will leave Amen Hale with everyone else," he said like it was already done and decided.

What the hell was he thinking? Had he forgotten why we came here in the first place?

"What are we going to do, Gannon?" I shouted back, angry and hurt. "Where are we gonna live!?" I yelled the words at him. "We came to Amen Hale because this was the only place we could be together, *remember!?*"

Gannon turned and looked out at my father who was standing at the foot of the platform beside my mother. "Mr. Ainsley, if Alana and I leave Amen Hale, will you let us live together under your roof as man and wife? Once I'm able to provide a place for us we'd move out, but till then, would we be welcome at your home?"

My dad's face lit up like someone had just thrown a drowning man a lifeline. "Absolutely!" he shouted. "If you can get her to leave this hell hole you'd be more than welcome to stay with us. Just do exactly what you said, Gannon. Marry my daughter, let's enjoy the reception, thank our hosts, and let's go home, son."

There were rousing shouts of "YEAH!" and the like from my family, all of whom were rising from their chairs, standing and hugging each other while the women wiped away happy tears. They seemed to be celebrating victory without me having said a word. I saw my mother stand and hug my father. She was smiling and looking relieved while Dad was grinning from ear to ear and my stupid brothers actually started to shout, "Gan-non! Gan-non! Gan-non!" like a bunch of idiots.

It reminded me of the way Gannon had moved the crowd in the fairgrounds after the fairy dance. With just a few words he had captured them and had them dancing to his tune like a magical, blue haired, pied piper—and now he'd done it again. All I had to do was go along with it and ride the wave and by tonight I'd be married and home with my family. And Gannon.

Niu gave me a squeeze around my waist and a prickling heat raced across my skin as I thought. What about the rest of my family? What about Niu? What about my Lion? What about Mary and Emma and Cathryn and Cornelius?

For some reason they already felt like my family. I didn't want to lose them.

Gannon turned back to face me like a conquering hero with a huge grin on his face and the crowd at his back. "Well, Alana. We'll be able to stay at your place and get out of here. Let's get married." He turned back to Cornelius and waved him over.

Cornelius came, still wearing a small polite smile even after the insults. I reached out and touched his wrist before he started.

"*I object.*" I tried to say the words but no words came out. I swallowed and tried again, leaning a little closer to Cornelius who bent down and gave me his ear. "I object," I managed to say, my voice barely able to make the words come out of my desert dry throat and mouth.

"What's wrong?" Gannon asked.

"I object," I said loud enough for Gannon to hear for himself.

Gannon looked shocked, but Cornelius gave me a kindly smile and backed away again as I faced Gannon. My family went quiet too, still standing as they watched with smiling faces frozen in place, totally confident of victory.

"What's the problem, Alana? We have everything we wanted and more. Marry me and let's go home," he said with a smile.

"I am home," I croaked.

Gannon kept his smile in place. "No, this is a place we visited. It'll be the first of many. We'll be old coots sitting in rockers together and we'll remember this place and we'll say, 'Now that was some *craazy* shit!'" He laughed happily, then reached out and touched my face. "Just let it go," he urged. "These people have you confused and turned around. Don't over think it, Kim. Just let it go and let's go home."

His using my old name was like a kick in the gut. My hand went to my waist and I touched Niu's ribbon and she gave me a squeeze.

"I have friends here I don't want to leave, Gannon," I said, my fingers playing nervously with the silky, cloud-like material of her ribbon arms.

"If they're real friends, they would tell you to go."

"*Stay*," came a soft high voice, so quiet that I barely heard it myself, and I was sure Gannon hadn't heard.

She gave me a squeeze and held it for a moment as if to say "*I will not let you go!*"

"There are people here that I love, Gannon."

"People you just met this morning," he sneered.

My brows furrowed and I tilted my head to the side as I gave back, "I just met you too. And I love you."

"Who is it, Kim? Tell me who?" He looked out at the crowd then back to me. "Do you love *Queen* Cathryn or *King* Cornelius more than your own mother and father?" He put a little sneer into *Queen* and *King*, making the titles insults.

I looked back at the man, standing quietly a few feet away and he gave me a kind smile as Gannon continued whatever it was he was doing.

"Do you love Princess Emma and Princess Mary more than your own brothers?" he asked.

"What's the hold up, Kim!" my older brother Nathan called from the crowd.

"Com'on, Kim," my other brother Doug shouted as if on cue to the blue-haired conductor of the band.

Gannon waved Cornelius back over. "Let's go," he told him, then looked back to me. "I love you, Kim. Me. Your Gannon. I. Love. You. Do you still love me?" he asked.

"Yes, Gan, I love you," I said, and I did, but I felt like I was about to break in half.

"Good!" He stepped forward and wrapped his arms around me and kissed me.

It seemed I missed some time somewhere.

Cornelius was talking again, continuing with the wedding.

I heard Gannon say, "I do."

I said it also.

I looked down, suddenly horrified to find my hands balled into tight fists wrapped in the ribbons of Niu's arms. My shaking hands moved in a panic as I tried to straighten the wrinkled ribbons and rub them flat again. Cornelius was saying something about rings, but I was so worried that I'd hurt her arms that I pulled the bow and undid the ribbon bow completely to get the kinks out of her arms, but as soon as the bow was undone and the ribbon was free both sides came to life and wrapped around me, holding onto me without being tied in a bow.

"I will not let you go!" Niu said.

"I don't want you to!" I cried as I wrapped my arms around the ribbon at my waist.

"Who the hell are you talking to?" Gannon asked, wide eyed as he looked at Niu's floating, billowing cloth body and the ribbon arms that held me. His face became an angry, suspicious mask. "Are you talking to your dress? Is that thing ALIVE!?" he asked, disgust and horror on his face.

"Niu is not a 'thing,' Gan; she's my friend," I said through my tears.

Gannon just shook his head and pressed on. He held a ring up, showing it to me. "Give me your hand, Kim."

I held out my hand and he pressed the ring into place.

King Cornelius then looked at me, clearly wondering if I wanted to proceed.

"I want to get married, Gan, but I will not leave Amen Hale," I told Gannon firmly. Finally saying how I felt.

"We can't stay here. It's not safe," he insisted as he slipped his own ring on his own finger, not waiting for me to do it or for King Cornelius to say the "with this ring" part.

"What do you think will happen here!?" I shouted.

"You *don't want to know*," he growled darkly. "Now let it go and let's finish this and go home with your family."

He took my hand and turned us to face King Cornelius who looked at me and raised an eyebrow.

"I will marry you, but I won't leave," I said again, quietly.

"I'm through with this," he said and rolled his eyes. "If you love this place and these people more than me, that's your choice. I won't stay here and watch what they do to you, Kim. It's not going to be pretty and I won't stay here and watch it happen." He took a couple of steps away from me.

"So that's it?" I asked.

"Yeah, that's it," he said flatly.

"But I love you!" I shouted.

"Then leave with me!" he shouted back.

"Stay with me! Live here with me! Gannon, please don't leave me!"

Gannon turned and walked down the steps, and I rushed to the edge of the platform.

"Where are you going!?" I shouted down at him, crying.

Gannon turned and looked up at me, his face angry and hard. "Come with me and find out, Kim."

I wrung my hands together trying to think of what to say to make him stay. "If it's dangerous here, you should stay and keep me safe! Stay and watch over me, Gan! Please!" I begged.

His eyes darkened. "You liked watching that blood bath this afternoon, *Alana*." He said my new name like a curse. "I almost puked my guts out, but you enjoyed it. I don't want to watch that every day for the rest of my life."

I shouted, "I gave myself to you, Gannon The Gray! I gave you my heart and my body! You belong to me!"

He turned and faced me and sneered, "Yeah, big deal, I wasn't your first."

"YES! YOU! WERE!" I screamed so loud his angry face showed nothing but surprise, and my family, who was getting rowdy, went still.

"We were in the water, YOU BASTARD! In the hot springs! You didn't see the blood!"

Gannon was already about thirty feet away from the chairs, and his mother, stepfather, and sister were already hustling along, quickly making their way toward the gateway escorted by one of the FBI men. My mother and father had already climbed up onto the platform and were standing at my side, letting things run their course, while my brothers and some of my other family were being held back from following after Gannon by the other FBI agents.

I stood on the edge of the platform and watched as Gannon turned, following after his family, but he shouted a parting shot as he left.

"I was your first and I'll be your last once Princess Emma touches you and turns you gay." He turned and waved over his shoulder as he walked away. "Have a nice life being a dyke witch. I tried to save you. I hope your family does better than I did."

"A witch," I repeated in shock.

"Me—a witch," I said again quietly.

My mother, my father, and Niu were all talking at once. I was so angry I couldn't hear anything. How could he do this to me? I loved him. I trusted him. *I gave myself to him!* And he treats me and my love like shit on his shoe. He'd had his fun and now he was done, he'd taken my virtue, my love, and my honor and was leaving me here in Amen Hale with my rotting broken heart. He called me a witch. I wouldn't want to disappoint him by not meeting his low expectations for me.

"I am a witch!" I shouted as loudly as I could. "I'm a witch! I'm a witch! I'm a witch! I'm a witch!" I shouted as hands tried to grab me and hold me down. I pulled free from the grasping hands and dashed to the edge of the platform, hopped down, and started to run.

Somehow Niu was still with me, wrapped around my waist and holding onto me. The train billowed out behind me as I ran barefoot in my wedding gown as fast as I could across the green lawn straight toward Gannon. He stood facing me from the other side of the gateway, standing beside the pool where we first met with his family behind him and FBI men gathered around watching as I charged toward them.

I stopped in the opening of the arch, one foot in my old home and one foot in my new home. Gannon's face was still angry as he faced me, not hopeful as if he thought I might be coming to join him, but grim. Done. Nothing but angry. I realized right then that he truly didn't want me to follow him. He was through with me. I hated the ache in my heart. I hated that I'd ever loved him.

"I have a gift for you, Gannon. An offering really. Something to remember me by."

Gannon's sister was pulling on his arm. "Don't talk to her, you idiot, let's go!" she urged.

"Go ahead, Alana, I'll give you the last word," he shouted back to me as she yanked on his arm.

"Oh no! Not words! You've given me quite enough words already. Lots of words. *Lots of lies!*" I hissed. "I have a gift for you, Gannon The Gray. It's cut and torn and bleeding and broken, but it will follow you until the day you die. I love you, Gan, with all my heart. But you're a monster, and I hate you. So take the filthy thing with you! I give you my heart."

"No!" I heard Niu's voice cry out.

My forehead tingled, but then my hands flew to my chest. I felt it burn!

Suddenly, I couldn't breathe!

I pitched forward.

Everything tingled, then the tingle turned into a burning, in my hands, my legs, my eyes, my head.

Burning! Burning! Head pounding!

Everything went black.

Black Rain

Our Lion

I WATCHED AS MY heartbroken Red Lamb ran across the lawn toward the gateway arch that Gannon and his family had just fled through. I willed myself to move there and appeared beside a nearby tree. I didn't want to disturb what was happening, so I stayed there and kept myself hidden. I'd heard the ugly things he'd said at the end of the disastrous wedding and now I listened as Alana spoke to Gannon.

I didn't fully understand what she was doing until it was too late to do anything but watch as she fell to the ground. There was already a crowd around her when I got there, but I was surprised that the new cloud person that I'd seen around Alana's waist as a wedding train was screaming like a banshee for everyone to stay back and fighting the FBI agents for possession of the body.

"Leave her alone!" it shouted in a high shrill cry. "Leave her be and I will save her!"

"Get off!" a man batted her away. "How will you save her, dammit!? She's not even breathing!" The man trying to do CPR continued his work while fending off the surprisingly strong ribbon arms that pulled at him.

"Still no pulse," announced another man beside the first with his hand on her neck.

Alana's father and her two brothers stood beside them, panting to catch their breath from running over. They stood helpless, horror struck, watching the FBI men work as others rapidly closed in from both Amen Hale and the Ainsleys' home.

"Stand clear and let the Child of Sky do what she can!" I ordered. "If she said she can save her then she speaks the truth!" I was careful to keep my voice at a loud, powerful human level. I had no idea what my voice would do if I truly shouted, but I didn't want to find out on accident. I would be more careful. Even now when I wanted to scream and shout with everything in me and rip the world in two as I watched my Red Lamb die.

Everyone backed away except for her father who only reluctantly released his hold on Alana.

"Please, help her, Niu!" he begged, tears running down his face.

"I will, Mr. Ainsley," she said confidently.

He nodded and moved away in time to grab Alana's mother as she arrived and hold her while Niu worked.

Others were arriving as well. Sky flew over and landed nearby but didn't interfere as Niu lifted Alana's head tenderly with her ribbon-like arms. We all watched the strange looking creature moving with such intent and care over Alana's still body. The Coven Mark that had appeared on Alana's forehead little more than a minute ago was already fading away. Niu blinked her blue jewel-like eyes that were set into the cloth, then she bent and kissed Alana's head, but what she did next left me with my mouth hanging open, catching flies. She shouted in her high pitched voice for all to hear.

"I am a Witch!"

"I am a Witch!"

"I am a Witch!"

She looked down at Alana and said, "And for my offering I give my friend my life. I will become a new heart for you, and I will live in you and I will never let you go. Let my soul and my life live in yours, best friend of my heart."

A circle with a crescent moon and four diamonds appeared on the cloth right between her blue eyes.

Sky screamed, "What are you doing!?" Then she clutched at her heart as if in pain. Believer, who had been standing at the edge of the crowd, rushed to Sky's side and collected her into his arms and held her as she wept.

Niu faded into Alana's flesh right before our eyes, her shimmering cloud-like cloth vanishing down into Alana's body until she was totally gone. Alana's body began to glow with a pale blue light. The coven mark reappeared on her forehead, and then her back arched and she gasped, deep and long, her mouth opening and closing like a fish out of water, her arms thrashed and she kicked with her feet as her whole body writhed.

Medics watching from the other side of the gate were about to rush over to start some idiotic treatment and I shouted at them to stay back. More of Alana's family arrived, gathering around, and we all waited and watched until Alana calmed and lay still on the ground.

Her eyes flicked open. There was no white or pupil at all. Her eyes were solid, brilliant blue that actually glowed, lit from within, like Niu's eyes had been. Alana didn't stand up like a normal person but floated up off the ground, hovering for a second before settling unsteadily to the earth. Her coven mark was clearly visible, and I saw that there was now a blue star where my black star had been. Whatever else she was, she was definitely a witch.

"Kim? Alana?" her father asked hesitantly as he stepped toward her, wanting to hold her.

Alana smiled and took a couple of tottering steps toward her father and hugged him.

"Oh Baby! *Baby! Baby! Baby!*" he wept. "You scared me to death!" He held her for a minute, then pulled her back to look at her. "Are you all right? Can you talk? Can you see? Your eyes are all blue." His worried face studied her, drinking in the sight of her.

"Call me Alana from now on. Alana Sky. Kim and Niu are gone." Her voice had changed. It wasn't Alana's voice or Niu's high, sweet trill, but something in between.

"Your voice is crazy weird, Kim. Are you okay?" one of her brothers asked as he stepped closer.

Alana turned her head his way and narrowed her eyes at her brother. She moved her hands in the air in a small over under gesture and her brother toppled onto the ground as if his feet had been knocked from beneath him while an invisible hand drove him down into the ground. He lay on his back in the grass, staring up at the sky with the wind knocked out of his lungs. Alana pulled away from her wide-eyed father and walked with halting, jerky steps to where her brother lay prone on the ground, trying to breathe.

"Sorry. You okay?" she asked in her new voice.

He nodded but didn't say a word.

"Call me Alana. My name is Alana Sky." She squinted, studying him with her glowing, blue eyes.

"Do I know you? Is your name Nathan?" She wrinkled her nose as she stared down at him.

"He's your brother," her father said as he came to her side. He pointed to her other brother who stood beside them. "And this is your brother Doug. You remember Doug, don't you?"

Alana screwed up her face as she studied him. "You're retarded and annoying."

"At least we know she hasn't forgotten the really important stuff," Nathan said from the ground, then had to squirm around as he tried to ward off Doug's attempt to kick him in his sore ribs.

"Enough! Cut it out!" their father ordered.

"He's retarded and annoying," Alana said, clearly puzzled. "Why do I love someone who is retarded and annoying?"

"Because he's family. He's your brother, Alana," her father said carefully.

"I feel strange." She held her hands in front of her face, looking at them as if she'd never seen her own hands before. "I have hands." She wiggled her fingers. "I have ten fingers, Dad!" The discovery was proudly announced in her new higher sweeter voice.

I stepped closer hoping she would remember me. "Alana?"

"My Lion!" she said, a huge smile on her face as she turned and struggled toward me like a toddler who was still getting used to walking, but she didn't reach me before she was swept up by her weeping mother.

I stepped back as her parents worried over her but then Alana started to shout. "Sky! Sky! Sky! I need my Sky!" She kept shouting until Sky came to her and Alana fell on Sky's neck and started to cry. The two older parents gave Sky her due and didn't begrudge her her place or the affection Alana seemed to have for her as a parent.

The three of them stole Alana away from the rest of us as they touched and handled and wept and puzzled and rejoiced. Not so much grieving the loss and change as they were rejoicing and overjoyed that they all still had someone to love.

Cathryn, Cornelius, Mary, Sky Dragon, Bethany, and Ryan were standing together a short distance away and I went to join them. Sky Dragon had Bethany in his arms but she didn't look well. Before they buried me in questions about Alana I asked my own.

"What's wrong with Bethany?" I directed my question to Ryan on purpose. It was the first time I'd spoken to him since our fight and I wanted to see how he'd react, but when he looked at me he seemed fine. Too fine. He was drunk!

"She's toasted," he said happily, the pot calling the kettle black. He pointed an unsteady finger at Bethany. "She drank four glasses of wine." He ratted her out with a smile.

"It was five," Mary supplied, looking serious, as she clung to Cathryn's arm.

I put a hand to Bethany's head and she moaned miserably. Her tail tried to reach me but gave up half way up and dropped, dangling straight down to the ground.

"Heeeadache! Make it go away," Bethany said weakly as she squinted her eyes at me.

"Did you try to heal yourself?" I asked her.

"I can't for some reason," she said, then shook her new bracelet at me. "And my kisses won't heal me either. I think I'm all out. I need some more!" She thrust her arm up at me drunkenly, nearly gouging my eye out with her long fingernails.

Sky Dragon just shook his head.

I touched her bracelet to see if she was right.

"You still have five kisses left," I said frowning. "There must be a reason my kisses didn't heal you. Can you think of what that reason might be?" I asked.

I met Cathryn's eye as she listened to me.

"No," Bethany said miserably.

"You disobeyed our mother."

Cathryn nodded, smiling, but she stayed silent, forcing me to handle it. This was new for me but I gave it a try.

"Cathryn only lets you drink one glass of wine at dinner and maybe one at a party, but you drank yourself silly, my Little One. Suffer and remember, and next time obey our mother," I scolded, my voice parental.

Bethany looked up at me with pain-filled eyes that I couldn't refuse and I reached for her and took her from Sky Dragon and cradled her little body in my arms with no thought in the world more important than holding her. I'd always loved Bethany as my friend and as a little sister, but as I held her now some new warmth that I'd never known touched me. Gripped me. She was my child now. She was our Little One.

"I'll heal you before we eat dinner, till then you can rest inside your father," I told her.

"Her father?" Sky Dragon asked in surprise, raising his eye ridges at me.

My tail pulled Bethany's tail up onto her chest so it wouldn't dangle or drag as we walked. "I'm not a witch anymore and she's not my little sister anymore," I told Sky Dragon as I rocked her in my arms.

"I claimed Bethany as my child. She's our Little One now, but don't worry," I looked over and gave him a smile, "she's still your Princess and you're still *her* Dragon."

Ryan was grinning stupidly and swaying on his feet as he spoke. "You've been a mom for less than a day and you already have a kid in AA."

My tail lashed out viciously and popped him upside the head so hard he flew backwards with a grunt.

"Damn girl!" Mary shouted.

"Oh shit!" I cried. "Sorry, Ryan! I didn't mean to hurt you, my tail just—" I looked at the angry thrashing thing.

"Bad tail!" I scolded it. It didn't seem to care and kept thrashing.

"Be patient with him," Cornelius said. "Ryan's had a bit too much to drink as well."

Cathryn seemed too surprised to say anything. She looked as if she'd had one too many herself, but I wasn't about to fuss at her for it; she'd had a rough day.

"I'm all right!" Ryan called drunkenly from where he lay, half buried in the hedge row he'd fallen into.

"I just forgot the most important rule," he said.

Sky Dragon looked down at him, shaking his head. "The tail is cool?" he guessed.

"Dat's it! Dat's the one!" Ryan pointed up at Sky Dragon and laughed drunkenly. "Dat's all you need to know, man!" He laughed then said, "Damn, where's my Sky? Let's put a tail on her ass too! Yeah. Yeah! She'd look hot with a tail." He started to struggle to his feet but fell.

"Rain!" Mary hissed. "Fix your brother! I don't want him getting experimental with my ass!"

"Yeah. Him I'll fix right now," I said as Sky Dragon helped Ryan to his feet. I willed the alcohol to leave Ryan's body and removed the haze of its effects from his mind. I healed his swollen and bleeding lip and charged him up with health and life, fixed his clothes and got him presentable again. Other than being embarrassed to death, he seemed fine.

After depositing one little drunken body into my husband, who agreed with my punishment, I explained what happened to Alana and Niu to my family. Ryan and Sky Dragon rushed off to join Sky but the rest of us hung back, letting Alana's human relatives huddle together there at the gateway arch, half in and half out of Amen Hale.

There were angry relatives who cursed at us and there were others who couldn't stop thanking Sky for her daughter's sacrifice. After about thirty minutes, the servants announced that the wedding reception/birthday celebration dinner was ready.

Those wedding guests who didn't choose to leave immediately moved into the house with us where the meal had been prepared in the manner that Amen Hale was accustomed to. Fancy, amazing, elegant, and laid out with more knives and forks and spoons than ever had a right to rest beside, above, and around a dinner plate.

Jane

Strange Flesh

"HELLO, MY LOVE. *How do you feel?*"

I was dreaming when I heard Dan's voice in my head and found myself staring into a pair of beautiful blue-green eyes only inches away from my own. I didn't move a muscle and I even stopped breathing as I looked into those eyes. We were facing each other, our cheeks pressed to the cool floor of The Hallow.

I'd been dreaming a strange and colorful dream. It was the first week of school and Dan was there. He was in all my classes. In my strange dream I was falling in love with him all over again. Other girls, popular girls and cheerleaders and the 'it' girls and even the damn female teachers at the school, tried to get Dan's attention, but day after day his eyes were on me, watching me. His sticky notes on my books and not theirs. His presence always in the perfect place to save me from embarrassment or inconvenience or some asshole guys, like my own personal, silent savior.

My dream was gone now, ended by his voice in my head, and the eyes in my dream were replaced by the eyes before me. Was there a better way to wake from a perfect, if strange, dream? I didn't think so.

"Were you enjoying my dream?" I thought to him in my head.

"*Immensely. I had no idea I was that cool.*" His mouth curled into a smile. "*Your imagination is very strange. Fun. Freaky. Exciting. Wonderful. Just like you. God, I love watching you dream.*"

"Why did you wake me then?" I asked as I smiled back at him, picking on my weird brain. I'd been enjoying my weird dream too.

"*I've been awake for thirty minutes and I was starting to get worried about you.*"

"I'm fine."

"Jane? Dan? Are you two awake?" my mom said softly in the dark room.

I sat up and saw that my mother and father had stayed with us while we slept. Dad was still out, snoozing away, but Mom was sitting up in her chair looking at me. They were lying in reclining chairs and had pillows and blankets. I saw off in the distance other guards, armed with weapons, keeping a quiet vigil over our sleep. Rain was being very careful with us while we lay helpless and vulnerable. It was nice to see.

"This reminds me of when we camped out at the lake," I told my mom, keeping my voice soft so I didn't wake Dad. "The weather was so nice we didn't even set up the tents, we all fell asleep in the lawn chairs."

Mom smiled. "How long ago was that?"

"It was three years ago, on the fifth of July at Goldhead State Park. You remember. Dad kept complaining that it was like shooting fish in a barrel because the water level in the lake was so low."

Mom smiled at me and studied me for a moment, which in turn was a long moment for me to study her. I searched her eyes and the lines around her mouth and the expression on her face along with the set of her shoulders and the clothes she wore. She looked tired, but I could tell she'd slept for at least a few hours.

"*We slept for almost eight hours, Jane. God only knows what's happened out there,*" Dan said in my head.

"Did you talk to my mom while you've been up or did you spend all your time hanging out in my dreams watching me and checking out what my weird subconscious was up to?"

Dan's silence was all the answer I needed.

"You know I don't mind, Dan, you're welcome to all I am," I told him gently.

"*I know and I love you for it.*" His arms slipped around me like I wanted.

"How are you two with this change? In diet?" Mom asked the question so carefully I had to laugh and the musical sound echoed around The Hallow. I looked over to see if I'd woken Dad but he was still out cold.

"Dan and I are actually quite happy with it. I feel less like a throat ripping monster and more like a person now. Not a human person," Dan reached out and began to straighten my bed head like I wanted, "but not your garden variety vampire either. We've changed. It's nice not to notice your wet, pattering human heart without really wanting to, and the sound of blood swishing through your veins no longer sounds like a siren song luring me onto the rocks but promising me sweet tasty things. Evil, but delicious."

"Geesh!" Mom shook her head and made a face.

Dan gave me a strained growl, complaining about making it so bloody/gutty but I ignored him.

"No more *human* bloodlust, that, I don't miss. Not at all." I stressed the word human. Because Dan and I still had bloodlust, just not for human blood.

"Is there *anything* you don't like about what's happened?" She was still asking about the sexual stuff. She and Dad had watched along with everyone else as Dan and I kissed Rain and bit her.

But I noticed other things in her face that I hadn't noticed before. What I saw stopped me cold. Something had happened. Something bad. Dan and I stood up. He stood behind me, his arms around me like I needed. She'd picked up her purse and was pulling out a comb. We waited until she looked up and her eyes tracked in on our new position.

"What happened to her while we slept?"

Mom frowned, disappointed that we'd seen through her calm face. I could see her trying to decide what to say. "It's hard to explain."

She looked strange. Whatever it was, it was all about Rain. Something weird had happened.

"*She's telling the truth, she doesn't know what happened*," Dan said in my head.

I'm done.

"We'll see you in a little bit, Mom. We're off to see for ourselves."

I left Dan to deal with Mom while I darted over to my father and shook him gently until his eyes opened.

"Jane!" he said happily with a smile.

"Hey, Daddy, I didn't want to take off without telling you we were fine, and I needed to do this." I gave him a kiss on the cheek. "Thanks for watching us while we slept. Why don't you and Mom go on up to your room now. These chairs had to be uncomfortable to sleep in and I doubt you want to go to the fancy dinner tonight. You and mom aren't cannibals."

"Wha—no, No. I'm up! I'm up! Your mother and I have lots to ask you about." He rubbed at his eyes, still coming awake.

"I love you, Dad, but I have to run. Let's talk about everything in the morning."

I darted over to Mom, planted a kiss on her cheek, and vanished as she was trying to grab me, her arms finding only open air where I'd been.

Every damn door was locked! Dan and I felt like double dumb asses as we circled the building trying every door until we finally went up to the balcony and out onto the one terrace deck that looked out over Amen Hale. There were torches lining the paths and decorations still in place for the wedding that happened earlier this evening, but servants were already putting away punch bowls and other stupid human items like the gigantic, chocolate fountain centerpiece.

We both noticed the magic archway on the lawn that opened to some place with a pool. There were government agents standing on their side and four of Amen Hale's own men dressed in black standing on our side of the opening. Dan was frowning as he watched what looked like an easy exchange of people passing from one side to the other. Two older people went back to the other side while a young girl returned from the other side and headed off toward the house at a fast walk, as if she didn't want to miss something.

"*Seems pretty trusting, doesn't it? For as often as the government has screwed us it seems strange to leave the door open with four humans guarding Amen Hale.*"

"Let's go see what the hell's happened," I said miserably.

We leapt down to the ground, thirty feet below, without making a sound and ran to the house and slipped into the dining hall. We found an out of the way niche by the wall to stand in where we could observe the room. The place had been decked out nicely, but Dan and I didn't care about the decor, we were interested in the one person in this room who could feed us and keep us alive.

We saw what had to be her, sitting at the raised table at the end of the hall. The table was one sided, with Cathryn and Cornelius in the middle and the others fanned out along either side facing the hall. It made it easy for everyone to see the Royal family and easy for us to see Rain. I took in her changed appearance in a glance but was having a hard time understanding what I was looking at. Maybe my brain was too scared to work right.

"Whatchathinkin?" I made my thought one spoken word. I hoped Dan's brain was working better than mine.

He shook his head looking both relieved and troubled as he stared at her.

"*Well, she looks calm and happy, and everyone at the table seems okay. The face bears a resemblance but the rest of her body is completely new. And she's a lot bigger now, taller.*" He shot me a weak smile. "*At least she's not a mass of slimy, squiggling tentacles and teeth. The demon horns and the creepy eyes are strange, but she's still beautiful. But one way or another, she's our food, and we need to find out if her blood can still keep us alive. If her blood has changed too we may be in trouble. And we need to find out if her attitude toward us has changed along with her shape. Demon eyes and demon horns might mean her heart's not quite what it used to be."*

"*Demon heart.*" Dan didn't think it but I did. My mind reeled as if I'd been struck. I hadn't even considered the possibility that she might change her mind! Or have her mind changed for her along with her body. What if her blood was fouled now? Demon black. And what if Rain didn't want to play "feed the poor vampires" now that she was all demoned up? What if my Black Lion didn't want her little, black lamb anymore? What if she'd rather eat us than let us eat her? Maybe "vampire mutton" is on the menu now, Dan! What if the rules changed while we were in la la land taking a siesta, dreaming stupid, weird dreams? And what the hell are we going to do if her blood is bad!? What if it's black, Dan! BLACK!

Dan's arms slipped around me and held me together, keeping me from flying apart into a hundred pieces.

"*I don't know what we'll do if her blood doesn't work,*" he said honestly as he looked into my eyes.

"We die!" I growled, my body shaking against his as ugly visions of black blood pouring from her wrist and neck played inside my head like a television that was showing a horrible, scary movie that you didn't want to see, but you couldn't find the damn remote control to turn the shit off! Dan held me as hard as he could and held my gaze with his blue-green eyes as he spoke in my head.

"*As long as I'm with you, my love, if we die, I'll die happy.*" Then he leaned in and kissed me gently, but when he pulled back he gave me an absolutely wicked grin and even showed a little fang. "*Maybe she'll taste even sweeter?*" His voice purred darkly in my head and my pent up emotions burst like a popped balloon and I laughed at my beautiful, optimistic bloodsucker husband, but now that he'd said it my overactive imagination started to wonder if such a thing was actually possible.

I looked across the room at her pale silver/white skin and wondered how sweet she would be—would her flavor be different? What would her blood taste like now? I tried to sniff the air, but across the room filled with hundreds of people wearing colognes and perfumes and tables piled high with human food it was impossible to smell a thing. But up close, what would she smell like? If all went well would she let me have her neck or her hand? *Please, please, OH PLEASE!* let it be the neck!

I watched her pulse pumping through the vein there at her throat from where I stood. What would it feel like to press my teeth into that silvery white skin? To feel that small part of a second when teeth finally pierced flesh—and then the blood, *the golden blood*?

Dan shook me by my shoulders and I looked up into his eyes, angry and hungry. He gave me a small tight smile. *"Are you through growling, my love?"*

I nodded. "Bastard!" I thought at him, still fighting my temper. Then I kissed him with all the anger and passion I had, but after less than a minute he started to pull away using all of his strength to try and hold my wrists down to my sides. I let him win and looked at him, confused.

"*That's the attitude we need, Jane, but control it, use it, and focus.*" His smile was gone now, he was totally serious.

Dan was right. I nodded. This first meeting with her in this new form might change everything. Or end everything. Our eternity hung in the balance and could go to hell right here and now. We had to do this right. We needed to think it through and plan it out.

"How do you want to go in?" I asked.

"We don't want to just appear beside her. We need to snail and take our time and be seen while we approach and make it part of her decision. And we need to go in looking good. Too good to say no to. Both of us need to turn up the heat as high as we can and look so good she won't even dream of saying no. You approach her first, Jane, I'll hang back and be your wing man."

Wing man? Oh shit! I knew what he was hinting at, and he was right. I was the hot ticket on our band wagon as strange as that was. We needed to court her again, win her again, and keep her. It made sense. We were vampires, and our bodies were made to be beautiful and attractive to our prey, to lure it in so we could feed. And now, that was her. The tall chick with the horns sitting on the other side of the room. She was our prey. Our only prey. I'd have to deal with my girl/sex issues, but another thought occurred to me.

"Dan, we've never really tried to look good around the humans before, we just do. If we actually *try* to look sexy with each move we make will we fry their little human brains?"

Dan considered that for a fraction of a second. "*You're probably right. The humans will be a problem. And I don't want to hurt these people if we don't have to. This is supposed to be our home. As long as they don't touch you they shouldn't lose their minds like Tom did; they'll probably stare at you like zombies if they don't try to grab for you. Let's do it this way, you be the beauty, I'll be the beast. I'll still look tasty but I'll turn up the fear and look scary enough to keep the humans from grabbing at you. You're the one that she finds attractive so we won't lose anything with me doing the beast.*"

"At least we know she's horny," I thought before I could stop myself from thinking something so stupid and juvenile. Just like a guy, Dan started laughing, his full, rich laughing voice so beautiful and clear that it was a mystery to me how he could laugh like that and not talk perfectly.

Half the room had already noticed us tucked away by the wall and Dan's laugh made even more people turn to stare at the two vamps, cuddled up by the window. More and more people pointed, looking in our direction as they spoke and ate and enjoyed their meal. It didn't matter. We wanted to make an entrance. It was time to bring the heat.

"Com'on, Dan, let's snail," I said.

"*I'll be two steps behind you looking scary and tasty,*" he promised, already putting on his Prince of Darkness face and looking out at the crowded room.

I stepped away from the wall, walking at human speed in human time. We called this *snailing* because it wasn't walking—it was walking, moving, and talking in tedious slow motion. Moving to the rhythm of creatures who lived in a different time than we did. It was a trick that we could play on our own minds that more or less slowed us down so that we appeared to fit in with our surroundings. My body moved slowly, but my vampire mind raced as I used every scrap of my ability to make myself as attractive as possible. Each movement and gesture, the expression on my face, my eyes, and the way I moved around objects and people was planned and calculated and done *just so*. I did not do it for the humans' benefit, but for my prey, wanting *her* to notice me, to see me and to want me.

As Dan and I passed by the tables, people froze and stared or pointed, some bowed to us awkwardly, curtsied or paled and backed away but absolutely everyone noticed us. I watched as the bolder or baser men would see me and smile at first and then a second later they would pale and back away as Dan's presence at my back kept them in line.

The slow steady walk, snailing across the entire Dining Hall seemed to take forever, but it did what we wanted; everyone at the High Table had stopped what they were doing and watched our creeping approach. The loud happy, boisterous talk in the Dining Hall faded and changed into a faint, whispering hiss of three hundred human snakes.

At the High Table, King Cornelius and Queen Cathryn sat in the middle with the others fanned out on both sides. On the far side of the table sat Sky Dragon, Ryan, Sky, and a new girl who must have been the bride, still dressed in the wedding gown, and the bride's parent. The bride had short, redish pink hair and alien eyes that looked like two brightly glowing blue jewels set into her eye sockets. She also had a forehead tattoo, which meant she was a witch. I let my vision zoom in and saw that Rain no longer had a Coven Mark on her forehead.

"This doesn't look good, Dan," I thought to him.

"*Don't worry about it, stay focused on Rain,*" Dan urged.

On our side of the long table Bethany sat closest to Cathryn and Cornelius, followed by Believer, Rain, Emma, Mary, and one older blonde woman I recognized as one of the servants named Hanna. Dan shadowed me as I ascended the side steps to the platform and walked up behind Emma's chair. The whole table on our side, even Cathryn and Cornelius looked mesmerized. Emma, Mary, Hanna, and even little Bethany had glazed, dreamy eyes and slack expressions though Believer's burning red eyes watched everything with a careful calm awareness, but surprisingly no menace. On the other side of the table I heard Sky and Ryan talking to the new girl, telling her to stay in her seat.

"Yes, the vampires are pretty, but stay here, Alana," Sky told the girl, speaking to her like a daughter.

"You can meet them later, but not now, we need to wait," Ryan told her as he wisely kept his back to us, looking at Sky and Alana. His voice somehow had a parental tone to it as well. Curious.

I pulled my mind away from the confusing conversation and focused on Rain. All my attention poured into her face, eyes, and every movement of her body as I thought of what to do, what to say, how to approach her.

"Dan and I were worried. You have a new body. You've changed. Have your feelings toward us changed along with your shape? Do you still love us, Rain?" I asked shyly. Going with the direct approach and looking as vulnerable as I felt. That, at least, was absolutely honest.

"Yes," she said with a small smile on her face. Hot red dots swam in the two dark seas of her eyes and in their depths I could see nothing but power, but her face looked honest and sincere.

"Will you still feed us and take care of us?" I asked.

"Yes," she said simply.

"You have a new body, Rain, and new blood in that new body. We were worried that your blood might not be able to sustain us now. We don't need to eat yet, but may I taste you?" I said plainly, without much emotion, and then waited to see what she'd do.

She seemed to think for a moment, and then she nodded and surprisingly I saw Believer nod as well, as if he'd been following the conversation and understood our concerns. Rain didn't make any gesture or say a word but her chair moved back about two feet by itself to give her some room and she held out one long arm, inviting me in.

"Come, Jane, taste me, and see if I am sweet or if I am bitter."

Just hearing her say it sent shivers up my spine. I slowly took the three short steps toward Rain, then turned around and sat back into her lap, almost as if I were a little child. She was so tall and her body was new to me in every way. I didn't know how to move around her yet. I watched as she reached up with her right hand and pulled her long black hair away from the left side of her neck and then leaned her head to the side, giving herself to me. It felt oddly ungrateful to just *bite.*

I leaned in but raised up and whispered into her ear, "Thank you."

She smiled but said nothing. I wanted some reaction from her. Some words or something. I'd been trying my hardest to look as scrumptious as possible, but maybe she didn't want me in that way anymore. Maybe she didn't like girls or wasn't as passionate as she used to be, but she'd been holding Emma's hand when I first walked up. I was both massively relieved and enormously worried. The thought that she didn't want me in that way, even if I didn't want her in that way, meant I had less control. That was a shitty attitude, but having her want me was important to our survival. It gave me leverage, something to use, something she wanted or even needed. My predator instincts pushed at me to keep this control even as I rejoiced at the thought that I wouldn't have to sleep with her.

"Do you still want me to kiss you?" I whispered into her ear.

"Do you want to kiss me, Jane?" she asked without seeing me, her head still tilted to the side, giving me her neck as I lingered by her ear. She'd given me her neck freely and here I'd crawled into her ear like a bug.

I frowned, confused by my own actions.

"*Yes, you are confused! Your head's a mess. Snap out of it! Say yes and kiss her!*" Dan shouted into my mind.

But for some reason I said, "I don't want to lie, Rain. Other than your blood, I honestly don't know what I want."

Her smile fell and she nodded. "That's all right, Jane. I know what I want."

"*No! Don't ask her that! Bite her!*"

"What do you want?" I asked while Dan shouted in my head.

"I want you to be happy, Jane. I love you. And you too, Dan, I know you're listening." She still offered me her neck, but now she slipped her left hand up my back and into my hair and pressed my face down to her neck.

"*Please, let it be beautiful for the ones I love.*" Her voice was soft and pleading, as if she spoke to herself.

My mind was gone, all reason forgotten, as my face pressed up against her silky smooth pale silvery flesh and I slipped my arms around her and closed my eyes as I nuzzled at her neck, savoring each amazing second. For once, moving at this slow human speed seemed like a glorious luxury as the couple of seconds of human time I took to roll in her wonderful smell and rub myself against her silky smooth skin was more like minutes to me.

It was so wonderful to be here in her lap and to have her hand in my hair, urging me to drink. I did not have to take her blood by force like a predator or a thief in the night, nor did I have to trick it out of her with my alluring wiles or lies, and I did not have to buy her blood with my body. Rain gave herself to me freely. Even if I did not know what I wanted, she knew what she wanted. She wanted it to be beautiful. Whatever that meant.

I placed my teeth against her neck—and bit.

As soon as the blood filled my mouth I knew that I'd bitten off more than I could chew. How could I swallow an endless ocean of power and not have my head explode right off my shoulders? It was already warm in my mouth. Would her blood burn me to a cinder from the inside out or make my head look like a spent match? If I ever swallowed it, would I ever be able to stop drinking it? Even for a moment? Would I ever get off her neck or would I hang here for all eternity like an oversized goiter?

"*Jane! Stop daydreaming and snap out of it! Just spit it out if you can't drink it!*"

"I'm not spitting this out!" I thought back, every cell in my vampire body screaming "HELL NO!" at the thought of letting one precious drop escape. I would have growled at him but my mouth was missing.

"*Jane! Think! Swallow what you got and lick her wound closed!*" Dan shouted in my head.

Rain moaned in pleasure and her hand caressed the back of my head, encouraging me to feed as something pushed its way up the bottom of my dress from under the chair, winding around my leg and squeezing as it climbed higher and higher. I stayed connected to her neck but my ass danced wildly on her lap while I evaded what I hoped like hell was her groping "tail."

I swallowed and the shock of the blood warming my cold flesh on its way down and the idea of where the tail wanted to go freaked me out so badly that I did the absolutely impossible *and let go.* Rain's body shuddered in protest as I pulled my teeth from her flesh. I quickly began licking the wound closed, catching each precious drop of bright yellow-gold sunshine that trailed down her neck as I worked to close the flesh. I managed to heal the wound and sit up before she started to complain.

"No! Please don't stop, Jane," Rain whimpered, still completely lost in the pleasure and ecstasy my bite had brought her.

She began to push me back down toward her neck, urging me to drink more. She was moving fast, but no where near our speed and I easily slipped around her hands while I held her tail pinned between my legs. I could feel her blood inside me like a glorious warmth, and already a part of my mind was questioning my actions and wanting to go back to her neck again. She wanted me back—

"*Jane! Snap out of it! It was a taste! Remember!?*" Dan cried out in my mind.

Rain's face filled with hurt and disappointment and unfulfilled need. She reached for me again, trying to draw me back to her neck but I eluded her arms effortlessly with a simple turn of my shoulder. I grabbed her naughty tail and pulled it out from under my dress as I positioned myself in front of her face so that I had her attention, shaking my head no, hoping that she'd snap out of whatever my bite had done to her brain.

Her face went from vexed, frustrated longing to the surprised hurt of a jilted lover, then spiraled straight down into a frightening, dark look that seemed more monster than human. Rain pressed her teeth together, fighting to swallow down her own black anger, but a low growl escaped her control. She squelched most of it, but the small noise that slipped out was enough to make the wine glasses rock and cups clatter and cause the fancy array of silverware to dance a jig up and down the length of the table.

"My God, Dan! What am I gonna do!?" I shouted wildly in my head.

"*Calm her down, Jane! Touch her face, talk nice to her, and stop pissing her off!*"

"How the hell am I pissing her off!?" I shouted back, in a state of panic myself. She gazed down at me with a face no longer filled with compassion and self-sacrificing love, but with hurt and anger and things I did not want to see.

"*Stop dodging her arms and let her hold you if she damn well wants to!*" Dan shouted back.

I fought my own desire to run away as I drew closer to her angry face and frightening eyes. I kept a steady stream of soothing words falling from my lips as I drew closer to her. I wrapped one arm around her neck and I pressed my face against her cheek as I whispered into her ear and petted and stroked and soothed as if my life depended upon it.

She'd only growled for a second, but I continued my labors, my hands moving, my voice whispering softly and my body no longer evasive but there when her arms slowly encircled me. Her tail returned, but this time it wrapped around both my ankles, holding my feet together as if it did not want me to get away. I stopped talking but kept petting while she held me like a possession, staring down at me as if I were hers.

Around us the small noises of activity began to resume though the others at the High Table wisely left me to my efforts, talking among themselves and around us as though Rain and I were invisible. I saw their looks. Emma and Mary, Cornelius and Cathryn, the servers. Frightened and worried for *me*, the vampire girl, trapped in the arms of a bigger, scarier monster.

I knew things would be simpler if I could just give myself to her and enjoy it, but without Emma's help, I didn't think I could do it.

"*Have you really tried, Jane?*" Dan's voice asked. "*You should try again. The one time you kissed her—*"

"Are you freakin' nuts!? You want me to get frisky now! With her husband staring right at me! And we're at a dinner in front of all Amen Hale! You want her to drag me onto the tabletop and do me right here!?"

"*Sorry,*" he said.

"And I don't think Rain would thank me for teasing her only to stop short *again* and say 'No, sorry, I was just experimenting!'" I shouted my frustrated reply inside my head.

"*Yeah. Bad, bad, BAD idea. Sorry, my love.*"

I tried to imagine what would happen tomorrow and the next day, and I was coming up with some pretty graphic images. After seeing what my quick bite did to her, I seriously doubted that Rain would be able to control herself during a real feeding even if she wanted to. Our bite affected her even more strongly now and left her with even less control of her passions and her anger.

And even if she was able to control herself while we fed, how long could I ask her to endure such a thing? Would it drive her mad, day after day, to be left wanting and unfulfilled? I remembered the hurt and needing look on her face, and I also remembered the angry eyes of the beast as it growled. The thought of denying Rain, over and over, while I enjoyed the glory of her blood was beyond ugly. It was blasphemous. And the thought of me or Dan being killed in a totally deserved fit of godlike angst seemed like a very real possibility.

I sat in her lap soothing the beast as I considered my future life and "this situation" while Dan listened silently.

Chef William Tanner

Eating the Dead

ONCE THE TWO vampires left the Hall, normalcy seemed to return to the world for the humans. The subdued mood in the room improved further as the main courses for the evening meal arrived. Chef Tanner had been given charge of the sacrificial human flesh, and he and his assistants had prepared and now presented an array of different dishes to the Princesses to see which were liked, which were loved, and which were not.

Bethany crawled into Rain's lap and together they tasted each dish and spoke to a very attentive Chef Tanner, who had his notepad in hand, eyes sharp and pencil moving as he ordered his staff to bring forward this dish or take something else to another part of the table to be enjoyed by others who might find it more appetizing. All foods prepared with human flesh were placed on or in special dishes that clearly marked the nature of their contents and were carried by servants wearing red dress coats.

When Andre, the head chef, presented Tanner with this position, the first thing Tanner did was arrange for the purchase of a very unique and extremely expensive set of bowls, platters, and serving utensils. The entire set was the work of the same macabre and gifted artist and every cup, bowl, platter, and even the serving spoons were fashioned of small human figures. Some of the plates and platters had happy, smiling, nude figures while others bore faces which cried out in pain and torment, and were unsettling to look at, let alone eat out of. The tiny bodies were adorned on the surface of the bowls or lying on their sides along the lip of a serving dish, shaped into the handle of a spoon, bent, twisted and cunningly crafted in eye jarring and shocking ways.

The dishes were a total surprise to Cathryn and Cornelius. They'd been expecting something divinely beautiful, not hideous beyond imagining. The King and Queen of Amen Hale stood behind Rain's chair with dour expressions and listened as Chef Tanner explained why he'd selected something so ghastly to serve their food on. Tanner was a small man, petite and girlish with rosy checks, wavy brown hair and huge brown eyes, but his skill, knowledge, and educated manner granted him the respect his stature and face tried to deny him. As it turned out, Chef Tanner had a very good explanation.

"There will be no mistaking the other beautiful bowls we use for these. Everyone who eats from the Parothki set will know exactly what they are eating. We must make it very clear because some people can make themselves sick just by *thinking* that they *might* be eating human flesh, or even thinking that they are eating out of a dish that once held human flesh. With these," he tapped the dish in front of him, "the Children of Amen Hale will feel comfortable that the food and dishes prepared in the kitchens by Chef Andre do not contain human flesh. But as the one who prepares your food, my Princesses, I also think of these as a last dignity. Each bowl or platter is a coffin of sorts for the flesh within it. We must never become complacent and forget that we eat the flesh of man." Tanner's big, doe colored eyes looked both calm and disturbing as he spoke.

Cathryn and Cornelius listened as Rain thanked Tanner for his wise foresight and said that she agreed with all that he had done. Hearing the glowing praise of their daughter, Amen Hale's King and Queen also thanked the strange little man, then excused themselves to go mingle with the dinner guests as Rain leaned forward and stared at the frightening platter in front of her.

Bethany took advantage of her head being so low to play with her horns as Rain held her face to the tabletop, looking at the intricately detailed glass figures.

"Each plate or dish or platter is totally unique and one of a kind," said Tanner, still glowing from all the praise. "The piece you are looking at is called 'Red Requiem' and has exactly one hundred individual figures."

"Each one is different, every single face," Rain mused as she stared at the plate. She briefly told Tanner about the Frenchman who came to Amen Hale earlier that day and his horrible reaction to the taste of human flesh she'd forced upon him and finished her story with a big regretful sigh, and her breath blew across the surface of the glass. And then the glass figures started to move.

Row upon row of bound and trussed miniature human figures that made up the base of the huge platter began to squirm. The bite-sized seasoned pieces of human flesh on the platter pitched and rolled upon a sea of small glass bodies.

"Oh wow! Can they come to life completely?" Bethany asked as she stared at the glass people, moving but still trapped on the plate like flies on flypaper.

Rain was utterly horrified; she hadn't meant to do whatever she'd done.

"Oh snap! Are those things really alive?" Mary asked as she leaned across the table to get a better look.

"They are alive," Rain breathed out as she stared down at them, "but they shouldn't be."

Small voices called out to her from the platter of living red glass, tiny hands clasping and unclasping, reaching in her direction.

"You really are a god," Tanner said as he stared at the platter in awe.

"My children of glass, come home to me, return to my soul," Rain told them and the tiny figures froze. The detail of the piece had increased a thousandfold. The figures had individual strands of glass hair, open hands with tiny fingers, eyes with eyelashes, mouths with glass lips, teeth, and open glass throats frozen in mid scream as what they were—*ended.*

The glass platter was now something that befuddled the mind as to the manner of its creation, as it terrified because of how real it looked. The little glass figures looked real, because they were real, but now they were nothing but a graveyard of dead glass corpses upon which rested the dead flesh of man.

"Did you have to kill them?" Emma asked. Her hands trembled as she reached out and ran her fingertips across the surface of heads and faces, backs and breasts of tiny red people. The others at the table watched as Emma raised her hand and sucked on her fingers.

"They loved you, Rain," she confirmed sadly. "They lived but a moment but they truly loved you." She gave Rain a pleading look, empathy for the children of glass all over her face. "Please." Emma touched the figures again. "Please bring them back, Rain." She began to weep.

Rain shook her head no. "They are back, Emma. Back inside me."

Bethany's tiny delicate hands touched Rain's grim face and her tail coiled affectionately around Rain's arm.

"Don't be sad, Rain, be happy, it's my birthday," Bethany's sweet, little voice pleaded.

Rain's own tail wrapped around Bethany but her words weren't happy.

"How can I not be sad, my cub? I killed a hundred innocent children because their birth was an accident. I'm just like Rain Marie. I'm no better than she was. I truly *am* the lighter of the Black Candle and the shedder of innocent blood." Her dark words and the red glass graveyard seemed to shroud everyone in a cloud of gloom.

All but one.

"Enough of this!" Believer bellowed, surprising everyone as he stood and loomed menacingly over the table with his burning red eyes focused on Rain.

"We both know that the Children of Glass are happy inside your soul, my love. If they loved you outside your soul, they will love you on the inside as well, it is how we are made, *you and I*. You would have been happy to stay with your Rain Marie and these children will be happy to stay with their Black Rain. You did not cast them out or send them away or ask them to kill, you brought them home, my love. You are not like Rain Marie Bryant. You are nothing like her."

Believer gave her a shocked moment to consider his words. The others watched as her face went from shocked to thoughtful, but Believer didn't wait for her to voice any opinion on his words. "No further distractions will be permitted. You and Bethany will honor the labors of Chef Tanner and the others who have prepared many dishes for you to sample," Believer ordered firmly, making both of them sit up straighter in their chair.

He directed his hot gaze to a wide-eyed Tanner. "Please continue, Chef Tanner."

"Yes, Prince Believer," Tanner stammered, still recovering from seeing a civilization created and ended before his eyes. The food tasting resumed and dinner at the High Table proceeded without further incident under the guard of Believer's watchful red gaze.

Katie Linn

Arts and Crafts

SUSAN THREW HER drink at the television and it slooshed everywhere.

"This is total bullshit!" she screamed. "Bullshit! Stop lying to us you mothafucking assholes!"

She jumped off the couch and surprised the guard with a vicious shove, knocking him to the ground. She overturned the table with refreshments and snacks, dousing the man and causing a tidal wave of ice and drinks to spread out across the rec room. Susan snorted (a clear sign of premeditation), turned and FIRED! right into Marcia's face as she came rushing up to do "something."

Marcia, the unfortunate soul tasked with keeping the teens happy and calm, stood there blinking, shocked beyond words, as Susan left the room in its newly remodeled state of post-apocalyptic ruin.

"Daaamn. Girl knows how to throw a fit," Shikith said as she stared after Susan.

"So do I," said Alfred darkly.

A flash of light and a "Ziit!" noise made them turn back to the TV just in time to see the screen go dark. Smoke seeped from behind the television.

Alfred, Katie, and Shikith sat on the couch in total silence for a moment staring at the dead screen. Marcia would normally have already been on them, trying to smooth things over, but she'd fled to the bathroom to wash Susan's loogie off her face.

"You know, it's like a gray canvas," Katie mused as she stared at the dead flat screen. "I'll get my stuff." She sprung up, leaving Shikith and Alfred on the couch. She darted past the drenched guard and out of the rec room.

They always had guards. There were cameras in every room and they listened to every word they said to each other. When the government people first spoke to her and her parents, Katie thought that they were nice and helpful. They told them all about Dr. Burgis and his pills and they explained that they would need to monitor her and the others teens to make sure the drugs didn't make them sick or cause them to go crazy like the one kid, Joshua, who had killed his whole family or like the girl who thought she was a witch or the ones who became vampires.

On Wednesday, they brought Katie, Alfred, Susan, and Shikith to this military base out in the middle of nowhere. There were doctors and tests and blood work and visits with shrinks they endured daily. The living conditions were nice in some ways. They set each of them up with their own special room. Katie had a huge art room with canvases, paints, clay to mold, blocks of stone to carve, and other things she didn't even know how to use. They also provided her with teachers who were excited to work with her.

They'd done the same with Susan, giving her a huge room filled with musical instruments and musicians to play with. Alfred Freeman they let go out to the gym to work out or go shoot guns and play soldier with the other soldiers like he wanted. But with the rooms came the cameras and the guards and the bullshit as they all called it. They didn't get to see any real news or use the internet or even talk to their parents except for pre-recorded video mail which seemed edited and cut up when they watched it.

Yesterday Alfred used his super skills to sneak off and spy on the soldiers. He overheard them talking about all the kids who took the pills. He heard a lot about Amen Hale, where the witch named Black Rain and the flying girl and the vampire kids had started their own little kingdom, calling themselves Princesses and Princes.

He also heard that the President was going to give a speech tonight about all the teens in the drug study and about what was happening in Amen Hale. It was supposed to be a Presidential Address to the nation. Alfred had words with their handlers and insisted on seeing the live television broadcast. They'd agreed, but now it was obvious that they'd lied. What they'd shown did not mention anything about the pills or Amen Hale or anything at all that had to do with the kids in the drug study; it was all the other problems and even that was edited and cut up.

Katie went to her art room, changed into her special pajamas, and grabbed the thick blanket off the bed, pulling it around her shoulders and then shuffling to her work table. She grabbed her flashlight and the little Dixie cup that used to hold her water for her paint brushes. She'd painted over the cup, making a new pattern.

She collected the scraps of colored paper she'd been working on, as she worked on other things that she wasn't really working on, to hide what she was really working on so no one would know she was working on it. Sometimes Katie thought everyone around her thought she was dumb, but she was smart enough to let them think she was dumber than what she was, which she thought was really smart.

She knew she lost it when she got into her art, and she knew her ADD was really bad right now because she'd stopped taking her meds, but she didn't want to start taking her meds again because that would mess up her art, and she didn't want to mess up her art, which was why she was doing what she was doing. She had everything concealed under her blanket as she shuffled down the hall and stopped at Susan's door.

Katie knocked. Waited. Knocked. Waited. Knocked. Waited. Knocked. Waited. Knocked. Waited. Knocked. Waited. Knocked. Waited. Knocked. Waited. Knocked. Waited. Knocked. Waited. Knocked. Waited.

One of the guards watched as she continued to knock and wait. He disappeared and Marcia came down the hall a minute later.

"Katie honey, I don't think Susan is in the mood to talk right now. Why don't you come with me?"

The door pulled open. "Come on in, Katie." Susan had tears on her face but she was smiling as she looked at Katie wrapped up like she was ready for a slumber party in her blanket. She could see by her sleeves that Katie even had her pajamas on.

"Fuck off, Marcia. Watch it on the cameras, you nosey cunt," Susan cursed at Marcia as Katie padded into the room dragging most of her blanket behind her like a long tail.

The door slammed shut in Marcia's stunned face.

Katie looked around the trashed room. Susan's rampage had continued here in her private music sanctum. Guitars were in pieces, amps busted, keyboards shattered, and sheet music littered the floor. When they first arrived Wednesday night, Susan had been able to sing like an angel and play every instrument she picked up, but all day Thursday she got worse and worse and then today it made her angry just to touch an instrument. Susan was losing her powers.

Yep. She'd come to the right place, had a good idea, done the right thing. Nailed it. Yep. Yep. Yep.

Out loud she said only, "S.O.S."

"What?" Susan asked.

"Go turn the radio up loud and come get under."

Susan stared at Katie's face and saw something there that made her act without asking why. She went to the radio, which had somehow survived her rampage and cranked the volume. She could see Katie's silhouette under the blanket; the flashlight she had on made the couch look like a big red tent. Susan lifted the edge and crawled under until she was sitting cross-legged on the couch beside Katie with an open space between them. As soon as she looked at what Katie had in her hands her eyes almost popped out of her head.

"Where did you get that?" she asked. Katie was holding a little cup; the pattern was the exact same little scrollwork of vines and pastel flowers that were on the cups Dr. Burgis used in his office to hold the pills.

"Take your pills. Be happy. Rock on." Katie handed her the cup.

Susan grabbed it and looked inside. Three white pills and one blue pill rolled around in the bottom of the cup. But then her brain started to ruin everything. They'd searched them and taken everything they had and given them all new stuff, so how had Katie gotten her hands on the pills? She rubbed the cup and felt the thicker texture of paint and she eyed the pills skeptically. They looked right but it was still impossible.

"Sue, you want to sing and play right?" Katie asked her.

She nodded.

"And I want to keep what I got. I made these pills, but they will work if we believe they will work. Hold on."

Katie took out a little pouch that held more pills and took out a blue pill and three white pills for herself and dropped those into the cup as well. She reached into her purse and took out a bottle of water and looked at Susan.

"Believe with me."

"You mean *make believe* with you," Susan said sadly. It was stifling hot under the blanket and she was already sweating and feeling horrid, and Katie was crazy, and this was a waste of time.

"I have my powers," Katie declared, giving her a satisfied look. "I made these pills and I believe they will work, but if you don't want my help then give me back the cup and the pills."

"No!" Susan pulled the cup to her chest.

"Be careful with the cup, don't crush it," Katie cautioned, like it mattered somehow if the cup were crushed.

"If you want to take the pills we need to get them ready, believe with me," Katie urged. She wrapped her hands around Susan's which held the cup and rocked back and forth, muttering, pulling Susan back and forth with her.

"I believe. I believe. I believe. I believe. I believe. I believe."

Susan copied her, not knowing what else to do and desperate enough to try anything, absolutely anything, even something insane and childish or absolutely crazy.

"I believe. I believe. I believe. I believe." On and on the girls chanted. After a while Susan stopped thinking about what she was saying and started thinking about how she was saying it, focusing on the sound of her voice, blending it with Katie's rote chant that was always the same every time as they held the cup and rocked back and forth, back and forth.

The chant continued, the heat made her faint, the stuffy, oxygen deprived confines under the blanket made her want to scream, but need made her stay. She had no idea how long she muttered but she was completely drenched with sweat when she noticed that she was the only one chanting, "I believe." She opened her eyes to see that the flashlight had faded to a dim glow that barely gave enough light to see by under the blanket.

"I believe the pills are ready. How 'bout you?" Katie asked.

"Yeah," Susan said, chilled by her own sweat despite the boiling heat under the blanket.

"I'll go first," Katie said. She reached into the cup and fished out her pills, opened the bottle of water, and took them one at a time then handed the bottle of water to Susan. Susan poured the pills from the cup straight into her mouth and quickly swallowed all of them at once, finishing off the bottle of water. She felt light headed and dehydrated.

"Don't tell anyone," Katie told her and shook the bag of pills at her. "Not even Alfred. He seems to be okay and his stuff is all fighting anyway and I don't like that. Shikith would kill herself or someone else if her powers came back so she can't take them either. Same time and place tomorrow. Deal?"

"Deal," Susan said.

Katie grabbed the empty bottle of water and stuffed a piece of paper in it and shoved it down between the couch cushions then tucked the pills and the cup into a pocket-like sash she'd sewn into the back side of her pajama top as Susan watched, amazed at the planning and preparation and *everything*.

"Now we gotta go eat," Katie announced.

"Eat? We gotta go to bed!" Susan said. "Shit, it feels late and I feel weird." It did feel late, she felt strangely unaware of just how late, and lightheaded. Perhaps it was from sweating so much.

"No. Remember, we have to eat after we take our pills or we might get sick and throw up and we don't want that. We Have To Eat." Katie said it like she meant it.

Susan was looking at her weird.

"What?" Katie had to ask.

"You're not really nuts at all, are you?" she accused.

"That would suck! The pills only work if you're crazy, and they worked for you at first, so you must be a little crazy." Katie waved her hands in the air between them like some mystical swami. "Just let gooo of your brain, let go and free your inner freak, Sue baby. Feel the music again and let it go where it wants to go, get your groove back, Stella."

Susan was still digesting that as Katie pulled the blanket off their heads. They were both absolutely drenched. They got off the couch stiffly and walked to the door and, of course, there was a guard just outside.

"Going back to your room, Katie?" Sherman asked. He was one of their better guards, smart enough to know he was on the other team and smart enough to not patronize and act like a real friend. He eyed them up and down.

"Shit, you guys are soaked, you two been doing jazzercise in there all night?"

"Pizza, pizza, pizza. Is there any pizza left in the Rec Room, Sherm?" Katie asked.

"They already cleaned up but I can go get you something," he offered.

"Hurry," said Susan.

Sherman eyed the two of them with a decidedly different look. More like a cop and less like a pretend buddy.

"Shit. You girls didn't get into anything you shouldn't have, did you? You both look tore up." He stared into their glazed eyes and slightly off expressions.

"Sherm," Susan put a hand to her stomach, "just go get us something to eat."

Before Sherman could move to the phone to call it in a voice spoke over the intercom. "We will have a pizza delivered to the Rec Room. Please escort them there, Sherman."

As soon as the girls left with Sherman, three men entered and searched the room and the sweat sodden blanket. They found nothing but an empty bottle of water stuffed between the cushions of the couch with a note stuffed in it.

Dear Invisible Rabbit,

I don't mean to be rude, but your crunching is getting on my last nerve. I can hardly hear myself think. Please find a new place to eat your salad.

Thank you,
Katie Linn

The Twilight Star

Breaking All the Rules

THE CRISP MOUNTAIN air was filled with countless little floating specks of light dancing above the shadowed shapes of tombstones and spread throughout the branches and brows of the surrounding woods. Magic made them appear as nothing more than the floating aerial soup of Mother Nature, but each dot of light held a life, with hopes and dreams and wishes and needs and fears. Many fears. Peffan landed on the white picket fence and dropped to his knees before his queen.

"Their truck is returning."

"Well," Taunwee said, then looked out into the night, awaiting the arrival of the vehicle.

Taunwee was an inch and a half tall and the white dress that clung to her curving form was so sheer and transparent it looked like the ghost of a dress and nothing physical that a hand could touch. The Queen's multi-colored hair changed with her mood and her mood usually followed the seasons unless she was aroused or provoked, and she had most certainly been provoked, but her ankle length hair was not red. Dark gray streaks and white rested on her head, colors that almost never adorned her hair. Gray and white, Confusion and fear, that all her people could see, know, and feel the same.

Standing with her on the fence rail were five of her consorts, each armed and ready to fight, hundreds of her soldiers hovered in the air nearby, and thousands upon thousands of her people filled the woods, watching and waiting.

Most of the year this graveyard was open and accessible to those few humans who sought the bones buried in the earth, but during the month of August this place became *another place* as Queen Taunwee, The Twilight Star, brought her court and her people here. They never allowed outsiders into the Summer Court as they sometimes did in other places.

But the girl and those with her had appeared out of nowhere. Taunwee was indecisive as to what to do about the breach of their Summer Court and the murder of thousands of her people. Even if done in ignorance, it was still horrible. She felt confusion; the workings of the universe she thought she knew so well now seemed woefully incomplete, or possibly even inaccurate. Fear of action and inaction gripped her. She was torn. She had seen many things, glorious things, and horrible things, and all those things made sense, but what she had seen this morning made absolutely no sense.

Her people had seen this mortal girl before, seasons ago. She'd come with her family to visit the graveyard while her court was away in other lands. The Twilin caretakers left here to tend this place watched the girl as her family visited the graves. They said that she was strange even then. That she seemed damaged, walking apart from the others and courting her own death as one already dead.

The air between the two joined trees shimmered once again and a gateway opened. It looked like a huge painting of some other place—a freeway billboard fallen from its perch and now framed by the wood of the trees that held it firm. The trucks had been coming and going regularly all day, but in all that time no one had ventured into the graveyard again or into the wood beyond.

This time, however, three men stepped through the gateway and headed in their direction. One of the men was older, with silver hair and a pear-shaped body. He was wearing common clothes. He stopped by the dirt path the trucks used and opened a folding chair he carried, lit a cigarette, and sat there by the gateway while the other two men continued toward the graveyard. One of these two men was younger, nineteen or twenty, also wearing common clothing, while the other was dressed in the black garb worn by the men who did not venture off in the trucks.

"They were going to have dancing after the dinner," the younger man complained. "I was hoping to dance with Arial. Or Keri. Or Lorenes. Ariel has too many guys after her but I'm sure I've still got a chance. A good chance."

"There'll be other dances, other feasts, other parties," replied the man in black.

"They were serving human flesh tonight. Real human flesh, cooked and fancied up and made into all kinds of different dishes. Manuel told me they had some super nasty looking trays and bowls that they were going to serve it in. He said they were the most gruesome things he'd ever seen."

The two of them were close to the fence and the entrance to the graveyard.

"Stop here, Benson. No one goes into the graveyard," said Reese.

"Why?"

"You heard what Lucius said, the place is sacred to her. If it's sacred to her, then it's sacred to me."

Benson kept walking but didn't step into the graveyard; he stopped right at the gate and leaned his full weight on the remains of the weathered fence that bordered the graveyard, his right hand resting two feet from where Taunwee stood, invisible and unseen.

"Don't lean on the rail, you dummy, it's old, it might fall."

Benson straightened. "Geesh, Reese, it's just an old graveyard. Let's go in, I want to go see the grave she laid on."

"Why?"

"Just to see it," Benson said casually.

"Then the answer is no."

The young man shot Reese a nasty look. "If I wanted to go pray to her or worship or something, then you'd let me, *right?*"

"If I thought you were serious, I might," he replied.

"That's bull. You're shittin' on me just because I'm still a Wiccan."

Reese chuckled. "I don't need a reason to shit on you. I'm your superior and you are my servant, I can shit on you any time I want just because I want to. You live in Amen Hale now, not America the Beautiful. You have no bill of rights that keeps me from shitting on you. The only right you have is the right to go tell the King and Queen I was shittin' on you."

"I still think it's stupid," Benson said, determined to have the last word as he stared out at the graves.

The two men were quiet for a minute. They watched the graveyard until Benson pulled his untucked flannel shirt tighter around him.

"I should have pulled a jacket from the closet."

"You still got time."

"Nah, I'll be fine once I'm in the truck and the heater's on."

"No, you won't." Reese took off his black leather jacket and handed it to the younger man. "It'll get colder tonight and you'll be in and out of the truck more than once. You'll get sick. With your jeans and flannel shirt the jacket won't stand out too badly, but be careful, hang back and let Mr. Thorpe do the talking."

Benson hesitated for a moment but then took the jacket and slipped it on.

They waited another silent minute while thousands of tiny ears and eyes listened and watched from all around with a keen attentiveness that made the night seem alive, even to dull mortal senses.

"This place does feel special. Like it's alive and watching us or something," Benson observed.

"How are you adjusting, Ben, you doin' all right?" Reese asked, his attention focused on the younger man.

"Well enough," he said, sounding unwell.

"What do you miss the most?"

Benson laughed. "The stupid shit. Having money. McDonalds. Convenience stores. Porn. Updating my Facebook status. I'm sure everyone thinks I'm dead by now. Being able to go to a movie on the weekend with a girl I just met. Feeling like I'm part of the rest of the world and not in a magical fishbowl. Freedom, like I could go anywhere with no one telling me what to do."

Reese took out a stick of gum for himself and offered a piece to Benson who waved it away.

"I was surprised you stayed when your folks left," Reese said with a careful neutral tone as he chewed.

"Me too," Benson replied with a rueful shake of his head. "There's a bunch of stuff I don't like about Amen Hale, but there's a bunch of stuff I do like. I don't *need* money here." He laughed because he missed having it and at the same time was glad he didn't need it. "I know where breakfast, lunch, and dinner are coming from and I don't have to think about it, which is actually pretty cool. I have real friends here, not idiots on the internet. I love being in the only place on earth with real magic. More girls would be nice." He grinned.

"What about freedom?" Reese prodded.

Taunwee watched the young man's face carefully as he sobered further, giving a passionate answer to the inquiry.

"I guess I don't mind being owned." He added a short moment later, "By the Queen."

Reese was studying his young companion, trying to figure him out. "You're in love with the Queen," he guessed. Benson's face confirmed his suspicions.

Reese groaned miserably, suffering for the boy.

Benson remained silent.

Taunwee watched. The tips of her hair turned green.

Another silence stretched out between the two men, but then the headlights of the truck turning off the main road onto the little trail drew their gaze. Wordlessly the two men turned and started walking back toward the gateway and the truck.

"What about the porn?" Reese asked with a gently teasing tone.

"I'm a better person without it. It weakens my heart," the young man answered Reese's lightheartedness with a totally serious reply.

"So mote it be," Reese intoned, serious as well.

In all her twelve thousand years of life there were few times Taunwee felt quite so put out. It was a simple thing, she'd been completely immersed in the conversation, interested in every word and nuance, and she was more than sad to have it end. Not angry. Hurt. The facts she was hearing of this strange girl with many names and godlike powers had been intriguing and needed. The information on Amen Hale and its Queen had been intriguing and needed. Every emotion on both faces had been intriguing and needed. Taunwee had been interested in not only their words, but in them individually, the minutia of their lives and how it all fit together like pieces of a puzzle. She rarely interacted with the children of Adam herself as some of her children did; very few could draw her interest. Taunwee paid no attention to her changeable hair, but her people did. They always watched her mood, which helped them serve her and anticipate her desires.

"Peffan, follow Benson. Keep him safe."

Without a word Peffan took flight, his point of light quickly traveling across the grass and weeds, winking out as he landed on Benson's shoulder.

Asadan Makir, Guiding Star of the Jasper Gardens, landed on the rail beside her with disapproval plain on his too beautiful face.

"What do you do?"

"As pleases me," she replied.

"You endanger us all." The words were gravely spoken.

Taunwee laughed. A quick series of beautiful tinkling trills. "Yes," she said.

He gave her a final scowl then turned and prepared to leave, grinding his teeth and fisting his hands so tightly that knuckles popped within his silken gloved hands. It was how Makir had expressed his displeasure in her court for thousands of years. If he'd been facing her he would have seen her hair and had some warning.

He bent his knees to spring into the air just as Taunwee's clawed hand closed around the back of his neck. She moved fast, pushing Makir forward until he crashed face down on the rail and then she straddled his back. Makir was a Child of the Dawn, the same as she, so regrettably she could not kill him even if she wanted to. Her consorts did not move to help her or restrain her.

Taunwee knew that Makir, like her consorts, expected some emotional tantrum or some physical violence which Makir would endure and then forget, but this was altogether different. With an unrestrained wildness she attacked, doing things with her magic she'd never attempted before upon one of her own kind. She violently clouded Makir's mind with all her power, not carefully, as would be done with a mind she intended to keep whole. She destroyed what he was and made him pliant and obedient. She left him some basic understanding of communication so he would still be useful, like a simple tool.

Asadan Makir's form shimmered and the mass of his body between her knees began to thin and lengthen and grow until the Queen sat astride a six inch long luminous white worm. She stroked the side of the pliant worm affectionately and it quivered under her hand. Its middle was still wrapped with Makir's fine silken robes though the rest of his belongings rested below his body on the wooden rail. The worm floated a scant few centimeters off the surface of the fence rail, the gift of flight still trapped within its magical body though it had no wings. Taunwee slid her hands across the undulating segments, giving Makir what would probably be the final touch of her hands until the end of all things.

Four of the smaller Lights had stood together at the Fall, choosing not to go with either side but to stand alone and apart. The other three bowed the head but not the knee to Taunwee, preserving themselves from her dominance while still pledging their *conditional* obedience. Over the years two had left. All the Dawn Children were made male in the beginning, but Taunwee changed her form to female. She'd changed herself but she'd never dreamed she could forcibly change another of her own kind. What she'd done was madness.

She opened her mouth and tasted sweet mountain air. Wildness and change was on the wind. She'd risen up against her brother. She felt no remorse, only joy, and a bone deep satisfaction. She'd hated him forever.

Taunwee, The Twilight Star, stroked the white worm's smooth flesh and smiled.

A worm.

How fitting.

"Let the craftsmen fashion saddle and stirrups, fasten it to his flesh, and drive a bit through Makir's head and affix a bridle that whosoever sits might steer him."

The wide-eyed courtiers hovering in the air flew away to fulfill her will. Her shocked people looked upon her as if seeing her for the first time. It was not the first time she had murdered, but it was the first time she'd raised her hand against one of her own kind. She sat astride Makir's body and watched them.

The night was utterly silent.

"I will name pairs!" she announced loudly. The response was automatic. Reactionary. Predictable. Reassuring.

None of them were fooled by the distraction, but *Pairs was Pairs!* The stunned crowd slowly built into the expected buzz of excitedly flapping wings. Floating dots of light crowded closer from all around, pouring in from the surrounding woods and the valley below as her words carried further out into the night from light to light.

"*She names pairs! She names pairs!*"

The scratching of crickets, odd clicking noises, snapping and chirping and other mysterious sounds merged into a mad cacophony of insect life causing the humans gathered around the truck to stop what they were doing. They looked out toward the graveyard and the swirling mass insect like specks of light that swarmed above the darkened tombs.

One of her consorts went to his knees, crawling to her with his head down facing the wooden rail. He'd never shown this much respect to her before, but then he'd never seen her turn one of the Shining Ones into a worm before either.

"Light of my Life, the men at the portal hear the sounds and see the lights. Perhaps we should quiet our people or shield what we do here?" He held his breath.

"Hide them not. Hush them not. Let them sing and dance and play. I agree with the girl. This is our place and I claim her words for the blessing they were. The humans already deem our graveyard sacred, and so it is."

She looked back, catching the sparking, blue eyes of one of her oldest and, until a few moments ago, most disfavored consorts. He was wingless, a human who'd become her consort in the days of Enos when man was new to the earth. For countless years he'd been like a cripple, which had made him bitter and difficult to deal with, but no more.

"Mammsik, disrobe Makir. Wear his garments, wield his sword and ride him; your eyes will match his blue robes. Hold for me his other valuables. They will be gifts for tonight."

Taunwee dismounted and left a smiling Mammsik to his work. He did not say thank you or anything else. She had acknowledged him, and spoken. It was enough.

Taunwee stepped to the edge of the rail and addressed the sea of excited faces already gathered above the graves. Thousands upon thousands hovered in the air or stood on the ground amidst the stones, but more were arriving every minute.

"Let the Promised gather and present! The rule is truth. Payment is in the telling. The gift freely given. Let the pairs tell us of their love, whose is deepest, whose is purest, whose is sweetest, whose is truest. Ninety Brides will be gifted, and ninety kisses I bestow, but to the pair judged most fine, ten more kisses shall be thine, and your house shall stand alone, prince and princess beneath my throne, not a slave to elder's bane, beneath my hand you shall remain."

The night went utterly silent with shock before exploding into frenzy unlike anything Taunwee had ever seen before from her people. The chance to be wed, have eleven children, and be free from the endless obligation and tyranny of Sires, Sire's Sires, and Sire's Sire's Sires, and so on would be a gift beyond all imagining.

Never had she dangled so sweet a gift before her children. Only a minute ago every one of them would have sworn such a thing to be impossible.

Taunwee laughed again, enjoying the wildness of this crazy night of impossible things. She looked back to the archway and the truck. Other men dressed in black had stepped through the portal and a group now stood, mouths hanging open as they stared at the graveyard and the bowl of open space hemmed in by dark trees. High in the night sky and hovering low over the graves and everywhere in between, lights twinkled and spun in a circle, as if a rotating galaxy of tiny stars had torn free of its patch of the heavens and come down to rest over this place. Though with the Twilin glamor in place, the sight was a bit less magical and a bit more disturbing for the humans.

Taunwee focused her ears to hear the conversations of the men who watched. The older man named Mike Thorpe, who'd been smoking as he waited for the truck, was speaking loudly to the others.

"I've been all through the everglades and Okefenokee and I've never seen a swarm of goddam bugs like that!" He gestured toward the Twilins with his lit cigarette.

"If they're not mosquitos or something that bites then they're harmless," said one of the other men in black. "It's gotta be a massive swarm of termites that only comes out once a year or once every seven years like locusts or cicadas. Must be every termite in North Carolina over there."

Reese nodded. "Someone go grab a can of repellant and some bug bombs we can set off while they finish unloading the truck. We don't want these things spilling through into Amen Hale."

Two of the men darted off to fetch the chemicals.

Taunwee shielded the growing light show from the highway but at the same time dropped the glamor that prevented the men from seeing their true forms. The swirling mass of Twilight creatures slowed and then halted in mid air to stare at their Queen in fear and confusion. The rules were plain, Satan had set them, stay away from man and let God and all things supernatural be forgotten. None could stand against him and his servants, those who avoided him endured, those who did not were purged. The same fear was on a hundred thousand faces as Taunwee spoke.

"Two thousand Twilin died this morning because their goddess thought us ants beneath her feet. If this girl goddess with many names kills more of my people, I refuse to let it be an act of innocent ignorance, done without thought and easily forgotten. Let murder be the ugly thing that it is. Though not as strict as we, these people seem to hold to the Ban. They disguise their men before sending them out into the world and they live in a walled, magical Kingdom. They are a hidden people."

Taunwee drew herself up and declared firmly, "This is our place and has been so since the floodwaters receded and we will not abandon it! And I refuse to be fumigated in my own home! We will let them see our true form and will be a people to them, not *insects*. Stay on this side of the portal. Avoid prolonged contact with them, do not harm them, crowd them, or provoke them in any way, but be friendly. We appear to be neighbors."

The croaking and insect-like racket changed now that the glamor was lifted. The strangely musical sounds of tinkling, laughing bells filled the night air as her people delighted in the joke, finding it very funny indeed. The Twilin people had no neighbors, only enemies, those whom they feared and others like man, whom they endured. The idea of neighbors was so totally alien it was comical.

Queen Taunwee turned her back to the staring men who gaped at a world changed before their eyes. The night sky filled with hundreds of thousands of tiny winged people instead of insects, glowing, singing, laughing, and playing.

Benson

A Pair of Queens

PEFFAN HEARD HER words and the injunction forbidding them from going through the portal. He was sitting on the shoulder of his charge as he allowed himself to become visible along with the rest of his people.

"Do you think she did this, made them, when she laid upon the grave?" one of the other men asked Reese.

"I don't know," Reese answered.

"The girl with many names did not make us," Peffan answered, not willing to allow that misconception to stand. The thought disturbed him.

"Who said that?" Benson said, looking up. Out. Around in a circle. They searched until one of the other men in their group spotted Peffan sitting on Benson's shoulder.

"Look!" He pointed at Peffan.

"Don't move Benson," Reese ordered.

They gathered around Benson who'd frozen, looking straight ahead, like a man with a poisonous spider on him who was trying hard not to make a sudden move and get bit.

"Shi-i-i-it!" a building crescendo. "Is it in my hair!?" Benson's hands twitched as he fought the urge to rake his fingers through his dense mop of brown hair and squeal in a sissified girl fit that he'd never be able to live down.

"Relax!" Reese ordered. "Just hold still! One of them is on your shoulder, but it's not doing anything, it's just sitting there."

Benson slowly turned his head and looked down at Peffan. He did relax as he studied the little figure, more puzzled than panicked. He was tiny. No. Not tiny. Miniscule. Less than two inches. He was man shaped, perfectly proportioned with a handsome face, puffy white shirt, tight black pants, and black boots. His eyes and facial features were normal, except for his dark green hair that reached just past his shoulders. A pair of purple wings were folded in, lying flat against his back, tucked down like a beetle's wings. Benson guessed that the white shirt had an open back where the wings connected.

"You, aaah, been there–on my shoulder–long?" Benson stammered nervously.

"Hello, Benson. I have been upon your shoulder since you walked away from the fence with Reese."

Peffan's voice wasn't mousey, high pitched, or effeminate but was average in tone and volume, though his manner of speech was slightly antiquated and at the same time punked up. Of course he was using magic to make his voice louder but the effect was seamless. He seemed completely at ease as he sat cross legged on the shoulder of Benson's borrowed black leather jacket.

"You're, aaah, on the wrong shoulder." Benson tried to fix things. "I'm not the one you need to talk to. You want Reese." He pointed at the man. "He's in charge, or Lucius or Byron or someone important."

"No. I'm on the right shoulder," Peffan said confidently. "And you are very important, Benson."

"Me!" Benson barked. "What makes me important?"

"Cats! I wish I knew!" The tiny man sounded genuinely curious himself as to Benson's mysterious eminence.

"What do you want with Benson?" Reese asked. "And what makes him so special to you?" He stared at the little man with a mix of worry and wonder, while still casting glances back to the mass of winged figures circling the clearing. There was more worry than wonder on his face.

"What do I want with Benson? The first question commanded. I want to keep him safe, the same as you, Reese." He nodded and said, "Arah," the odd word a punctuation at the end of his sentence.

"What makes him special? The second question commanded. Benson has stirred the love of two queens, you," Peffan poked a finger at Reese, "his master, care for him and his happiness," he looked back to Benson and said gravely, "*which is no small thing.*" His words sounded sincere and heartfelt, but no one had a chance to explore this comment as Peffan turned back to Reese and continued. "And by my count he has three girls he hoped to dance with this night alone and they are only distractions as he reaches to the heavens—*and the heavens reach back*," he added ominously. "I'd call that special!" Peffan gave Benson a respectful, almost awed look. "Benson's got *it*," he declared soundly. Then he said, "Ferah."

"*It? Benson?*" said an incredulous voice. It was one of the other young men standing with them. He'd kept the two words separate, making "Benson" and "it" mutually repellant, like oil and water. Peffan noticed the dark look he directed at Benson. He was the same height, but bigger and more solidly built than Benson with his whimsy frame.

"Receive the gift of free advice," Peffan addressed his words to the bigger boy. "Envy will steal your joy and eat your flesh faster than a bat on the wing. Be at peace. Benson is not your rival." He looked up at Benson with a companionable, friendly smile.

Benson blinked and swallowed, uncomfortable with the odd protectiveness of the little man sitting on his shoulder. Even embarrassed by it. He didn't notice it, but he was earning queer looks from the other men as their gaze bounced from Benson to the creature on his shoulder.

Reese spoke up before any more could be said on the ludicrous subject of Benson's mysterious mojo or his not so hidden love for his Queen. "Cooper, go report to Lucius immediately and tell him what's happened. The rest of you guardsmen get back to Amen Hale and get this truck ready to move. I want it unloaded and ready to roll in ten minutes!" he ordered.

The group of men broke up reluctantly, heading back through the portal as Reese turned back to Benson and his visitor. "What are you?" Reese asked the little man.

He stood up and bowed gracefully, balancing easily on Benson's shoulder.

"The third question commanded. I am a Twilin. My name is Peffan." He nodded, then declared, "Tath!" with a big smile on his little face. "Truth was asked, payment given three times. Arah. Farah. Tath. You owe me the truth, child of Adam." He gestured back to the portal. "The young girl dressed in black that came here at mid of day and slept upon the grave, tell me of her."

Reese pondered what to do. He felt as if he'd stepped into a trap by asking a few simple questions. Now he apparently owed this little fairy man an answer, but he didn't want to say anything that would endanger Amen Hale or the Black Lion. He had no idea who or what these things were.

"Please ask a different question," he asked, his face pained.

Peffan nodded "yes" but said "no." He held up a finger, "If asked a question that is prickly, pick distant fruit for the meal but that which grows upon the same vine, something connected and yet safely shared." He cocked his tiny head to the side making a sour face. "Don't trim the verge too tightly though, it *is* discourteous. I answered as servant to master, three to one, to slight me further than I slight myself would be churlish indeed."

He stood with his hands on his hips, tiny face expectant.

"Trim the verge?" Reese mumbled, unfamiliar with the antiquated metaphor and unsure of the first part of what Peffan said as well. The only thing he was sure of was that he was in deep shit.

Peffan saw his confusion and grimaced, time marched on and language changed so quickly. "Do you speak any other languages?" Peffan asked. "German perhaps? French?"

Benson came to Reese's rescue. "I think he means, don't beat around the bush too much when you give your answer or he'll think you're nothing but a stingy shit." Benson looked down at Peffan and quirked his lip. "Is that it?" he asked.

"Well spoken, Benson!" Peffan laughed. His voice was normal but his laugh was not; it was a strange, higher pitched trilling that reminded him of little bells. "I told you he's got it," Peffan announced merrily. "I rarely meet a human I like, but I like him."

Reese ignored the little man's ramblings and directed his stunned gaze to Benson.

"What!" Benson said defensively. "So sue me, I like Scrabble. Just give him something vague, Reese, some stuff that he probably already knows. Things that won't matter but are still interesting to know."

"The Black Lion is many different things to many different people," Reese began, trying to be vague and still give something to end his obligation to the little man. "To some, she is now a god called the Black Lion." He obviously included himself in this group and wasn't ashamed of it. "To others she is Princess Rain of Amen Hale. The outside world knows of her as the Black Witch, and to her friends and family she is called Black Rain." Reese stopped there, reaching the limit of what he'd willingly give.

Peffan bowed. "Well," he said, but looked as if he considered this answer thin and considered Reese a stingy shit after all.

Reese looked back to the massive throng of glowing figures; the majority still spun in the vortex circling the clearing but there were others who had drawn closer while they spoke. A few hundred hovered mere yards away, gathered in colorful clouds of little bodies, watching with curious eyes, whispering together as their wings buzzed behind them in a blur of shimmering colors. Reese also noticed that the ground was covered in a moving carpet of tiny creatures walking on their feet. These were wingless Twilins, most migrating toward the graveyard but many lingering nearby, gathered in groups of ten and fifteen. Each of the groups had similar colored hair and wore similar clothing, like clans or families. The wingless ones were watching as well but kept a more careful distance. The only Twilin closer than a car length was Peffan.

"Our people mean no harm, Reese, they are only curious." Peffan drew Reese's attention back to him. "None of them will come near the portal. It has been forbidden, and we obey our Queen. The Children of the Twilight Star and the Children of Amen Hale are much alike. We are both hidden peoples. We both have Queens. We both have magic. We both share this place." Peffan pointed to Reese. "It is special to your young goddess and it is special to our Queen, and it is the home of our Summer Court."

The white rental truck rumbled to life and pulled out of the archway, stopping beside them. Mike Thorpe, the older man at the wheel waved for Benson to get in, but Benson wasn't watching the truck, he was looking at the spinning mass of lights, watching as the closest Twilins flew by. Some of them were couples, holding hands as they spun through the air while others flew alone or in groups, whirling and spinning through the air as they passed by, circling the clearing to the sound of tinkling bells.

"Are they dancing?" Benson asked.

"Yes. They are dancing. There will be Pairs named tonight. Weddings. They are happy," Peffan answered but gave him a curious look. "Why do you ask Benson?"

"We had a wedding tonight too. They're dancing by now in Amen Hale, and they're dancing here." He scuffed at the ground with his boot. "Both Queens are dancing, but my ass will be stuck in a truck for the next ten hours." He turned and looked at the truck and frowned. "I gotta go, Peffan, but could you do me a favor?"

"It depends on the favor, Benson. I do not grant wishes, and I am not your master or your servant."

Benson laughed, his glum expression brightening. "I haven't seen your Queen and I don't know a thing about her, and I'm in love with Cathryn, which will never change, but please tell her that I think she has a very pretty name. Taunwee. Taunwee." He said the name like he was trying it out, sampling the sound and shape, seeing how it made his mouth move to form the sounds and say the name.

He smiled approvingly. "I would dance with Taunwee before I danced with Ariel or Keri or Lorenes, her name alone is prettier than those other girls."

"Cool it, Benson!" Reese ordered. "Zip it and keep it zipped! I think one impossible dream is enough. Go get in the truck and get your ass out of here, you're already late. And be careful tonight. Keep your mind on what you're doing and not on dancing queens."

Benson pointed to Reese with his chin. "Time to switch shoulders." Peffan hopped into the air and landed on Reese's shoulder. The awkward, gangly twenty-year-old boy walked around the truck and swung himself up into the passenger seat.

"I must leave as well," Peffan said.

Reese looked down at his own shoulder where Peffan now stood.

"It was good to meet you, Reese." Peffan gave him a small bow. "Fare thee well."

"Wait! If we want to talk to you again, what should we do?" Reese asked quickly.

"Tonight our Queen is busy picking Promised pairs, it would probably be best to wait till tomorrow for a formal meeting, but all you need do is approach the railing and announce yourself and we will speak to you. Queen Taunwee has declared that we are neighbors to the people of Amen Hale."

The green-haired man vanished, one second there, the next gone.

The Wayward Heart

Bloody Kisses and Sweet Nothings

GLASS SHATTERED IN the back of the Suburban.

"Sit down, Gannon! Get away from the window!" yelled Agent Swartzman.

"Go get him! We can't let him jump! Go!" Whidby, the driver, yelled at Swartzman, the agent who sat in the passenger seat hesitating. The sound of more glass breaking got Swartzman moving toward the back where the crazed blue-haired teenager and the witch's beating heart were waiting.

Whidby and Swartzman had been there when Gannon and his bride-to-be traded a few final bitter words at the gateway before she collapsed, clutching her chest. Fearing a reprisal, they'd rushed Gannon and his family through the house and out to the parked vehicles, trying to get them far away as fast as possible.

When Gannon opened his door he found a human heart, bloody and beating, lying in his seat. He slammed the door and stepped away. Whidby and his men loaded the family into a different vehicle as the lab boys gathered around the animated body part. They got a mile down the road before the heart vanished from its evidence bag and reappeared in the second vehicle, on the seat beside Gannon's leg, fit in between him and his sister like a part of the family.

On and on it went. Every time it was removed from the boy it simply returned. Anyone who touched the heart without protective gear felt a numbing chill that lasted for hours. Anyone who touched Gannon when the heart was in his lap also felt the chill. When they questioned him during a period of calm when the heart had just been removed he told them that it wasn't cold to him, that it was warm and alive.

The decision was made to take the boy to the location in Montana where the other unusual teens were being held while his mother, stepfather, and sister were sent back to their own home in a separate vehicle. It was assumed that the heart would follow. The last glimpse Gannon's terrified family had of him was through the darkly tinted glass of an FBI SUV. They pressed their faces to the glass trying to force their shaking, cold numbed hands to cup around their eyes and help them peer through the reflective glare. Gannon lay stretched out in rear seat. He was asleep, soundly sedated, his hands behind his back in cuffs. The heart lay on the seat beside him, pressed up against his chest, glistening wetly and dripping blood as it beat happily along.

It was strange to think of a body part as having emotions, but Swartzman and Whidby both thought this particular organ had them in spades. Happy when it was where it wanted to be, which was pressed up against the kid, pissed and downright angry when separated from the kid or when the kid tried to hurt it, although it never stayed mad at him for long. It seemed to forgive him quickly for any offense.

So far the kid had thrown it on the ground and tried to stomp it to death, he tried to squeeze the life out of it with his bare hands to keep it from beating, and he'd actually stabbed it with a small knife he had on him, then tried to cut it into little pieces. It was after the knife incident that Whidby drugged him, cuffed his hands and feet, and left him in the back seat to the mercy of the heart.

Both Whidby and Swartzman had felt the heart's chill touch more than once as they wrestled the bloody knife away from the boy who swung it wildly as he attacked the heart in his other hand. After that incident both men had the same clear goal: they didn't want to touch it or him again. Until they reached Dallas and handed him off at the airport, they'd do whatever they had to do to keep the witch's heart happy. There wasn't a thimble full of mercy between the two of them for the blue-haired kid.

"He's fucked!" and "Fuck him!" was the consensus of the two agents. Although they held him in low regard, they still needed the package to be alive when they hit Dallas, so suicide was off limits, which meant no diving out the windows.

"Just sit down, kid!" screamed Swartzman as he climbed through to the second bench seat and got a good look. The kid had lain on his back to kick the window out, and now he'd flipped back around and picked up the heart with his teeth, biting it on one of its protruding valves. Gannon faced him, wild eyed with blood all over his face and a pulsing organ clenched in his teeth.

Swartzman backed up and let the kid lunge head first for the window. He waited as long as he dared then grabbed his legs and drug him back into the SUV, cutting him open in a number of places on the ragged glass still in the window. Gannon was cut up and bleeding, but he didn't care. He was laughing and happy as he flopped back onto the seat. They pulled to a stop on the side of the road and two men from the following vehicle rushed up, quickly opening the doors and surveying the mess.

"Get the first aid kits; we need to tape some of the bigger cuts shut now! Quick!" Swartzman shouted to the reluctant men. They swarmed over Gannon, stripping off his shirt and searching for cuts and lacerations. Everyone moved with a strong sense of urgency.

"Two minutes thirteen seconds," called Whidby, still behind the wheel as he kept an eye on the time.

"We need to move him to the third seat, too much glass!" one of the men shouted.

"Keep working on the cuts, do that last!" ordered Whidby.

They all worked faster, the plunger on another syringe of drugs was shoved down with speed, and various methods of wound closure were employed in the next forty-five seconds.

"Thirty seconds! Move him!" shouted Whidby.

They lifted him up and pitched him over the back of the bench seat.

"Ten seconds!"

One overachiever was still repositioning the boy's body when the heart found its way home, appearing right on top of Gannon's bare and scraped up shoulder. The agent screamed and jumped back, holding both his hands out as if his palms had been burned.

"Damn!" He shook his hands. He walked off, shaking out the chilled members, flexing frozen fingers as if this might bring them back to life.

The three men around the boy exchanged looks before Whidby made a call.

"That's it. No one touches him again. I still can't feel my fingertips and it's been hours. We'll wait here for a military chopper or a hazmat unit or something, but we're done. We don't have the equipment or training to deal with this, and if we keep drugging the kid, we'll kill him. I'm calling it in."

Gannon The Gray lay in a stupor on the leather seat. He was resting on his side now with his hands handcuffed behind his back. Balanced on top of his bare shoulder was Alana's heart, no longer separated by a shirt, but naked flesh to bloody, naked flesh. He felt the warmth of the thing. Drug-induced darkness was coming, but he wanted it off him. He could feel it beating away. It was happy. Very happy. It loved him. This thing, this hunk of flesh, this piece of putrid, pulsing meat.

He sent out the command to his drugged shoulder and arm, trying to move just enough to upset her delicate perch and send her careening down into the floor board. Oh how she hated that! His brain sent the message and he got the desired movement from his shoulder, but she rolled up instead of off. The heart landed on top of his head, covering his ear and cheek, the dangling valve dribbling blood across his lips like a wet kiss. Gannon tried to turn his head but the towels they'd placed around his head for support and comfort trapped him in position while they cradled her comfortably to the side of his head.

As Gannon slipped into darkness and madness, the rejoicing heart whispered over and over the same words with the only voice it had.

Tha tha, tha thump. "I love you, Gan."

Tha tha, tha thump. "I love you, Gan."

Tha tha, tha thump. "I love you, Gan."

Tha tha, tha thump. "I love you, Gan."

Tha tha, tha thump. "I love you, Gan."

Tha tha, tha thump. "I love you, Gan."

Alana

A Little Accident

ALANA STOOD BESIDE her mother and father, one hand in each of theirs as the three of them watched the dancing couples winding in and out in a long chain across the floor of the Cathedral Hall as the musicians played a merry tune that seemed more fitted to castles and kingdoms of long ago.

"They're doing a Farandole, Mom." Alana's blue eyes sparkled as she watched Sky and Ryan pass by.

Her mother pulled her arm down to keep Alana soundly on the ground. She tended to float a few inches off the floor now which made walking a clumsy affair. Her penchant for incidental levitation had been disconcerting at first, but the Ainsleys were a tough lot, adapting quickly, which was what they were doing now. They had no choice.

"I know that dance! I can do that. Isn't it beautiful?"

Her mother gave her a strange look. "And when did you ever do the—Faranhole?" She mangled the odd name. "You've never had formal dance training; you were always too busy with track and field."

Her father added, "And who even told you what the Farandole is?"

"Mo-om!" Alana whined.

"Good Lord. Is that Reggie and his wife out there?" her father spotted some of his relations happily joined in the dance and mixed in with the strange people of Amen Hale. "Reggie?" He chuckled. "Look at that. They're doing good, Karen."

"Please!" Alana pulled on her mother's hand.

"No. You're having trouble walking, you're not ready for dancing," her mother said firmly. "Take it easy. You've been through a lot today. Too much."

Alana pulled her hand free from her father and held her stomach. "I feel weird, something's in my stomach. No. Not in my stomach. Lower."

Her mother and father shared a glance but didn't answer or respond because they had no idea where her mind was going. Her next sentence could have been anything. Absolutely anything. She'd been talking to herself nonsensically since her incident at the gateway. Her mind was muddled, not recognizing or understanding some of the most everyday things and knowing other things that she couldn't possibly know. Like the Farandole apparently.

Her eyes had changed, and she had the witch's mark and she could move objects about, cups, saucers, plates, and forks seemed to obey her every whim. Those things they could see and deal with, but the Ainsleys were more worried about the things they couldn't see. Alana was not acting like herself. She was confused and changeable. More than changeable.

Changed.

Alana's facial expression shifted, she looked embarrassed. "Oh no! I think I need to go to the bathroom!" she said loud enough to turn nearby heads.

She shook her head no. "I'm holding it in, I want to go dance."

Her face flashed to utterly grossed out. "Holding it! I don't want to hold that! Euw!" She looked around the room, hopping up and down between her parents. "Where do I go, what do I do? Where do I put this! Gross!"

"I'll take her," Alana's mother said. "The bathroom's this way." She started to lead her away to where she knew the bathroom to be but Alana planted her feet and pulled to a stop.

"But I want to dance," She whined.

"I need to go to the bathroom!" she shouted at herself. "What!? What!?" she said, her eyes becoming two huge blue circles, her face shocked, looking about in confusion. "What's wrong with me!? What's happening!?" she screamed.

"Alana, calm down! Just come with me to the bathroom!" her mother said as she tried to hold her in her arms and pull her toward the restroom. Alana fell to the floor crying, curling up into a tight sobbing ball.

She lay on the floor, crying, with her white wedding dress stained yellow and her legs soaked with urine.

"We need to get her to a hospital!" Her red-faced father seethed as he lifted her from the puddled floor. A crowd was gathered around them, including some of the FBI agents charged with minding the wedding guests.

"A moment, Mr. Ainsley, if you please," Cathryn said firmly.

He gritted his teeth but held her while she and Sky put their hands on Alana's head, feeling her brow as they spoke together about her condition, but whatever was said it did not please her father.

"What she needs is to go to a hospital. Now!" Richard Ainsley yelled right in Cathryn's face again.

"No," Cathryn said calmly. "She needs to be cleaned and comforted and she needs time to adjust to what she has lost." She scanned the crowd. "Beth, go and prepare my shower for Alana."

"Right away, Queen Cathryn." One of the women standing nearby in an evening gown curtsied and rushed away.

Cathryn looked to Mrs. Ainsley. "Would you care to join us, Mrs. Ainsley?"

"Join you?" Karen Ainsley asked suspiciously.

"Our daughter needs to be cleaned and she needs rest. We need to bathe her. And then you can sleep with her in her bed."

Mrs. Ainsley looked even more confused and worried. "Why would she need me to sleep in the same bed with her?"

"Because your daughter is a witch. She'll want a body in the bed with her to comfort her and a familiar face to see when she wakes."

Karen didn't get a chance to reply before her husband shouted his thoughts on that course of action. "Alana's not going anywhere with you people!" He repositioned his daughter in his arms, took a deep breath then bellowed, "Everyone get the hell out of our way!"

An unmoving wall of people, monsters, witches, royalty, and a darkly frowning deity stood between them and the door. Mr. Ainsley turned his gaze to the three FBI agents watching like silent witnesses.

"We're leaving with our daughter, now get off your sorry asses and walk us out of here!"

The three agents gathered around the Ainsleys and the growing knot of family and friends as if they intended to help them walk out with Alana.

Cornelius stepped up and addressed the tight packed group amiably before things went further awry. "Mr. Ainsley, I understand that it's been a trying day, but our daughter is where she needs to be. Alana is a witch."

"Kim is NOT a witch!" Mr. Ainsley shouted. "And she's not *our* daughter, she's *my* daughter! Now get out of my way, you sick, demented bastard. I won't let you touch *my* daughter!" He looked over at Cathryn. "And she's not taking a shower with you or your gay witch either! You're all nothing but a bunch of sick pedophiles!"

In the shocked second after, as people blinked in surprise, one female voice shouted out. "As above and so below!" The words were amplified with magic and people jumped as a quick charge of energy tingled through the room like a static shock.

Mary raised her hand high over her head drawing every eye to her open palm. "Your voice I take!" she clenched her hand into a tight fist.

Heads turned and watched as Mr. Ainsley tried to say something. No sounds came out. His family gathered around as he tried again. Nothing. He went red in the face, trying to scream or curse or make a sound but it was useless.

Mr. Ainsley's eyes, along with the rest of the eyes in the room, watched Mary as she stepped out and danced her way into the circular gap of open space between the Ainsleys and the surrounding crowd of onlookers from Amen Hale. She took her time and did some graceful circles and spins, leaping and dancing her way across the room, treating her closed hand (the captured voice) as the centerpiece of her graceful movements until she knelt before her father the King and presented the voice like a gift.

She opened her hand. "And set it so," she said, as she rubbed her open palm on the toes of his fancy, black dress shoes. Mary stood and looked back at Mr. Ainsley with her glowing eyes. *"If upon your knees you bend, and kiss his feet, you'll speak again. If you're filled with too much pride, mute you'll be until you die. As above and so below, I call the curse and set it so."*

The glow in Mary's eyes faded, leaving her dazed and confused as her normal green color returned. She gazed about at everyone looking at her and then looked back at Cornelius. "What happened?" she asked.

"You brought me a gift, my child."

"I did?" she frowned but then grinned hugely. "Did you like it?"

Cornelius chuckled and so did many of the others from Amen Hale. "Yes, my child, it was exactly what I needed. Now come here, touch me and see what mischief you've caused." He held his hand out to her and Mary took his hand, nodded, then turned into his embrace, placing her back to his chest so she could face the Ainsleys.

"Be careful, Mr. and Mrs. Ainsley," Mary said to them from the shelter of Cornelius's arms. "Alana is a witch, twice marked and twice dead. She will have accidents and do things without even meaning to. She will be crazy. And if she wakes in a hospital surrounded by soldiers she will call upon her god, and the Black Lion will *roar*." Mary's smile faded; she turned and looked toward Rain who stood against the wall, already looking angry. The rest of the room followed her gaze.

"Good luck with that." Mary's voice said quite plainly that they would need it.

"AND THANKS FOR VISITING!" Mary's unexpected happy shout made people flinch, step back, and spill their wine. She and Cornelius both moved to the side and the crowd behind them parted like a drawn curtain, opening a way for the Ainsleys to make their FBI-escorted exit.

The way was wide open, but Mr. Ainsley wasn't about to leave with his voice smeared on Cornelius's shoes instead of in his throat where it belonged. There was a tight huddle as family and friends rallied around the Ainsleys. They whispered, backs to the room and heads pointed inward like a football team arguing about which play to call because the captain couldn't speak.

After almost five minutes the huddle broke. They were ready to run their play. Q.B. Grovel. Mr. Ainsley handed Alana to her older brother and went to stand before Cornelius. He dropped onto his knees in front of him. There was no music or dancing now. That had ended a while back.

Everyone in Amen Hale not set to other duties watched as Mr. Ainsley humbled himself. His whole body quivered with rage as he brought his lips down on Cornelius's shoes, planting one good mouth smooch on the tip of each toe top. He twitched as if shocked then grunted and made a few low experimental noises and mutterings, testing his voice before getting up off his knees and rising to his feet, looking Cornelius in the eye.

"Be very careful with your words," Cornelius cautioned. "The kindest and gentlest of my daughters has corrected your discourteous tongue, sir. If you persist, Bethany will give the next lesson. You don't want that." Cornelius didn't elaborate; his face was enough to make Mr. Ainsley take it down more than a notch, but as he cooled Cornelius seemed to heat.

"Alana is dangerous," he affirmed. "I understand she already surprised your son. I hope he wasn't hurt." Cornelius paused to glance over at the boy who held Alana in his arms. "I assure you, Mr. Ainsley, that was the least of the accidents your daughter will have. You won't be able to control her or keep her from hurting herself without drugging her into a state of unconsciousness and keeping her there for the rest of her life."

A deep peal of thunder rattled the windows, and heads turned toward Rain who still stood against the wall. She appeared barely in check of her emotions; her disturbing eyes stared at Mr. Ainsley as Believer stood beside her, trying to calm her. Believer moved and stood in front of her, blocking her view of the room and the room's view of her.

"You can't control Alana," Cornelius began again. "But more importantly, you won't be able to keep her safe. The last witch that left Amen Hale was captured by evil men. They did horrible things to her before they burned her alive. Alana is safer here with us than she is with you."

Karen Ainsley grabbed her husband's arm and turned him about before he could speak. The two of them began to argue and kept at it. Long minutes later, Mrs. Ainsley, the victor, spoke for both of them. "I will stay here with my daughter while the others return home."

"So mote it be," said Cornelius. He looked to the FBI agents, pleased to see that Agent Trisha had arrived. He spoke while the Ainleys argued some more. "Trisha, would you please escort the rest of the wedding party from Amen Hale? Mrs. Ainsley will remain with us for the time being to care for her daughter."

Trisha stepped out of the crowed and stopped in front of Cornelius in the high heels and lovely gown that she hadn't had the chance to show off. She dropped into an impressive curtsey. She'd practiced it for a solid hour. Her superiors had kept her busy at the Ainsleys' home, handling one problem after another pampering self-important government flunkies instead of letting her go to Amen Hale. And then the strange events at the gateway between the bride and her wanna-be-groom tied her up. Agent Trisha arrived just in time to see the end of the evening without having had a chance to mingle and show off her dress or dance with anyone. She felt like an unfortunate Cinderella; the clock had already struck midnight and it was time to turn around and go home. She was trying not to frown as she spoke.

"Thank you for the wonderful evening, Cornelius. I'm very sorry I missed it."

"As am I, Trisha." Cornelius stepped forward and took her outstretched hand and brought it to his lips. "You look absolutely stunning in your gown, my dear, and I apologize for curtailing the evening. When next we entertain I will owe you a dance."

"And a kiss," said Cathryn from where she stood a dozen paces away, her face totally serious.

Trisha blushed like mad but the eyes she turned to Cornelius said quite plainly that she was game.

Mr. Ainsley made a disgusted sound and rolled his eyes and mumbled something under his breath about "*tax dollars hard at work.*" Cornelius would have been embarrassed but his ire at Mr. Ainsley's poor manners steadied him as he spoke to Trisha.

"So mote it be. Until then," he told her and released her hand so she could usher the wedding guests out of the Cathedral Hall and out of Amen Hale.

Black Rain

The Golden Gate

BELIEVER BADE ME remain quiet and still, telling me to let my family and the others take care of Alana, but watching people argue over what was mine made me want to scream. As soon as the last of her crazy family passed through the doors, I moved, stepping around Believer and those in front of me with a speed that left the room a momentary blur. Before leaving they'd handed Alana to Byron and I stopped in front of him.

"Give her to me."

Byron took a step back as if he would refuse me. Like most of Amen Hale, he was still uneasy with my new appearance, but I'd had enough of waiting. Mrs. Ainsley, my mother, and Sky watched as I stepped forward and lifted her from Byron's arms without waiting for him to offer her to me. I closed my eyes and held my Red Lamb close, enjoying the feel of her in my arms even through the ruffles and folds of her wet wedding dress.

"Will she be all right?" I asked whoever could give an answer.

"She will be, Rain. You know it's always hard in the beginning. Now take her to my bath," my mother's voice answered.

"Yes, Mother." I opened my eyes and carried Alana in my arms toward the wall of the Cathedral Room that held the big silver mirror. The glass misted as I approached then opened to show a view of the Queen's bathroom on the other side. The high angle came from the mirror that hung above the long bathroom vanity.

A naked woman stared out at us, too surprised to do more than watch as I stepped through the silver frame and out onto the open air above the marble vanity without pausing. I walked my way down to the floor of the bath as if the air beneath my feet were a gently sloping ramp. Beth curtsied, totally unbothered by everyone seeing her in a state of undress. We waited for my mother and Mrs. Ainsley.

"You will not fall, Karen. Follow me," I heard my mother say as she stepped through the mirror.

From inside the bathroom, Karen Ainsley stood at the open portal of the mirror and looked down at us, fear on her face. She pushed through the mirror and took that first step out onto nothing as if she were stepping off a cliff to certain doom, only to be pleasantly surprised as she took a second, and a third step. She was smiling broadly by the time she stood on the floor beside my mother but got distracted right away as she looked around the bathroom, raising both eyebrows.

"It's nice, Cathryn, but very dated. Surely you can do better," she said critically as she scanned the place.

My mother laughed. "It will be nice to have you with us, Karen." She turned to me. "Rain, our clothes please."

"Yes, Mother." I noticed my husband standing in front of the mirror out in the Cathedral Hall, trying to ensure our privacy. He turned his back to us and faced the Hall so he wouldn't see us either. Believer was always so sensitive about our privacy.

I closed the gateway then turned my attention to our clothes. Alana's wedding dress, my mother's gown, Mrs. Ainsley's dress, and even my loin cloth and breast bands vanished and appeared, folded and resting neatly atop the vanity.

Alana's mother made no comment.

I walked forward into the gargantuan shower and placed Alana on the padded table in the center of the room. I stayed at her head, trying to keep my eyes and hands only on her face, which was hard to do as my mother and Beth moved her about and washed her body, rinsed, then massaged her limbs with hot oils.

Mrs. Ainsley seemed to relax as she saw that both my mother and Beth moved and worked in ways that showed practiced experience and skill and were in no way sexual. I was surprised to find that I couldn't look at Alana's body without being aroused, which was worrying me. I didn't know that I wanted her in that way and it was truly freaking me out. Alana was my lamb.

Beth asked her mother to select a fragrance from the scented soaps that Alana would like and I joined her before the section of shower wall that held a massive selection of bath stuff. My eyes lit up as I saw some soap labeled as "peach blossom."

"Why are your nipples blue?"

She was eyeball to nipple, so I guess it was a valid question. Still an odd way to start a first conversation. No names, no nothing, just "what's up with your nips?"

"They changed to blue because those who loved me like blue." My hand reached up to worry at my blue lips.

"Do you change for everyone who loves you?" she asked as her eyes traced up from my breasts to my horns and then back down to my tail. Tail stopped waving about and wrapped around me as if her gaze had made it shy.

"That habit may turn you into a real mess after a while," she added.

I thought about that. It wasn't everyone who loved me that changed me; I realized that it was the other way around.

"I only change for the ones I love the most." I turned back to the soaps and grabbed the bottle of peach blossom and opened it, taking a sniff. It was a bit flat and bland. I reached for a bottle labeled peach divine.

"How much do you love Alana?" she asked.

"With all my heart," I answered without thinking. I opened the bottle of soap and shoved it into Mrs. Ainsley's face. "Do you like this one?" I asked quickly.

She sniffed at it and nodded weakly.

"Have you changed for my daughter?" she asked, refusing to be distracted from whatever she was after.

I nodded and kept my trap shut. I grabbed a bottle labeled morning glory and opened the top and wrinkled my nose; it smelled strongly of chemicals. No morning and sure as hell no glory. My nose was so sensitive now, this was going to be hard.

"How have you changed for her?" she asked doggedly.

"Please, Mrs. Ainsley."

"I have no please in me, girl," she said firmly and looked up into my eyes, which very few people did now.

"How have you changed for Alana?"

"You won't understand."

"We shall see," she said ominously.

Mrs. Ainsley grabbed a bottle of soap labeled "Winter Garden Floral" as she dropped the bottle I'd given her back onto the rack.

"Kim." She frowned. "Alana," she corrected, "prefers floral smells." She walked over and gave the bottle to Beth and came right back.

"It's foolish to have all of us standing around in here naked with you pretending not to look at Alana. It's practically like having a boy in the bath with her. Your mother and the maid can manage while you and I finish our talk outside where you'll be more comfortable and less aroused. Come," she called over her shoulder as she walked out of the shower.

I followed a moment later, after I was sure the shocked expression on my face had more or less returned to normal. Mrs. Ainsley had a towel in hand, drying herself off when I stepped out of the shower. Her body reminded me of my mother's in how she still held that beauty of youth, though she held it stiffly, in muscled defiance against the forces of Mother Nature instead of Cathryn's grace and eternal natural beauty.

I thought of her being dry and she was, from head to toe though her hair dried in every direction. She looked up at me with the usual questioning face people gave me when I messed with them, but I kept messing all the same. I had her own undergarments appear back on her body, cleaned and freshened. I robed her in a plain white gown made from magic fabric and she couldn't keep from smiling as she touched it. I knew that the very feel of the fabric would fascinate her because it was unlike anything else on earth, light, airy, stretchy, and sinfully soft.

I added a fine blue sash tied around her middle and I styled her hair and combed it back. Her hair only hung to her shoulders in a short business cut and I resisted the strong urge to change its color or lengthen it or alter other things on her person. I turned and walked out of the bathroom before I got experimental. The urge to mess with her hair was strong. It needed kung fu.

I didn't dry myself. I ran my hands though my wet hair and down the length of my body as I walked into Cathryn's parlor enjoying the feel of my own hands on my new magical skin. My fingers traced up and down making me shiver as I walked to the table. Vampire skin felt every sensation so much more than human flesh ever could; it made even casual touch much less than casual and oh so pleasant.

My tail slung trails of water around the room, flailing about like it was writing its own name in water ink upon the walls. Rain's tail was here! I sat at the table in the parlor and a moment later was joined by Mrs. Ainsley.

As soon as she was seated, the chamber maid approached the table, a plump woman in her mid to late thirties. Her poorly dyed blonde hair was pulled back in a tight, unappealing braid. She stared at me with dull brown eyes hiding under bushy black brows that were badly in need of waxing and tweezing. Major unibrow.

"Is there anything you require, my Ladies?" She was so nervous she was actually shaking.

"Wine. Anything but red," Mrs. Ainsley said. She watched the trembling servant curiously, noticing the way her eyes flitted to me every second or so.

"Water please. No ice." I spoke first to save her from having to speak to me.

As she moved about preparing our drinks, I let her thoughts come into my mind to see what on earth was happening inside this poor woman's head. The name that popped into my thoughts was "Beetle." A nickname that she went by. Even thought of herself by.

Just pour the drinks and go to your place. Just leave it alone, you fat, stupid cow! Stop shaking! Pour and serve. Pour and—the cork! Stupid cork! Stuck! Oh darn!

I willed it to come free gently.

It did.

Good. Oh no! She's watching me. Should I have gotten her water first? No. Byron said guests are always served first.

"Will you be getting dressed, Rain, or will you be speaking to me in the nude?" asked Mrs. Ainsley crisply.

"Not until I must," I answered.

If I looked like that I wouldn't get dressed either. I wish I had a chilled glass for her. She deserves a chilled glass. I'll go with them tonight.

She filled the glass with water and set it on the table in front of me.

"Do you usually walk around in the nude?" Mrs. Ainsley asked rudely. "Was what you had on earlier your version of formalwear? A loin cloth?"

"Yes and no." I sighed. She was just like her husband.

"Why does Alana call you her Lion?" She leaned in, giving me the darkest of looks. "I've heard others try to explain it, but I'll hear it from the horse's mouth if you please. Out with it. What does she mean when she says that?"

"I am her god."

Mine too.

"That's blasphemous!" Mrs. Ainsley growled at me.

"Yes. It is," I agreed seriously.

That stumped her for a minute.

It's not blasphemous to me! This is getting good! I'm so glad I won the second shift!

"What on earth makes you think you're her god? Alana is Catholic."

Is, was, wasn't—not anymore! Hehehe.

I fought off the smile that threatened to come to my face from hearing Beetle's thoughts, like cat calls from a watching audience. In front of me, Mrs. Ainsley was pressing her thin lips together so tightly they were white, what lipstick she'd once had was lost to the shower. And as for Alana's religion, going in and out of a church building didn't make you anything other than well exercised unless you're there for yourself. I'd gone to church three times a week.

I tried to explain. "When I was a human girl—"

"Foolishness!" she cut in. "Don't sling that childish drivel at me! You are still a human girl!"

She's crazy.

"You've taken those vile pills and they've changed you, but you're not a god! You are a tall, silly, teenage girl with white skin, horns, and a tail who likes to parade around butt naked and sleep with girls. *That* is what you are!" she finished crisply, then surprised me by reaching out and pulling my hand from my horn and holding it in both of hers on the table, giving me a compassionate, almost motherly look as she continued.

"I understand that you have mental issues, Rain, and I will not belittle you for it. Alana is on Zoloft too and she hasn't been taking her meds either, which needs to change for both of you. I'm sure that's part of her problem right now. So let's talk this through together. Why do you think you're a god?"

Because she is a god, you silly, old shrew.

"This afternoon, during the human sacrifice, I told a story about lions and lambs. After the sacrifice, your daughter prayed to me, Mrs. Ainsley." She snatched her hands away from mine and leaned back in her chair, narrowing her eyes at me.

Oh! She didn't like that! Her precious daughter praying to the Black Lion. Here it comes! She's gonna go ape!

I waited until Beetle's commentary ended to begin again.

"Alana prayed to me as if I were the god in the story I told, a god called the Black Lion. I answered her prayer as if I were the Black Lion." I looked up into her eyes to make sure she heard this next part, though I could see by the expression on her face that she was hearing but not caring. I said it anyway for Beetle's benefit. "As within, so without. I must be true to myself. Five minutes after I answered your daughter's prayer I burned to death, the Black Witch died, and the Black Lion took her place. As within, so without. I am on the outside as I am on the inside. I am what I am."

"Don't say that, Rain. That's very, very blasphemous."

I nodded. "I know. It's still true."

Mrs. Ainsley stood up, drained her glass, and held it out for Beetle to refill, which she did promptly. She left the table and began to pace the room.

Her hair is so beautiful. I wish I could touch it.

I reached up and raked my fingers through my still mostly wet hair.

"Could you fetch me my mother's brush and comb my hair while I talk? If you don't mind," I added.

A big delighted smile came to her plump fleshy cheeks and she curtsied. "Gladly, Princess Rain." She rushed off to get the brush.

Mrs. Ainsley returned to the table and sat back down, frowning. "Just how many people are you sleeping with now? Even if she consents you'll end up giving

Alana an STD." Her mouth twisted into an ugly crooked line. A mockery of a smile.

I thought for a minute and was shocked by the answer as I gave it.

Where's the brush. Where, where? No. No. Where? Dang it! Ahah!

"The body I'm in is brand new, only hours old, I haven't slept with anyone since I became the Black Lion, so in a way, I'm a virgin."

She breathed out a quick huff of air. "And who and how many did you sleep with before you changed to this?" She swirled her wine around in her glass and eyed me as if I were a deviant in denial. I spoke as my brain added it up.

"I was married on Wednesday to Believer and I had sex with my husband that night. Yesterday I did not have intercourse, though I did orgasm a few times because of being bitten by the vampires. It feels good," I said to her disgusted expression. "Today I haven't had sex other than being bitten by the vampires. I'd count it as sex, but not intercourse. So to answer your question, I have only had intercourse once, and that was on my wedding night with my husband."

She looked skeptical. "So what is all this I hear about you and all these girls? From the way you were acting in the shower you clearly want to have sex with my daughter."

Is she still going on about sex? Give it a rest, lady!

Beetle slipped behind my chair, and my tail wrapped around her waist, holding her.

She's holding me with her tail! It's almost like she's hugging me. I wonder if she did it on purpose or if the tail has a mind of its own. It seems pretty independent.

She reached down and petted my tail.

My tail gave her a squeeze.

Hmm. I think her tail likes me. Wow, she has such full, thick hair.

I leaned forward and she gathered my hair into her hands and let it hang down the back side of the chair.

"Are you going to have sex with my daughter?" Mrs. Ainsly asked plainly.

Oh my god, it's like silk it's so soft. And thick! And it smells so wonderful. Like roses. I wonder what shampoo she uses. I bet it's expensive. It's not fair. She's got all this and I got nothing but a damn rat nest, so wiry and blah.

"Tell me the truth. Are you planning to sleep with her?" she asked again.

I'd been distracted listening to Beetle go on about my hair but I answered Mrs. Ainsley's query, giving her my full attention.

"If Alana had married Gannon and lived her life as a servant among us I would have left her to her husband. I would have loved her as her Lion and she would have been my Red Lamb, but I wouldn't have slept with her. But she has come as a witch. Whether she sleeps with me or not isn't really the point, sooner or later she will fall in love with Emma, and then she will want me in that same way."

Mrs. Ainsley's murderous glare rolled away as the comb passed through my hair. It felt so wonderful.

I shouldn't have eaten the sacrifice meat. I bet it's gonna give me the shits tonight. I'll probably be living on the toilet for the next two days, sitting and shitting my shitty life away.

"Quite unfair, don't you think!?" she said angrily. "It's a horrible punishment for a single moment of poor judgment and a few hasty words spoken as her groom walked out on her! If you cared about her at all you'd let her go home with me. She is not gay. She will not want you like that, and it's wrong to use magic on her to turn her into something she's not."

Blah, blah, blah, blah, blah. Her hair smells so good. I'll pull some from the brush and make myself a prayer charm.

"I know what you're saying and in a way I agree. It is horrible, but it is what it is. I didn't have a single gay bone in my body till Emma touched me. Now I like girls, and I love Emma. I am bewitched and I wouldn't change it if I could. I am happily enchanted and held in the thrall of the White Witch of Amen Hale."

Mrs. Ainsley continued rambling on about how unfair it was and how I should reconsider. On and on and on. I tuned her out as the comb passed through my hair again and again. I listened to the quiet, peaceful, dreamy thoughts of Beetle as she moved the brush.

She's young, but I don't care. I wonder if she'll even want me. I'm not pretty like the new princess. I'm getting old and fat. Fat, old cow. Good grief, that old windbag is still at it. She's acting like her daughter is going to die if she sleeps with the Princesses. Sigh. Here she is, alone with her, and all she can do is prattle about silly things and talk about her daughter. I wish I were at the table and she were back here combing her hair. I'd talk about things that matter. We common people never get alone time with her. I wish it was just me and her, all alone, completely alone. I want her all to myself. I don't want to share. I want to be greedy. I want to steal her away from the world and have it be just me and her without another soul around for miles.

But what would you do if you had her? I slipped my question into her thoughts, matching the sound of her own internal voice so she'd think it was her own query.

I would ask if I could be her lamb. I want to be her lamb. I should have joined the others in the garden last night. Oh, that's a big one. Hmm. She's got a lot of knots. I'll go tonight.

"You're not even listening to me!" Mrs. Ainsley shouted and brought the flat of her hand down hard on the tabletop.

I opened my eyes. I'd had enough. "Mrs. Ainsley, as bad as you think it is—it's worse."

"Thank you, Beetle. That's enough for now." I stood up and Beetle slid my chair back for me.

I turned and looked at her and gave her a warm smile.

"Are you ready to go?" I asked. My tail reached out and wrapped around her wrist and hand.

Her eyes became two huge white circles. "Princess? I'm not sure what you mean? Go where?"

"You need not go to a garden to find me, I'm right here. I will give you what you want. All of it, and more than you can imagine. Right here, right now."

Two tall antique cabinets and some other furnishings moved on their own, shifting to either side to clear a ten foot wide expanse of bare wall. The image of two thick, white columns appeared on the wall like a drawing, and then began to push their way out from the wall. There was no violent shower of busted wood and shattered plaster. Everything moved smoothly and quietly, reshaping itself as needed like malleable clay. The twin columns reached from floor to the twelve foot ceiling high overhead with a connecting transom across the top forming a massive square doorway instead of a circular archway.

Already the floor popped and groaned against the weight and I willed the doorway to bear its own weight so it wouldn't fall through to the downstairs, and since weight no longer mattered I changed the whole damn thing to gleaming, solid gold. Stars, moons, and suns appeared, carved into the gold up and down the length of both sides.

"Rain!" Mrs. Ainsley shouted. "What have you done?"

I cast out with my will, out into the night, into the air and beyond, out into space. I felt the moon and passed it by, out and out until I found what I wanted. I called an arch of stone to rise on the surface and willed a bubble of air to surround the place and matched the temperature and conditions to the room in which we stood. The open space in the golden gate shimmered and bright reddish light poured into the room, the color reflecting off the red surface of the sandy ground beyond the portal.

Mrs. Ainsley took a bold step closer to peer through the portal and I put my arm out to stop her. "Only Beetle and I will step foot onto this world. She and I have business to discuss and you are not welcome."

She nodded, blinking and looking up at me as if she'd never seen me before in her life. She stayed where she was, trying her best to look around me at the alien landscape. "Is it Mars?" she asked.

I ignored her and put a hand out to Beetle, the serious face I'd given to Mrs. Ainsley vanishing as I looked at this woman who wanted me.

"Come, Beetle. Come and do all that you said you wanted to do. A whole world with just me and you and not another soul around for thirty eight million miles."

She was crying before my tail drew her hand into my own. We stepped to the square doorway and looked out at the rocky barren expanse together. With a thought I raised a circular area of white, natural looking stones on the other side of the doorway for us to walk out onto. I raised a foot high fringe around the white circle adorned at the top with lions in different actions and poses, some walking, some lying down, some running, some hunting, and some having sex. The bordering wall and figures atop it changed to a sparkling green that looked like jade because it was jade, all one solid piece. I shaped a kneeling bench, like a prayer altar and in front of the bench a chair pushed up from the ground that looked like it was formed of the weathered and ancient bones of Mars itself.

We walked out onto the surface of this far away world and I willed the gateway behind us to shut, the scene of my mother's parlor vanishing. The matching twelve foot high stone arch on Mars now framed a plain square section of red desert.

We turned in a circle, taking in the endless rust colored expanse. I felt very alone with her. Had two souls ever been so alone? I knew that the answer was yes. In the beginning, God made Adam and it was just God and Adam, alone in the garden and in all of creation. So God had us beat. I did not mind and I was not jealous.

I did not make it to the chair and she did not make it to the bench. She fell onto my feet and held me. Beetle wept and cried. I told her that the White Lion was better, but she said she wanted me. I told her that I was flawed and weak and that I would surely fail her. Still she wanted me. I told her that I wasn't the kind of god that would be listening every second of the day and see every slight and feel every hurt. She said she understood and that she would be grateful for what she could get and she promised not to complain.

I told her that I would change her and remake her how I wanted. She said that she would be whatever pleased me. I heard her thoughts as she told me that she loved me; they matched every word. I knelt beside her and lifted her face to my face.

"From this day on you will be my lamb. Your name is no longer Beetle because you will crawl no more. You will be," I studied her face. She waited, expectant and excited. What did I want to name her? This moment reminded me of Rain Marie. She made me and left me nameless so that I had to name myself.

"Marie. From this day on you will be Marie, and you will no longer flinch or slouch or cringe but carry yourself as befits one whom I have chosen and named. You are beautiful, and you are mine."

With a thought I cleansed her marred complexion and then I fixed her horrible teeth. I stripped her of her clothes and had her stand, so that we both stood naked while I shaped her body, making it lean and healthy and comely. Although the work I did was nothing like what I'd done with Emma, the change was still breathtaking. I released her hair from its tightly bound prison and made it fuller and healthy and changed the color to a deep brown with auburn highlights. She had chin stubble, a unibrow, and hair in places where no hair would be best, or even *normal.* I removed all of it permanently, leaving the rest of her clean and smooth except for the hair on the top of her head and some nicely crafted dark eyebrows. Her dull brown eyes I changed into a warm chestnut brown that complemented the rest of what I'd done.

Finally I gave her a new white and brown dress made of magic fabric and a pair of open toed shoes to wear. I made her a keepsake necklace with stones from the surface of Mars that I smoothed down into perfect round circles and strung on a golden chain. I took one rough red rock as a souvenir for Bethany before looking around one last time. Marie stood beside me, her arms wrapped around my waist and my tail wrapped around us both as I turned the rough red Martian rock over in my hands.

"Tell whoever you need to tell that you have tomorrow off. Tomorrow is the first day of the rest of your days as mine. Forget old grudges, let the past go, and enjoy yourself, Marie. You are my lamb and I love you. I know you won't be perfect and I don't expect you to be. Try to be a good lamb, and I will try to be a good god, and we shall live, day by day. That's all I can promise."

"So mote it be, my Lion," she said back to me.

We stared out at the barren empty world, both of us enjoying the view and the time alone together.

Dan

Jedi Mind Trick

JANE AND I stood out in the hall as Hanna emerged from Emma's room. She looked from Jane to me, not afraid of us as most people were when they saw us. We could see the relief on her features, around her eyes and mouth; she was hoping we would watch Emma while she was gone. She didn't want to leave her unattended but she had to go. I could also see that she was seriously torn up. Her eyes were an unfocused mess. She also reeked of Emma's magic like she'd wallowed in it, which I was sure she had. It was not a bad smell. Actually it smelled wonderful to me and it smelled wonderful to Jane also, which was why she hadn't noticed Hanna's eyes and I had. Jane was focusing on the smell, breathing it in and enjoying it as Hanna finally got her words out.

"She just laid down, my Lady, but she'll want to see you. Could you—"

Jane put a finger over her lips. "Shush," she hushed her. "Yes, Hanna, we will watch over her. Go home."

"Mary will be here later this evening, my Lady. Thank you."

She curtsied again and rushed away like she was in a hurry to go.

"Jane, I better follow her to make sure she gets home okay; Hanna's a total mess. Did you look at her eyes?"

"No. Sorry. I didn't. I missed it completely. Go after her, Dan."

My body vanished from beside my love to follow after Hanna, and I was glad to be going; I wanted to give her the appearance of privacy. Without my body there she relaxed some, even though she knew I was still there in her head. Somehow, having me stand beside her and look at her seemed more invasive to her than having me stand inside her and look out of her. I knew she wanted some privacy and someone needed to walk Hanna home so it fit perfectly.

I appeared on the stairwell, ghosting along behind the love-struck maid as the rest of my soul resided inside Jane. She was still in the hallway, staring at Emma's door as she listened to her return from the bathroom and settle into the bed. The sound of sheets moving about. A pillow being fluffed. A contented sigh. A stretch. I could feel how much she wanted to open the door and go in and how much she dreaded the fact that she wanted to go in at the same time. Her emotions swirled around inside of her like she'd thrown parts of herself into a blender; it was a whirling mess of different things. Jane's self-image, her idea of herself was not dealing well with Emma and Rain and even Mary now.

It seemed pretty easy to me but I wasn't being asked to sleep with a bunch of guys either. The thought of the shoe being on the other foot wasn't appealing. If I had to sleep with some dude named Ronald (Rain) and some other gay guy named Edgar (Emma)—maybe both at the same time—I think I'd hurl. Correction, I know I'd hurl. Before, after, and most certainly during. I have a gay uncle and I didn't see anything wrong with it, but I wasn't gay or bi.

I know Jane's gag reflex had acted up more than once in the past few days but the really crazy part of all of this self-torture was that none of it was necessary. She didn't have my problem. I knew her soul better than I knew my own. I'd searched it, combing through her memories, and in all her life there were only two truly repressed memories that I'd found. Memories that she didn't even let herself think of or remember correctly.

The first was when she was eight years old and her Uncle Billy had walked in on her when she was in the bathroom. Instead of turning around and leaving, he'd exposed himself to her and told her to touch him. She did. Billy lost his nerve and left after just a few minutes and only did it once. Jane had taken that particular memory and dropped it into a box labeled "DID NOT HAPPEN!" At the early age of eight she took that box and the ugliness inside it and stuck it somewhere in her mind and then promptly forgot where she put it because she did not know how to deal with it. As far as she was concerned it never happened.

I found the box and looked inside but I knew no good would ever come of messing with it. If I could have erased it altogether I would have, but our vampire minds didn't work that way. We remembered everything, perfectly, forever. Which meant that the lies we'd told ourselves when we became vampires also carried over. I could expose it for what it was, but I could not expunge it.

The second memory that she'd repressed was about the night she'd met Emma at a slumber party. She'd repressed most of what really happened that night as well. I would never have found the real memory if I hadn't have relived that particular day, moment by moment and seen it as it truly happened. If Jane knew what had really happened that night I don't think she'd have ever told me to relive the memory that she'd painted over with lies.

Jane still stood out in the hallway, but when Believer and Lucius rounded the bend at the end of the hall, that moved her to action. She opened the door and slipped into Emma's room. Emma was already abed, curled in the sheets, and Jane stood there and watched her. Her thoughts pondered what to say or how to approach her, and what to do if she reacts this way or that way.

My attention drifted back to my body. Hanna was approaching the guest hall but there was a group of men gathered out front, smoking and laughing. They were watching her closely and with Hanna in her condition I knew this might be trouble. I appeared before the men, and they jumped. I panned around with a quick warning glare as I pushed open a door, holding it for Hanna.

She stopped at the door and looked at me, but I frowned and shook my head no and pointed down the hall, like a parent to a wayward child, sending Hanna to her room.

"Yes, my Lord," was all she said before turning and moving down the hall. It was a few minutes past eleven but the hallways and meeting areas of the place were crowded, so I cheated and crawled up the wall on my hands and feet and traveled along the ceiling just above Hanna like a spider. I let my eyes glow and the effect was frightening enough that everyone cleared a path for Hanna as if she had the plague.

Up two flights of stairs and down the hall we came to a halt before room three fifteen. Hanna got out her key and unlocked the door then looked to where I hung on the wall, my hands and bare feet splayed out wide to give me good purchase.

"Thank you so much for walking me home. Goodnight." She opened the door and stepped inside.

I waited until the door shut and the lock clicked into place, then the good folk of the third floor who were gawking at me were left with a less interesting blank patch of wall to look at. I appeared outside Emma's room and froze there like a statue positioned in the hall as I poured even more of my awareness into Jane.

Jane had circled the bed and stood, looking at Emma as she slept. My hopes flared as Jane brought to her mind the memory of when she first met Emma. She was remembering that night, when she and Emma had retreated from the "boring slumber party" down the street to sleep at Emma's house. She was remembering the lie that she'd told herself and not the truth. As gently as possible, I pulled just one small part of lie away so she would see that something was not quite right with her memory of that night.

"What was that!? What are you doing?" Jane thought to me inside her head.

"*Oh. Sorry.*"

"What are you playing at, Dan!?' she yelled at me in her head. "What the hell are you doing to my memories?"

"*The way you remember it is a little different from what I saw. If you want to remember it that way, cool, I'll leave it alone. Sorry.*"

"Remember it what way!? What other way is there to remember it? What the hell are you doing in my head, Dan!?"

"*Sorry! Sorry! Sorry! If l ever find another repressed memory I'll leave it alone. Believe it however you want to. Just be happy, Jane. Oh shit. Hanna needs some help, people on the stairwell, be right back.*"

Out in the hallway I smiled as I lied my ass off to the woman who was my entire world. I'd lie, I'd cheat, I'd do anything to make Jane happy. Her mind was rolling the phrase "repressed memory" around and around. Now that she knew the memory was "*off*" she wouldn't be able to help herself, she'd pick at it. Like an itchy scab or a zit right on the tip of your nose with a fat, nasty head screaming to be dealt with even though you know you should leave the thing alone.

I smiled as she started to worry at the edges of the memory where I showed her the lie.

"Fine!" she growled inside her head for my benefit. She knew what I was doing, but it didn't change anything. She pulled at the lie, but she couldn't get anywhere with it. She didn't have the ability to remove it. She'd been the one to put it there in the first place and for her it was impossible.

"*I can help if you want,*" I told her.

She thought about it. Toyed with the idea of just leaving it. "Will this mess me up, Dan?"

"*It's not a memory that I'd want you to be without.*"

"So the answer is yes," she said. Her thoughts drifted away. She was tired of all this. For a second she thought about what it would be like to have stayed a human girl, to be in school with her friends or home in her old bed, asleep by now. But then she thought about not having me there with her, not having me inside her head right that instant, about being alone inside the quiet of her mind. The thought terrified her. She needed me in her as much as I needed to be in her.

She thought of me. Of us. Of what we were and what we had. She didn't want anything to come between us and she was scared to love anyone else because she wanted to give everything she was to me.

"*I'm right here,*" I said into a quiet space when she held no thought other than emptiness.

"Hi." She was happy as she gave me back my best pick-up line. At least that was how she thought of it.

"I love you, Dan. Just show me a little and I'll let you know if I want more."

I let her remember that night, when she'd left the slumber party and slept over at Emma's house. She was lying in the bed beside Emma, but instead of just bored and tired now she felt all the abuse she'd taken from the girls before she and Emma left the slumber party. She felt her emotional state at that moment. Real pain, real abuse, and other feelings she had no name for, nothing like her comfortable lie. After years of telling herself it wasn't that bad and nothing happened, she actually believed it hadn't been that bad and that nothing did happen. This memory and these feelings made absolutely no sense with how she remembered the rest of that night. She couldn't stop there.

"That's messed up. Are there other things inside my head like this?"

"*This is the only one I saw, Jane,*" I lied. "*And I wouldn't have found this if you hadn't made me relive the day as it happened moment by moment. It freaked me out some when I saw it too but I didn't know what to do with it.*"

She thought for a while on what I'd said and was reassured that this was it.

"Show me the rest of it. Show me what really happened, Dan."

I opened those memories. I watched as she relived that day the way it really happened. I didn't mind if she loved Emma more because of seeing the truth. I actually hoped she did. It would make her happy. It would make us both happy. We could love her together. That would make me happy. What could be wrong with that?

Black Rain

Making Marie

I OPENED THE GATEWAY and saw that I had a crowded room to return to. They were all standing in the parlor and not charging through the gateway, so Mrs. Ainsley must have told them to stay out.

Marie gave a tug on my hand to get my attention. "You need to get dressed, my Lion. There's men out there. And Prince Believer is out there too."

"I guess I should," I said. I knew Believer would want me to be decent. I donned my breast straps and my little silver chain and the dangling loin cloth, calling them to appear on my body. I held my lamb's hand as we peered through the portal and the waiting crowd. I was excited for her and worried for her. And worried because a crowd this large usually meant a new disaster.

"Be brave, my Marie, be brave. Dare. Speak. Be bold. You are mine," I told her and she straightened beside me, looking determined. We walked through the doorway and out into my mother's crowded parlor. Cathryn, Cornelius, Lucius, Believer, and about ten others wearing the black of our security officers were standing there to receive us. My immediate reaction was dread.

"What's happened?" I asked my mother who stood directly in front of us.

"Be calm, Rain. Nothing horrible or bad has happened. We haven't been attacked and no one has died." She spoke to me but her attention was being fuddled as she kept looking at Marie. "We have some new neighbors apparently."

"Neighbors?"

Cathryn and Cornelius both nodded and smiled.

"It seems there was more magic in the world than we knew." Cathryn stepped forward to stand before Marie. She reached out and touched her face and hair and stared into her new chestnut brown eyes, inspecting her while she spoke to me. "At the graveyard in the mountains where the new gateway opens. It appears that you stumbled upon a community of small Fae-like creatures. They are very small, each only an inch to two inches tall, and most of them can fly. Lucius tells me that they look perfectly human, but with wings. And they have magic."

Marie kept a firm hold on my hand and kept her head high and her back straight as Cathryn walked around her, looking over every inch of her.

"But why didn't I see them when I was at the graveyard?"

Lucius answered the question himself. "They disguise themselves as insects with their magic. The first time you opened the gate, Mistress, they were there, we just didn't notice them for what they were. You remember that the field was crawling with bugs and flying insects."

"Insects?" I asked, "But—" A wave of pure horror washed over me. I'd killed bugs in the graveyard! I thought through exactly what I'd done. I recalled how all the sounds of bugs had gone quiet as I reached out with my magic but returned when I told them (the bugs) that all was well. My mind flashed on the odd red ants and the penny-sized hole beside the grave. Had those ants actually been little people?

"*Love and laugh and play,*" I had said, and then I murdered them. Goosebumps rose on my arms at the idea of how evil it must have seemed. How evil it was. Had I killed hundreds? Or thousands? Or millions? Is this what it meant to be a god, an increase in the extent of my horror? I no longer killed or murdered one or a dozen in a day, now I murdered in mass, whole civilizations and peoples wiped out as I blundered along like an ignorant colossus, oblivious to the heartache I left in my passing. My idle thoughts destroying, my every step causing sorrow.

"Blessed Be, child, what's wrong?" my mother asked as she stared at my face.

I ignored her question and turned to Lucius. "Did they say anything, Lucius? How did they act? Were they angry with me? Were they upset?" I asked in a rush, not caring how I looked or how I sounded.

Lucius deferred to one of his men who was on his knees right beside him. "They seemed in good spirits, my Lady. Not, angry at all. A small man with green hair, nicely clothed appeared on the shoulder of one of our young men. He seemed to be an ambassador or a spokesman for them. He said his name was Peffan and that his people are called the Twilins. There are hundreds of thousands of them. He was friendly and he said that they mean us no harm and that they want to be our neighbors."

Lucius spoke up, adding matters he thought of immediate importance. "They are ruled by a Queen named Taunwee. This Peffan said that their queen has forbidden her people from approaching the gateway or from coming through, but I have ordered that the gate be closed at all times when a vehicle is not entering or exiting and I posted a guard on the gateway at all times. While I was there they remained a respectable distance away from the gate, though they are a curious bunch. I spoke with a few of them myself who were standing close by, watching us. They are quick and very intelligent and very determined to know more about you, Mistress." Lucius gave me a look that he wanted to make into a hard stare but couldn't seem to complete as he looked at my face. He gathered his thoughts and pressed on, "They also asked about Prince Believer and your mother the Queen."

"But didn't they seem sad or angry or upset?" I asked again. "They must be angry with me. They have to be."

Lucius and Reese both shook their heads no, confused by my continued distress. I hadn't spoken when I'd killed the ants, I'd killed them with nothing but a thought. They didn't know what I'd done to the little people.

"What is wrong, my love?" Believer asked me.

"I need to go see them now!" I said firmly.

"Now is not the best time, Rain," Cornelius cautioned.

"My Lion," Reese spoke again, still on his knees, "Peffan made a point of telling me that the Queen would be very busy tonight with weddings. If I understood him correctly." He looked like he had some doubt about that.

"I'll see her right now!" I said firmly. "I will not wait."

"No, Rain." Cathryn stared at me hard, not sparing for my distress but demanding as she spoke. "This Taunwee is a Queen of her own land, my child, and she has said *not* to come. She has magic of her own. We will respect her wishes. You will go nowhere tonight. I forbid it!"

I let go of Marie's hand and pushed past Believer roughly to kneel before my mother as my tears and the heartache finally broke free and heaving sobs racked my body.

"Mother! You don't understand!" I wailed, my words mangled as I cried. "I have to go. I have to tell her I'm sorry for what I did!"

Cathryn's cool hand touched my face as Believer's cooling touch stroked my back and my distraught tail switched from writhing in agony to coiling itself around his leg as if it needed to hold onto something solid and the cloud was the most solid thing it could find in my world at that moment.

"I do not understand your distress, but you should obey our mother," Believer rumbled from behind me. "If you have sinned against Taunwee then make this right on the morrow, but not tonight when she has asked we leave her be. Do not add another transgression to what you have already done, although I do not see how you could have sinned against her when you did not know she existed until a moment ago." He still sounded confused even as he tried to reason with me with practical, common sense and logic that my brain completely rejected.

My insides felt on fire as I thought about what I'd done. Visions of tiny, dead bodies buried in sand paraded through my mind.

"My Lion!" Reese practically begged. "The entire valley is filled with their people and they are busy with some ritual, perhaps it's these weddings Peffan spoke of, perhaps something else. I love you, my Lion, but please, wait till tomorrow to visit the Twilins. Peffan told me that tomorrow afternoon would be best when I asked him when we should meet." Reese bowed his head and kept his eyes on the floor.

I stood there and shook and cried while all around me my family and friends and lambs listened as I told them about my trespass. About my sin against the Twilins. Cathryn, Cornelius, and Believer tried to console me, telling me it was an accident and that I was not to blame for what happened. Their logic, though sound, gave me no peace. The thought of waiting until morning made me want to die. How could I wait until morning? How many had died in the ground?

Women, children, and infants would be the ones down below where they thought it was safest. Little children or toddlers, perhaps the size of a pill bug? Dead now. Tiny sightless eyes and teeny, tiny fingers that would no longer grasp the fingers of their mothers. These people were not mine to kill. They were not my children.

I obeyed my mother while at the same time I made her pay for my obedience as I cried all over her, bringing new meaning to the word INCONSOLABLE.

"I will go! I'll go for you! I WILL GO!" A clear shout rose above the din of comforting words.

The room quieted.

"Send me!" she shouted again.

I turned and joined the others already looking at her. Marie stood a few short steps away. Dan had come in while I was crying and he stood with the rest of my family adding his worried face to the mix. Marie stood straight and tall in the midst of all the torn up, worried faces. I'd stopped listening to her every thought, but now I listened again, though she spoke with her mouth and not her mind, out loud for all in the room to hear.

"Make a beautiful tiny, table for me to carry and a tiny, little cup to set upon the table. Make the cup as fine and wondrous a thing as you can imagine. And we can put one of your tears into the cup, and I will take the cup to Queen Taunwee tonight and tell her that you are sorry, and that you could not sleep without telling her you were sorry. I am your lamb, I have your name. *I*," she declared boldly, "will carry your sorrow and bear your grief. That way you can sleep in peace. I'll tell her that you didn't know the ants were people. And I'll tell her that you plan to visit her tomorrow."

Other voices in the room chimed in, quickly and loudly supporting the plan like it was the most brilliant and inspired thing they'd ever heard. Happy, smiling faces surrounded me, but I listened only to the voice inside Marie's head.

And if the cup with your tears is not enough, I will offer her my life if she must have it in payment for the lives that were accidentally taken. I don't mind. So mote it be.

I heard the rest of what she kept in her heart and I closed my eyes so she could not see in my eyes that I knew.

If Taunwee took her from me it would be fair, I'd taken thousands from her—but I did not want to lose her.

I loved Marie. As I thought about what she was willing to do for me I couldn't imagine that even a million Twilins were worth her life. I would not trade her for anything. Nothing was worth her life.

Not even my own.

She was *my* lamb.

Mine.

Marie

Cup Bearer

MY LION WEPT and wept and wept as she kissed me on my head and told me she loved me again and again. That was when I thought for sure she knew what I was planning to do. She had to know. Why else would she weep so?

"I've placed magic on your hands, Marie, the cup and the table won't fall or tip as you walk."

There was a warm glow around my cupped hands, protecting the precious, shining offering. Resting in my palms was a miniature, glittering table that looked like it was meant for a tiny doll. The table itself was made of a powder blue colored crystal carved of super tiny butterflies, all combined together to create the shape of the table, at least that's what she told me. The detail was completely lost on eyes like mine, I just couldn't see that well.

On top of the table rested the tiny diamond goblet that looked as if it had been made by magical spiders, who'd spun it into being one liquid crystal strand at a time. It glittered like a little star atop the table, and again, the detail and beauty of the cup were lost to me. What was in the cup was more beautiful than the cup could ever be. One of her tears. She'd taken it from her eye and held it on the tip of her finger and whispered her sorrow, regret, and shame into it, and I suddenly felt so out of place, and unworthy.

I shouldn't even be here, I don't deserve this. What am I doing!? I'm just "Beetle." Just a fat, old cow.

The old thoughts that tried to surface inside me burned to ash and blew away as she spoke of how much she loved me, adding it into the teardrop before lowering her finger to the cup.

"Tell Taunwee that I'm sorry. I love you, my lamb."

She stepped away and Cathryn and Cornelius kissed me goodbye. They were weeping as if they knew my plan as well and were unsure of my safe return. The others in the Queen's bedroom gave me strange looks as I passed by and I wondered if everyone in the entire room knew, and if they did, how *did* they know. Had I been that obvious?

As I passed the men dressed in black I noticed Frank Cline among them and I felt an unexpected swell of joy inside me to see that Frank was one of the four men who were on their knees. He belonged to my Lion. I'd always thought he was so nice and I'd admired him from a distance from the first day I arrived here. He'd been kind to me the few times I'd bumped into him, but I hadn't really spoken to him other than as needed by my job. I was an invisible person. A beetle, crawling by, quietly doing my duty. *The beetle died on Mars,* I reminded myself. I am Marie now. Frank's eyes followed me as I passed, staring at me, noticing me. Wanting me? I walked out the open door and into the hall.

Out in the hall, I'd only gone a dozen steps when I heard the sound of marching feet. The four men who had been on their knees, the four that were hers, caught up with me and took up positions around me. Dan, the Dark Prince, appeared in front of our little procession out of thin air.

The sound of my Lion's voice whispered into my ear as if she stood right beside me. "These shall be your escort as you bear my cup."

Everyone cleared a path as we marched through the house and out the doors, down the path between the buildings and into the underground garage that housed the new gateway arches. I walked as if in a dream, paying little or no attention to those we passed. Earlier tonight I had combed her hair and dreamed a dream of being hers. What does a person do when their cup is too full? What does a person say who is too happy to sing? Too content to sigh? Too amazed? Too thrilled? Too, Too, Too much of everything.

And after all she'd done for me, I now had a chance to do something for her. Something that needed to be done. And I'd thought of this all on my own. Me. *Marie.* She'd told me to be bold, and I had been. More than anything, the thought that I'd pleased her carried me forward.

I floated along, a small smile on my face that was my own as I focused on the path, placing one foot before the other, as I held my cupped hands and her cup, close to my heart.

Taunwee

Dividing the Kisses

THE DAM BEFORE her stopped speaking and bowed her head as a group of guards alighted beside Queen Taunwee.

"The gateway has opened, a group approaches," one of them reported.

Taunwee considered the couple standing before her. What to do with them? The Roe and the Dam had been doing quite well before the interruption, perhaps she would yet give her a chance to prove herself.

"Quickly. Approach me, Deeka of the Shir-Bran."

The diminutive figure left her young Roe's side (who looked both worried and frustrated) and ran to her without question. The girl was a wee thing, the top of her head would not reach Taunwee's shoulder, but she was lovely. She had short, cropped brown hair that was common to her tribe, and large dark eyes like twin pools of midnight. Taunwee knew that some roes preferred small and petite and this girl was both, as well as serene and daring.

"Onto the leaf," Taunwee ordered when Deeka hesitated to dare approach so close without invitation. Once the wingless Dam stood on the leaf, they lifted off the ground and flew through the air followed by a massive cloud of attendants, guards, and servants.

She guided her leafy craft above the tombstones which glowed white with moonlight and with the brighter glow of the Twilight created by her people watching and rejoicing in the giving of Pairs. She guided the leaf and set it down on the fence rail where the humans were approaching. Her guards flew out from the rail and let their wings glow, creating an effect almost like the runway lights at an airport, guiding the humans down a luminous path to stand before her.

In front of the procession that marched toward them was a frightening creature. She had never seen its like before. It had no heartbeat or life of any kind that she could discern, although it was animated and filled with dark power. A slight, red light glowed from the eyes and Taunwee could see by its movements that it possessed a massive potential for damage. Alien and strange, like an animated piece of stone. The shell was magnificent in appearance, pale and white and molded in the fashion of a young, attractive man child. Even the smell it radiated was intoxicatingly attractive, yet the creature was an abomination.

Taunwee's gut instinct was to send it away and have nothing to do with it, but she was simply too curious to trust her gut. She wanted to find out what "*it*" was. How many of these nightmare things were in Amen Hale? Was it a mindless warrior or was it an actual person? Where did it come from? Who made it, and more importantly, why on earth were they sending it to her? Did they mean to unleash this demon upon her children?

Her unease grew, her hair changed color, her guards closed in. Without her even saying a word the floating lights rearranged themselves so that the procession would be halted ten feet from the rail upon which Taunwee stood.

She had only a moment to look past the golem to consider the rest of the group. Four men dressed in their usual black escorted one girl between them who cradled something very carefully in her hands. Instantly the Queen's hair changed color again, a happy warm brown. This looked interesting in an entirely familiar way. It looked like an offering. A gifting. She'd seen it countless times from civilizations and peoples long dead and forgotten in the days before the ban, when they could interact freely with the children of Adam.

She noticed the broad grin on Mammsik's face; he too saw this as an offering approaching. He'd brought her an offering every season for almost two hundred years until he came before her with no gift but himself. The bit and bridle, saddle, and straps had already been placed onto Makir and he sat astride the white worm, ready to serve her as she saw fit.

This gifting was a surprise. Taunwee did not think that these people saw themselves as beneath her or beholden to her in any way—but perhaps they did. Some strange superstition or belief. She watched as they approached, uncertain what would happen next.

As they approached, the golem stood to one side, allowing the others to pass until he took a position at the rear of the party, watching over them with his glowing, red eyes. Taunwee recognized Reese as one of the men and it was he who stepped forward, bowed, and spoke to the attendant that hovered in front of the group.

"We apologize for interrupting the Naming of Pairs, but we bear an urgent message for Queen Taunwee from the Black Lion." He was nervous and unsure if he was speaking correctly and his eyes kept shooting to the rail where Taunwee stood with her consorts.

She looked like the rest of the Twilins in size and shape, but she shone brighter and was more beautiful and more stunning in every way. She was the Twilight Star and had fascinated the sons and daughters of Adam since they first walked upon the earth. Peffan was away, riding in the truck with Benson, and one of her other attendants named Cassadan now hovered in air, treating with Reese.

"Do you yourself bear this message, Reese, or does the woman?" he asked, his voice formal and courtly.

"She bears the message."

"Queen Taunwee, the Twilight Star, will receive *her* and *her* message."

Reese nodded, getting the point. "So mote it be." He stepped to the side. He looked dire, as if this girl child intended to offer herself as a sacrifice.

Taunwee's hair changed to a shade of blue, her confusion evident to all her people. The line of hovering lights opened as the girl approached and closed after she passed by. The girl child had a glow about her, an awed and uplifted look that Taunwee had seen many times as men stared upon her beauty or others of her kind, but the expression on this girl's face was not of her doing.

Taunwee's hair was a bright, almost glowing blue by the time she stopped before the rail. The girl did not bow but remained straight and purposeful, hands cupped around the glittering offering and a happy light of what Taunwee would have to call "love" or "madness" gleaming in her eyes as she looked down at her on the weathered rail.

"What is your name, child?" Taunwee spoke first, her voice filling the valley like warm welcoming sun, full and sweet and powerful. Most humans felt compelled to comment on her voice or tremble or bow down before they could say more, but this girl did not. She had a strong reaction, but not one due to Taunwee's voice.

A rush of joy ran through the girl, her whole being practically quivering in rapture.

Bafflement!

Taunwee, Diviner of Secrets, Witness of the Dawn, the Winged Oracle, Mother of Knowledge Untold, donned shades of blue that never before had graced her head. How could this question create such a reaction? All she'd done was ask the girl her given name! According to Peffan, the boy, Benson, had been enamored with her name as well. *Perhaps names were very, very important to these people?* she guessed wildly. She watched as the girl tried to reign in the sea of emotions which threatened to drown her so she could bring herself to speak.

"I am Marie," she finally said. Her voice said quite plainly that she thought the name to be more than just a name, but a gift more precious that words could describe. Taunwee's own people hovering all around them reacted to the emotion in her voice, their wings beating faster.

The Queen recalled that the goddess with many names had once been called "Rain Marie" when she first visited the graveyard seasons ago with her parents. With this thought, the reaction to the name made more sense. This one bore the dark goddess's own name. She must be important and very special to her. Some brown wove its way through the electric blue atop her head. The Queen was pleased that she would be speaking with someone important and not a mere servant. Very, very important, she guessed.

More brown. Less blue.

"I am Queen Taunwee, the Twilight Star." She held her hand to the side, pointing to Deeka. "Your arrival has interrupted Deeka as she tried to win for herself the chance to marry and bear a child. What message is so urgent and what burden is so precious to cost her a chance to be wed to her true love this night?"

The girl's face fell some, saddened for Deeka, but still resolute.

"Queen Taunwee. When my Lion was here this afternoon, she killed some of your people who looked like ants. It was an accident. She didn't know they were people. She is heartbroken."

Taunwee watched as tears shone in the girl's eyes as she spoke. Not yet falling but soon to spill free.

When the young goddess killed her people around the tomb and began to reshape the earth, she'd been so surprised and just plain old frightened that she'd run and hidden behind a leaf, right along with the rest of her people and watched in fear as the strange girl slept on her bed of freshly made grass, resting atop her dead children as the cloud spirit watched her.

It would have been possible to let the breech go if the goddess had remained ignorant of what she'd done, but now that she knew, Taunwee could not ignore it. The blood of her children cried out to her loudly now that the ugly scene was fresh in her mind. Names and faces in her memory. Bright crimson adorned her entire head seasoned with streaks of white. Her voice was harsh as she spoke to the girl.

"Why did she not come herself if she is heartbroken!" Taunwee did not stomp her foot but she leaned in toward the girl. "Why does she send you? Will she not speak to me face to face after she has killed my children?"

Taunwee watched as the happy light in the girl's eye dimmed. Blue crept back into her hair. The girl spoke to her without fear or trembling, though she had plainly shown that she was angry with her. A faith burned in her and it sustained her and would not be shaken. Taunwee realized right then that this girl did not think of her goddess as less than she, but more. Greater. She spoke calmly when her words came.

"There was a—disagreement." She frowned, a line creasing her brow. "When my Lion heard that the insects at the graveside were actually people in disguise she wanted to come right away, but her mother forbade her and would not spare her though she wept and wept." And then the tears fell from the pools of her eyes as if they'd waited for that exact moment to roll in thick lines down her face.

"She wanted to come but could not, so she sent me to bring you this." She held her hands out and opened her cupped palms to reveal the table and the glittering cup. She carefully stepped forward and set the table and its cup onto the rail beside the Queen then sank to her knees beside the fence, her eyes and nose rising above the faded 2x6 that topped the old fence but her mouth now out of sight.

She was eye to eye with Taunwee and watched as the Queen approached the offering, for offering it was. Taunwee looked at the table in passing, beautiful, a godling thing, not made with hands. The cup was sized well, though a little large. It was not exceedingly ornamental as most men were apt to make them. She leaned over and looked down into the cup at the clear liquid and she smelt the magic and power it contained. She looked to the huge brown eyes only inches away, watching her closely.

"What is in the cup?"

"One of her tears. It carries her regret, her sorrow, and—" She hesitated for a moment. "Her love. Her regret, so you'll know it was an accident. Her sorrow so you'll know how heartbroken she is. And her love for me. My Lion is sorry, and she wants you to forgive her sin. And she wants your people to forgive her sin. She was crying."

She swallowed, the two huge eyes closed and pressed tight, squeezing out fresh tears. "She wants forgiveness, but if you can't forgive her, I will take her punishment. If you must have blood then I will give it. I will die for her if that's what it takes. Please," she pleaded, "I beg you for my Lion, forgive her."

Taunwee eyed the contents of the cup. She did not doubt the tale, as bizarre as it sounded; it all fit and made sense. If someone were to make up a tale, this would not be it. Her mother forbade her from coming so she sent one who bore her own name, and she sent a gift and her tears. But something about this still tickled at her as being off.

"Did your Lion ask you to offer your blood for her sins?" Taunwee asked the girl, sure she already knew the answer.

The eyes smiled; though her mouth was hidden below the rail the smile was easy to see.

"No. She planned only to ask forgiveness and send her sorrow and regret so you would know it was an accident. I didn't tell her what I planned to do. I kept, secret, all in my heart." Her eyes looked down, ashamed. "But when she put her love for me into her tear, along with the rest, I knew that she knew."

Odd colors played through the Queen's hair, purple woven through with cotton candy pink and bright neon green.

Taunwee was *envious.* What on earth did this girl goddess do to inspire or deserve such love and devotion from this girl? She wondered how many of her own people would show such selfless devotion to their queen. A short list, that, and would it truly be selfless? It would be tit for tat.

Taunwee reached out and took the cup and felt the strength of its manufacture. Made of diamond, not crystal. Hmm. Both the table and the cup were beyond her. Working with organic materials was easy, but she could not shape diamond. She held the cup to the side.

"Deeka, drink from the cup."

The Dam obeyed without hesitation, clearly determined to shape bitter events into sweet rewards and win her Roe and child. Deeka took the cup from the Queen, using two hands to grasp it like a bowl instead of holding it by the stem. She tilted and drank. Her eyes held a shocked expression when she rose from the cup. She managed to hand the diamond vessel back to Taunwee before she started to shake.

"What do you feel?" Taunwee asked her.

"Much," the girl said quietly, dark eyes wide as she struggled to master her trembling limbs.

Emotions played across her face one after another, and then she was moving. She walked to Taunwee and embraced her.

Queen Taunwee stood rigid, unsure what was happening or what to do. NONE dared approach her unbidden! Only the thought that this goddess child was channeling herself through Deeka kept her still. Was Deeka possessed of her spirit? She did not want to seem unresponsive. She allowed Mammsik to take the cup, his hand there, anticipating her need, and she embraced Deeka. She felt the small girl's arms encircle her, so small she was almost childlike, though she was a hundred and twenty years old and of an age to have a child of her own.

Taunwee waited while Deeka apparently luxuriated in the embrace, but after a moment it seemed she realized what she was doing and with whom she was doing it, but still did she did not move away. She straightened and wiped at her eyes and stayed beside her, small arms around her, as if she fully intended to stay right there until sent away like a clinging bit.

"It was an accident," Deeka spoke as she held her. "Her goddess did not mean to hurt us and she is heartbroken. Suicidally so. But do not touch this one." She uncoiled one arm to point a finger at Marie who watched from mere inches away. "She loves her far too much. This one may be a willing offering, but if we shed her blood I think her goddess would go mad."

Taunwee felt the delicate shrug of doubt from the diminutive shoulders pressed against her. "Perhaps not, perhaps her goddess would endure the loss better than I think, but she tastes more than half mad already. She values this one more than every last one of us put together. Her goddess loves her more than her own soul."

Deeka's arm went back around her and she rested her head on her breast. Taunwee heard her people all around as they hummed quietly with their wings and sang softly while they gazed upon this girl child with curious eyes. The Queen was not the only one envious. Taunwee could imagine what they were thinking. What was so special about this one that could make her goddess love her so? Was she rare or unique or peculiar in some other way? Was she her biological child, or a goddess herself in disguise? What? Why? How?

Some of her people were becoming careless, drifting closer and closer as their curiosity pulled them toward the girl like moths to a flame. A small clutch of bits even played with a stray length of her hair that was caught on the wooden rail. They stroked it in their hands and hid in it, peeking out through the brown strands as they gazed at her.

Before moving forward, Taunwee removed Deeka from her middle and had her stand at the edge of the leaf. The Queen then turned her attention back to the human girl.

"Will you accept my judgment, Marie of Amen Hale, and put yourself at my mercy for her sin?"

"Yes," she said without delay.

"Bring Reese."

One of her attendants flew off to summon him closer, and Reese came up to the rail and bowed.

"Your goddess seeks forgiveness and Marie has offered to do whatever I require to obtain that forgiveness."

Reese frowned and his brows bunched up above his eyes not liking the sound of that.

"Marie will be my guest until I see the Black Lion face to face. Tell your goddess to stop her weeping. I forgive her. Done is done. It was horrible, but it was an accident. She may give gifts to the tribe she most harmed when she visits with us tomorrow to reclaim her beloved. I will have Cassadan go with you to advise you on what would make appropriate tribute. Having some direction for her grief may help her recover herself and it would be a boon to those who suffered. I have words for the Queen of Amen Hale as well, Reese. Words for her ears alone."

She tilted her head, waiting for Reese to respond.

"For the Queen's ears alone," Reese agreed.

"Tell her she was right to make the child wait and not to give in to her weeping, that this would have been more easily settled tomorrow. The dead would still be dead and the grieving no less bereft. But tell her also that her child bears close watching tonight. Her tears tasted suicidal."

Reese's face lit up like he'd been stuck by a pin and he began to dance from foot to foot in his anxious haste to go. A simple man. Taunwee thought his was a good reaction to such grave news, even if it was a little undisciplined.

"Cassadan," she called, and the little man appeared on Reese's shoulder. "You may go, Reese." She dismissed him.

He retained the presence of mind to bow and thank her before rushing off with his entourage. The frightening golem creature made his own bow before following the men through the gateway.

"Marie, you will serve me tonight," Taunwee told the half face that rose above the fence rail like a half risen human moon.

"Yes, Queen Taunwee."

The shiver of pleasure she felt at hearing this human speak those words almost made her angry. Almost. She could have asked any of the Twilins and they would have said the same. Her hair remained a nice shade of brown.

"You will help me pick Pairs. Together, we will decide who gets to marry, and who does not."

The girl's eyes smiled and Taunwee smiled with her but it was a sad smile. The girl did not know.

"You seem happy, Marie, but long before this night is through you shall be weeping. I wish tonight would be a joy, but everyone wants love, and there's only so much love I can give. My people do not die unless they are killed, and I cannot allow them to breed like flies or the whole earth would be covered in our people. So marriage and children are allowed only as I give the gift of life with a kiss."

Taunwee walked to the edge of the rail and the girl leaned in obligingly. The Queen ran her hand over the girl's right eyebrow and stroked her cheek.

"Tonight you and I have the thankless task of deciding who gets to kiss me and who does not."

Black Rain

The Great Escape

DAN APPEARED IN the room and gave me a quick, worried glance as he handed my mother a note. She read it, looked up, and screamed.

"I FORBID IT! You *will not* kill yourself, Rain!" She marched up to me and tried to stare up into my face, but I was too tall.

"Get on your knees before me! Now!" she ordered in a way she'd never spoken to me before.

I obeyed.

Believer came over and stood behind me as I knelt before her, but he was not on my side. I knew he was on hers. They were all on hers. I heard the worried voices in the room as Cathryn grasped me roughly by my horns, using them like handlebars designed to hold my head as she stared into my eyes, putting her face close to mine.

"I will hear your voice and your promise, daughter mine," she growled, determined and ready to fight. "I buried my mother today! I will not bury my daughter! You will not kill yourself! Tell me you will obey me." She waited.

"I will obey. I will not kill myself. I will live forever. You can all calm down."

No one calmed. Perhaps it was my voice. Perhaps it was my answer. Perhaps it was everything. Cathryn took one long look into my eyes and went to the next level of nuts and started ordering people around like she knew what I planned. Perhaps she did. She was a witch.

But then she showed me Taunwee's message. I hadn't thought that she would get so much just from tasting my tears. I'd never met her, but already she was all up in my shit. Taunwee had ratted me out and now I'd have to deal with all the drama of seeing the funeral before my body hit the floor.

Cathryn told Dan to hold one of my hands while Believer held my other and she stood in front of me, crying and touching my face and pleading with me. They rotated, each of them taking a turn, weeping and telling me that they needed me and loved me and telling me why I should not die, why I couldn't do myself harm. Dan even tried to use his vampire powers, his eyes glowing white as he tried to force his way inside my head but I'd already shielded myself. When magic didn't work Dan got out his notepad and tried to reason and cry like everyone else.

I had to look away, my facade crumbling. For some reason his efforts touched me more than the ones who had a voice to plead with, and that was a mistake; my moment of weakness confirmed everyone's fears. The eyes in the room that stared at me were forlorn and wildly desperate. God himself might be able to walk hand in hand with man, but I couldn't seem to do it without killing them or maiming them or causing them to go mad or become addicted to my blood or my body. God could, but it seemed "gods" like me could not.

What happened to Taunwee's people confirmed it for me and now that I'd figured a way to go and not kill Dan and Jane, it was just a matter of doing what needed to be done. I'd been on the edge of doing this off and on for a while but always I'd pulled back or been talked out of it. One person or another or some situation or obligation would keep me from doing what needed to be done.

The door opened and Jane entered the room with Emma.

"Dammit, that's not fair!" I growled.

Jane smiled and arched a lovely eyebrow at me. "Vampire," she said, like that gave her all the excuse in the world to be wicked. Jane was too smart sometimes.

There were so many bodies packed into the room Emma couldn't run to me, but people were clearing out of the way quickly. I'd been putting it off, but it was time to let go. Emma's glowing, copper gold eyes were fixed on me as she made her way across the room. She could not kill like Bethany, with a look and a word, she could not touch someone and know all their secrets like Mary, and she could not do all the things I could do. Emma was not a god, but none of that mattered. She was stronger than me, so I did the only thing I could do. I ran.

I'd delayed and stalled and listened greedily to my family, more to hear the sound of their voices one final time than to hear them tell me through all the tears how much they loved me. I wish I could have done the same with Emma but I couldn't. She'd tie me around her little finger like a pretty ribbon. I loved her too much.

My body collapsed between the arms holding me as my soul rose out of my body to hover safely near the ceiling. I did not let myself hear, I did not want to disobey my mother, and I knew she would be shouting for me to come back, but I did give my disembodied self sight. I watched the yelling and screaming below me for one brief instant and had to look away.

I fled to the bathroom and left my message upon my mother's mirror. I needed to finish what I'd started before something happened to stop me. I had to do this. This was the only way to keep them safe from me. To keep the world and everyone in it safe from me.

I glided back into the room and had to do an about face and float my ghostly ass back into the bathroom. The scene had been too much to take. I took a minute, gathered my conviction and steeled myself for what was in the next room and went back in. Heads were tilted back in silent howls and people and creatures were running around like mad. I was glad I hadn't given myself the ability to hear yet because everyone was crying or screaming.

Believer was not like the others who crowded my body; his eyes searched high and low, looking about the room. Suddenly his red gaze stopped right on me. He looked heartbroken but determined; he had not given up. I thought for sure he saw me, but then he looked in another spot. I felt my resolve start to crumble like a sandcastle smacked by the first strong wave of the approaching surf and I knew if I stayed any longer I'd crumble completely. My resolve would be washed away by all their need, but what the world needed most was for me to go away.

I drifted through the golden gateway that stood momentarily forgotten on the side of the room while everyone lamented over my body. The gate was still open, the red alien landscape still visible to the room. As soon as I passed through I closed the portal and willed the stone arch on Mars to crumble so Lucius and my sisters would not be able to follow.

I drifted above the small circle of white stones where I'd stood with Marie less than two hours ago. I would have wept if I had eyes to weep with. I did not. I had tears to shed and no way to shed them. I still felt as if I were crying. I had no heart, so I failed to comprehend how what I did not possess could pain me. A phantom organ? Phantom tears? Served me right.

I welcomed the pain as proof of having once had a life that mattered. I released the bubble of air that covered the immediate area like a dome. The oxygen rich air I'd created and held here rushed out and the thin Martian atmosphere rushed in, creating a red swirling sandstorm. I watched until the dust cloud finally settled.

The small encircling jade wall and its carved lions were covered with a thin but concealing layer of red sand. The circle of white stones, the white bench, and the white, bonelike throne blended into the red landscape. I'd thought of changing it all to dust but it seemed as if there was no need. Mars had put its own red scab over the alien wound on its skin. So mote it be.

My soul ghosted over the barren wastes of red earth and rock. My heart felt as empty and formless and hopeless as the barren, red world beneath me. I pushed away the urge to go home, go back to my body but the compulsion grew as I glided over more and more endless nothing. Growing and building.

What if I did go back? What would it hurt?

But how many would die tomorrow if I went back?

That thought stilled the churning inside my mind. I had no body or way to feel a chill, so how did I feel it?

Had I imagined it? I did not know.

Was Mars cold? I did not know.

I did not know a lot of things. But I did know one thing for sure—Mars was lonely.

Jane and Cathryn

Mirror, Mirror

JANE SUPPORTED CATHRYN, holding her upright as they looked at the mirror in her bathroom and the words written on the glass with Cathryn's own red lipstick. The stick still lay on the vanity as if Rain had taken her time about it. Dan said she never went into the bathroom from what he'd seen.

At night, inside my cloud.
By day before my lambs.
Let my beloved feed daily.
I will never run dry. I will never die.
I love you. I wish I could stay,
but the world is safer with me this way.

Cathryn's head moved, a quick birdlike cock to the side. "Where is Mary? Where are the rest of what is mine? I want them here. I what them with me. I want to see them."

Jane answered her, "Dan told me Bethany went to sleep in the guest hall with some of the other young girls tonight. Dana and David are abed and have been for some time. The twins have joined the others and are now weeping with the rest. Believer has already assigned two guards to watch Izzy for signs of suicide. Mary is in the prison, doing as Rain asked her, probably touching the last of the prisoners by now. I doubt she knows what's happened."

Cathryn licked her dry lips, her eyes jerked around wildly, thinking, thinking.

"Send Dan to gather Bethany to me and lay her in my bed. I want what is mine close this night. You go and watch over Mary. She will not handle this well. Bring her to me and lay her in my bed as well. I'll have guards keep watch over Sky and Ryan in their rooms. I don't want them unwatched but Emma is so wild, she just might touch them."

"And what about me, Mother," Jane asked.

Cathryn blinked and looked, really looked at Jane. She had golden/red tears running down her face.

Cathryn threw her arms around Jane and they both wept.

"You are mine. You and Dan will be in our bed with the rest of what is mine."

"But we do not sleep," Jane said as she cried.

"Tonight, neither do I, Jane." Cathryn comforted. "Tonight, neither do I."

Mary

This One Goes Out to The One I Love

I TOLD THE GUARDS thank you and goodnight and left the final prison cell with Jeffery Frouden still stretched out and shackled to his own bed. I noticed the time on a clock mounted on the wall at the top of the stairwell; it was well past one a.m. After touching all of our prisoners and enduring their trapped panic, I wanted nothing but out. I wanted trees around me and sky above me, and I wanted to feel nature and life that did not have sad stories to tell me.

Most of the captives had lives with rough beginnings, shitty middles, and a fast approaching end in a stew pot. Seeing Rain earlier in the day as she made their fancy new prison had freaked our captives out badly. When they were sitting in the old, uncomfortable house they'd felt hopeful and optimistic, but now they just felt like dinner. And now that Rain had horns, a tail, demon eyes, and was seven feet tall, even the macho guys started to cry like five year olds who wanted their mommies. They didn't want to play anymore. To say they were depressed wouldn't do it justice.

My head felt stuffy and cramped, like I was still sitting in a little eight by ten room and had been for years and would be until they came for me. Came to kill me. I gave myself a shake as I pushed open the doors and stepped outside into the cool night air. Most of the men in our little prison had already served lots of time in some of the most horrifying hellholes the world had to offer, and knowing every second and every horror they'd endured as though I'd lived through it myself made me want to puke and scream at the same time. Touching the prisoners was nasty, but it had been the right thing to do, and it *had been* filling. Good, bad, or indifferent, I'd gained from touching each of the sixty-four prisoners and from touching eighteen of Alana's wedding guests and sneaking a touch on two of the FBI goons who came with the guests.

With every new life I collected I gained experience in countless little ways and I gained magic. On the plus side for the evening I did find a few who deserved grace. Two of the men were completely innocent, just poor deluded idgits in the wrong place at the wrong time. They had no clue of what they were into. Eight others were borderline and most of these had kids who needed them more at home than we needed them in our meat locker, so that brought the mercy head count to ten. It still left us with fifty-four prisoners. I'd already taken what I wanted from them, the Lions and the lion-like of Amen Hale would eat the rest.

I pushed all the other people crowding my head back, back down into their place, down! Down! DOWN!

I closed my eyes and did my housecleaning, putting people on shelves inside my head and cleaning my mind and wiping down the corners before I brought out my most precious possession, Mary! I had not noticed before today, but when I began to feed on more than one or two people in succession, Mary tended to fade down into the background and hide until I called for her again. What was driving the bus while Mary was away was more witch and instinct than girl until the feeding frenzy ended. Perhaps it was just my mind trying to protect itself from being washed away, but I'd missed her, and the moment I set her in the front of my thoughts again I felt better. Much better.

I was silly, crazy, happy, airheady Mary again. Seventeen-year-old witch girl Mary. Fun, flighty Mary. Kissy, huggy, touchy, flirty Mary. Her own distinctive ticks and mannerisms were more important than ever now that I held inside me the ticks and itches and urges to scratch at every crevice on my body. The combined nail biting, nose picking *yuck!* from almost a thousand lives.

My fingers played with the one stripe of green hair that always hung down into my eyes. Other girls in other lives had played with their hair in almost the same way, but only I had white hair with a green stripe. It was totally unique and totally, 'me'. I felt better, more myself, more Mary with each passing moment.

With my eyes still closed I pushed out with my magic and felt the prison behind me with its inhabitants and guards, but my attention was grabbed by two figures hiding in the woods off in the new garden area. I recognized the feel of these lives, Peter (sixteen) and Teela (fourteen) were busy little bunnies. Teela was as pretty as she was gullible and Peter was surprisingly experienced for a sixteen year old. He did like her, it wasn't just him taking advantage (though he was taking advantage). Too young, bad match, it was very ill advised, *but that's the way of life.*

I thought about my own first time with tall, dark, and hunky Luke Hosterman. I'd been fifteen and he was eighteen when we hooked up in the cab of his cramped, stick shift, pickup truck. Luke had been more experienced than me as well, and on top of that I was jail bait at the time. Stupid. But I'd had a good time, not magical, but good.

For Teela tonight might be the most magical night of her young life, possibly her whole life. Quite often it was that way for girls, the first time is remembered in a special way. For Peter it may be the most magical night "so far." I wouldn't know how they felt until I touched them, but I was curious to find out. *Later,* I promised myself. I left them unmolested by my magic and added the rhythm of their hearts and passion and sweet young sweat to the rest of the life around me as I reached out farther with my senses, feeling the life around me.

I felt a crowd of people in one part of the new garden. I'd already touched some of these folk earlier in the day so knew what they were up to. Yesterday evening was the first night that the people of Amen Hale, who saw Rain as a god, had gathered in any numbers in a specific place. Today, those who could get away had met at twelve noon and then again at twelve midnight.

Four of them were leaving now, spread out on different parts of the trail, but twenty-seven remained in the circular clearing that held her statue. I danced down the trail in their direction with my eyes closed as I listened to the music of the life all around me. There was nothing that I wanted or needed to do at the moment, so I let myself go there. I'd never been a deep thinker and preferred to eat the fruit of life's joys when I found them and not spend my time thinking about who planted the tree the fruit grew on. I did not worry if "*he*" or "*she*" or "*it*" watched me as I ate the fruit and smiled if it was sweet, or cried or cussed if it turned out to be nasty or had a big, squiggly worm in it. I went with the flow and took what was there and enjoyed it.

I'd never thought of myself as a spiritual girl. I enjoyed life and lived, spun, danced, hugged, talked, laughed and loved. That was me. That was Mary. But what I'd done today with Rain, I'd done as Mary, and that had changed me. I wasn't sure how, but *changed* I was. My feet carried me to a strange, unfamiliar place to do strange, unfamiliar things, but it was where they wanted to go. I did not worry beyond that because "*that*" was Mary. So mote it be.

I left the path and moved through the wood, taking a short cut. I stopped at a large, flat stone that I was sure Rain had made and set here for decoration. An oddity off the beaten path meant to be discovered and marveled at. (Florida didn't have stones like this.) First I pulled warmth from the stone with magic, making it cool. Then I wrote on the stone in nice big letters. I let the paths where my fingertips traced on the stone grow warm with my magic and left a message that the infrared cameras and satellites would have fun with before I moved on down the trail. I'm sure it would show up as nice, red type on a blue field in their cameras.

SO RUDE!
to Stare
From way up
There

I think I was being shy. I'd never been to church before and the thought of them watching me as I did whatever it was I was about to do creeped me out, but it did not stop me. I moved on until I reached the clearing with Rain's statue and her worshipers. Most were gathered around her statue with a few hovering at the fringes of the circle, watching shyly or speaking in hushed tones. The gathering had such a somber, hushed, serious feel, like a church service in a really stuffy church or a funeral or a Sunday dinner when important company was over and mom had me, dad, and my sisters dressed in fancy clothes and made us eat like civilized people. Those dinners always sucked and so did this.

I wasn't feeling it, but I did not know what to do. Their way did not feel right to me. *Their way would not be my way,* I decided. I could have searched the thoughts on what it meant to have a god from all my lives but I did not want their thoughts to mess up my own. I was Mary, and I did not know, and that was right. That was me. I'd never done this before, this was new for me. New, awkward, weird and exciting, and a little scary.

The people closest to the statue were on their knees and paid me no mind as I walked into their midst. I circled the clearing, and walked around the statue. The odd pile of stuff placed at the foot stood out in my special vision, the auras glowing brightly. I saw a pair of glasses that glowed a bright gold. A shoebox that held something. A cut and curled section of hair tied into a loop with some red ribbon caught my eyes with its strange red aura. A strangely carved block of wood. My heart tightened up when I saw the drawings made by children with crayon.

In Wicca we often brought small offerings to the god and goddess or the guardians when we made a circle. I wished I had a knick knack, something to leave behind, some offering. I didn't have my purse and even if I did I didn't own any trinket or doodad special enough to place at Rain's feet. Something small and important only to me.

A thought popped into my head. "The fork." But I didn't have it. I wish I'd thought to grab it as a keepsake. It would have been perfect. I thought of when Rain and I stood in the kitchen of her trailer the day after she lit the Black Candle. We were doing dishes together at her sink. She'd been washing, while I did the rinsing and drying. She told me then that I was special and I hadn't believed her. She'd reached out and grabbed a plastic fork from the strainer and held it up between us. "If I think this fork is gold," right before my eyes the white plastic fork turned to gold, "it *is* gold."

I remember her telling me, "If I think you are special, then you *are* special." Rain had made me special and I loved her for it. But I'd loved her before she made me special because she was my best friend. All that I was I had because she loved me.

My steps became quicker and I closed my eyes and spun in slow circles in a graceful dance as I moved around the statue. Soon I'd let myself go. I danced and I sang, but not with words, I just let my voice rise and fall and flow with the rush of my steps and the pulse of my heart. Some of the others joined me and others moved out of our way.

I was surprised to feel Jane join us. She didn't say a word to me, she just danced with us and I heard her sweet voice join mine as together we sang to our god. Her voice was so desperate! And so filled with need! So passionate! It surprised me and made my own heart hurt. I felt her longing and ache as I sang and danced and cried and even worshiped with her. I danced for Rain and sang for Rain and loved her. I wanted to give something, but I had nothing but "me"—so that was what I gave.

I pulled it up, like drawing water from a deep well, starting way down at the tips of my toes and pulling it up through my legs, past my chest and up. I drew the power and magic within me, all of the life and magic that I'd collected from the eighty-two souls that I'd touched today. My eyes were closed but I could see the brightness through the thin flesh of my lids. I called all that power and life and magic that I'd gathered today and brought it into my mouth. I did not shout or scream but simply prayed my three words that would be my offering to her.

"I love you."

Black Rain

Wooing a God

FOR A WHILE I hovered there above the dust-covered remains of what I'd made, nothing but a presence in the air. Had it been thirty minutes, an hour, a day, a week, a year? How the hell would I ever keep track of time to even know? Would I end up marking lines into the rock for each time it grew light and dark? Was a Martian day twenty-four hours? Mars was smaller than Earth and farther from the sun so—*twenty-four? Forty-eight? twelve?* I could have the knowledge. Let my self know it. If I wanted it. But did it even matter?

The sad truth was—no, it did not.

I glided along over the surface of the planet, passing mile after mile of red earth. From time to time the landscape managed to catch my eye as I passed by a ridge or over a gully or an odd looking mountain. But it was a dead world. There was no life, no plants, and no moving water. Next to nothing in the sky. On and on.

Something glittered on the horizon. I looked again and saw the same metallic flash. Immediately I headed in that direction, my curiosity roused. I came closer and—shit.

Space junk.

It was the bottom half of some landing craft. There was a ramp leading from the hunk of junk down to the surface. Whatever little robot or lander it carried had long since rolled away and gone off to take its pictures and dig little holes in the dirt. I didn't see any tracks leading away, but where there's a will there's a way and I had a will to know the way, so I simply headed in the direction that felt right.

The little vehicle had gone a fair distance. It was motionless in the bottom of what looked to be a dry riverbed, but there were no rivers on Mars. The top was one big, flat solar panel. The entire thing was about the size of a small coffee table.

I floated down beside the little rover. It had an American flag decal on the side. I felt no true connection to the flag. It wasn't my flag anymore. My country did not have a flag. I would have smiled if I had a face and mouth. A phantom smile. America was the first country to put a man on the moon but would anyone ever know that Amen Hale was the first to put a girl on Mars? My Marie.

Thinking of her brought the phantom pain in my phantom heart but I let myself think of her. Of all the people that I could be thinking about, my husband, my mother, Emma, my child, people that I knew better and loved longer, it was Marie that filled my mind and I'd only known her for a few hours. I brought her here, to this empty, lonely place because she wanted to be alone with me, so it seemed wrong to ban her memory from my mind in her own special place.

I recalled her private thoughts as she thought shamefully to herself, "*I want to be greedy*" as she looked at me, wanting me. My phantom smile for the happy memory faded to pain in the center of what I was as I remembered the rest of what I did here with her. I changed her from "Beetle," the slumped, sad, little woman she'd been and made her into my "Marie." I had promised her that I would *try* to be a good god to her—and now I'd left her. I sent her off to Taunwee to pay for my sins and then I left her, just like Rain Marie had done with me.

You have your reasons.

You keep killing people.

You don't belong with men, gods do not walk with men without crushing them.

It was an accident!

It doesn't matter if it was an accident, they're still dead! Dead and gone!

Reasons and reasons and more reasons I reminded myself and argued with myself. They all sounded a lie.

I remembered Believer telling me earlier tonight that I was nothing like Rain Marie, and here I was, doing exactly what Rain Marie had done.

A flash of red light broke my thoughts free.

What was that!?

I looked back down to the little rolling robot. Blink—a flash of red. One lone flashing LED still functioned. It seemed to go off once every ten or fifteen seconds. The red light was the only moving, living, or working thing on the planet and it held me in its grip like it was the most fascinating thing I'd ever seen. The tiny red light blinked. Blink. Blink. Blink. Blink. Blink. Blink.

That my world had reduced down to one blinking light made me want to cry.

Blink.

Blink.

Blink.

Blink.

Blink.

Blink.

Blink.

Blink.

Blink.

Blink.

Blink.

Blink.

Blink.

I felt something odd as I stared at the little light, but that was impossible because I had no body to feel with. Was I imagining it, another phantom feeling? The area around me started to glow with a greenish light and I felt something inside me, something that spoke to me without words, and yet it spoke to what I was. It was simply there. It pressed around me like a warm, loving embrace and pressed into me what it wanted me to know.

"I Love You."

It was from Mary. I knew it. I could feel it. It was like a magical postcard with just three words. My phantom smile came back. Somehow she had found a way to reach me even here with her magic. But the surprising thing was what she'd chosen to say. She hadn't said, "Why!?" or "Come Back!" or "Help!" or "Don't Go!" She'd simply said "I love you."

Blink. The red light seemed to object to my attention being diverted by this rude intrusion into his world.

"What about me?" it seemed to say.

Do you love me? I asked it with my phantom voice.

It blinked, it seemed to say that it did.

I didn't trust him. He'd just find a pretty rock or some other rolling coffee table and—

Blink.

Yeah, I bet you tell that to all the lost gods you meet.

Blink.

The mysterious green light around me faded and vanished, the message delivered. Mary's presence faded too.

Blink.

My moment of madness faded with the light.

Blink.

It was just a stupid light again. For a minute it actually had felt as though I had company. A conversation with Mary, who wanted to tell me she loved me, and my red, flashing, digital suitor that was so jealous of my attention.

Blink.

My mind spun. My phantom eyes wept. My phantom heart broke.

Blink.

My digital suitor continued to press his cause, flashing louder and brighter as the sun set and night swallowed day. Perhaps he raised his voice because he was afraid.

Blink.

Black Rain

Dream Sweet Dreams

I LET MYSELF FALL down, but not into the red, sandy ground of Mars, but back into my body.

My last sight was a final red flash.

Blink!

Then I was gone.

I lay still. I kept my eyes closed but I could feel my body again. It felt so good to have a body again. My body. For a while I just lay there and breathed. I was surprised to feel I was in Believer's arms but not inside his body. I'd left instructions as to my sleeping arrangements at night. I wondered why I was on the outside of my love and not on the inside. I opened my eyes and found two glowing red eyes staring down into my own.

Two glowing red eyes.

Eyes that did not blink on and off. They shone.

I felt myself smiling. My phantom smile was a real smile again.

"Why do you smile, my Lady?" he asked quietly, gently, as if he did not want to wake others. I answered just as quietly.

"Your eyes are prettier." I reached up a hand to touch his cloudy face around his eyes. Dark lines formed in the clouds around his eyes, adding emotion and character to his voiced words. Confusion.

"Prettier than whose?" he asked quietly.

"Prettier than the Martian who tried to steal me away from you."

Believer's expression darkened, an ugly frown cut across his face and his eyes became a hot red.

"Shh, my love," I soothed gently. "Don't worry about him. He was short and squatty, and he had only one red eye and he kept blinking. It was annoying." I touched his frowning slit of a mouth as if I could reshape it with my hand. "I am married to you, this is where I belong."

He looked doubtful, and I couldn't blame him. I'd already left once. He took a while to consider what his next words would be before he spoke again.

"What brought you back to us, my love?"

"Where are we?" I asked instead of answering. He was so huddled around me and looming over me I couldn't see anything but him. He straightened so I could see the room. We were in my mother's parlor. The golden gateway to Mars stood just ten short feet away from where Believer held me in his arms.

"Is everyone okay?" I asked, worried and guilty over causing more drama.

"For now."

"For now?" I looked back up into his face quickly, not liking the sound of those ominous words.

"Do you plan to stay with us or leave us?" his quiet voice challenged as his red eyes stared into me. "Tonight they all sleep in the Queen's bed by her orders and remain under the careful guard of the vampires. Our mother is very wise. I did not understand why she did this at first but soon it became quiet obvious that Izzy and Mary are of a mind to do themselves harm. And if Izzy goes, Lizzy will follow. And if Mary goes, Emma will follow her."

That was what would have happened if I had stayed away.

"Believer, what should I do?" I asked him as I wiped at the tears that started to run from my eyes.

"I have thought much on why you would leave," Believer's deep voice rumbled kindly.

"I saw you," my weepy voice interrupted. "Before I left, you were the only one who was thinking and looking for me away from my body, looking around the room. You looked right at me and I thought you saw me and I almost went to you right then." I covered my mouth and finished my words from behind my hand. "You almost ruined my whole plan."

"And when you felt your resolve weakening you fled through the portal," Believer finished my tale for me giving me a small smile. "I thought as much when I saw the gateway close." His smug smile and satisfied tone warmed my heart.

"You were right, my love. Be right again, tell me what I should do," I asked him.

Believer's smile remained as he spoke, but it was a sad smile. "I cannot tell you what you should do because I am hopelessly in love with you. I have only one answer, stay here and love me. *That* is what I want you to do. Whether that is what you should do is not my concern." He gave me a gentle squeeze with his arms. "I have my life returned to me, what care I for the world?"

His smiling face faded and fell all the way back to serious.

"Please, Rain. Do me a kindness," he asked.

"What?" I asked, filled with worry by his turn of mood.

"If ever you decide that you must truly leave this place and choose not to take me with you, do not tie me to your body as a caretaker. I cannot do it. To have you and hold you, but hold nothing in my arms but memory and dreams is more than I could bear."

Drops of wetness fell from his eyes to land hot on my face. Each drop made me want to scream but I spoke instead.

"Izzy and Mary weren't the only ones who were thinking of doing themselves harm."

He nodded. "You are right, my love," he confessed in his deep sad rumble.

"You would ask Sky to unmake you," I guessed.

He nodded.

"And Bethany would not survive the loss of both of us," I guessed again.

He nodded again.

My mind took off from there, connecting the logical dots. Alana, my red lamb, would surely die without me. And Cathryn would die after enduring as much as she could, and if Cathryn died then Cornelius would be close on her heels. I thought about those of Amen Hale who loved me. Like Marie. And like the young girl named Shelly whom I met on the path earlier that night pushing carts of dirty clothes from the prison to the laundry room. Would that sweet young girl take her own life just because I was gone? She seemed so smart, so independent and self-possessed, but maybe she would. How many of the others who dropped to their knees would die I wondered—would it be mass suicide? Would they get together in a group and hand out the poison, spiked kool aid?

"Shit," I said.

"I agree," Believer cussed with my mouth, which was the closest I'd ever heard him come to the real thing.

"What do you want to do right now?" he asked me, changing the subject.

I smiled, glad to move on to other things. "It does not matter what I want. You own my body at night, that *is* our arrangement is it not?"

He laughed, casting a glance toward my mother's bedroom as he struggled to keep his rumbling mirth in check. I'd surprised him with that little statement which delighted me to no end. The brightness in his laughing eyes and his smile were like life to me and filled me with hope.

"What I want is for all the ones we love to know that you are back and well and safe. Tomorrow we shall be together, but tonight I want more than anything to watch you as you sleep with our family." He started walking toward my mother and father's bedroom.

The bedroom door opened before we got there, and I saw that a smiling Dan was holding the door. Jane's bright eyes met mine from the other side of the room. She was not smiling, she had tears on her face. I looked away from her eyes to the huge bed loaded with people. My father had Bethany lying on top of him and the twins, Izzy and Lizzy, lay beside him on the far side. They were all asleep. My mother lay in the middle, arms tightly wrapped around a very distraught and wild looking Mary; neither were asleep. They stayed still and quiet, watching me as if I were a skittish deer that might startle and bolt if they moved. Emma lay on the other side of the bed with her arms wrapped around Alana.

I scanned the rest of the room, the chairs, the floor, but Mrs. Ainsley was nowhere in sight. Perhaps she'd gone back home or gone to a guest room. It hadn't taken Emma long at all. Emma and Alana were both sleeping soundly.

Believer set me back on my feet and steadied me as I got my balance on legs that seemed longer than I remembered my legs being. I wobbled forward and crawled into the bed. I tried not to wake anyone, but there wasn't a lot of room so I still shook the bed as I crawled forward. Mary and my mother scooted apart and I crawled up into the nest they'd prepared for me between them. I turned awkwardly, being mindful of my horns as I did so, and lay on my back between them as they both looked down at me, each propped up on an elbow.

"Mary," I said quietly.

"Yeah," croaked a voice hoarse and raw from crying.

"You found me. You brought me back. You're my Prince Charming."

"I am?" She still looked doubtful. Sheets were between us and she hadn't touched me yet so she didn't already know.

"I would have stayed on Mars and changed myself to a rock or a shooting star or a cloud and drifted forever if you hadn't told me you loved me. You saved me, Mar."

Finally a smile touched her face.

"Touch me, Mary," I whispered to her in a voice that said how much she meant to me and how much I loved her. "Touch me and know all of it, my prince."

She touched me then and after a moment she smiled—and that was when Cathryn came alive.

"Why did she leave us, Mary? Tell me what she was thinking." She was mad and I didn't blame her. She didn't even bother to ask me.

Mary was smiling now and calm but her voice and body were battered. I knew it must have been bad; she had a bloody spot in her eye from broken blood vessels along with scrapes and scratches on her cheek. Cathryn looked like hell too. I healed and doctored and touched up both of them as Mary spoke to my angry mother.

"She's worried about the kill count. When she was the Black Witch she would kill one or two a day, but today is her first day as a god and she's freaked out at how many people died." Mary flipped her green stripe out of her eyes and began to list my sins for the day as if she were ordering off the drive through menu at Mickey Dee's.

"First, she made sure the human sacrifice guy got greased, even when Bethany didn't seem to want to grease him, then she killed our Gran in the garden which was kinda nasty." Mary made a yuck face before continuing the litany. "Then she had the accident with the children of glass which was a hundred people, then she killed hundreds or maybe even thousands of tiny, Fae people in Taunwee's little kingdom." Mary leaned down and kissed me, pressing her lips to mine.

At first I was so surprised I just lay there as her lips worked against mine, but then I kissed her back and was sad when she pulled away. She smiled down at me and looked me in my eyes.

"The prisoner was a bastard, Rain, our Gran choose her own fate, the children of glass are inside you, so they are happy, even if they had a short life. And Taunwee needs to post a damn sign or something that says, 'Ants are people too!'" Mary had gotten a little too animated and more people were waking up.

Cornelius looked over at us, gave a brief start, and then smiled. "Good to have you back, my child."

A sleepy Bethany opened bleary, teary eyes.

"Parents don't leave kids," she said acidly, giving me an evil scowl. She crawled over the pile and attached herself to my leg like a vicious leech without another word and snuggled in, not even giving me a chance to explain or to say I was sorry. Our tails intertwined as if they agreed with her.

And then I felt movement on the bed and looked down, surprised to see Jane crawling in. She attached herself to the other leg in much the same way Bethany had. She stretched a hand out behind her and laid it on Emma's back and gave her a gentle shake.

Emma turned and looked at me, surrounded by everyone, and frowned fiercely. I, and the rest of us who were awake watched her, waiting for her explosive outburst that would wake the dead, but it didn't come. Instead she just looked to Jane.

"If she tries to leave, bite her," she growled.

"Yes, Jane," Cathryn said with a nod. "I think that would be best."

"But I'm not going anywhere, Mother," I whined quietly.

"Don't trust her, Mom, she's crazy," came a voice from the other side of Cornelius that had to be Izzy or Lizzy.

"Yeah!" came another voice that sounded the same as the first.

Jane had her arms wrapped securely around my leg and her face pressed to the flesh of my leg, right at the curve of my hip. It was close to other things and I felt her cool breath gliding across my skin and shivered.

"None of that, Rain," Cathryn finally spoke to me. "This day is done, now go to sleep."

"My hair, Mom," I complained.

She and Mary together pulled my long black mane from where it was pinned under me and laid it out above us piled up against the headboard and then they both settled in on either side of me. I lay in my parents' bed, surrounded by the people who loved me most in the world, blanketed in all the love anyone could ever hope for, and I worried if I'd made the right choice. Tomorrow was a new day for the Black Lion to walk among men. How many would die?

"Stop thinking things like that or I'll have Jane bite you," Mary growled, then kissed me on the cheek.

"Told you not to trust her!" hissed one of the twins.

"Yeah!" echoed the other.

"Shh! Girls. To bed. Mary's listening to her head and Jane is listening to her heart and Emma is with us. We will know if her thoughts turn toward something foolish. We will be ready. We will not lose her tonight."

"She's like me." I was sure it was Izzy's voice.

"Yes, Izzy, in some ways she is," was all Cathryn said.

I thought about what my mother just said. I knew I was crazy, but—was I really like Izzy?

Mary kissed my head. "Sorta kinda. Dream happy dreams, my Lion. Dream happy dreams."

She and my mother both stroked my hair and Mary hummed a lullaby.

My last thought was of a blinking, lonely light on a sad, red world. I was glad I was not there, still looking into my Martian lover's eye.

I slept.

www.ingramcontent.com/pod-product-compliance
Lightning Source LLC
Chambersburg PA
CBHW080726280626
47162CB00019B/2994